THE
Queen's Handmaiden

THE Queen's Handmaiden

Jennifer Ashley

BERKLEY BOOKS, NEW YORK

THE BERKLEY PUBLISHING GROUP
Published by the Penguin Group
Penguin Group (USA) Inc.
375 Hudson Street, New York, New York 10014, USA
Penguin Group (Canada), 90 Eglinton Avenue East, Suite 700, Toronto, Ontario M4P 2Y3, Canada
(a division of Pearson Penguin Canada Inc.)
Penguin Books Ltd., 80 Strand, London WC2R 0RL, England
Penguin Group Ireland, 25 St. Stephen's Green, Dublin 2, Ireland (a division of Penguin Books Ltd.)
Penguin Group (Australia), 250 Camberwell Road, Camberwell, Victoria 3124, Australia
(a division of Pearson Australia Group Pty. Ltd.)
Penguin Books India Pvt. Ltd., 11 Community Centre, Panchsheel Park, New Delhi—110 017, India
Penguin Group (NZ), 67 Apollo Drive, Rosedale, North Shore 0632, New Zealand
(a division of Pearson New Zealand Ltd.)
Penguin Books (South Africa) (Pty.) Ltd., 24 Sturdee Avenue, Rosebank, Johannesburg 2196,
South Africa

Penguin Books Ltd., Registered Offices: 80 Strand, London WC2R 0RL, England

This is an original publication of The Berkley Publishing Group.

First edition: October 2007

Library of Congress Cataloging-in-Publication Data

Ashley, Jennifer.
  The queen's handmaiden / Jennifer Ashley.—1st ed.
    p. cm.
  ISBN 978-0-425-21732-0
  1. Elizabeth I, Queen of England, 1533–1603—Fiction. 2. Nobility—Great Britain—Fiction.
3. Great Britain—History—Elizabeth, 1558–1603—Fiction. I. Title.

  PS3601.S547Q44 2007
  813'.6—dc22

                                                                                          2007021344

PRINTED IN THE UNITED STATES OF AMERICA

10   9   8   7   6   5   4   3   2   1

Acknowledgments

I'd like to say special thanks to my editor, Ginjer Buchanan, for the opportunity to write this book and for her guidance and enthusiasm throughout the project. Also to my family, who were so supportive of the time it took to research, write, edit, and proof. I couldn't do it without you! Readers can find more information and reference sources about the Elizabethan world at www.jennifersromances.com/tudorhistoricals.html.

THE
Queen's Handmaiden

I

I WAS BORN in the same year as my lady Elizabeth, in the year of our Lord 1533. My mother found this auspicious; she, like Doctor Dee, puts much faith in the stars and the dance of the heavens and predicted that my life would be filled with wealth and happiness.

My grandmother cynically observed that I was a sickly child and that arriving in the world five days before the lady Elizabeth seemed to give me no advantage. Grandmother died the year Queen Mary arrested Lady Elizabeth and put her in the Tower for treason, and at that sad time I thought perhaps her cynicism had been justified.

My association with Elizabeth began years before the day of her arrest, when she was still the small daughter of King Henry, and Aunt Kat took me, Eloise Rousell, to live in Elizabeth's household. I would be something of a playmate and companion to Elizabeth, Aunt Kat told my grandmother, although events unfolded in an altogether different manner.

Aunt Kat, then Katherine Champernowne, had been appointed

as Elizabeth's governess the year before. Aunt Kat was a learned woman and loved teaching a bright pupil who picked up complex mathematics and languages like others collected flowers. At the time Her Grace was only Lady Elizabeth, not princess, because her father had declared her a bastard when he sent her mother, Anne, to the block and married Jane Seymour. Not until Henry's marriage to Catherine Parr was Elizabeth again hailed as her father's daughter and third in line for the throne of England.

My own life did not begin to take shape, carved into the sharp patterns it would become, until the day in 1547 when we learned that old King Henry was dead. Both Elizabeth and I would be fourteen in September. Her recent portrait showed her in a gown of scarlet damask over a sumptuous gold underskirt and sleeves, and a pearl-studded French hood—all sewn by me. My talent as a seamstress, my only talent thus far, had manifested when I was about twelve and sewed gowns for Aunt Kat and other ladies of the household. Elizabeth, who loved clothes, praised my work and began to request, then demand, that I make gowns exclusively for her.

The day dawned like many others in January, crisp and cold, clouds from the previous day's rain tearing and fleeing before a fresh wind. We were at Enfield, north of London. Elizabeth had breakfast in her chamber, then lessons with William Grindal and Aunt Kat.

Aunt Kat knew Latin and Greek and astronomy and history and was as intelligent as any of Elizabeth's male tutors ever were. I was a bit slower, but then my father had the misfortune of being an actor. He was quite a good actor, I was told, and when his troupe came into a town, all flocked to see him. But if you are a member of a highborn family like the Champernownes, you should not marry an actor from a traveling troupe, as my mother learned to her distress.

After her marriage, my mother was turned out by her family and told that if she was fool enough to marry a strolling player, she could lie in the bed that she made. By all accounts, my mother and father were quite happy and had been deliriously in love. She traveled with him and his acting troupe for a few years, roaming the English countryside.

Alas for love. When I was a year old, my father succumbed to the unromantic illness of influenza and passed from this earth. My mother tried to hang on with the troupe, but if you cannot work in a troupe of strolling players, they soon have enough of you. My mother and I were left behind in Winchester at the same time Jane Seymour lay dying, and the troupe went on.

My mother is rather a helpless person. (I learned this at four years old, when she fell into a crying fit because she could not find a pair of shoes. I found the shoes, she told me I was uncommonly clever, and sunshine was restored.) But after the troupe abandoned her, she somehow made her way back home to Devon. My grandmother, still displeased, nearly refused to let her in, but Grandmother felt sorry for me, poor fatherless girl, and let us stay.

My mother, as I said, was not very strong. Soon after the instance of the lost shoes, she met a man—of the correct lineage this time—and married him.

She fell easily in love with Sir Philip Baldwin, but I do not believe he ever loved her. He wanted a family connection and a pretty lady to sew his shirts and impress his neighbors, nothing more. If my mother realized this, it did not bother her in the slightest. She enjoyed playing lady of the manor and shook the dust of the troupe from her feet with a speed that frightened me.

There was no room in this domestic bliss for me—the child of the actor who'd eloped with my mother. The validity of my mother's first marriage was called into question, and by extension, my legitimacy.

My grandmother indignantly said I was no bastard, but my stepfather was not interested in admitting an awkward girl-child into his house. So at age five, I was fostered to my Aunt Katherine—who was a cousin of my mother on her father's side, but whom I always referred to as *aunt*—and went with her to Hertfordshire and the lady Elizabeth.

The ladies and gentlemen of Elizabeth's household accepted me and more or less let me do as I pleased. Aunt Kat had a rather privileged position, and the household servants treated me with some indulgence. I was neither servant nor lady, but rather a hybrid who waited upon my aunt, played with Elizabeth when she wanted me, ran errands, and stole off to do as I pleased.

I lived an unusual but not unhappy childhood. Elizabeth was an imperious girl, ever more so than her sister, Mary. Mary was old and unhappy by age twenty, given to melancholy looks and much time on her knees. Elizabeth, in contrast, accepted every morsel of food, piece of clothing, and curtsey or bow as though it were her due, and as though those bestowing it should feel honored to do so.

Even Elizabeth deprived of her rank as princess never changed her demeanor. She was royal to the core. When her will was crossed, she grew at first haughty and cold. Then, if things did not improve, she grew red in the face, her dark eyes sparkled, and she lashed out.

She twisted words into scathing reprimands I never could achieve, and to prove her point, she sometimes used her fists. Afterward, the storm receded, and she would be apologetic, even generous, but never ashamed.

The first years in Elizabeth's household passed comfortably enough, life flowing in easy routine. When I was twelve, in 1545, my aunt married John Ashley, a gentleman of Elizabeth's household, but this was hardly a bump in the road. John Ashley was a grave and courteous man, and I liked him. They were married, I called him uncle, and that was that.

About the time Aunt Kat married, my own talent for needle-work blossomed. I'd always been a clever sewer, but now whenever I buried my hands in a piece of fabric, a vision came to me of the completed garment, down to the tiniest detailed seam and brush of velvet. I could draw this garment and then cut and sew it exactly as I had pictured, and the result was always beautiful.

The morning in January when all our lives changed, I was sketching an idea for a new gown for Elizabeth. I wanted to try something in the French fashion, the sleeve caps puffed above the shoulders and stuffed with wool. I was not certain the style would become Elizabeth, who had fine white shoulders that looked well in the red damask I had made for her portrait, where the sleeves slipped the slightest bit to reveal bosom and shoulder.

"My brother has come," Elizabeth announced from a window embrasure. "Why has he come?"

She peered out into the bright afternoon, which was already clouding over for more rain. Her red-gold hair hung long from a high forehead, parted in the middle to reveal a straight white streak of scalp.

"Someone else is with him. Those are not my brother's banners." Her pale lips thinned, and her brows drew together in disapproval.

I left my unsatisfactory drawing and came to the window. The milk-white skin of her throat smelled of lemons as I drew close to look. "Aunt Kat, come and see."

Aunt Kat threw me an irritated glance. She had set her plump form before the fire, her feet on a stool, her book in a lap. Had it been only me in the room, she'd have stayed seated, but Elizabeth frowned down into the courtyard, impatient and curious.

Aunt Kat heaved herself to her feet. She came to the window, her wide skirts swaying, and looked over Elizabeth's other shoulder. "It is Hertford," she said crisply. "The Earl of. Edward Seymour."

Disapproval weighted her tone. Hertford was the older brother of Jane Seymour—Jane, who had caused Elizabeth's mother to be sacrificed so that she could bear King Henry a son.

Aunt Kat had never met Anne Boleyn before her fall, but Aunt Kat's love for Elizabeth extended to animosity to those who had hurt her, even indirectly. Jane's hold over King Henry had caused Henry to declare Anne an adulteress, execute her, and proclaim Elizabeth a bastard and no heir to the throne. After Henry's marriage to Catherine Parr, however, he restored Mary and Elizabeth with another act of succession, though Aunt Kat always grumbled that he took his time to do it.

"Why Hertford?" Elizabeth asked.

The question was not naïve; her voice held calm determination to work out a puzzle. Her brother Edward coming here to Enfield was not strange. Edward and Elizabeth sometimes shared a house, with his entourage as a royal prince, with hers as Henry's daughter, with Mary's as princess, and with Jane Grey's, granddaughter of Henry's sister.

Not strange that Edward should be with his uncle Hertford. Still, there was something sinister in the way the banners closed around the small prince on his horse, surrounding him and cutting him off. Elizabeth scowled down at them, then turned away, the puzzle not forgotten.

"I will dress to meet my brother."

Elizabeth was already perfectly splendid in a blue velvet gown and gold kirtle, but she would never allow herself to be seen in less than her best on any occasion. The presence of Hertford made her determined to present herself in regal form.

Something was wrong. I sensed it, Aunt Kat sensed it, and one of Elizabeth's gentlewomen, hastily sent for to help me dress Elizabeth, sensed it as well. While a servant lit candles, we slid a blue kirtle over Lady Elizabeth's shoulders and helped her fasten on bodice and sleeves. I sewed a small tear in the blue satin sleeve, passing the silk thread through my mouth to make it slick. I turned Elizabeth to the window so I would have more light, and continued my stitching.

She looked out at the courtyard, where the horses and riders of Hertford's entourage lingered. Blossoming candlelight reflected her in the glass, clear as a mirror. She had a long, rather narrow face, a small nose, slightly hooked, and pale lips. Her eyes, intelligent and alert, flicked from the men to the horses. She stroked one long finger down her bodice but not nervously.

In the reflection, I saw myself and Aunt Kat standing to either side of her, robust contrasts to Elizabeth's aristocratic slenderness. Aunt Kat was a large woman. Her stiffened bodice pressed her belly into a narrow line, but her skirt belled from her ample hips.

I took after Kat, being a little too plump, though my young body was not much larger than Lady Elizabeth's. But while I looked as though I had a healthy appetite, Elizabeth was always thin. Her hair was red-gold, her father's hair. I had my father's hair, too, but a dull brown-black. Aunt Kat and I had the same eyes, round and blue, both of us gazing at the world with frank interest.

Aunt Kat had much learning, as I said, much more than I, but the pair of us shared a curiosity that everyone but us found unusual. Aunt Kat assuaged hers by reading books and learning languages; I assuaged mine by poking into things that did not concern me.

I and the gentlewoman pulled Elizabeth's overdress over her, a robe-like garment that draped back from her silk kirtle in folds of velvet, soft as lamb's wool. Despite Elizabeth's preoccupation with her brother and his arrival, she scrutinized every inch of the gown and inspected the tear I had mended.

"My thanks, Eloise," she said, as though I'd saved her favorite dog from drowning.

I did not follow the princess and her train of ladies through the house and downstairs for the meeting with Elizabeth and her brother the prince, but I did not long fret at being left behind. As soon as Elizabeth descended, Aunt Kat caught my hand and pulled me along the gallery. Hand in hand, silent as conspirators, we tiptoed along to another set of stairs down to the ground floor and approached the great hall from behind.

On the dais, where the high table would sit if used, was a barred screen. The purpose of this was to provide a place to keep food warm while the servants served, but now Aunt Kat and I used it for the purpose of spying on those in the hall. We peered out through the slats just as Elizabeth and her retinue entered.

I had seen Prince Edward before, though not for many months. I always thought him a lackluster boy, even at only nine years old, and I did not change my opinion now. Fair-haired and pale-faced, Edward had a weak chin and a weaker mouth. He was not sickly, but an air of malaise hung about him even though he moved with a robust manner. He did not wear finery but riding clothes and eyed Elizabeth's gown, sleek hair, and pearl-studded French hood with some aspersion.

Elizabeth halted and curtseyed to her brother. He politely bowed in return, and then his gaze moved to his uncle next to him.

Tall and bearded, Edward Seymour, Earl of Hertford, had an animated gleam in his dark eyes. Even from behind the screen I saw that he held his mouth straight with effort and moved his hands in an agitated manner.

Elizabeth waited for Hertford to acknowledge her. She was a king's daughter; he merely the brother to a deceased queen. Hertford bowed to her almost as an afterthought, which I could see displeased her.

Before she could say anything to him, or even to her brother, Hertford dropped to one knee before Prince Edward.

"Your Grace," he said. "The King, your father . . ." He faltered.

I pressed my face to the bars. I saw that Hertford struggled to keep his mouth turned down, to present sorrow, but he was pretending. His fingers twitched, and his eyes sparkled with excitement every time he forgot to shield them.

"Your Grace." He took Edward's hand and pressed it to his lips. "My lord of England."

Edward gasped, his pale face whitening further.

Elizabeth moved forward, skirts swishing across the geometric stones. "What are you saying? What about our father?" Her sharp voice held none of the hysteria of childhood, clearly seeing through Hertford's posture of sorrow.

"My lady. Your Grace." Hertford collected himself and settled his face into grim lines. "Your royal father is dead. I am the first to call His Grace King."

Two things flashed through my mind: first, shock that King Henry, who had seemed stubborn enough to live forever, was gone. It seemed unbelievable. Second, that Hertford hadn't told Edward right away. He'd waited until the boy was with his sister. Out of kindness? I studied Hertford's face. He certainly did not look at Edward kindly.

At that moment, Hertford bowed his head over Edward's hand. "I swear to protect him from this moment with my life and give him my wisdom as though he were my own son."

Beside me, Aunt Kat gave a loud, decided sniff.

No one in the tableau heard. They froze, all three of them. Elizabeth, grand, upright, her back straight, her face hard as marble. Edward, small, thin, and vulnerable. And Seymour, Earl of Hertford, crouched between them, his back a blank plane to Elizabeth, his face pressed to Edward's hand. Edward, the new King of England, Ireland, and Wales, began to cry.

✦

JOHN ASHLEY SLOSHED another stream of purple hock into a cup and pushed it across the boards to me.

"Not too much, John," Aunt Kat admonished him. "You'll make her tipsy."

John Ashley smiled at his wife with a benevolence that hadn't dimmed with two years of marriage. " 'Tis not every day a child-hood playmate becomes a king."

"He never thought of me," I said, idly twirling the cup. I did not care; I had never been much interested in Edward. Elizabeth at thirteen did nothing without calculation, even in a temper. Edward, four and a half years younger, always seemed to need someone to guide him. I was being unfair—he was only a child, after all—but I could not help feeling he would be an easy king to manage.

"It was touching," Aunt Kat put in. "To see them weep together. My lady has tender feelings for her brother and her father."

"Lord Hertford was glad," I said.

Kat and Uncle John ceased speaking and looked at me. I sipped the hock, liking its sour bite on my tongue. "Lord Hertford is glad Henry is dead," I continued. "He acted sorrowful, but he was not."

"You should not gossip about your betters," Aunt Kat said,

but absently, as though she admonished me out of habit and not from any conviction that I was wrong.

I gave her an innocent look. "Everyone is my better here, auntie. Who am I to gossip about?"

"Mind your tongue, miss." Uncle John grinned at me, drained his glass, and reached for the bottle. "You are not wrong, Eloise," he said. "The Duke of Norfolk overplayed his hand, or *he* would have knelt to Edward today to break the news, *he* pledging himself to guard the King. But he cannot from the Tower, can he?"

"Norfolk?" My interest in politics at this point was negligible unless it directly related to Elizabeth. On the other hand the arrival of a trade ship from Amsterdam or Spain excited my interest, because a ship might bring silks from the East, which Elizabeth would buy or be given, and then they'd be handed to me to work. My greatest joy was rubbing my hands over exotic fabric, even burying my nose in it to inhale its dyed scent. My grasp of Latin and French might be crude, that of Greek nonexistent, but with a needle in my hand I could do anything.

I knew each of Elizabeth's gowns the way I'd know my own children. I knew that the azure gown we'd dressed her in today had been made of satin from Milan, silk woven in an oriental city, lace sewn by young ladies in Liege. I knew that the satin shimmered because the warp threads were green while the weft was blue, making the skirts appear as liquid light when she moved.

Lady Elizabeth would need new gowns now, I thought in anticipation, first for mourning her father, then for her appearance in Edward's court. I had no doubt that he'd ask her to attend court, the brother and sister were so close. She'd need court gowns, ball gowns, gowns for dining with ambassadors, gowns for hawking and hunting with her brother.

I thought of the coming days with relish. Lady Elizabeth would become an even more important personage as the King's sister. I imagined her in ermine-trimmed robes; in cloth of tissue and cloth of gold; tight, pointed bodices of brocade; skirts of damask and velvet and silk. I imagined sleeves of a gold brocade folded back to reveal undersleeves in scarlet silk. My fingers itched to get to my drawing paper and chalk.

"His son's severed head," said Uncle John.

I jumped, my visions fading. Aunt Kat looked at me in disapproval, wanting me to accord John Ashley the attention and respect I'd give a father. "Forgive me," I squeaked. "What on earth are you talking about, sir?"

"The Earl of Surrey," John repeated. "That damned Howard family has no idea how to be subtle. They wished to control Edward's Regency, and tried to take their power before old Henry was even dead. The King would have none of that. But Surrey stuck his nose in the air and said that power was his due. So his head was parted from his body. Poets!" He shook his head as though writing couplets alone had led to the death of the Earl of Surrey.

"His father is still in the Tower?" Aunt Kat asked him.

"Norfolk will win his freedom. The wily old man has been in and out of favor so often that turning coat is second nature to him. He knows exactly what words to say to boost himself from the muck. Henry was to have signed for Norfolk's execution but conveniently died before he could. Norfolk has escaped the chop once again."

I shook my head with him. I was a gentle soul and hated violence of any kind—I would catch bees in a cup and put them out the window rather than smash them and disliked hearing of executions. But I also had little patience with impatient men. The Duke of Norfolk and his son Surrey had pushed forward to take what they wanted. Because of their haste, they'd let a rival family, the Seymours, swoop down and seize Edward.

The Seymours had literally seized him. This very night Lord Hertford had taken the boy King by the shoulders, hastened him out the door, and hoisted him onto a horse. They needed to get to London immediately, he had said. Edward, dashing tears from his eyes, had obeyed.

The games will begin in earnest now, I thought.

Prince Edward was a Seymour, Lady Elizabeth descended from the Howards—she was the Duke of Norfolk's grandniece and the dead Surrey's cousin—and Princess Mary had Spanish royal blood. Even I, not astute at politics, realized what a boiling mixture that would be.

❖

I DID HELP make Elizabeth's new clothes, to my delight, but not for a funeral. Elizabeth did not attend King Henry's funeral and neither did her brother, but nor did she attend Edward's coronation.

As it turned out, the first sumptuous clothes I made for Elizabeth were for a wedding. Her stepmother, Catherine, the widowed Queen, wed none other than Lord Hertford's younger brother, Thomas Seymour, who had, with the ease of a dancer, stepped into the position of Lord High Admiral. Thomas Seymour proposed to Queen Catherine, and Catherine, in love like a girl, quickly accepted.

The boiling had begun.

2

I FELL IN love with Thomas Seymour of Sudeley, Lord High Admiral of England, the moment I saw him. How I fell out of love with him again changed me from naïve child to wary woman.

Seymour was tall, strong-limbed, and robust, with a full red beard that outlined sensual lips. His eyes were dark and filled with fire. When he smiled, or better still, laughed, he warmed the room.

Aunt Kat and my lady Elizabeth fell in love with him, too, I saw in the softening of their eyes when they looked at him. Queen Catherine had been in love with him well before she'd married King Henry, and only a few short months after the King's death, she became Thomas Seymour's lawfully wedded wife.

Seymour's older brother, now Duke of Somerset and Lord Protector of England, was furious at the marriage. He proceeded to exclude Catherine from court, making his own wife first lady of England, although Catherine, stepmother to the King and widow of the former King, should have had that right.

But I do not think Catherine cared about losing her place. Court formality and playing nursemaid to a wretched, gouty old man was behind her—she'd landed the man she loved in marriage and lived with him now at Sudeley Castle and in their large home in Chelsea.

I watched Thomas Seymour take supper in the great hall at Chelsea with the Queen and Elizabeth, while I hovered to wait on them with Catherine's waiting women and Seymour's gentlemen. I feared that my bold gaze at Seymour would gain me dismissal, but I realized that all other ladies' eyes were likewise fixed on the Queen's new husband, and I was not noticed.

He was a man made to be admired. Since King Edward's coronation, he had been made Lord High Admiral of England, which meant he commanded the navy and the seas. He and his brother, Somerset, ran Britain between them for the boy-king Edward, although Somerset, Lord High Protector and flaunting it, gripped most of the power. Thomas Seymour was left to bedazzle this household of ladies and succeeded admirably.

Next to him, dowager Queen Catherine smiled, pleased as a cat. She was old now, being thirty-five, but she was still stately and pretty. She drank wine and smiled and laughed, ready to let happiness enter her life.

John Ashley did not admire him. "That man is trouble," he said darkly one evening as we sat in his chamber for our usual after-supper gossip.

"Nonsense," answered his wife, taken with Thomas Seymour and not ashamed of it. "See how fond he is of the Queen. She deserved to marry for love. He is a breath of fresh air."

"Cat in a henhouse," John Ashley muttered, then said no more of it.

Later that night I carried a pile of new cloth to Queen Catherine's chambers. She liked my work, and she had asked for me to assist her lady of the wardrobe in constructing new gowns for her as Lady Sudeley. Catherine, for all she was a modest lady of the Reformed religion, dressed well, and I looked forward to creating gowns for her.

I had a love affair with fabric. Nothing else on earth, not even the eyes of a handsome man, could make my blood sing and my skin tingle like a finely woven piece of cloth. The velvet I carried sang in my ears and smelled of rich blue. I could taste and smell fabric as a cook could herbs, knowing which was exactly right for which dish.

The moment I touched this velvet, I saw a gown for Catherine take shape—a belled skirt tucked at the waist, paired with a bodice of cloth of silver over a kirtle of blue satin. So infatuated was I with my velvet that I never noticed Thomas Seymour until he was before me, filling the dark passage to the Queen's antechamber and blocking my way.

My heart did a double beat. First the velvet, then encountering the very handsome Seymour alone thrilled my girl's heart. I had not yet seen him close up and had not realized how very tall he was. My head went back of its own accord, my neck craning so that I could take in all of him.

"Is that a pile of cloth with legs?" he asked, his voice muted but rich as the velvet I held.

I curtseyed, knees shaking, and nearly overbalanced my load. A broad hand landed on top of the cloth, steadying it.

His dark eyes danced as he peered down at me, and his smile showed teeth that were white, though crooked. "What are you?"

"I'm a g-girl," I answered.

A foolish answer in a foolish stammer. "I see 'tis so. But you have the bosom of a woman. Where is your husband?"

"I am not married, my lord."

"Ah, poor mite." He leaned over the clothes, his handsome face coming close to mine. "Would you like to be?"

I was thoroughly bewildered. Why such a highborn man would even notice me, a seamstress and a governess's niece, let alone speak to me so familiarly puzzled me greatly.

"I am too young," I managed.

"You are not, indeed."

He moved closer to me, and I backed up a step. He grinned like a wolf. He took another step forward. My left foot slid back. He took another, and I another, until my heel contacted with the stone of the wall.

"You are a woman, young . . . What is your name?"

"Eloise," I said faintly. "Eloise Rousell."

"Are you French?" he asked in that language.

"*Non, monsieur.*" I resumed in English. "I am not French. My father had a French name."

Grandmama vowed that the man's name was Russell, plain and simple, but that he'd given himself airs and changed it to the French spelling.

"Better still, a good English girl. The King, he is a good English boy, son of my English sister and the very English King Harry."

"Yes, my lord." I agreed, although at this moment, I'd agree if he'd said his sister had been a mad Amazon from Saracen lands.

"Where are you taking all those cloths, Eloise of England?"

His breath smelled heavily of wine, and another smell clung to him that I could not identify, warm and sweet and cloying. He was not drunk, but his eyes were heavy and his cheeks red.

"To the Queen's chamber," I said.

"She is no longer the Queen. She is plain Lady Sudeley, my wife. Do you find her plain?"

"Of course not, my lord. She is most beautiful."

"For her age."

"She is no longer young, but . . ." Queen Catherine had a dignified beauty that I admired. She also had a kind smile and a way of speaking to those inferior to her that made them want to serve her.

I could not express this while her new husband had me backed against the wall, smiling in an odd manner. I feared to offend him and so be punished. Perhaps gentle Queen Catherine would grow angry at me for displeasing her beloved husband.

"Young, that is the thing," Thomas Seymour went on. "I like a young lady. How young are you?"

"Fourteen in September," I faltered.

"An excellent age. Ripe for marriage. The Lady Elizabeth, how young is she?"

"She will be fourteen as well, my lord. We were born five days apart."

His eyes gleamed. "Now, there is a fact. I will remember it."

He seemed to wait for my answer. I blurted, "Will you, my lord?"

"I will. Fourteen is a woman, Eloise of England."

He reached down and squeezed my left breast, hard. In that moment, my childhood ended and my adult life began.

I saw myself, him, the passage, and the cloth in my arms in brutal clarity. He was no longer a handsome man to be admired, but a man of licentious tastes, who thought nothing of accosting a girl of the household not ten feet from his wife's chamber door. I saw myself, small and innocent and sheltered facing him on quaking legs. I'd encountered no other men in my life than my Uncle John, William Grindal, and other gentlemen who waited on Elizabeth. Their gatherings were serious and quiet, punctuated with discussion on philosophy and the scriptures, in which my Aunt Kat and Lady Elizabeth took full part.

At Enfield and other places Elizabeth resided, we had never had the presence of a full-blooded male, a man who wanted life and power and desire. *A breath of fresh air,* Aunt Kat had called him. I called him a hurricane, a force to flatten the unwary.

If Thomas Seymour forced himself on me, he would walk away, whistling. I, if I could not hide it, would be blamed for being loose and lascivious. Queen Catherine might grow furious and turn me out. Lady Elizabeth would be disgusted. Even if Aunt Kat forgave me, she could do nothing to help me. My mother did not want me. My grandmother would say that blood would tell.

I looked up at Thomas Seymour's smiling face. No longer a handsome courtier, he'd transformed into a monster.

I could not step away from him, since he had me flat against the wall. Screaming would only bring the Queen from her chamber to see me beguiling her husband in the passage.

Since I could go neither backward nor forward, I dropped straight down. The cloth flew from my hands. I bumped my nose on his hard thigh, my forehead on the top of his boot.

Startled, he sprang backward, then recovered and grabbed for me.

I scuttled out of reach, snatched up the cloth and ran, trailing fabric. The beautiful blue velvet snaked its way around my ankles, and I tumbled to the floor. Heart racing, I turned over, my hands burning from the cold, rough stone.

Thomas Seymour stood over me, mouth open in surprise and anger. Then his grin returned, as did that gleam in his eye that terrified me. I scrambled to my feet. Abandoning my precious cloth, I fled.

His chuckle followed me down the cold corridor. "Scamper, little kitten. One day, come back and find your tom." He laughed softly, a sound that carried down the passage and up the stair as I ran for the safety of my own rooms.

✠

THE NEXT DAY Aunt Kat seized me by the ear. "Whatever came over you, Eloise? Leaving costly cloths lying in the middle of the floor! The velvet was as good as ruined. What were you thinking?"

"I saw a ghost," I said. "It frightened me."

Aunt Kat released me but frowned, her plump face severe. "What ghost?"

"I could not see," I said glibly. "I heard her screams."

Aunt Kat frowned further, but she darted a superstitious glance at the ceiling above us. "Nonsense."

"No, Aunt Kat. It is the truth. It came from the upper gallery. I heard her wailing and shrieking."

I closed my mouth then, afraid of overembellishing. I did not actually believe in ghosts, being much too hardheaded for superstition, but Aunt Kat believed in sorcery and astrology and ghosts aplenty. Besides which, the dark and windowless upper gallery was unnerving.

"Mention none of your ghosts to Lady Elizabeth," Aunt Kat said. "She sometimes has bad dreams, and I do not wish to worry her."

" 'Tis the ghosts," I said. "They give her the bad dreams."

Aunt Kat gave me a gentle slap across the cheek. "Enough, you silly girl. Go on with you."

I curtseyed and left her to return to my sewing. I'd diverted her attention from the ruined fabric and from speculating why I of all people had let it be ruined.

From then on, I took care never to be caught in the halls alone. If I had to travel to dark corners of the house, I trotted in the footsteps of the housekeeper or other maids, and when I sewed, I did so in the presence of Aunt Kat or Lady Elizabeth or the dowager Queen and her entourage.

This was made easier for me because the house was quite full. The dowager Queen had her ladies, at least a hundred of them; Lady Elizabeth had ladies and gentlemen to wait on her, and maids and Aunt Kat. We began to be rather cramped, which suited me, because I could always stay in a crowd and avoid Thomas Seymour.

The morning after our first encounter, he'd caught sight of me in the great hall. His eyes rested on me, and he smiled. Panicked, I pretended not to notice. When he happened to pass close to me, he mimed a cat with claws and murmured, "Run away, little kitten."

After that he said not a word, nor even looked at me. He seemed, to my relief, to forget all about me.

I could not avoid Lord Seymour altogether, try as I might. He was the man of the house. He had his own retinue, which crowded us further, and he expected his orders to be obeyed before his wife's.

The servants, fiercely loyal to whatever master or mistress they served, fought among themselves.

"That wine is for Her Grace Elizabeth."

"No, 'tis to go to the Queen dowager."

"Her Grace Elizabeth always has *this* wine."

"It is the Queen dowager's private stock."

"No, it was purchased by Her Grace Elizabeth's household."

Then a stentorian voice. "His lordship commands it be brought for him. It will be given to his lady or the lady Elizabeth at his pleasure."

Thus endeth the argument.

※

IN FINE WEATHER, Elizabeth walked in the gardens. I walked with her, being one of the few women her age in Queen Catherine's household, and she'd professed me a favorite, her liking for me heightened by her affection for Aunt Kat. I never made the mistake that Elizabeth thought me an equal, I not being even as highborn as the countesses and baronets' wives and daughters, but she did like to confide in me things she would not the others. Harmless Eloise the seamstress did not tell tales.

One particular morning in 1548, when the sky was as blue as the kirtle I was sewing for my lady Elizabeth, she and I wandered the gardens in an aimless fashion. We walked arm in arm, she in silks, I in serviceable linen and wool. But though I wore sensible fabrics, my skill with the needle transformed them into beautiful lines.

Our wandering surprised me, because Elizabeth usually laid out her plans for walks like a general preparing for battle. "Where are we going, Your Grace?" I asked.

"I do not know. Where shall we walk, Eloise?" She slanted me a half smile, a strange light in her dark eyes.

"The gardeners have bedded out geraniums in the front walk, Your Grace," I offered. "They are quite beautiful, scarlet against the green."

"No." She gripped my arm and half pulled me toward the far end of the gardens and the river. "I would like to walk among the hedges."

"As you wish, Your Grace."

I acquiesced, first because she employed me, and second because it was clear she'd drag me wherever she wanted to walk. She propelled me along toward the long hedges, no more strolling.

"What think you of this gown, Eloise?" she asked. "Does it suit me?"

"Of course, Your Grace." The gown slid from her shoulders to bare a small bit of white bosom, flattering her slender frame. The bodice was modest, because Aunt Kat would let Elizabeth wear nothing but a modest gown, but her white throat, slim shoulders, and small breasts made it somewhat alluring.

A nubile lady, it announced, within whom first longings have begun to stir. Untouched, untried, waiting.

"I made certain of it," I continued.

Her lips twitched. "Your talent is formidable, as is your pride. Guard against pride, Eloise. It will be your downfall."

"Aye, Aunt Kat says the same."

She showed her teeth in a smile. "Cunning is better. Remember that."

She had lost me, but I murmured, "Yes, Your Grace."

She stopped so suddenly that my momentum propelled me forward a few steps before her arm dragged me back.

"Is someone there?" she asked.

I saw movement among the hedges, but the walk was bathed in shadow. The hairs on my neck began to prickle. "A gardener?"

"No." Her eyes glittered, but not with fear. "Let us catch him, whoever he is."

"Take care, my lady," I said, alarmed. "It might be a robber."

She laughed. "Not in my stepmother's gardens. They would not dare."

They would, I thought. I'd heard of earls and ladies set upon at the edges of their own estates if they were not careful. Some bandits did not care how highborn their victims, as long as they made off with goods and did not get caught.

The fact that Elizabeth hurried forward to confront such a man, with no more weapon between us than the scissors in my pocket, horrified me.

"Your Grace," I protested.

She would not answer. Her breath quickening with our pace, she dragged me on toward the hedges.

Let it be a rabbit, I prayed. *Or a gardener. Or a rat.*

It was my lord Thomas Seymour.

He sprang from behind a low hedge, roaring and growling like a bear, waving his arms like a madman. Elizabeth screamed, but with the squeal of an excited girl. My own scream tore from my throat in genuine terror.

"Your Grace, run," I shouted.

Still shrieking in the high-pitched bursts of a lady pretending to be afraid, Elizabeth dragged me around and began running down a side path. Not back toward the house, and not very quickly.

"Your Grace," I panted.

"Let us run, Eloise," she said, delightedly. "Or he will be upon us."

Thomas Seymour, still growling, pursued us. Did he run slowly, or was that my imagination? Elizabeth ran slower still. I wanted to scream loud and long, to rip my hand from her and flee to my tiny room, high under the eaves. Elizabeth held me fast. I'd need ten soldiers, armed, to pry myself from her.

We rounded a corner. I saw ahead, unbelievably, Queen Catherine herself, bobbing up and down on her toes, laughing like a girl.

"This way, my dears," she trilled. "Hurry."

She motioned with her arm to us, and we scampered after her. "Come along, come along," she called. "Else he catches us."

And what shall he do if he does? I thought suddenly. Surely, with Queen Catherine there, he could do nothing.

Months ago, I would have believed it a harmless game. But I remembered the dark, cool passage, the soft cloth in my arms, the sour taste of fear in my mouth, and the feel of Thomas Seymour's warmth on my body. I remembered his fingers squeezing my breast, the brush of his fingers on my skin.

There are three of us, I thought stoutly. *We can hold him off.*

"Come along, come along," Catherine shouted.

We ran after her, skirts flying, Elizabeth occasionally screaming, then laughing.

Catherine led us down another path, then round a corner to a dead end. A high green hedge faced us, the edge of the park. Here a stone bench offered the passerby a place of peace. For us, it was a trap.

I shrieked, "The other way!"

Too late. Thomas Seymour charged around the corner, penning us like calves herded for slaughter. I faced him, mouth dry and eyes wide. Catherine and Elizabeth collapsed into laughter.

Thomas came forward, growling and lurching, still playing bear. Catherine flung her arms around Elizabeth from behind. "I caught her, darling," she said breathlessly. "I've caught her!"

Elizabeth whooped with laughter. Catherine held on. Elizabeth's long hair came free from her French hood and fell about her in a cloud of red-gold.

Seymour ignored me completely, intent on Elizabeth in his wife's arms. His eyes glittered with a feral light. "You've caught us a lovely fawn, my dear." He swatted playfully at Elizabeth's hip. "Naughty fawn, to run away."

Elizabeth smiled widely, her eyes alight. Thomas wound a

lock of her loose hair around his fist. "What shall we do to punish our pet, my dear?"

Catherine laughed, the love in her eyes painful to see. "Naughty girl," she said, hugging Elizabeth. "Naughty child."

I stood in a daze, my back against the hedge, my hood slipping over my ear. I realized three games were being played here before me. One was Catherine's—she merely happy to be lighthearted and laughing with her husband. The second game was Elizabeth's. Catherine could not see her look at Thomas, the one that admired him as a virile man, not a stepfather. Elizabeth liked that he chased her, and she liked, better still, that he'd caught her.

The third game belonged to Thomas Seymour. He had exactly what he wanted, Elizabeth cornered with his wife's help. I watched a play, and only Seymour knew all the parts.

His eyes slid sideways, took me in. "Needlewoman," he said. "You must go nowhere without your needle and thread, eh?"

"Yes, my lord," I rasped.

"And your scissors? What needlewoman is without scissors?"

"Yes, my lord."

"Hand them over."

I froze in astonishment. Catherine's eyes lit up. "Yes, dear Eloise, give them over."

Elizabeth struggled in some earnest, though she laughed through her words. "No, no, do not cut off my hair."

"Give them." Seymour swung a glare on me that burned like ice.

Quickly I dipped my hand in my pocket, drew out the scissors, and held them out. Thomas snatched them from me. The face he turned back to Elizabeth and Catherine was teasing. "Hold her, my love."

"No," Elizabeth cried. "I beg you, not my hair."

"Very well," Thomas said. "Your hair is safe."

He snatched up a handful of her skirt and began to snip it.

I cried out in anguish. I had labored over that skirt and knew every stitch of it. The intricate gold and silver pattern had been difficult to match, the black velvet overskirt so fine it was like gossamer. I had been proud of that gown, which I'd made to be both beautiful and modest. I watched, open-mouthed, as Thomas Seymour proceeded to ruin weeks of my work.

Snip, snip went the scissors. Catherine laughed. Elizabeth laughed. Thomas concentrated on his task, his breathing hard, his eyes fixed and glazed.

I stood against the hedge, the twigs prickling my head and neck and shoulders. Pieces of skirt fluttered to the earth, to lie like bright, fallen flowers of gold and black.

Thomas Seymour kept on cutting, a mad light in his eyes. In the end, the ground was carpeted with cloth. When Seymour finished and tossed the scissors aside, Elizabeth had nothing to cover her loosened stomacher and chemise but her stepmother's cloak.

3

 "For shame," Aunt Kat scolded.

Elizabeth, sitting in a dressing gown in her bedchamber and drinking the sweet herb tea Aunt Kat had brought her, at last looked stricken.

Only Aunt Kat could scold Elizabeth. She'd outgrown listening to any other long ago. But Katherine Ashley held a special place in Elizabeth's heart and could speak her mind.

"The shame of it," she repeated. "Every person's eyes agog when you came in. Thank the Lord the Queen was with you, though she ought to know better. She held England safe through months of war, and then to throw away dignity on a silly romp in the garden."

" 'Twas only a game, Kat," Elizabeth said. She sipped tea, her slim shoulders drooping. She had returned to being a guilt-stricken little girl, not a young woman who wanted a man.

"You may have thought so," Aunt Kat sniffed. "But there are others who do not. As the King's sister you must jealously guard your reputation. He'll likely make a good marriage for you, but if your reputation is in shreds, you will have to make do with the dregs."

Elizabeth looked sullen but with a defiant gleam in her eye. "I could not prevail against the both of them."

"Mind that you learn how." Aunt Kat gave her another stern look, and then her expression softened. "He's a fine-mannered man, his lordship, used to flirtations at court. You are *not* used to it. He does not know this. Young ladies your age are married off already and know how to comport themselves. His lordship is not used to a simple household and does not understand."

I, my mouth full of pins and my lap full of Parisian silver netting, did not agree. I thought that Thomas Seymour knew exactly what he was doing and exactly how far to push his wife to get it.

I assumed, at that time, that he simply wanted a dalliance with Elizabeth. I could understand why. She was slender and beautiful, with her red hair and dark, flashing eyes, combining the best of her father and mother. I had never known Anne Boleyn, the woman for whom King Henry had nearly destroyed England, but I had seen her portrait, and I had heard gentlemen who knew her wax eloquent about her.

Dark hair, pale face, not really much to look at, until she turned her eyes upon one and smiled. Anne's eyes had been starred with silver lights, and she could hold a man with her gaze (the gentlemen claimed) and make him her slave.

Henry himself had been robust and handsome in his youth, with red-gold hair and a physique envied by gentlemen in England and beyond. He had been strong, loud, restless, arbitrarily cruel or generous, a slave to his own passions, and unforgiving of passions in others.

He'd been attractive and fiery and so had Anne. Between them they produced a daughter with a strong, handsome face, a graceful body, a sense of elegance, a presence like a whiplash, and a calculating mind.

Aunt Kat had a fond belief that she controlled this girl, and to a point, she did. Elizabeth listened to Aunt Kat. But only to a point.

Thomas Seymour had designs on her, and Elizabeth was not unhappy with those designs. She loved her stepmother, of course—Elizabeth was very fond of Queen Catherine—but a handsome man, very interested in a young woman, could cloud that young woman's mind. I well knew this.

I prayed that Elizabeth would not go so far as to betray Queen Catherine. I burned inside with my secret knowledge of Thomas Seymour's character, but I did not want to confess it in the presence of Elizabeth.

I waited until later, after Elizabeth had gone to bed and Aunt Kat was alone in her chamber, reading. I knelt at her feet and told her about my encounter with Thomas Seymour. I bowed my head, afraid and ashamed as only a girl of fourteen can be.

Aunt Kat closed her book with a snap. "And what were you doing traipsing the galleries at that time of night?"

"Carrying the cloths to the Queen's chamber. Well, her antechamber. I assumed her asleep. I was anxious to begin."

Kat looked at me, her usually shrewd eyes going deliberately blank. "You must have mistaken his intentions."

"No, aunt." I remembered the pressure on my breast, the unclean feeling in my belly, and the startled wonder that a man had touched me familiarly.

"You were mistaken," she repeated. "He is a rogue, and he smiled at you. It excited you."

"No, aunt. It disgusted me, rather."

"Do not say such things about your betters, Eloise. People will think I have raised you with no manners."

"Please, listen—"

"I do not wish to listen. You were mistaken. Say nothing more of it."

"I thought you would wish to keep Elizabeth safe."

"I do. I want that beyond everything." The shrewd light returned to Aunt Kat's eyes. "There is more to this than what you see. Say *nothing*, for Jesus' sake, or you could bring disaster upon us all."

"But poor Queen Catherine," I tried.

"Eloise, to whom are you loyal?"

"To you, aunt," I said, bewildered.

"And?"

"Uncle John."

"And?"

"Lady Elizabeth."

She nodded, satisfied, and plied me with no more *ands*. "Keep your thoughts to yourself," she said, "and your mouth closed. Close your eyes as well, if need be."

"I understand nothing of this."

She looked me up and down and sighed. "I suppose it comes of your mother marrying low. I had expected you to grow up a bearer of false tales, like your father. Instead, God has gifted you with a straight tongue and shining honesty. Unfortunately, these gifts are not always useful in the world of the court."

"You would rather I learned to lie?"

She patted my cheek. "Of course not, dear. But I would like you to discover the meaning of the word *discretion* and apply it well."

"Discretion." I repeated.

"Yes, dear." She shook her head, as though bemoaning my slow comprehension.

"Are you saying, Aunt Kat, that the occurrence today was political?"

"I am saying nothing, you silly girl. I already know how to apply discretion."

I stared at her. "But Queen Catherine is married to him."

"Yes, dear, I know that. But my first loyalty is to Elizabeth. What is best for her is what is best for me. And you."

I closed my mouth, worked my aching jaw. "Perhaps you ought to send me home to Grandmama."

I winced, because I had no desire to come under control of that sharp-tongued old lady. She liked me rather better than she liked my mother, but that did not say much.

Aunt Kat patted my cheek again. "Nonsense, dear. I want you here with me. I'd miss you terribly."

"You would?"

Aunt Kat was an affectionate woman, but she had never told me she was happy that I was about. I thought of myself as rather a nuisance, except when there were gowns to be made. I warmed.

"Indeed." She lowered her voice. "I need you. Be my eyes and ears, Eloise. I want to know every word Thomas Seymour speaks to Elizabeth in my absence. Every word. Do you understand?"

"Yes, Aunt Kat."

I kissed her, left her chamber for my own chilled room, and sat up far into the night.

I had gone to Aunt Kat supposing she would listen to my tale, grow horrified, and insist that Lady Elizabeth and she and Uncle John (and I) leave immediately. Instead, she'd behaved as though the event in the passage were simply bothersome. An unlooked-for incident to be suppressed at all costs.

You do not understand, Eloise, Aunt Kat had been saying. *You are slow. You understand neither Greek nor Latin nor the subtleties of the court.*

I wondered, as I blew out the candle, what Uncle John under-stood.

�֎

IN THE MORNING, I woke a wary creature. I performed the same rituals, rinsing my face, brushing my unruly black hair. I cleaned the grime from under my fingernails and rinsed my mouth, chewing a bit of anise to make my breath pleasant after my morning mead. I ate yellowish bread smeared with thick, sweet butter and took a few bites of the porridge that Aunt Kat had regularly forced upon me since age five.

I lifted a dull-blue kirtle over my head, and a maid laced the bodice in the back. Over this went a robe of plain brown, with sleeves folded back to reveal the white linen of my chemise. The pointed edge of my stomacher was laced to a skirt that flared from tucks that I had taken pains to make exactly even. A maid pinned my hair under a French hood—a wide band that pushed my hair back from my forehead and a cloth that covered the length of it.

One ring, plain and silver, adorned my finger. My mother had given it to me, saying it had been my father's. The band was thin, beaten, and worn, not much value in it. But it was my one link to a man I'd never see again, and I wore the ring every day.

Attired and breakfasted, I took my sewing basket and made my way down to Elizabeth's chamber. All as usual. But I could not put the events of the day before out of my head. I remem-bered the almost savage look on Thomas Seymour's face when he cut up Elizabeth's dress. I remembered the strained laughter in Queen Catherine's eyes as she abetted her husband in flirting with another woman. And Elizabeth, glaring at Aunt Kat and insisting she had done nothing wrong.

I slipped inside Elizabeth's chamber and took my place on a

bench near the window. Soft late-April air slid through the window and surrounded me in pleasant scents. I removed the satin bodice I had begun the day before and laid it across my lap. I had stitched in the boning, and now I needed to sew the side seams. It must be carefully done, or the points in front would not match, and I'd have to start all over again.

The chamber was filled with Elizabeth's ladies, old and young, pretty and plain, highborn and gentry. Elizabeth was dressed, but two maids hovered around her, one trying to settle her French hood, the other shaking her skirt to let it lie straight.

Elizabeth was in a sunny mood, making jests as she chewed on red strawberries, bright as jewels. She seemed content, but I could not be. I worried for her. I worried I would say the wrong thing to her about Thomas Seymour; I worried should she ask me of him, and I would not be able to say a word for fear of speaking the wrong ones.

I made one last stitch and beckoned to a maid. "Tell Her Grace that we must have a fitting."

The maid nodded and returned to her mistress. I saw Elizabeth brighten, which relieved me. Sometimes she did not like to leave her books and her ladies for any reason, but she usually did like to try on clothes.

The maid loosened her gown and pulled it from her shoulders. I stood up, shaking out the half-made bodice I'd just stitched. At that moment, the door burst open, and Thomas Seymour strode in. He was dressed for hunting, in riding boots, swirling half cloak, plain doublet and tunic, and trunk hose.

The maids screamed. Elizabeth gave him one startled look and dove behind a screen.

"How now?" Seymour said loudly. "Do you hide from your step-papa? Is the lady so modest?"

Only I seemed alarmed. The other ladies giggled or flashed

Thomas ready looks. They banded together and formed a gig-
gling mass in front of the screen so that he could not get at the
half-undressed Elizabeth.

"You challenge me, ladies." Seymour laughed, a warm, boom-
ing sound. He laid a firm hand on one of the younger girls. "I
have touched you. Now you may not sit down until you have
touched me. But you must catch me, first."

The lady responded to the game with glee. She lunged at Seymour, who sidestepped with another great laugh. The ladies
joined in, trying to corner him. He ran and dodged in the large
room, with a trail of ladies chasing him about.

I stood in the corner and stared. Elizabeth remained behind
the screen, but I thought I heard soft laughter emanate from it.

It was a bizarre scene, this grown man chasing ladies about
like a stage villain in my father's troupe. They screeched and ran
here and there, while I froze in the corner, Elizabeth's half-made
bodice clutched to my chest.

Thomas Seymour dodged by me and tore the bodice from my
grip. I reached for it, but he held it above his head, smiling playfully. A cold light lurked deep in his eyes, as though, like yesterday, this foolery meant something deeper and more dangerous.

"Tell your mistress to come out," he said to me. "Else I'll rip
it to shreds."

"Your lordship, no, please."

"Come and get it, kitten," he said, his eyes narrowing with
dislike.

He knew I could reach the bodice only by climbing him, and
he knew I would never do such a thing. He had read my character when I'd fled from him in the passage many nights ago. I had
seen through his flirtations and had rejected him, and he did not
like this.

"Tell her to come out," he commanded.

Mutely, I shook my head.

He clutched the satin in his large grip, and then, with a heart-breaking sound, he ripped it in two. I cried out and clapped my hands to my mouth. He ripped it again, all the way down, tearing out the painstaking seams I'd spent the morning sewing. I watched my work rendered ruined beyond repair by a man who valued it not.

Elizabeth would not come out. She liked the game, if the laughter that recurred meant anything, but fortunately she was too prudent to emerge in her undressed state.

Seymour tossed the pieces of satin to the floor, where they lay unmourned by all but me. The ladies continued the romp. Seymour, I saw, was growing bored.

I believe he simply would have shoved the screen aside to reveal his stepdaughter, had not Aunt Kat entered the room. Despite her lecture the night before that we should let Seymour do as he pleased, she looked horrified.

"Ladies!"

Her stentorian tones cut through the melee. The young women stopped their squealing and looked chagrined, though not too much so. They seemed more sorry that Aunt Kat had come to spoil their fun than ashamed they'd been doing it at all.

Seymour's eyes flashed. Anger, deep and dark, revealed itself in the set of his mouth and the flick of his fingers. "Mistress Ashley, you do ruin our little entertainment."

"Perhaps best 'twere left for another day, my lord."

I understood then what Aunt Kat meant when she'd said there was more to this than a man wanting a young girl. Seymour was dangerous. Aunt Kat stood resolutely before him like a hen before a wild boar. The look in his eyes was deadly, but my aunt raised her head and met his gaze square on.

Aunt Kat was always a brave woman, too much so, I thought

at times. But she loved Elizabeth like a daughter and would fight for her with the fierceness of a she bear protecting its cub.

"Mistress Kat, shall we step out?" Seymour gestured to the chamber door. Aunt Kat gave one frigid nod of her head and stalked solemnly through the door to the antechamber.

Seymour followed. Fearing he'd raise his fist to my aunt once they were out of sight, I snatched up the pieces of the bodice and scuttled after him before they could disappear.

They stood together in the antechamber, Aunt Kat looking in no wise worried. I closed the door to the bedchamber and retreated to a window embrasure to watch them.

"I seek only to protect my lady Elizabeth's reputation," Aunt Kat began. "You charge too quickly for her."

"I mean no harm by it," Seymour answered, his tone disdainful. "I'll not leave off. A man cannot romp with his daughter?"

Not in the way you wish, I thought, closing my fingers around the shredded bodice.

Aunt Kat looked prim. "I only give advice, my lord."

"I'll not be ruled by a pack of women." He shot a glare at me, though I'd said nothing, and stormed from the room.

I reflected that in this household, he could not escape a pack of women. The women here were family, and he was the stranger.

❄

LORD SEYMOUR DID not leave off. Aunt Kat watched him and admonished me again to tell her of his behavior. I was a dutiful spy and reported when I saw him slip the key from Elizabeth's bedchamber door into his pocket.

"Should you tell Queen Catherine?" I whispered.

"My dear, the Queen has much to occupy her," Aunt Kat returned. "She is with child. Let her think her marriage idyllic for now."

I did not see how she could. Thomas Seymour stalked Elizabeth with the single-mindedness of a hunter after a prize buck, claiming that all he did was play.

Aunt Kat at least took the precaution of having me sleep nights in Elizabeth's chamber. But my presence did not keep Lord Seymour at bay, nor did I think it would. Three nights I stayed with Elizabeth, lying awake to hear her soft breathing and the call of night birds below. I slept fitfully, waiting for her ravisher to burst in at any time.

He did not appear until the morning of the fourth day. I heard the key in the lock and sprang from my cot, knocking my foot against the bed railing and wrenching my ankle. Behind the bed curtains, Elizabeth stirred and muttered a cross word.

As I hopped, clutching my hurt foot, Lord Seymour, clad only in a nightshirt and slippers, his legs bare, strolled into the room. He did not even notice me, his eyes fixing on the closed curtains of Lady Elizabeth's bed.

Queen Catherine entered behind him. She, too, was clad in night rail and robe, and she smiled. I relaxed, but not entirely, remembering the scene in the garden when Catherine had held Elizabeth for her husband's machinations.

Lord Seymour yanked open the bed curtains and put one bare knee on the bed. "Sleepyhead," he said, and guffawed. "Is our precious daughter awake?"

Elizabeth, startled, scrambled for the other side of the bed and pulled the bedclothes to her chin. But the eyes that stared over the top of the covers sparkled with mirth.

Seymour crawled to her. Queen Catherine, still smiling, climbed upon the bed behind him. He sat still, letting his wife reach Elizabeth first.

"Tickle," Queen Catherine said. "Our daughter is most ticklish."

Elizabeth squeaked and cringed from her. Catherine pounced. She tickled Elizabeth until she laughed. Before my horrified eyes, Thomas Seymour's brawny hands closed around Elizabeth's waist, groping, wriggling, touching.

Elizabeth squealed with laughter. I set my weight gingerly on my hurt foot, wondering whether to run for my aunt. What could she say if the Queen played right alongside Lord Seymour?

Elizabeth finally rolled away from the both of them and out the other side of the bed. Laughing, her stepmother and stepfather pursued her. Elizabeth dodged behind me, using me as a shield.

My weight came down on my twisted foot, and tears sprang to my eyes. Elizabeth laughed her happy, throaty laugh.

Seymour danced around the both of us, slapping Elizabeth on the hindquarters. I tried to block his blows, but Elizabeth slipped away surreptitiously, allowing him to get to her more easily.

Queen Catherine laughed, pushing the loose hair from her eyes. "My dears, we must run in the garden. 'Tis a fine day."

"A splendid idea," Lord Seymour said. He glanced at me for the first time. "You. Ready her. We will return."

Elizabeth stood shoulder to shoulder with me, out of breath, flushed, laughing. Lord Seymour reached around and gave her one final swat, his hand half landing on my buttocks in the process. I flinched and Elizabeth giggled.

Queen Catherine sashayed out the door, Lord Seymour following. Before the door closed, before I could move to Elizabeth's dressing room and find her a gown suitable for a garden romp, Seymour returned.

"Leave us," he shot at me.

I did not dare. I remembered Aunt Kat facing him down like an indignant hen, and stood my ground.

But Aunt Kat had a far more formidable presence than I. She had the weight of years, wisdom, and respect. I was a fourteen-year-old waif, product of a bad marriage, here on Aunt Kat's charity.

Lord Seymour ignored me. He moved to Elizabeth, and she backed from him until she rested against the high bed.

"Daughter," he said, his mouth in an ironic twist. He laid his hands on either side of her, resting them on the bed.

Instead of looking alarmed, Elizabeth's eyes half closed. She relaxed and did not fight when Lord Seymour eased his thigh between hers. He cupped her face in one hand, lowered his head, and kissed her lips.

I could not decide whether to beat him with a bolster or run for Aunt Kat. If I struck him, a high lord, I could be flogged, or much worse if he took against me. If I ran for Aunt Kat, hobbling on my wrenched ankle, he might ravish her several times over before I could return.

Seymour kissed her again, a small thing, but then it turned deeper. Elizabeth opened her mouth for his intrusive tongue.

The decision of what to do was taken from me. The door swung open again to reveal Queen Catherine, still in her bed attire, returning with Aunt Kat.

The Queen gasped. Thomas Seymour sprang away from Elizabeth, but his glib words died on his lips.

There was no denying what Catherine had seen. Her face whitened, going nearly gray. I saw all hope that Seymour's attentions to Elizabeth were a game die, as well as all hope that after three marriages she'd at last found a man with whom she could be happy.

Seymour had been fairly caught, but I saw no shame in his gaze. His expression held only annoyance that his wife had chosen to enter at the wrong moment.

Queen Catherine turned and walked from the room.

Later that morning, I helped Aunt Kat pack Elizabeth's things. Catherine had decided Elizabeth could not stay.

That afternoon, we left for Cheshunt in Hertfordshire, to the home of Aunt Kat's sister and her husband, leading Elizabeth into her first exile.

4

CHESHUNT. I LIKED the lilt of the name and hummed it often to myself, although I knew to Elizabeth it meant shame. Whatever our reason for the sojourn, those June days were golden to me, in the soft air of Hertfordshire, with quiet days and serene nights. No more dangerous games, no more fear of Thomas Seymour coming upon me in the dark, no more watching with worried eyes while Seymour planned and schemed.

I had little doubt that Seymour continued to plan and scheme—he was that sort of man. But perhaps with the absence of Elizabeth and bathed in the sorrow of the dowager Queen, he would grow remorseful, or at least more cautious.

For me, life returned to the simple pleasures of day-to-day living. Lady Denny, Aunt Kat's sister, known to me as Aunt Joan, became Elizabeth's appointed governess. Aunt Kat was in disgrace for not stopping Seymour's pursuit of her charge, and Protector Somerset had demanded her replacement. Elizabeth would not hear of Aunt Kat being sent away, so though Aunt

Kat was no longer Elizabeth's official governess, we lived cozily in Sir Anthony Denny's house and continued a quiet life.

"Jealousy," Aunt Kat said one evening after Elizabeth had retired. She and I and Aunt Joan sat in Aunt Kat's chamber, I sewing busily, Aunt Joan reading. Aunt Kat pretended to write letters, but after every two or three scratched words, she'd raise her head and stare moodily at the fire.

"What *do* you mean?" Aunt Joan asked, lifting her thin nose from her book.

"Her Grace the Queen. I was there, you know, when the Queen interviewed Her Grace Elizabeth and explained why she had to depart. She'd not have me leave her side. Her Grace Elizabeth, I mean."

Aunt Joan pursed her lips. She was as book learned as Kat and had been quite pleased to condemn my mother, her cousin, for her silliness and frailty, and again for marrying a Catholic. The Champernowne women were as unalike as they could be: Aunt Joan liking learned conversation with her husband more than anything; my mother, who couldn't be bothered with books; and Aunt Kat, somewhat between the two, reading Latin and philosophy but adoring gossip. Aunt Kat and Thomas Parry, Elizabeth's cofferer, gossiped like two old women in a market, which John Ashley did not like, but he might as well have tried to push back the tide with a broom.

What the two sisters did have in common that my mother lacked was their love of the Reformed religion. They could wax eloquent on the subject to the point of tedium. My mother was of the disposition that if her husband told her she must return to the old religion, she would without a murmur, but Kat and Joan Champernowne knew their own minds.

"The Queen explained that my lady Elizabeth must guard her

reputation as she would guard the most precious of jewels," Aunt Kat went on, "because how she presents herself to the people of England is of vast importance. She might be Queen someday."

I thought this a remote possibility, but I did not venture my opinion. Edward was a healthy young man who would marry in a few years and produce an heir. After that came Mary, who was also young enough to have children. Most likely Elizabeth would be married off to some foreign prince, and Aunt Kat and I would travel to France or some cold place in the north of Europe to serve Elizabeth, or else would be forsaken and left in England. Thoughts of such a prospect cut into my happy simplicity, so I kept them at bay.

Aunt Kat leaned forward, eager to continue her story. "Lady Elizabeth was much abashed and I daresay ashamed. Her fondness for Her Grace the Queen is unrivaled. They embraced most affectionately. But I saw the jealousy. The Queen now knows her husband fancied Elizabeth first and married Queen Catherine only when the Council interfered with his chance at Elizabeth's hand. But mark my words, it is my lady Elizabeth that the Admiral prefers."

"And you condone this?" her sister Joan asked coldly.

"Well, of course not!" Kat sat back in her chair as though quickly reversing her position both physically and in words. "Never would I advise Her Grace Elizabeth to marry without permission of the Council. Such a thing is tantamount to treason. The Lord Admiral married Catherine the Queen and that is that." She picked up her own sewing with a little shake.

"And that should remain that," Joan finished. " 'Tis dangerous and wrong to suggest otherwise."

Kat widened her eyes. "Think you I would stand against the wishes of the King of England? Even if they come out of the head of His Grace of Somerset."

"Do guard your tongue, Kat," Joan said. "Your tongue will be the death of you."

I shivered at the words and the cloth under my hand moved. I suddenly saw a cold room, Aunt Kat in tears, a paper spread before her on a table, a man in a chill voice demanding she sign it.

The vision spun away, but it stunned me like a slap. "Yes, do take care, Aunt Kat, for heaven's sake," I hissed.

She stared at us both. "Gracious I speak only to my family, and I'd say not a word of this to Her Grace. 'Tis only a bit of harmless gossip, indeed, Eloise Rousell."

"Who else do you tell it to?" I pressed her. "Thomas Parry?"

"I have good, comfortable talks with Master Parry, yes. But he insisted that he would be torn asunder if he repeated ought I said to him."

I shuddered and suddenly could not warm myself. "It might come to that," I murmured. "It might come to it."

❧

LADY DENNY, MY Aunt Joan, had cause to travel to Sudeley, where Queen Catherine now resided, and she sent us news of everything that happened there. The Queen made ready for the birth of her child in September and spoke with much hope of its being a son. A son would please her husband and provide him an heir, and perhaps assuage his ambitious interest in Elizabeth.

Catherine's anger at Elizabeth had died quickly, Aunt Joan reported, and she missed the girl quite keenly. Catherine confided in Aunt Joan that after the birth of her child, when the scandal had blown over, she'd send for Elizabeth to live with her again.

Elizabeth, for her part, never spoke a word about what had happened with Thomas Seymour. I knew, however, that she thought of it a great deal. When twilight came and she could no longer see the words in her books, she would lift her head and stare out the window, her eyes betraying chagrin and unhappiness and anger.

She wrote letters of affection to Queen Catherine and sent her small gifts, praying for her and her unborn child. That she felt remorse for hurting the Queen, I was certain, but what I could not decide was whether her remorse was for letting the flirtation go too far or for being caught at it.

"What think you of marriage, Eloise?" Elizabeth asked me one day toward the end of August. Summer had passed its height, and the last days of August cooled into balmy softness. Summer flowers ran riot among the hedges at Cheshunt, bleeding their last color before autumn would send them into dormancy.

"Marriage?" I repeated. "I try to think of it as little as possible, Your Grace."

I was not certain whether Elizabeth was in one of her whimsical moods, when she'd skewer every person within earshot with her wit and expect her answerer to be equally witty. Or she might have asked in all seriousness, wanting to provoke a philosophical discussion.

"I believe I shall never marry," she said, her mouth firm. "It seems to me a rather dangerous endeavor."

"My Aunt Kat likes it."

"She married for love, and was allowed to. A lady of a high family marries for politics or gain and usually not at her choice."

"They marry for duty," I agreed. "Perhaps sometimes duty and love come together?"

Elizabeth gave me a sideways look. We were the same age, she and I, but she looked on the world with eyes older and wiser than mine. "It can happen," she said doubtfully. "But not very often. My stepmother Catherine married for love this time, but when she married for duty, she was much happier."

I opened my mouth to argue. I remembered Catherine as Henry's wife, a patient woman keeping her emotions in check, and I imagined she'd been the same in her first two marriages. When she'd married Thomas Seymour she'd dared to be happy, laughing and jesting like a girl. Her serious demeanor, which Henry liked, had gone.

Henry had also married Catherine for her beauty, unmarred by two widowhoods. That beauty remained, and I do not believe Seymour was immune to it. I suspected his interest in Elizabeth had to do more with the fact that she was now third in line to the throne of England than in her young beauty, although I did not discount her charms. I remembered Seymour's hot breath on my face, his rough hand on my breast—he was plenty lecherous enough to want Elizabeth for her body.

"I shall not marry at all," I said with conviction. "A man is expected to rule his wife, and I dislike the notion of being ruled by a husband. It is natural to obey a mother and father, even an aunt and uncle, but most husbands, I believe, take advantage of their power."

Elizabeth gave me a thoughtful look. "Would that be true, think you, if the wife were a Queen?"

"I am afraid so," I said. "Not much stops husbands wanting mastery, I should think."

"Must it ever be? The husband would be the Queen's subject, would he not, if she ruled England herself?"

"But a woman has not ruled England," I pointed out. "Not for centuries. There has always been a male heir, who marries and produces at least one son, unless there is a war. A woman has never been Queen in her own right."

"True, but if my brother does not have a son, Mary will be Queen. My father willed it."

She did not say so, but the implication was clear. If Edward had no sons, nor Mary, Elizabeth would step into the shoes of the monarch. I studied her firm jaw, her no-nonsense eyes, the tilt of her head that suggested arrogance. Arrogance could become a detriment if it were taken too far—as the Earl of Surrey had learned on the chopping block. But it could also be an asset, an air that set a person apart from others, that forced awe from those who beheld them.

"But Mary would take a husband," I said. "Whoever her Council and the English people thought best. I would think a queen has less freedom than any other woman when it comes to choosing a husband."

"But she would be Queen. And others must obey."

"True. But in my experience, Your Grace, the people of England do not swallow things readily. England is not like the Saracen lands in which the people live in absolute terror of their kings."

I could not claim complete knowledge of Saracen lands, but this is what I believed. I did not bring up the fact that when King Henry had put aside the beloved Catherine of Aragon, his first wife, to marry Elizabeth's mother, rebellion had boiled under the waters of the then-placid pond of England. Henry had executed plenty of men who would not support the divorce of Catherine or the acts of succession that made Anne's issue first in line for the throne. Anne had been reviled, openly hissed at in the streets, and in danger of the mob whenever she went out. A monarch marrying badly carried dire consequences in England.

"England is a different place," Elizabeth said. "The people have affection for their queens, and for their princesses."

"They do cheer most heartily when you ride out," I agreed.

Elizabeth's look became thoughtful. "That is not an affection one should take for granted. A reputation must be guarded."

I thought back on what Queen Catherine had said to Elizabeth, as related through Aunt Kat: she must always look to her reputation and how others perceived her. The words seemed to have had impact. This was the closest Elizabeth had come to discussing the reason she'd been sent from Catherine's household, the first hint, and I feared to upset her by remarking on it.

"You are wise, Your Grace," I murmured.

Elizabeth gave me a sharp look, sensing I knew more about her situation than she'd told me, but she let the matter drop.

August ended on a brisk wind, the trees already sending showers of golden and red and orange leaves to the ground. With the end of August came word from Sudeley Castle that the dowager Queen Catherine had delivered to Thomas Seymour a girl.

We rejoiced Catherine's good fortune, and Elizabeth's hope grew that Catherine would send for her soon. But the rejoicing was short-lived. Another message came from Sudeley hard on the heels of the first, that Queen Catherine herself had died of childbed fever.

5

 QUEEN CATHERINE'S DEATH plunged Elizabeth into illness so severe that Lord Protector Somerset sent a physician from court to attend her. Elizabeth liked me to sit beside her while she lay abed, and I saw the change in her day by day. Her illness made her thinner, but the lines that appeared around her mouth were laid by wariness and grief. Instead of rendering her opinion on each and every thing as she liked to do, she grew quiet, watchful, as though she knew some terrible occurrence approached.

Catherine Parr was buried at Sudeley, Thomas Seymour's home, Seymour appropriately grieving. But reports I heard of Catherine's death itself horrified me. Servants' gossip and Aunt Joan's confidences to Aunt Kat revealed that Catherine in her delirium had raved that the love she bore her husband had been ruined, that he was false and had used her for his own ambition. He'd pursued Elizabeth under her nose and wished Catherine to die—had he poisoned her?

Then Catherine would come to herself and say that no, she

had not been in her right mind when she accused him of adultery and poison, and stoutly declared that she loved her Thomas dearly. In the end, Catherine had left him everything she owned and had died with words of forgiveness on her lips.

The news alarmed me not a little. Even wading through the layers added as the rumors passed through servants left a message that was ominous. Queen Catherine had clearly seen Seymour's ambition, and her fever had brought to the surface ugly truths that had kept their heads down ere this.

Despite the ominous gossip and sorrow over the Queen's death, I was happy we returned to Hatfield, where Elizabeth would have her own household. I was sorry to leave Cheshunt, a peaceful if rather dull place, but Hatfield had possibilities. Elizabeth would be a princess in truth with her own entourage and gentlemen-at-arms, and she would manage her own estates willed to her by her father. Despite whispers that Seymour was once again trying to gain more power at court, I hoped happier times approached.

Hatfield was a fine redbrick house in Hertfordshire, twenty or so miles directly north of London, north and west of Cheshunt. It had long country lanes and good hunting in the forests nearby, and was isolated from the rigorous pace and stink of London but close enough for an easy visit to Whitehall or Greenwich. Elizabeth professed to be fond of the place, where she'd spent innocent days of babyhood.

"Thomas Seymour will ask to marry her," Aunt Kat said a few weeks after we'd settled Elizabeth into the new house. "Mark my words."

"I thought you disapproved." I was sorting new cloth for Elizabeth's gowns, preparing for court visits to her brother, which would likely come more often now. Elizabeth was fifteen, an adult by royal standards, and an arranged marriage would likely not be long in coming. Given Thomas Seymour's and the Lord Protector's rivalry, I doubted the Protector would extend Seymour's hand to Elizabeth.

"If he offers to take her to wife, what can there be to disapprove of?" Aunt Kat retorted. "He is a handsome man, wealthy and intelligent. I happen to know that before he married Queen Catherine, he had his eye on our lady Elizabeth. I'd rather she marry Thomas Seymour than any other man in the kingdom."

"He has spoken of it to you?" I asked, my mouth full of pins.

"Nay, why should he speak to me? Not to me but to Master Parry. I told Elizabeth she ought to write a consoling letter to Lord Seymour, and do you know what she said?" She hesitated long enough for me to give her a curious look, then she trundled on. "She gave me a look that held much excitement, then told me she did not dare write, for then people would think she meant to woo him. She knows the lay of the land better than most."

I thought back on Elizabeth's speculation on marriage and wondered. "So she will not write?"

"No, which will make him pine for her more."

"She is much younger than he is," I said.

"She is at a ripe age to marry. And he is not so old that he is not still fine of looks and prowess."

I began pinning together the layers of velvet and silk that would be sleeves folding back to reveal gold brocade. "I believe he has charmed you, Aunt Kat, and gotten you firmly on his side. Perhaps more than is prudent."

She flushed a dark red. "Nonsense. He has said naught to me about it, not one word."

She clamped her lips firmly shut, but I worried. I had become immune to Seymour after what he'd done to me in the hall at Chelsea, but I could see the fascination he held for others. Aunt Kat had not believed my story, and she now had swung the other way about his attentions to Elizabeth. Kat's words implied that Seymour was busily beguiling Thomas Parry as well, cofferer of Elizabeth's household—Thomas Parry for knowledge of Elizabeth's finances, Aunt Kat for knowledge of her person.

As our stay at Hatfield lengthened, Elizabeth's health gradually improved. She resumed lessons in Greek and Latin under a new tutor, Roger Ascham, William Grindal having sadly passed away. She penned affectionate letters to her brother and walked in the growing chill of Hatfield's gardens in winter, and still said nothing about Thomas Seymour.

November skies grew gray and bleak. I was soon glad to stay indoors near the fire and look through windows at the bare trees against the white sky. Aunt Kat spoke very little directly about Thomas Seymour, but she spent more and more time in seclusion with Master Parry, and when Parry took a journey to London, Aunt Kat shot bold hints that things would change for Elizabeth once he returned.

"What is your aunt conspiring?"

I jumped in the darkness of my chamber as John Ashley paused in the doorway and fixed keen eyes upon me. The chill made the needle hurt my fingers, and I set it down and rubbed my fingertips in the velvet in my lap.

"Is Aunt Kat conspiring?"

Ashley shut the door against the draft and came to sit close to me. "My wife is a good woman, but she cannot leave well enough alone. She loves Elizabeth as she would a daughter, and like a mother with a daughter, she would do anything to advance Elizabeth's position and happiness, even if she sends herself to the block for it."

"The block?" I asked in alarm. "Why do you say so?"

"Because the Lord High Admiral is ambitious, niece. He will thwart the Council and the Protector and do as he pleases.

He did so to marry Catherine, and he has received all her lands for his pains. He is ruthless and will overreach himself, and Kat will be caught in his betwixt and between. And he will catch Elizabeth with her."

"It can only be nonsense where Aunt Kat is concerned," I said, hoping I was right. "Lord Seymour will never offer, and Elizabeth is indifferent to him."

John Ashley's gaze was sharp enough to cut. "You have more intelligence than that, Eloise. Look at me again and declare there is nothing in this. That Her Grace Elizabeth does not blush finely when Seymour's name is spoken, that she does not smile at any who speak highly of him. Tell me this."

I glumly shook my head. I knew it time to cease pretending; I could read the signs as well as he. "What do we do?"

"We extract your aunt from danger, and we warn Elizabeth to take care. I have much affection for Kat, and she has a good heart, but sometimes . . ."

"Yes," I agreed. "Sometimes . . ."

Sometimes a good heart led to a downfall. Seymour's sojourn in Catherine's household and all that followed had forced my eyes open to a new world. I could not be a naïve child forever; I had to keep my wits about me in this whirlpool that ever surrounded the Tudors. This was a world of ambitious men not hesitating to use a young girl to achieve what they wanted. And perhaps Aunt Kat had ambition, too, to be able to point to Elizabeth's rise and say, "I did that."

A new world, and a dangerous one.

✠

"DURHAM PLACE WAS to have been mine." Elizabeth scowled at Master Parry a few days later, her red-gold brows pinched. Slim and tall, she turned from the window, consciously moving so the beam from the winter sun touched her unbound hair. "I was promised it. Does my lord Somerset not remember this?"

Master Parry, his fat face red, twisted a gold chain in his hands. He was not nervous facing his mistress, but angry along with her. Elizabeth had learned not long ago that Lord Somerset had procured Durham Place, her London residence, for his own use, namely to set up a mint. Master Parry's recent mission in London—the one Aunt Kat had hinted to me meant more than it seemed—had been to look into the matter.

"He claimed he needed it, Your Grace. There he squats, coining more money to spend in the name of your brother the King."

Elizabeth's ladies looked interested at Master Parry's outburst. Elizabeth's nostrils flared, her mouth white and pinched. "He presumes."

"He does indeed, Your Grace." Parry bent his head, a sly look entering his eyes. "I spoke to the Lord Admiral about it, and he was most sympathetic."

"The Lord Admiral." Elizabeth stopped, her gaze growing fixed. She moved slightly out of the sunshine, her studied pose vanishing. "Does he apologize for his brother?"

"He does indeed. The Admiral very kindly offered you the use of his own residence when you come to London so that you would not be inconvenienced."

"Very kind." A hint of frost touched Elizabeth's voice, but I was close enough to see her eyes. Their dark centers widened and fixed on Parry. "What else?"

"The Lord Admiral was quite interested in all your properties, Your Grace, and whether the Council had finished their bequests to you. He declared it shameful when I told him they had not. And he liked to offer advice on how you might make savings since the Council has not bestowed on you everything it should."

"Did he? And what did he suggest?"

"That you look over your books yourself. That he could help you in these matters. That . . ." He lowered his voice almost to a whisper, his eyes as hard and focused as Elizabeth's own. "That you might make savings by the two of you sharing resources. He has many houses and men at his disposal, and could help you obtain those that are rightfully yours."

"What did he mean by all this, think you?" Elizabeth's voice was low, sounding more like a calculating man's than a young girl's.

"That perhaps he might have you, too? You know he did not break up the household of Queen Catherine, but changed his mind and kept her ladies and gentlemen together."

"To wait upon Jane," Elizabeth said quickly. "He did it so that Jane Grey might have a household."

Because, she did not say, Thomas Seymour wanted Jane to marry Edward the King. I had heard Aunt Kat and Parry and even John Ashley discuss that fact often enough.

"Perhaps." Parry smiled like a fishwife with a secret. He took a step closer to Elizabeth, out of earshot of the ladies across the room. "And what would you say, my lady? If Seymour offered for you? Would you have him? If the Council approved, of course."

He added the last hastily. Edward's Council had frowned on Seymour's last attempt to ensnare Elizabeth, and well she knew it. Marrying without their consent not only would displease her brother but would keep her from the succession and result in her forfeiting all those lands that the Council was taking its time about giving her in the first place.

I saw these thoughts spin behind her eyes, a lady weighing the consequences of being able to love a fascinating man against forfeiting all possibility of inheriting the crown.

I could have lent an argument if I'd dared, that Seymour had blatantly chased Elizabeth while he was married to Catherine and pursued other dalliances as well. Not a man who would consider it necessary to be true to his wife. Many men were not so nice when it came to fidelity and were quick to break their wives' hearts.

I had no way of knowing whether Elizabeth counted this as an argument. I'd met more than one woman in love with a philanderer who held absolute conviction that if said man were with *her*, he'd philander no more. Many ladies harbor these false and impossible dreams.

Whatever debates hummed through Elizabeth's head, when she opened her mouth to speak, it was in the tone of a lawyer who had calculated every word beforehand.

"If what you imagine comes to pass," she said to Parry, "then I will do as God shall put in my mind."

A lovely answer, saying neither yea or nay. Parry widened his eyes. "Of course, Your Grace."

Later when Parry had scuttled off to his office and coffers, I fitted Elizabeth into the dress I was creating. Her hands were ice-cold, her pupils dilated, and she scarce seemed to notice me and my maidservant pinning the velvet to her frame, that is until I accidentally poked her.

She jumped then slapped my face, but not hard. "Do take care, Mistress Seamstress."

I apologized humbly, words of apology now rote on my lips, so often did I have to apologize to Elizabeth. Her hands and mouth shook, but I saw a gleam of excitement in her eyes, a woman who knew a man wanted her, and liked that wanting.

"Master Parry is a prodigious gossip," she said suddenly. "Are you fond of gossip, Eloise?"

"Me? No, never, Your Grace." I stuck my tongue in the side of my mouth after I said it.

"Liar." She laughed, the note shrill. "What a liar you are, seamstress. I am surrounded by liars."

I had no idea what she meant by this, so I did not reply. She then growled with impatience at the fitting, so I and my maid unpinned the gown and laid it aside for another time.

Later that evening I came upon Parry closeted with my aunt in her chamber. Chatter, chatter, chatter—they chattered away about my lady Elizabeth and Thomas Seymour, nattering and gossiping as though they had every right to arrange the lives of two important people of the realm.

I liked Aunt Kat's chamber, small and cozy, softly lit with candles and warmed with a fire. Because Aunt Kat was a favorite of Elizabeth, she had candles made of fragrant wax, a fire built high, a bed as plump as she was around the middle, cushions for her benches and stools, plates and goblets of her own, and the best food sent from the kitchens.

I remembered how when I'd first joined the household, when Elizabeth's status had still been that of king's bastard and a forgotten one at that, the ladies and gentlemen of her chamber had ordered sumptuous meals to be served in the dining room in order that they could feast themselves. A small child could eat only a little of the spread, and the ladies and gentlemen heartily enjoyed the remains, doing as they pleased.

Aunt Kat put a halt to it, claiming the rich foods bad for Elizabeth's health, much to the annoyance of the spoiled ladies and gentlemen. Now that Elizabeth was no longer a child and had been restored as princess, we all dined well and slept in comfort, lucky in our positions. A far better life, I always reminded myself, than I would have living with my mother and her priggish Catholic husband, who liked to pretend I did not exist.

As a child, I had amused myself drawing pictures on scraps of discarded paper of the Catholic husband and then sticking him with my scissors. I would hastily burn the papers, afraid anyone finding them would think me practicing witchcraft, but as far as

I knew, my stepfather never took harm from it. Now, I simply pretended he did not exist either.

Neither my aunt nor Parry ceased gossiping as I seated myself at Aunt Kat's table and helped myself to a thick slice of bread, which I used as a truncheon, heaping warm meats and sauce all over it. A watchful servant brought me a goblet and a large measure of hock.

All the while Parry and Aunt Kat moved their mouths, so intent on each other that they never noticed me. Which was to my advantage as I snatched the last sweetmeat from the tray and quickly stuffed it in my mouth before the servant could take it away.

"What think you of all that, Mistress Ashley?" Parry said, his chins bobbing and wagging as he held in a giggle. "The Lord Admiral wants to marry Her Grace. I knew it as soon as I saw him in London. His interest was avid."

"I've known for much longer," Aunt Kat sniffed. "No reason she should not have him to husband. I've said so all along."

I thought of Uncle John Ashley's warning. "Aunt Kat . . ."

She took as much heed of me as though I were a buzzing fly— less, because a fly she would swat.

"You've known no such thing." Parry laughed, confident in his news.

Aunt Kat leaned over the table. "I have. Why do you believe we left Queen Catherine to tarry so long at Cheshunt? You knew of the one incident of the kiss, which could be put down to misunderstanding if need be, but there was far more to all of it, my friend, far more."

"You invent tales," Parry said.

"I do nothing of the kind. The Lord Admiral was always taken with our lady, and why should he not be? A lovely girl Elizabeth always has been, so poised and regal. The perfect lady, not like others I could mention, though they be close to her."

I stopped eating to listen. She did not go so far as to name Princess Mary, who was short and stout and looked Spanish, but this was exactly the sort of talk in which John Ashley did not want his wife to indulge.

Parry rolled his wine goblet between his fat palms. "We have ever been friends, have we not, Mistress Ashley?"

"Of course, Master Parry."

This surprised me a bit, because these two had quarreled in the past, and Parry dipped his fingers into Elizabeth's money from time to time. We all knew it, even Elizabeth, but we looked the other way. Only Elizabeth could dismiss him, and she had indicated no inclination to do so.

"Then you will tell me, will you not?" he went on. "As we both have our lady's best interests at heart, and you know so much about it."

Aunt Kat loved to be flattered. An intelligent and well-read woman, she still had a woman's weakness toward flattery. She gave Parry a delighted smile, then to my horror proceeded to tell Parry the entire story of Elizabeth's encounters with Thomas Seymour when he'd been married to Queen Catherine. Every morning romp, every tickle and pinch, the cut-up dress, Seymour's visit to Elizabeth's chamber in his nightshirt, the Queen's tacit condoning of his seduction until she could shut her eyes to it no more.

Thomas Parry lapped it up as a dog would a dish of scraps. He and Aunt Kat leaned closer and closer until I thought they would touch over the table, their sleeves and collars in danger of ruin with stew.

"So he has wanted our princess," Parry hissed. "A fine feather in her cap, he would be, such a rich man, and highly placed."

"And a handsome one. And the King loves him, and he is of the Reformed religion. The household when he was in it was a different place. Lively and happy and everyone laughing. A fine dancer is the Lord Admiral and always full of jokes. But pious for all that, always reading scripture with the Queen. Much better than his stick of a brother, who is miserly and dull."

"Aye, perhaps the King likes his Uncle Thomas a little better than his Uncle Edward?" Parry said.

"I grant you, even if the Council does not like the match, when King Ned is of age, he will certainly smile upon it."

I burst out, "But surely he is too old, Aunt Kat. Thomas Seymour." By the time the King reached his majority, Seymour would be well along in his forties.

Aunt Kat fixed me with a gleaming stare. "You do like to go on about his age. He is of an age with me, Miss Impertinence, none too old for Her Grace. What young lady does not want to marry a man of wise years, and for all his great age as you call it, he is slender and strong and fine haired. And I saw his limbs when he went bare legged into my lady's chamber. No quarrel there, I imagine."

"Aunt Kat!" I put as much shock into my words as I could, because she was red with wine and excitement.

Chatter, chatter, chatter. They were plotting and planning a marriage for the lady Elizabeth, a woman for whom it was illegal to choose her own husband. Aunt Kat shot a guilty glance at Parry. He closed his mouth at the same time, his breathing loud through his nose.

"You'll not repeat a word of this, of course," Aunt Kat said.

Parry sat back on his bench with a thump, shaking his head hard. "Never, never, Mistress Ashley. I'd never tell a soul about our lady Elizabeth. I have assured you time and again that horses will pull me asunder before I repeat a word."

He looked very sincere, and after a moment, Aunt Kat gave him a decided nod. The two exchanged a secret smile, lifted pewter goblets of wine from the Rhine valley, and drank to it.

6

 I LEFT AUNT Kat's chamber torn in my mind whether to report the conversation to John Ashley. I went to bed without seeking him, reasoning that Aunt Kat and Thomas Parry might talk for hours about Elizabeth, but what harm could it do? They told tales of Elizabeth's youth, nothing more, and she'd left those days behind. Remembering Elizabeth's illness after Catherine's death, I concluded that Elizabeth had much remorse over her silliness and would not succor Thomas Seymour again.

Aunt Kat and Parry, no matter how fondly they might think of their position in Elizabeth's household, had no true power to affect Elizabeth's choice of bridegrooms. That was up to the Council, the Protector, and Edward. Idle chatter about a man's legs would not bring down King Edward's reign. I also had a headache and did not fancy running to Uncle John to tattle on his wife, so I kept my thoughts to myself and slept the sleep of the guiltless.

How John Ashley got wind of the conversation I do not know,

but when I rose in the morning, I heard him almost shouting in Aunt Kat's chamber. I dressed quickly and went to see what was the matter. It was most unusual for Uncle John to quarrel with Aunt Kat—they bore much affection for each other. But this morning his voice rang out, his displeasure made known.

"Gossip and meddling," he shouted as I approached the door to Kat's chamber. "Have nothing to do with the Lord Admiral, for the love of God. Nothing good can come of it, do you understand?"

Aunt Kat had never been a meek woman, nor readily obedient to her husband. She had a good opinion of herself and a strong will and a voice as loud as his. She shouted back that she meant only good for Elizabeth, and he, John, was the party who needed to understand.

Uncle John banged out of her chamber, his hair mussed and his eyes glittering with rage. He caught sight of me and savagely beckoned me to follow.

My head gave an extrahard throb as I descended the stairs with him to the wide hall. "Uncle, do not look at me so. I cannot stop the Thames flooding, and I cannot stop Aunt Kat when she wants to talk about something."

He turned to face me at the bottom of the stairs, his cheeks still red, but he modulated his voice. "I do not blame you, Eloise, but you must understand—that man is dangerous, and all his smiles and beguiles do not make him less so."

"I know he is dangerous, uncle, you do not need to convince *me*."

He looked at me sharply. "And why are you so certain?"

I did not want to talk about the awful evening Seymour had forced his attentions on me. I could still feel the pain of his large hand on my breast, smell the sticky sweet smell of his breath.

"I see through him," I said glibly. "Not all women are fools."

"Your aunt is, in this instance, and I have told her so. I am for London. You will report to me any meddling she thinks to do as soon as you learn of it."

I clutched his sleeve. "Why not stay and watch yourself? Or take her with you?"

"I have business," he said in clipped tones. "I have no time for a wife who embroils herself in dangerous gossip."

He turned and strode away, barking at a servant to come and help him ready for his journey, leaving me squarely in the middle of a husband-and-wife quarrel.

Aunt Kat sulked for a day, angry at John and at me, calling me no better than a gaoler. The next day she began to repent, admitting that her tongue wagged too much and she gave far too much interest to affairs not her own. She blamed Master Parry for dragging the story out of her but conceded she should have not allowed him to goad her.

After several more days dragged by, Kat became quite unhappy and remorseful. She missed John and lamented that she'd so angered him. She wrote him a letter and waited eagerly for reply, but had none. After that, there was nothing for it but that she go to London and make things up with him. Her arm was sore, she told Elizabeth, and she'd like a physician to see to it. Elizabeth saw through the excuse for the journey, but she gave Kat a cool nod and permission for her to leave for a short while.

Wanting I suppose to reconcile with me as well, Aunt Kat bade me accompany her to London. I went readily, because not only did I want to see Kat and John patch their quarrel, but the countryside was gloomy in the dark of December, and London, though muddy and cold, would at least be interesting. It was too cold for plague in the city, vendors would be selling hot nuts and cider, and there would be street entertainment. Though Aunt

Kat told me that tumbling men and performing bears were low forms of amusement, I liked them, and I noted that she could not look away from them either. Elizabeth too enjoyed bears and tumblers, and troupes such as that to which my father had belonged often stopped at Hatfield.

When we reached London, I hoped to tarry in the lanes and shop a little, but Aunt Kat went with haste to the dwelling of her friends and there we stayed. The house was large but dark, and the fires did not draw well, making the rooms smoky and my throat sore.

"Will you not see a leech?" I asked the next day when Aunt Kat showed no sign of leaving her chamber, let alone the house.

"I cannot go out, Eloise. I have nothing to wear."

True, Aunt Kat had not packed very much above her travel garments, and she seemed not in the least bothered by this. She had the firm look of a woman who meant to stay the whole day indoors with her feet propped on a stool by the fire.

"Perhaps I will see the leech," I suggested. I could also linger at the markets, looking over fabric brought in from all over the country and the world.

"Do go, Eloise, you are restless as a sparrow," Aunt Kat said. She returned her brooding attention to the fire, clearly uncaring about what I did.

I conscripted a maid and young lad to accompany me, it being unfit for me to wander the muddy streets alone. They resented being dragged out into the cold and muttered to themselves as we walked along.

The house in which we stayed was situated near the Strand, and I walked along that avenue filled with vendors selling everything from sweetmeats to trinkets from far-off places, shops of books for learned men, and houses of the nobility.

Durham Place, which should have been Elizabeth's had the

Protector not wormed his way into it, was a pile of elegance situated on the Strand not far from the Lord Protector's own Somerset House. The gates of Durham Place were open as I passed, and I glimpsed a huge courtyard with arched openings leading to the house set far back from the street. The house, a vast building with its apartments looking directly onto the Thames behind it, was lovely for a London residence. I could well see why Elizabeth did not like to let the Protector hoard it.

Further along the Strand, near where it became Fleet Street at Temple Bar, a troupe of acrobats performed, and I stopped to watch. Wind blew down the lanes, so close to the river, and the chill crept up my skirts and into my gloves. The troupe, dancing and tumbling, were smiling and rosy, but the audience stamped feet and blew on fingers.

Behind me came the tramping of heavy feet moving more or less in unison, which betokened an important personage coming our way. The audience dispersed, hurrying out of the way of the liveried and armed men, and I did the same. I hadn't gone more than three steps before a familiar voice said, "It is too cold to be abroad, kitten. Is your mistress so cruel that she does not allow you to laze by the fire?"

Thomas Seymour, Lord High Admiral, stood upright among his guards, his mouth smiling behind his long red beard, his dark eyes glittering. Why he, the exalted Lord High Admiral, should be on foot I could scarcely tell—presumably going about some business, but it was far easier to move about London on boats and barges than tramping through the streets.

I curtseyed and said neutrally, "My lord."

"I asked you a question, seamstress. Does your mistress not keep you busy sewing?"

His eyes glinted as he took in me, my two servants who had scuttled a little down a side lane, and the absence of any other person or retinue. Clearly he wanted to know whether I was protected and whether Elizabeth was in London, but I had no intention of telling him.

"You are too cold," Seymour announced. "You must come with me and get warm."

I remained still, pretending that the etiquette that prevented me from entering a conversation with my betters kept me quiet and rooted in place. My fear of him had evaporated into rage. He had intruded on me, I did not trust him, and he was busy manipulating Aunt Kat and Thomas Parry and, by extension, Elizabeth to get what he wanted. A lofty man not caring whom he stepped on to make himself still more lofty.

Seymour's teeth worked his lower lip, making his beard move slightly. He seemed in no hurry to sweep me away, and his men assumed the stoic expressions of soldiers awaiting orders.

"I saw you looking in the gates of Durham," Seymour said. "A magnificent house, even if the stink of the river mars it."

He paused for some response, so I murmured, "Yes, my lord."

"She would rejoice to see it once more for her use." He leaned toward me as he spoke, a note of cunning entering his voice. "As I discussed with her clever Master Parry. It shall be, and so much more, very soon."

He gave me a nod, expecting me to grow excited perhaps, to indicate I'd rush back to Elizabeth and tell her the intriguing hints Thomas Seymour had dropped in the middle of the Strand. I contrived to look blank, pretending not to understand him, and his ingratiating smile vanished.

"You will come with me, little seamstress. I have need of you." He did not touch me, but jerked his head at a man to take charge of me. Seymour then said something I could not hear to the leader of his guards, and they all wheeled about and proceeded to march with me back down the Strand the way they had come.

I was small and agile and thought to slip away, but I was hemmed in by men with swords and pikes. I had no idea what Seymour would do—take me to one of his own houses and keep me there until he made me reveal everything he wished to learn about Elizabeth? He had flattered Parry until Parry had spilled details on Elizabeth's household finances and property holdings; perhaps he would pry from me knowledge of Elizabeth's habits and small ways he could infiltrate her trust.

Or were his designs on me worse than simply wanting information? I believed Thomas Seymour not above holding me captive until Elizabeth agreed to aid him. Speculating what he would do to me while he held me captive awakened my darkest fears. He was a ruthless man, and I was no one very important.

"Eloise Rousell, where do you go?"

Never had my uncle's deep voice sounded so beloved. The tall figure of John Ashley broke through Seymour's retinue, the most welcome sight in the world. "Why are you in London, niece?"

Seymour scowled at the interruption, but he knew John Ashley for a trusted gentleman of Elizabeth's household, and he checked whatever sharp words had sprung to his tongue. "Ashley."

"My lord." John bowed diffidently.

I wondered what excuse Seymour would offer for kidnapping me, but he did not deign to explain. Instead, his flattering, beguiling smile returned.

"The seamstress is a credit to you and your good wife."

"Your lordship is kind," Ashley replied.

"I will make you a gift, some trifle. To express my appreciation for looking after Her Grace so well."

Alarm flickered through me, and I saw it reflected in Uncle

John's eyes. Accepting a gift, even a small token, could construe loyalty to Seymour, and pledging loyalties was a dangerous pastime. If anyone needed our loyalty, it was Elizabeth.

"You are kind, my lord," John repeated. "Serving the princess is reward enough for me."

Seymour gave a negligent flick of his fingers. "A bauble, perhaps, that your niece might like to present to the princess. I will send a messenger to Whitehall."

A man of single-mindedness was our Seymour. He sought even now to learn whether Elizabeth had traveled to London with Ashley and her seamstress, and where she stayed.

"Her Grace is not at court," Ashley said. "I left her in Hatfield."

Seymour gave me a sharp look, and I did my best to appear innocent. I nodded a little, to affirm my uncle's words, but said nothing.

Having ascertained what he wanted to know, Seymour said a few more niceties so that Uncle John could repeat to Elizabeth what a pleasant and courteous fellow he was. He signaled to his retinue and walked off once more toward Fleet Street, giving us a dark look before turning away.

As soon as Seymour was out of sight, Uncle John seized me by the elbow and steered me in the other direction. The two servants emerged from around a corner, stuffing sweetmeats into their mouths. I bent a glare on them, but they showed no remorse. If I dragged them out into muddy London in the cold, they thought it their due to run off and gobble food when my back was turned.

"What are you doing in London, Eloise?" John Ashley demanded. "Where is the princess?"

"At Hatfield, as you said," I replied. "I came here with Aunt Kat."

"Why?" He looked horrified. "Never tell me it was to see *Seymour*. What is she—"

"Not to see the Lord Admiral, but to see you." I let my voice soften. "She misses you, uncle, and is quite sorry she quarreled with you. She made the excuse that she needed to see a physician, but she has made no move to do so. She is waiting for you."

Uncle John's grip relaxed, and I hoped I saw tenderness enter his expression. "She is foolish sometimes."

"Perhaps, but she is willing to be guided by you."

He gave me a sidelong glance. "Stop when you have won, Eloise. Your aunt is not the most obedient of wives, but I prefer her that way. In truth, I miss her."

"Come back to the house with me now, then. She is staying with the Slaynings. She will be glad to see you."

He nodded, and we fell into step together, but my assurances did not stop his questions. "If she came to London to make it up with me, why were you conferring with his lordship?"

"Hardly conferring. More being kidnapped." I told him what had happened, and he looked grave.

"He is scheming something," Uncle John concluded. "I hope whatever it is never touches us."

I fervently shared the wish. The conspiracies of the highborn could be dangerous, indeed, and I knew Seymour for a dangerous man.

Aunt Kat was indeed so pleased to see her husband that she smiled at him and welcomed him as though all differences between them were forgotten. He stayed to supper, which was a happy reunion, and other friends, including Anthony Denny, joined us. By tacit agreement, neither I nor Uncle John spoke of my encounter with Seymour.

After supper, Aunt Kat retired with Uncle John to her chamber, and they did not emerge again until well into the morning.

I admit that before I went to sleep myself I pressed my ear to their chamber door and was happy to hear the bed bumping and scraping against the floor.

In the morning Aunt Kat and I broke fast with Uncle John, and Thomas Parry, who was in town on other business, came to take breakfast with us. Again, we made no mention of Seymour. After the meal Aunt Kat agreed to return to Hatfield, and so we departed.

We went first to Fleet Street to pay a visit to another lady, where Aunt Joan met us. Aunt Kat and I left on horseback with our servants and rode north through London to Smithfield and on toward Hatfield.

Behind us, down the Thames, as I was to learn later, Thomas Seymour had begun a dangerous mission, wishing to use his position as Lord Admiral to overthrow his brother and the stranglehold the Protector and the Privy Council had on King Edward, and to lure Edward into his grip.

7

"I AM ALL amazed," Aunt Kat told Anthony Denny as he supped with us on a cold January night. "It must be a mistake."

"The Lord High Admiral was found to be in collusion with pirates and obtaining money by fraudulent means," Sir Anthony said over his glass of wine. "Money he planned to use to raise a force of men-at-arms and take control of the King's person. I am afraid he has been arrested and confined to the Tower."

Kat exchanged a bewildered look with Parry, who shifted in alarm. I remembered Seymour on the streets of London when I'd been there with Aunt Kat, walking purposefully to do who knew what. His eagerness when he tried to discover from me where Elizabeth was that day took on a sinister cast. He'd nearly kidnapped me; would he have done the same to her?

Anthony Denny had arrived at Hatfield that afternoon, accompanied by William Paulet, who had been comptroller of the household for King Henry and now served Edward as his chief steward. A graying man with a shrewd, canny eye, I stood in a little awe of Paulet, who had been one of those who'd carried out the arrest of Elizabeth's mother, Anne Boleyn. He had acted out of duty then, and he acted out of duty now, but that made him no less formidable.

The first emotion I felt upon Anthony Denny's revelation was relief. Elizabeth was well quit of Thomas Seymour, safe from his riding up to Hatfield, beguiling smile in place, to coerce her to marry him. Having already made Aunt Kat and Thomas Parry his allies, he might have persuaded or even forced her into marrying him.

"It's scarce to be believed," Aunt Kat repeated. Parry relapsed into silence, and his wife, Lady Fortescue, cast Sir Anthony fearful glances.

"Unfortunately, 'tis all true," Denny said, slowly twirling his goblet. "He tried to woo the King to his side with gifts and money, but I am afraid his overly obvious bribery simply annoyed the boy. And now with the evidence that Seymour was funding a private army . . ." Denny raised his eyes and shrugged. "Somerset is furious. The King is furious, the more so because the man duping him was his favorite uncle. It is quite embarrassing to discover one has been the victim of charm and cunning."

"Indeed," Paulet added.

Denny set down his wine and licked his lips. "You can imagine I did not like this errand, today."

Aunt Kat jumped a little. "We are always pleased to see you, Sir Anthony. I am sorry you have missed John; he is detained in London."

"But we will travel to London together, Mistress Ashley," Anthony Denny said. "I am afraid that the Lord Admiral's plan to marry Princess Elizabeth has come to light, and coupled with his wooing of other nobles—not to mention pirates—and arming himself against his brother . . . well, it does not look nice.

I am afraid you, Mistress Kat, along with Master Parry, have been named accomplices in this matter."

"What?" I cried in indignation, and all heads turned to me. "How could anyone believe such a thing?"

I knew full well how they could, of course. Parry had not kept quiet about his talks with Seymour, proud that Seymour had deigned to discuss Elizabeth's finances with him. Aunt Kat had wanted Elizabeth to write to Seymour and encourage his advances, and only Elizabeth's natural caution had nipped that idea in the bud.

Mistress Parry did not help matters by bursting into tears. "I knew no good would come of it," she sobbed. "Will I ever see my husband again?"

She was sitting next to me, and I pinched her hard. She yelped, but at least she stopped talking. I knew little of the law, but I had learned from observation that court life could be dangerous and saying as little as possible was always best.

Aunt Kat simply sat, her mouth open. I doubted she'd fully understood Seymour's true corruption—she'd seen only a handsome, powerful man interested in her charge. If Elizabeth married Seymour, the Lord High Admiral of England, Elizabeth would be honored and titled and, more important to Aunt Kat, remain in England. Far better, in Kat's view, than Somerset or King Edward marrying Elizabeth off to some foreign prince and Kat never seeing her again.

Despite my worry for Aunt Kat, I felt just a little bit glad that my suspicions of Seymour had proved right. My self-satisfaction, however, quickly evaporated.

"You will accompany us to London this night," Denny said to Aunt Kat and Parry. "I will give you a little time to prepare yourselves, but we must leave right away."

At this, Mistress Parry cried the louder. Aunt Kat rose in agitation, her ample hips rocking her stool backward.

"I cannot simply leave. My lady Elizabeth . . . I must see her, I must speak to her . . ."

"No, madam," Paulet interposed. "You must not. I will see that word is taken to her of your departure after you have readied yourselves. Perhaps you would like to prepare now."

There was a look in his eyes that the agitated Parry and Aunt Kat failed to grasp. Paulet would not say so out loud, but he was giving them time to prepare out of sight of himself and Denny, perhaps to collude their stories about all Seymour had done. And perhaps deliver the set story to Elizabeth?

From what I'd heard of Paulet, he was canny and wise, and always knew which way the political wind blew. If he was doing what he could now to keep Elizabeth from being implicated in Seymour's schemes, she might have a chance.

"May I accompany my aunt to London, sir?" I asked of Anthony Denny. "She will be distressed to be alone."

"No, child." Denny's look was kind, but firm. "Your lady Elizabeth will need you more. There is nothing you can do in London."

Aunt Kat nodded vigorously, though her eyes filled with tears. "Stay with her. She will need the comfort and counsel of her favorite ladies."

Take care of her for me, she was begging me. *See that she is protected.* I understood the danger. Seymour had been plotting against Somerset and the King, and marrying Elizabeth, it was clear now, had been part of that plot. Seen in that light, Aunt Kat's conspiring to helping him marry Elizabeth against Somerset's wishes would be considered treason.

Traitors died terrible deaths; I had seen their bodies after such an execution and their decaying heads displayed on pikes. I wondered if they would also accuse poor Uncle John, or would he simply have to live through the horror of his wife's execution?

As I helped Aunt Kat from the room and led her to her chamber, my stomach roiled in fear. I had to help, but my thoughts were frozen and I did not know what to do. I was a seamstress, not a thinker, not a wise counselor like Denny.

Words could condemn Aunt Kat, or words could save her. The right words said at the right time, or words omitted at the right time. The Council, guided by Somerset, had so much power—the power of words, the power of life.

I entered Aunt Kat's chamber and began to help her don her cloak and riding shoes. An idea hummed through my brain, but I had no way to predict whether it would work.

"Aunt Kat," I said in a low voice, making sure the bustling, weeping maidservants did not hear me. "You had no intention of going against the King's and Council's wishes in this, did you? You thought only to marry Elizabeth to someone she would admire, but not if it meant displeasing the King."

"No, of course not. But I did not know. I did not know. John was right when he told me not to meddle."

"That is all you must say," I hissed. "It is true that you thought Seymour would be a good husband for Elizabeth, but you never dreamed of her marrying anyone against the Council's wishes. She would abide by the law always."

"Yes, but . . ."

"Aunt Kat." I put my face close to hers and stared into her eyes. "You never, ever, once thought to see Elizabeth marry Thomas Seymour against the wishes of the Council."

She gaped at me a moment, and then I saw understanding dawn. Her mouth closed and she drew a long breath. "Quickly, I must speak to Parry ere I go down."

I nodded, my heart thumping in hope, and I ran away to find him.

When I parted from Aunt Kat in the muddy yard thirty minutes later, I could not stop myself bursting into tears. Aunt Kat gathered me into a hard hug and told me to mind myself and Elizabeth.

Aunt Kat, Parry, Denny, and Paulet rode away in the mud and the dark, surrounded by outriders. They disappeared soon, hoofbeats dying into silence, while Lady Fortescue and I watched with tears streaming down our faces. I turned back to the house, my heart heavy, my mind whirling. I had been advised by Denny not to go to Elizabeth with the news of Aunt Kat's arrest, but after the riders disappeared, I turned around, entered the house, and told her anyway.

❧

WHAT DOES A woman do when she discovers that the man with whom she's fallen in love has been using her only to get something he wants? Especially when it is her first love? Does she bow her head, ashamed, and accept the inevitability that suitors of certain rank are more interested in the money, power, and connection of his fiancée's family than of the woman herself? Or does she become hardened and angry, vowing to never feel such disappointment again?

When I spoke to Elizabeth that night and told her all, her face grew whiter and whiter but her jaw hardened and a new light entered her eyes. Tears wet her lashes, but she held them back, not from bravery, but with an anger brighter than any I'd ever seen from her. The temper tantrums of a child suddenly made way for a fierce, adult anger that she honed into a weapon as I watched.

"Say nothing, my lady, I beg you," I whispered. She sat on a chair, I on my knees at her feet. "Aunt Kat is innocent; they may send her back home on the morrow, and this will pass us by."

"Perhaps," Elizabeth said, not really listening.

I told her of my words to Aunt Kat, about how she could say that she had never once thought to go against the wishes of Edward's Council, and how Denny and Paulet seemed to approve. Her look turned even colder.

"Sir Anthony is a very shrewd man," she said.

"Would you like me to stay with you tonight, Your Grace?"

"No." Her anger was grim, and I wasn't certain to whom she directed it—me, Aunt Kat and Parry, Thomas Seymour, Denny, the Protector, perhaps all of us.

As she looked down at me the ice in her eyes frightened me more than anything ever had, even Thomas Seymour forcing a seduction on me five feet from his wife's bedchamber door.

"Stay away from me, Eloise," Elizabeth said, "so that I do not succumb to the temptation to speak of this with you before all is known. Silence is best."

I nodded, wiping my eyes. "Others will wonder if we do not speak at all. It is known you confide often in me."

"Then I shall pretend to be angry with you and not wish you by my side."

"I understand." My heart beat a little faster, for some reason excited by this duplicity, by a secret Elizabeth shared with me and no other. I was ashamed of myself for my satisfaction, but it remained.

Elizabeth slapped me, not a contrived slap. Her fingers stung my face and my hair bounced wildly into my eyes. The ladies on the other side of the chamber looked up in interest. I had little trouble bursting into tears as I fled the room.

※

I SPENT THE next several days pretending that all was well, that Aunt Kat and Parry would return right away, that Somerset would admit his mistake about their complicity and send them home. Seymour might be leaning toward treason, but my aunt and Parry would never dream of that.

Elizabeth walked with her ladies, took her meals as usual, studied as usual, played music and read and prayed as usual, and did not allow any discussion of Aunt Kat's arrest. Ostensibly, she knew nothing about it. Somerset's instructions, according to Denny, had been to tell her nothing.

But Somerset was a fool if he thought servants would not gossip about anything that happened in the house, especially something so extraordinary as an arrest. They might not disobey and tell Elizabeth directly, but they could certainly discuss it when she was within earshot, and the most loyal of her servants would make certain she knew somehow.

One blustery, cold, and dark afternoon not long after Aunt Kat's arrest a contingency of people rode into the yard at Hatfield. The outriders wore the emblem of the Duke of Somerset, and they surrounded several gentlemen and a lady who demanded to see Elizabeth.

Face white, Elizabeth determinedly stuck to her studies, reading out loud a passage in Greek to drown out the commotion downstairs. One of her gentlemen ushers entered the room apologetically and explained that Sir Robert Tyrwhitt had arrived and had requested to speak to her.

"I will see him when I am finished," Elizabeth said coldly. Lines pinched about her eyes and mouth, but she resolutely turned her face to her books. The gentleman withdrew, looking troubled.

"Tyrwhitt, Tyrwhitt," Elizabeth said when he'd gone. "I've always thought his name sounds like a cheeping bird. Tyrwhitt, Tyrwhitt, too-woo."

She whistled a little and the ladies laughed, though my throat was too tight for laughter. So was hers—she put her hand to it and swallowed.

I perceived that her nervousness did not stem entirely from fear but also from anger. The outrage that her governess and financier could be arrested under her nose infuriated her. So did the idea that Seymour's duplicity had been brought to her door. She was well aware that not only had Seymour used her, but Somerset now used her to build the case against his brother. I saw frustration in the set of her lips, a burning in her eyes as she longed for the day when she was not a pawn on the chessboard.

She kept Tyrwhitt kicking his heels for a good long while before she condescended to see him. When he came up to her outer chamber, she was every inch the regal princess in crimson damask kirtle and velvet overskirt and Tyrwhitt every inch the impatient suitor.

Robert Tyrwhitt had once been Master of Horse to Queen Catherine, and he'd obviously used the wealth of that lofty position to grow comfortable and stout. His wife, who was the lady I'd seen arrive with him, had been lady to Queen Catherine. Lady Tyrwhitt was nowhere in evidence now and likely had been left downstairs so that she would not soften the interview to come. Elizabeth, on the other hand, insisted that her ladies stay, at which Tyrwhitt looked pained.

"It ill pleases me to announce it, Your Grace," he began, "but your governess, Mistress Ashley, and the treasurer of your household, Master Thomas Parry, have been detained at His Majesty's pleasure in the Tower of London, during investigation into the improper pursuit of a marriage between yourself and the Lord High Admiral."

Elizabeth watched him coldly. I saw thoughts flicker behind her eyes, deciding what would be the best way to receive the news. What did she want him to report back to Somerset?

Lifting her hands to her face, she began to cry. Tyrwhitt stared at her in astonishment, as though this were the last reaction he'd expected. Had he thought he'd find her cold and brittle, I wondered, or perhaps sly and guilty? He hadn't had much contact with Elizabeth as a child, despite his role in Catherine's household, and probably had no notion of her true nature. Perhaps he'd expected a seducer, one who beguiled with smiles and glances, perhaps reasoning that she'd be like her mother, the supposed whore Anne Boleyn. Instead, he'd found a young princess, straight backed and no-nonsense, who cried when she learned that her governess was in danger.

"Now then," Tyrwhitt said, clearly uncomfortable with the tears of a fifteen-year-old. Nervously he laid several sheets of paper on the table before him. I saw a signature at the bottom of one, my Aunt Kat's handwriting, and felt cold.

"Katherine Ashley and Thomas Parry have made their first confessions," Tyrwhitt said. "They signed their names to their statements. It would be best, really, Your Grace, to confess straight away and let this all be done with."

Elizabeth sniffled and pressed a handkerchief to her white face, but the hand that reached for the papers did not tremble. "May I read them?"

Tyrwhitt gave her a thin smile. "Perhaps you will tell me what you know, and then we may read them together."

Elizabeth withdrew her hand and laid it in her lap. Her fingers curled into her palm. "Mistress Ashley is a good woman, and would do nothing to deceive my brother the King, or His Grace of Somerset. Or myself."

Tyrwhitt's smile became strained as she reminded him just who she was, and he shuffled the papers, clearing his throat. "Thomas Parry hints that the Lord High Admiral was familiar with you, and Mistress Ashley says nothing to deny it."

"The Lord High Admiral never offered marriage to me, if that is what you mean," Elizabeth said, keeping tears in her voice. "I never made pledge to him. I would never agree to marry without the King my brother's consent, and I trust he believes so."

The second reminder of her position irritated Tyrwhitt. He huffed. "Do remember, Your Grace, that though your brother is ruler of this realm, you are but a subject."

"Of course." Her chill manner returned. "Which is precisely why I would not have chosen my own husband. The Council and the Lord Protector and my brother must approve. Mistress Ashley knew that very well and would not have advised me otherwise."

I wondered again what Tyrwhitt had expected as he grew more and more irate. That Elizabeth would throw herself at his feet and beg for mercy? That she'd confess she'd conspired against the King? She'd never have admitted that, even were it true.

I learned much in that room as I watched her match wits with Tyrwhitt, a man more than twice her age, and win. He tried to cajole, to be stern, to threaten, to cajole again, but Elizabeth never flinched. She repeated over and over that she had no intention of marrying outside the wishes of the Council and declared that the romps Kat Ashley and Thomas Parry may have described were nothing more than childish games, which Queen Catherine herself had joined.

As Tyrwhitt lost patience, his words became cruel. "My wife was in service with your stepmother, as you know. She waited on the Queen in her last days, was in the bedchamber when she died. The Queen, in her delirium, declared her husband had betrayed her. And Master Parry says you were sent away from the Queen's household when"—Tyrwhitt smoothed out a paper and read from it—"'one time the Queen, suspecting the often access of the Admiral to the lady Elizabeth's grace, came suddenly upon them when they were all alone, he having her in his arms, wherefore the Queen fell out, both with the Admiral and with Her Grace also.' "

Elizabeth sat as though carved of marble. Any reminder of how she'd hurt Catherine upset her, and coming from the self-satisfied Tyrwhitt made it doubly infuriating.

"I admit a misunderstanding with Her Grace the Queen," she said in a brittle voice. "But it was cleared up soon after. There was ever great affection between us, as our letters to each other while I stayed at Cheshunt will show."

Tyrwhitt frowned, annoyed at her answer, and shuffled his papers again. "You realize that your governess and treasurer will remain in the Tower until this matter is cleared. My wife, Lady Tyrwhitt, will take the place of Mistress Ashley as your governess."

"I see not why she should," Elizabeth snapped. "Mistress Ashley is innocent and quite dear to me."

"Mistress Ashley has told your secrets," Tyrwhitt said. "I wonder that you'd want her near you ever again. She has betrayed you."

"She has done no such thing."

Tyrwhitt more or less shoved the papers at Elizabeth. "See there, in her own words."

I saw the triumphant look in Elizabeth's eyes and realized she'd gotten Tyrwhitt to do as she liked, let her read the confessions. She skimmed through Parry's with a frown and tossed it aside, and then her expression softened as she read Aunt Kat's words.

I was close enough to read over her shoulder and saw what she did, that while Aunt Kat had admitted that Seymour had liked to play with Elizabeth and her ladies, he'd not given her much more attention than he had her cousin Jane Grey. Aunt

Kat had also stated quite firmly that she'd had no intention of persuading Elizabeth to marry outside the Council's wishes. Parry had repeated the same thing.

Elizabeth hid a small smile of satisfaction as she pushed the papers back toward Tyrwhitt. "My aunt is innocent of duplicity. She has written here the same that she told me, that my brother's wishes are what we would follow in matters of marriage."

Tyrwhitt gathered up the confessions, the paper rustling like dry leaves. "Nevertheless, my wife and I will remain here, and I will discuss this further with you. I suggest that you think it over, Your Grace, and speak with me again on the morrow."

Elizabeth gave him a frosty nod and a little gesture of dismissal. I suppressed my glee when Tyrwhitt bowed and went away as though he were the accused and *she* the interrogator.

As soon as his footsteps faded, however, Elizabeth put her hand to her face and declared her head was splitting in two. We put her to bed where she remained, ill and unable to rise, for the next several days.

8

TRUE TO HIS word, Tyrwhitt tried, every day Elizabeth could stand to leave her bed and meet him, to make her say what he wanted her to. He never succeeded. With the precision of a dancer, Elizabeth evaded his questions and brought him back to the fact that she would obey the King her father's last wishes and never think to marry without advice of Edward's Council. Whatever Seymour's plans had been, she implied, she'd had no intention of participating in them herself. She held herself aloof, apart.

I knew as I watched and listened that Elizabeth had fallen out of love with Seymour. When once her eyes would brighten at the mention of his name, she now spoke no word in his defense nor made any sign of protest about his arrest. She had finished with him. She could not stop what happened to him now, and so she strove to remove herself from the incidents.

Tyrwhitt, faced with her coolness and her iron will, seemed all amazed by her. The only human feeling she had, I heard him mutter to his wife, was for her governess, Kat Ashley.

"They *must* have collaborated on a story," I also heard him say. "They sing the same tune, the three of them."

"She will have counseled them," Lady Tyrwhitt said darkly. "The princess, I mean."

"She is a girl!" Tyrwhitt exploded. "God's grace, she is but a fifteen-year-old child, for all her book learning. I will wager it was Parry who advised her." He sighed. "Though Sir Anthony Denny and Sir William Paulet swore that they never allowed Ashley or Parry to speak to Elizabeth after their arrest. I do not know how they managed it, but they must have."

I went away then, a smile on my lips.

A piece of news that came to us soon after that brought Elizabeth out of her cold aloofness and sent her into a towering fury.

"It is untrue," she told Tyrwhitt hotly when he came to her chamber. "As you can see." She spread out her arms, showing her slender figure hugged by one of my gowns. I'd sewn the bodice long and to a point in front, oversleeves of blue velvet folded back to reveal undersleeves of finest gold satin.

Tyrwhitt winced. "It is rumor only, Your Grace. Gossip. No one will believe it."

"Of course they will believe it, I am not a fool. Here I am, shut away from the world, unable to speak. Take me to court, and let me show myself. 'Twill be easy to make a mockery of the story that I am heavy with the Admiral's child and locked in the Tower if I am seen at court."

"I have not been given permission to allow you to leave Hatfield," Tyrwhitt said miserably.

Elizabeth swept books and papers to the floor. Secretly I was pleased to see her in a fine rage, because the coldness I had perceived in her the last days unnerved me. I was used to her shouting and her hot tempers; her icy control was new.

"Then I will write to *His Grace* Somerset." The lines about her mouth told me it was all she could do to give Somerset the honorific. "And I will ask him myself."

"My lady . . ."

Elizabeth sent him a freezing glare. "My reputation is at stake, Sir Robert. The people of England shall not be laughing up their sleeves at me, or pitying the princess who has fallen so low. I have *not* fallen, and these slanders are insulting. How dare he allow them to persist?"

I well could guess how he dared—it would be in Somerset's interest to paint Elizabeth as a whore and his brother as a whoremonger. The two ready to take over the kingdom—easily stopped by Somerset, of course.

Elizabeth won. She wrote her letter, and Tyrwhitt had it delivered to the Duke of Somerset's cold hands.

"Master Tyrwhitt and others have told me," she wrote, "that there goeth rumors abroad, which be greatly both against mine honor and honesty . . . which be these: that I am in the Tower and with child by my lord Admiral. My lord, these are shameful slanders, for the which, besides the great desire I have to see the King's Majesty, I shall most heartily desire your lordship that I may come to the court after your first determination, that I may show myself there as I am."

I heard that when Somerset received this letter he turned green with fury. His wife too snarled at the impudence of Elizabeth, she who'd behaved so wantonly, nearly committing adultery with her own stepfather. What right had she to write so peremptorily to Somerset, the first lord of the land, while she herself was one step from being condemned as a traitor? Somerset ground his teeth and wrote a curt and severe reply.

Thus began the battle of wit between Elizabeth and the Duke of Somerset.

✣

WHILE ELIZABETH EXERCISED her fury at Somerset, I worried about Aunt Kat. She remained in the Tower, how sequestered I did not know. Lady Tyrwhitt assured me she was fine, but one of their men told me Aunt Kat had been put into a dungeon and made to sit in chains.

I worried for her and also Uncle John, who was still in London, and I begged Elizabeth for leave to journey to London and see him.

Elizabeth was at first not inclined to let me go, but after a time she changed her mind. "You will keep your eyes open and tell me what truly goes on in the Tower and at court. John Ashley will know some things, and you are clever enough to invent a way to learn more."

I had intended to question Uncle John thoroughly and try to gain admission to the Tower to see Aunt Kat, so I had no trouble agreeing to her stipulation. I doubted I'd succeed in speaking to Kat herself, but I meant to discover everything I could.

I rode to London with some of Tyrwhitt's and Anthony Denny's men, who had been dispatched on errands and to deliver messages to Somerset. We rode at a swift pace—very unlike the stately journeys I took with the princess—and entered the gates of London late that night. Two of the guards were persuaded to ride with me to the house where John Ashley lodged.

"Eloise," Uncle John exclaimed when the servant saw me in, travel worn and dirty faced. "What do you here?"

"I worried for you," I said.

John Ashley looked gray and weary, his face lined, his hands shaking. "Worry not for me," he said, "but for poor, silly Kat." He dragged me into an embrace and for a moment, we both shed tears for Kat Ashley.

I drew away and wiped my hand across my face. "Surely Edward would not condemn his sister's beloved governess. He could not be so cruel."

"Not he." Ashley had me sit down and the servants brought us warm, spiced wine. "But Somerset might. He has fixed all his jealousy and suspicion on Thomas Seymour, and he will pull in any he believes will help condemn his brother. Somerset has always been the bland, do-good Seymour while Thomas got the charm and attention. Naturally that rankles."

"Hardly fair to punish Aunt Kat because Thomas Seymour is more dashing than his brother. That is not her fault."

"But Seymour is a traitor, or as good as one," Ashley returned. He sighed heavily. "Apparently his plot, as far as I can learn, was to marry either Mary or Elizabeth, overthrow Somerset, and rule behind the throne—both Edward and his offspring, with his wife aiding and abetting him."

"Mary or Elizabeth?" I repeated. "So it made not much difference to him which princess he chose?"

"I imagine that he preferred the pretty and young Elizabeth," John said dryly. "But yes, either would do."

I looked at my shoes. "Elizabeth fell in love with him." I did not mention the brief, foolish time I'd been in love with him, too. But it gave me an understanding of his charm.

"I know she did. But that is neither here nor there. A princess may fall in love and break her heart with no one to condemn her—as long as she keeps it to herself. But any action on that love determines her fate. The question is not that Elizabeth fell in love, but whether she promised to marry him and so aid his schemes."

"She did not."

"And that is why they are evil to our Kat. To make her admit that Elizabeth did agree, with Kat's help."

We sat in silence, hearts heavy, thinking of the woman we loved sitting in the Tower. John had tears in his eyes—he and Kat quarreled sometimes, and he felt her too impetuous and too ready to pry into things she should leave alone—but he cherished her. Theirs had been a match of love and friendship, and I regarded it as an example of what a good marriage could be. I was brokenhearted, but John must be doubly so.

"Will they let us see her?"

"I have tried. They fear I will pass messages to her or advise her what to say."

"Perhaps I can. I am a seamstress—I can invent some excuse to enter the Tower—"

I broke off when John gripped my arm hard. "I'll not let my niece traipse into the Tower like a heroine and be arrested as a conspirator. 'Tis a foolish idea, Eloise. Let me hear no more about it."

His fear for me was genuine. I subsided. "But how can we sit here not knowing what is happening to her?"

"I do have *some* information. Not everyone belongs to Somerset, and men tell me things. Men who do not like Somerset's complete control over the King."

Some of my fears gave way before curiosity. "Who are these men?"

"No one you should trouble yourself about," he said curtly. "Never say I said this, but I believe Somerset's days are numbered." He stopped, looking uneasy, as though he feared that spies of Somerset lurked behind the walls. "We will dine, niece, and you will rest. You look worn out with your journey."

I obeyed him, seeing he would say nothing more.

�֎

I STAYED WITH Uncle John a few days, trying to live a normal life while Aunt Kat's imprisonment remained a shadow over us.

I usually enjoyed excursions to London, liking to look in shops at things brought from the strange lands of Africa and the East. I loved to see the fabrics that had come on the great merchant ships, the silks and velvets, the damask and satin from the Continent and beyond. Even the more common fabrics of lawn and linsey-woolsey could usually gain my attention, but this time I could find no interest.

The third day of my stay with John Ashley, we had our fears confirmed. Kat had indeed spent her nights in a dark cell, and when she was released, she'd talked and talked and talked to the eager secretary of Edward's Council, who took down her every word.

Guards belonging to Protector Somerset came to Uncle John's house and asked us not to leave. It was from the guards, bored by their assignment of standing near the house, that we learned most of what happened; they gossiped readily with us to relieve their tedium.

Aunt Kat, they heard, had yesterday told the interrogator, Sir Thomas Smith, many stories about Princess Elizabeth, how Elizabeth had let Thomas Seymour cut up her dress in the garden, how Seymour had run into Elizabeth's room in the mornings "bare legged," how he'd teased and tickled her, and how he'd been found kissing her by Catherine the Queen.

Also, they'd heard from the court, rife with gossip, about Elizabeth's letter to Somerset denying she was pregnant by Seymour and offering to show herself to stifle the rumor. Somerset had written back to her, telling her that she should name her accusers so he could punish them.

Somerset had gone into a rage at Elizabeth's reply—that she would not be considered the sort of person who pointed fingers and punished rumormongers. This news had perforce filtered through nobles to their servants, and in turn our guards, so I could not tell how embellished all had become before it met our ears. But I saw in the stories of Elizabeth's letters to Somerset a grain of truth—that Elizabeth had stood up for herself and her damaged reputation, laying it fully in the Protector's lap to prove she'd done anything wrong.

Elizabeth won with regard to the rumors that she carried Seymour's child. Somerset did issue a statement saying that such stories about the princess were untrue and should not be spread on pain of punishment. I sensed an acid tone in the proclamation, but it was done.

Uncle John and I were, except for this news that filtered through the guards, mostly in the dark about the happenings surrounding Seymour. I stayed in London with him for most of February, a cold and dreary month, neither of us allowed to communicate with the princess. Uncle John convinced me it was foolish to try, and so I conceded.

And then one day in March the guards were sent home, and I was allowed to leave again for Hatfield.

I reached Elizabeth's house on a cold morning, to find the princess in another rage. "The Protector could get nothing from my fine Kat," she snarled. "She is innocent of anything but having a foolish tongue. But he dares to replace her with Lady Tyrwhitt, a woman of foolish mind. Kat is *my* mistress. I have done nothing to demean myself so much that the Council should now need to put any more mistresses upon me."

Calling for paper, she sat down to write her anger to the Protector once again. I imagined the tall, thin-faced Somerset, his white lips folding in on themselves as he read yet another tirade from Elizabeth. She well knew how to write, and she had no hesitation in reminding him who she was—a king's sister and a king's daughter. She wrote to him like the upstart he was, and I guessed that the Protector took every slight to heart.

"What of Kat?" she asked me later that night when her rage had brought on a headache. Elizabeth lay in bed with a cloth scented with chamomile resting on her forehead. Elizabeth's headaches made her angry, her fear made her angry, and her anger could wind her into illness. "What do you know of her confinement?"

"Only that she is confined," I answered.

"Why should they hold her?" Her voice had quieted, worn out with rage. "She has told them all she knows; Seymour has been condemned and his lands seized. Why is that not the end of it?"

"I do not know," was all I could say.

Elizabeth had let me read the papers Aunt Kat had written herself in the Tower:

". . . my lord Admiral did cut her gown in a hundred pieces, and I chid Her Grace . . . And she said the Queen held her while my lord did so . . .

". . . And good Master Secretary, speak that I may change my prison. For by my troth, it is so cold I cannot sleep in it and so dark that I cannot in the day see, for I stop the window with straw; there is no glass . . ."

I cried when I read the last, and when I went to bed that night, I wept some more. This was the most terrible thing that had happened in my young life, and at fifteen, I could not imagine worse. The woman who had raised me, who had taken me in cheerfulness from a home where I was unwanted, now suffered in the cold and dark with no surety that she'd ever see daylight again.

Elizabeth cried for her as well, and she wrote the Protector a strongly worded letter the next day, explaining that Kat was more important to her than a mother and to please relieve Kat's suffering—send her home, and be good to her.

Tyrwhitt accosted me that afternoon, having read Elizabeth's letter thoroughly before he dispatched it to London.

"You are close to Her Grace," he said. "How is it she loves Mistress Ashley so well? Here is a woman who confessed all manner of lewd behavior on Her Grace Elizabeth's part, embarrassing her, if clearing her from the Admiral's plots. I would think Her Grace would like never to see the woman again."

"The princess loves few people," I explained. "Indeed, I think she is impatient with most of humanity. But those she loves, she loves very deeply and she will not abandon. My Aunt Kat loved her and stayed with her when Elizabeth had nothing—when she had no status as princess and was declared illegitimate. Aunt Kat loved her anyway. She will never forget that, I think."

Tyrwhitt looked at me in perplexity. He went on his way after that, clearly not understanding.

9

On March 20, 1549, Seymour was led from the Tower to his execution. Elizabeth and I were at Hatfield still, awaiting news of Aunt Kat's fate. It was Tyrwhitt who brought the news to Elizabeth of Seymour's death. He entered the chamber where she studied of days and cleared his throat.

Elizabeth let him wait a few moments before she condescended to raise her head. "Yes?"

"His lordship, the Admiral, has been executed on Tower Green," he said in his dry voice. "This morning."

Elizabeth waited a moment, her pale lids lowering only once over her dark eyes. She sat very still, her hand unmoving on the page of the book she'd been reading. "I see."

Tyrwhitt waited. I worked in the corner, unhappy that Seymour's death did not upset me. I was a bit shocked that the Protector would execute his own brother, but Seymour had been a cruel man, using charm to beguile others into serving his every need. I did not know if that feeling made me an evil person.

Elizabeth dipped her head, acknowledging the difficulty

Tyrwhitt had in delivering such news. He waited for her reaction, clearly wondering if she would burst into tears and fling herself to the floor, weeping for her dead lover.

She disappointed him. She looked at Tyrwhitt calmly and said, "This day died a man of much wit and very little judgment."

Tyrwhitt's lower lip pulled down. "Indeed, Your Grace." He met her gaze a moment longer, but had to turn away in defeat. At the door, he stopped.

"Another bit of news, Your Grace." He swept Elizabeth a bow. "Your governess, Mistress Ashley, and cofferer, Thomas Parry, will be released forthwith and allowed to rejoin you here."

Again Elizabeth made no reaction but to nod to him in dismissal. I dropped my needle and carved silver scissors as relief flowed through my body. Aunt Kat was all right. She'd come home, and life would return to its usual happy pace.

Tyrwhitt at last took himself off and only when his footsteps faded into the distance did Elizabeth rise from her chair. She peered into the corners of the room until she found me, and then she beckoned me. "Come here, Eloise."

I threw down my sewing and went to her, my heart beating hard with happiness. Elizabeth gave me a quick embrace and a kiss on each cheek. "We shall be happy that Kat Ashley is coming back to us. Shall we greet her with splendid gifts?"

I fervently agreed and spent the rest of the day happily helping her plan the celebration for Kat's return. But that night when I sewed alone in Elizabeth's outer chamber, I heard Elizabeth in her bed, weeping for a long, long time. Her sobs of despair near broke my heart.

❧

THE MOST NOTABLE change after Seymour's death was Elizabeth's deportment. I suggested she change the manner of her dress, moving from sumptuous fabrics and colors to rather plain, dark clothes. When I offered the suggestion, her eyes sparkled.

"You think shrewdly, Eloise," she said. "I shall show the King and the court that far from being a wanton, what a sober, quiet creature I am."

We shared a smile. I looked through my old pattern books and new ones that had arrived from London that spring, and decided to emulate the French and Spanish styles of a surcote, a sleeved overgarment that closed at the throat and flowed open over the bodice and skirt in an upside-down V. The skirt and bodice beneath were of plain white taffeta, the stomacher pointed over the front of the gathered skirt. A high collar enclosed her throat, and her French hood held back her sleek hair.

She wore this costume and others like it to court when Edward sent for her again. Another gown had the surcote decorated with lines of fur on high-capped sleeves, a little more ornate for the occasion that called for it.

Her gowns drew stares, but they were stares of approval from the people who mattered. Princess Mary and her ladies still dressed in gowns cut low across the bosom with sleeves sliding seductively from shoulders. They glittered in jewels that covered throat, fingers, and wrists and ornamented the bands of their French hoods.

Courtiers compared them, favoring Elizabeth. Elizabeth carried herself with decorum, they decided, as a Protestant princess should, while Mary with her Catholic leanings liked glitter and extravagance. Elizabeth showed a composure well liked in a young lady, especially appropriate in a sister to the King.

Elizabeth and Edward resumed terms of affection, though rather stately affection. She gave him a portrait of herself, and he invited her to spend Christmas with him.

Life in Elizabeth's household settled down, with Katherine

Ashley restored. Somerset, the boor, had lost much popularity by beheading his own brother. No matter how much perfidy Thomas Seymour had been plotting, Thomas had been well liked, and many a person thought that his overthrowing Somerset would not have been a bad thing. Elizabeth, ironically, became much more popular than Somerset, and when she went about with her retinue of armed riders, people cheered her. Elizabeth of England was all a princess should be.

Somerset, poor fool, was overthrown not many months later. I remembered John Ashley telling me that Somerset's days were numbered, and he was proved right. John Dudley, Earl of Warwick, convinced the King that he would make a much better Lord Protector than Somerset ever had, and the young Edward, tired of Somerset's high-handed stinginess, agreed.

The Earl of Warwick was a popular general, father of the handsome Robert Dudley, Elizabeth's childhood friend. Not long after Somerset sent his own brother to the block, Somerset was out, and Warwick filled his place. Elizabeth, when she heard the news, barely looked up from her books.

The other change was that though Thomas Parry also resumed his post as Elizabeth's treasurer, she never again trusted him as she had in the past. She went over his account books herself, signing her name in the margins, a practice she maintained for the rest of her life. She also asked William Cecil, who was Edward's secretary of state once Dudley took over, to manage her vast properties, all of which the Council finally relinquished her in the year after Somerset's fall.

I sewed her somber gowns, Elizabeth grew in prosperity, and Aunt Kat, Uncle John, and Thomas Parry and his wife assumed their comfortable gossip, though they were careful not to mention marriage again. Roger Ascham continued to teach Elizabeth until they quarreled, and he sadly left her.

As the months passed I grew taller, my hair became less unruly and wild, and my figure thinned from chubby youth to slender womanhood. I began to let my gaze linger on handsome young men, but I kept this firmly to myself. Aunt Kat was responsible for my virtue, and I told myself I should not make things more difficult for her. So I watched a man's muscular body from afar and pretended that I felt as Elizabeth did—that for now the unmarried life was preferable.

Elizabeth's friends, on the other hand, began to enter the married state. In the spring of 1550 Elizabeth learned that Robert Dudley was to wed a young lady of Norfolk, one Amy Robsart. Elizabeth was to attend the ceremony, and so would Edward the King.

"Money," Elizabeth told me as we traveled in the warmth of early June to the wedding. "Sweet Robin needs money, and he must needs marry it. A fifth son can expect little from his father, for all he's Lord Protector now." She sniffed. "Lord Protector might mean he holds a larger purse, but he holds the purse strings all the more tightly."

I was not certain Elizabeth approved of this marriage. She'd known Robert Dudley—or Robin, as she liked to call him—since they were children studying together at court. Robert had loved mathematics and astronomy, Elizabeth Latin and Greek. Robert had been charming even then, with his lopsided smile, dark good looks, his lavish bows, and his devotion to Elizabeth.

They were nearly the same age—they liked to pretend they'd been born on the same day in 1533, but in truth Robert was about a year older, now eighteen to Elizabeth's nearly seventeen. I knew they liked one another well, and after Elizabeth had made her quiet return to court, they'd renewed the friendship.

It pleased me to see her with Robert at Edward's court, sharing dances and talking and riding together. She showed none of the strange infatuation she'd given Thomas Seymour, although

I noted that Dudley and Seymour bore a resemblance, as far as handsomeness and studied charm went. Dudley seemed a bit more practical than Seymour had despite the charm, more resigned to his place as younger son.

I was surprised at Robert's choice in Amy Robsart, who was a pretty enough girl, but pale and wan. She had none of the robustness of Elizabeth and barely looked at Robert at all as we gathered the day before the ceremony at Richmond. Elizabeth did not speak to her, Amy being nothing more than the daughter of a country squire albeit a wealthy one. Elizabeth had bestowed a few gifts on her and would congratulate her at the ceremony, but their worlds certainly did not mix.

The ball that night was lavish. Warwick spared no expense to marry off his son, pleased that he'd found a girl of childbearing age who stood to inherit a fortune. Her dowry must have been large, I speculated as I watched the dancing ladies and gentlemen, entertained by musicians who played suspended by ropes in the air above us. The musicians looked nervously at the hard floor beneath them and clutched their instruments as they floated about. The music was a bit strained, but the dancers did not seem to mind.

I danced myself with several gentlemen, including Robert Dudley himself, Robert's brother Guildford, and a young man called James Colby who was tall and red-haired, introduced as one of Robert's friends. Colby danced well, but he seemed to have little interest in me. I preferred dancing with Guildford, who'd inherited some of the Dudley charm.

Very late that night, indeed in the early hours of the next morning, I wandered an upstairs gallery, trying to find the chamber I shared with several gentlewomen including Aunt Kat. I rounded a corner and saw, in a dark window embrasure, Princess Elizabeth snug in Robert Dudley's embrace.

I stumbled to a halt. My heart beat hard three times before I realized they were not kissing, but talking. However, Robert's arms were firm around her waist and she smiled up at him, making no move to push him away.

If they saw or heard me, they made no sign. I decided, after a few sickening moments, that I had better stand at the end of this passage to make certain no one else came this way. I would say nothing, but I could not imagine what scandal would befall Elizabeth if she were discovered in the dark in the arms of a man who planned to marry another woman on the morrow.

"An interesting choice of brides, sweet Robin," Elizabeth was saying. "As I told you before."

"She will do," Robert answered.

"She is rich and from good stock."

"You make her sound like a soup."

Elizabeth chuckled. "May you have many, many offspring from your soup. That is why men marry, is it not?"

"Men with ambitious fathers," Robert said darkly.

"Come now, this occasion is happy. In the hall you danced on light feet."

Robert finally laughed, the dour note leaving his voice. "Do not tease me. Ever you tease me, dear Lizzie, as though you live to torment your Cock Robin."

" 'Tis a pleasant thing to live for, teasing one's friends."

"But you tease me specially," he said. "Come, admit it. I am your favorite tease."

I tried not to roll my eyes at his obvious flirtation, and I debated making some noise so they would stop. But if I interrupted, Elizabeth would be embarrassed and furious. I also did not sense the danger in their silliness as I had in Thomas Seymour's romps. Elizabeth and Robert were old friends—natural that some flirtation had grown between them.

"Your women will be looking for you," Robert pointed out, as though he sensed my agitation at the other end of the passage.

"They do fuss," Elizabeth agreed. "They forget that they work to *my* demand."

"Ever the imperious princess. I am certain they quake in their shoes."

"Your tongue speaks nothing but nonsense. It is silver coated."

"Then stop my mouth. Kiss me, to wish me good luck on the morrow."

"I wish you all the good fortune in the world," Elizabeth replied, and then she went quiet.

I could not resist turning around and peeking toward the window embrasure. Robert had bent over her, his tall frame dwarfing her smaller one. Their faces hovered an inch apart for a moment, and then Robert's lips met hers.

He pulled her up into the kiss, his bent knee sliding between her legs, until her body flowed into his. It was not a friendly kiss, not a kiss for luck, but a passion that had grown between them that they did not bother to hide. I sensed that this was not the first time they had kissed; they seemed familiar with the exact feel of each other's bodies.

Robert's tongue swept into her mouth, and Elizabeth smiled with it, a woman enjoying the taste of her lover. As they broke apart, I swung around and hid myself.

Elizabeth must have heard some rustle, for her crisp voice rang down the hall. "You may come here now, Eloise."

It was a command, made in a tone I could not disobey. I moved on cold feet along the passage to the window. They stood apart, Robert lounging against the carved stone arch of the window, a smile firmly in place.

" 'Tis only Eloise," Elizabeth told him. "Who knows how to keep her thoughts to herself."

"The pretty seamstress." Robert tugged a lock of my hair. "Would you like a gift, pretty seamstress?"

"No," I said abruptly, and then at his irritated look I softened it with a curtsey. "No thank you, my lord, you are most kind." One was not rude to the Lord Protector's son, even if he had been wantonly kissing a princess of the realm.

"She does not need you to shower her with gifts, Robin," Elizabeth said, annoyed. "She is a dear friend who can keep her own counsel." She held out her hand. "Walk with me to my chamber, Eloise. The halls might be filled with lecherous men."

Robert laughed out loud. He gave my hair another tug, letting his finger trail along the shell of my ear before he pulled away.

"Take care of my lady," he said and winked. "Stay ever vigilant by her side."

Elizabeth seemed to tire of the game. She frowned at Robert and jerked me to her. "Good night, Lord Robert. My felicitations on your nuptials."

She began to walk swiftly away with me, and I strode fast to keep up. Behind us we heard Robert's laughter floating in the darkness.

"Not one word," Elizabeth hissed. "No tales to Kat or John Ashley, and never speak of it to me."

"Of course I will say nothing," I said, offended that she'd even think so. "But will you tell me—are you in love with him?"

Elizabeth bathed me in a glare that could have seared me from the inside out. "Of course not," she said in a chill voice, and then she dragged me at a near run all the way to her chamber to prevent me asking more.

�֍

ROBERT AND AMY married the next day. Robert was red eyed, an indication he'd not gone to bed after I'd last seen him, but likely remained awake to drink more. Elizabeth sat serenely in the seat set aside for her comfort, her expression never changing as Amy Robsart became Amy Dudley.

After the ceremony Elizabeth coolly kissed Amy and wished her good fortune, then bestowed an equally cool kiss on Robert. I saw the two friends exchange a glance, their bland countenances barely moving as they acknowledged one another and their secret.

Throughout the banquet and the ball that followed, Elizabeth watched Robert, but the pair of them never made any sign that they were more than good friends sharing memories of childhood. Elizabeth only once smirked at my discomfort.

When I leaned over her chair to refill her glass she said, "Close your mouth, Eloise. You gape like a fish. When I asked for your discretion, I did not mean for you to frown upon us like a disapproving nursemaid."

I grew angry. "You put yourself in danger," I hissed. "Have you forgotten how close you came to arrest and ruin?"

Her eyes narrowed to slits. "I am not a complete fool. It has gone no further than what you saw. He is a dear friend, a trusted friend, and now he is married. That is that."

She turned away, finished with me. I straightened up, my hands clenching the jug of wine so that the pattern on the silver indented my fingers. I saw Kat Ashley staring at us from across the room, and I contrived a neutral expression though I seethed.

To my intense relief Robert and Amy left the next day for Norfolk, and Elizabeth returned home and to her usual routine. We saw little of Amy Dudley after that but whenever Robert came to court at the same time Elizabeth visited, I slept very little.

✠

SEASONS PASSED AS did years. Edward ruled and became more and more Protestant. John Dudley, Earl of Warwick, got himself made Duke of Northumberland. His son Robert lived in Norfolk with his new wife and was elected to Parliament by his Norfolk constituents.

Archbishop Cranmer presented Edward the King with a revised edition of the Book of Common Prayer of 1549. Young Edward took religion quite seriously and approved of Elizabeth's somber attire, which I continued to make for her. "Sweet Sister Temperance," he called her, and Elizabeth did nothing to disabuse his perception of her. I could not help but remember "Sister Temperance" with her fingers entwined in Robert Dudley's dark hair, but outwardly, as far as I saw, Elizabeth behaved herself.

Edward ground his teeth over Mary, who refused to give up the Catholic Mass and who, when Edward blatantly forbade it, had it said in secret. Elizabeth read the Bible in English and discussed scripture intelligently with Edward and earned praise.

Despite my worries about Elizabeth and Robert Dudley, life moved along calmly enough for the next three years until Edward, who as a boy had been athletic and robust, suddenly grew sick and then sicker. Then it was put about that his life was in grave danger. Elizabeth, riding to St. James's in early 1553 to see him, was turned away and had to retreat home. Catholics dusted off their icons and prepared for the country to return to the old religion under Mary.

But Edward, as sick as he was, had another card to play. When he laid down his last hand, he shocked us all, and plunged Elizabeth into danger for years to come.

10

IN THE MIDDLE of a sticky night in July in 1553 a servant came to Aunt Kat with news. I was sitting in her chamber with my lap full of velvet, blue as the sky with a raised velvet pattern of flowers exploding from a vine that grew from vases. I saw in it great beauty and regality, but behind my usual excitement at a new fabric, I felt faint uneasiness. I sewed the gown for Elizabeth's next visit to court, whether to be to hold the hand of her sickly brother or to attend her sister Mary at her coronation, I could not tell. Either way I worried.

The servant came to Aunt Kat first, although he was in the employ of Thomas Parry and by rights the first person to hear news of this sort should have been Elizabeth. But perhaps he felt safer confronting two women rather than facing the uncertain temperament of Elizabeth and the annoyed glares of Parry.

"Disaster, Mistress Ashley," the manservant said breathlessly. His name was John, as were so many servants named because it was easier to remember one "John" than think of the names of them all. "The King is dead."

Aunt Kat rose hastily, her skirt knocking over a small table with a candle. I rescued the candle before it set her skirt alight, placed it on a safer shelf, and righted the table. Aunt Kat slipped the bolt over her door and closed the shutter against the night, even though the July weather was close and the room stifling.

She resumed her bench and bade the servant kneel at her feet. "Now, tell me. No embellishments, I want the entire truth."

I leaned in to listen. Young John ceased looking nervous and instead seemed flattered at our attention. "I heard from a servant outside the bedchamber that he vomited black bile and coughed horrible sputum from his lungs and died in grave weakness."

I felt momentary pity for young Edward. He'd been so pre-occupied with his Reformed religion and had been led first by Somerset, then Northumberland. The court had not had much of *him* in it, but much of those who used his position to gain power. They'd given away his lands and spent his money and let him die. I pitied him his death but at the same time I was still impatient with him for letting Somerset nearly destroy Elizabeth.

The manservant wasn't finished. "I heard tell that the high lords of the King's chamber do not want news of the death to come out. They seek the King's sisters: Mary, Mary of the pop-ery, and . . ." He broke off, feeling Aunt Kat's eye on him. "His other sister."

I said, "But if he is dead, then Mary is Queen. She must know by now, and if not, she must be told."

"Nay, for neither sister will be Queen now." John's eyes rolled in enjoyment. "Bastards they be, by royal decree."

Aunt Kat grabbed his ear in a tight pinch. "You lie. Mary is Queen and after her Elizabeth. 'Tis old Henry's will and that has never changed. If there had been a change to the succession, we would have known. There would be a Parliament called and an uproar heard all the way here."

"No Parliament but the King's bedchamber. We have a new Queen. All hail Queen Jane, long may she reign."

I was growing tired of the swain's poetry. I fixed him with a cold gaze. "It must be a lie. A rumor grown by idle servants with nothing better to do."

John grinned, now loving his position of talebearer. How else would a young man have two women leaning over him, our bosoms hanging before his face, rapt on his every word? "'Tis no lie, Mistress Rousell. The grand Northumberland, who has married his son to Lady Jane, made Jane Queen of all England. The King himself struck his sisters from the list and wrote the words *Jane Grey* at the top of the new list. Then he died."

Aunt Kat and I sat up and stared at each other. "He cannot have," Aunt Kat breathed. "'Tis treason."

I wondered briefly if she meant the King or Northumberland. I did not understand much about politics, but I understood hole-in-corner dealings. The King could not change the succession without approval from Parliament, but the Duke of Northumberland was a cagey man who twisted events and persons to suit himself.

"What will happen?" I asked, half to myself. "Will Mary stand being ousted by Northumberland? Her will is as strong as Henry's ever was, for all I've seen."

We leaned back to our informant, but alas, he'd run dry of information. The gist of the matter was that the King was dead, he'd named Jane Grey as Queen at Northumberland's instigation before he died, and Northumberland was searching for Mary.

Aunt Kat and I looked at each other, realizing the same thing at the same moment. If Northumberland wanted to secure Mary before news of the King's death leaked, he'd want to secure Elizabeth, too. Kat's dark eyes met mine, and we looked back at John Messenger.

He never knew his danger. Aunt Kat grabbed one arm, and I the other. John was too surprised to protest, and I swear the ridiculous man thought we sought to thank him for the news by smothering him with kisses. He laughed a half protest as we pulled him to the storage cavity behind the fireplace, tossed him on his arse on the floor, then banged the door closed. Aunt Kat locked it, and we dragged a large chest in front of the door.

John yelped when he discovered the trick and banged on the door in outrage. I sat down on the chest. "Shush yourself," I said. " 'Tis only for a day or so. You'll be fed."

I understood, as Aunt Kat did, that no one could know that Elizabeth knew the truth. Unless the cocky servant made up the story to make himself important, danger now cloaked the house.

Lady Jane—innocent little Jane, Elizabeth's schoolroom friend, who would have thought? Grandniece to Henry and granddaughter of his sister Mary, Jane had a claim to the throne, but a tenuous one. Northumberland, being no fool, would realize he had to control Mary and Elizabeth before he could proclaim Jane Queen, that the daughters of Great Harry would not meekly step aside and let Jane assume the throne.

And so he'd hunt them and bring them to heel and possibly to the block.

My blood chilled. Aunt Kat's face too was ashen. "It must not happen," she said in a dark voice. "It will not happen. We will not let it happen."

We put our heads together and began to scheme.

❧

ELIZABETH'S REACTION TO the news when Aunt Kat broke it was predictable. She waited, white-faced, while Aunt Kat explained in a low voice what the servant had said, turning to me to confirm it. Once Kat was done, once Elizabeth had glared at me in rage, she picked up a pretty glass ball and hurled it hard through the window. Sunlight glittered on the sphere as it arced out to the gardens followed by splinters of the window pane.

"He cannot," she snarled. "He can*not*. Where is Mary? Does he already have my sister?"

"We do not know," I answered. "As far as we can discern, Mary is still in East Anglia and we do not know if she has even heard the news."

"Find out. I want to know everything. I cannot simply sit here and wait for Northumberland to decide what he will do with me . . ."

She trailed off, then suddenly screamed in rage. A fall of books, papers, pens, and pots of ink rained to the floor. Aunt Kat and I, the only ladies in the chamber with her, backed away until her tantrum wound to its close. She put her hand to her head and cried out in pain and anger, and I knew one of the headaches that she'd fallen prey to more and more often had come upon her.

"I hate the silence," Elizabeth said later. She lay in bed, her face white, the headache upon her so hard she could eat nothing and drink only a little wine. Her rage had worn into cold anger, her eyes bearing the calculation of a cornered fox. "I can send no messages and receive none. I must pretend ignorance. I can only wait and wonder."

"And plan," I said. I had my feet on a hassock, and I stitched again on the blue velvet. The manservant John was still locked in Aunt Kat's chamber. We had thought to bring him food, but feared he would overpower us if we opened the door, so he stayed, hungry and complaining. "We must plan what to do should the worst come," I said.

"The worst," she repeated. "You mean my death. I will face the worst with dignity, but I will do everything in my power to keep it from happening. Damn Northumberland." She flopped back onto the pillows. "And poor Edward. Thank heavens," she added, "that Robin Dudley married himself off to that stick, Amy Robsart."

"You believe that he would have been the one chosen to marry Jane?"

"Very likely. Robert stood to inherit nothing and would have been dependent on his father." She wrinkled her nose. "But no, Guildford Dudley is more compliant and never said nay when his father ordered him to marry Jane Grey. The Duke of Northumberland and the Duke of Suffolk, marrying their children to each other's to gain England."

The marriage of Guildford and Jane at Durham Place this spring had surprised us, but neither Elizabeth nor I had foreseen that Northumberland would push Mary from the throne with Jane Grey. I wondered if Guildford and Jane were yet husband and wife in truth, Jane ready to produce the necessary heir. When the two had married, vicious gossip, happily repeated by Aunt Kat and Elizabeth, said that Jane had quietly rebelled and not yet let him into her bed.

"Poor Jane," I mused. "I wonder what she thinks of all this?"

"Thinks?" Elizabeth scoffed. "She thinks nothing but what her father and mother tell her to think. If Henry Grey says, 'Be the Queen of England, Jane,' she will curtsey and say 'Yes, Father.' If he says, 'Be a washerwoman, Jane,' she will curtsey and say, 'Yes, Father.'"

I could not disagree. I remembered Jane from when she had studied and played with Elizabeth in Catherine Parr's household. She'd loved her books best of all and been meek and quiet about everything else. Jane had been closer to Edward's age than Elizabeth's, and she and Edward had liked each other well. I had thought Northumberland and Suffolk would succeed in marrying Jane to King Edward, and if Edward had lived, perhaps they would have.

"When I am Queen, I'll have wise men for my advisors, not landed men seeking the crown for their own heads," Elizabeth declared.

"I scarce see how landed men can be avoided, my lady," I said, biting off a thread. "Gentlemen always want more, more, more. The Duke of Northumberland is powerful, I am sorry to say, and many men owe their positions to him."

"But he has put aside the true succession," she said. "He has overturned the right way of things—God's way of things—has dared to interfere with the body politic and the great chain of being."

Elizabeth was always interested in the great chain of being, because she, if she became Queen, would be somewhere near the top.

"God, angels, kings, then lesser men," I said. "Essentially. Is there room for displaced princesses and seamstresses?"

Elizabeth raised her head again. "You forget yourself, daughter of a strolling player."

"I do not, my lady." I busied myself making tiny stitches in a seam. "I never forget who I am."

She burst out laughing, my lady Elizabeth, ever changeable. "That is why I like you, Mistress Eloise. You and your Aunt Kat. You ever speak your mind, but you have shown great loyalty to me, and I will to you. Never forget *that*."

"I will endeavor, my lady."

"Impertinent jade. Read to me, Eloise, the light blinds me today."

Obediently I put aside the velvet. As I reached for the discarded book, she opened one eye and looked interestedly at the gown. "What is that you sew? The blue velvet for me?"

"Yes, my lady."

"What do you see in it? Will it be a shroud?"

"No," I said quickly. "I do not see that. The cloth does not speak of death."

"It is cloth, Eloise, not the stars. My astrologers see better than you."

"Yes, but—" I pinched off my answer.

"Ha. I know what you think of astrologers, and you ought to keep those opinions to yourself. Now read to me."

"I do not read Greek well, my lady. I can pronounce with your guidance only." I opened the book, the archaic words strange to my eyes.

Elizabeth's mood changed like lightning. "Then send me someone who can. I tire of this."

She moved to throw back the bedcovers, and I lifted my hand. "But you are ill, my lady. Wretchedly, miserably ill and can bear to see no one but myself and Aunt Kat."

I thought she would fly at me. It would be my duty to bear her blows, to let her play out her fit of pique, but at the last minute her foxlike eyes narrowed. "Yes, I am quite unwell." She put her hand to her forehead and fell back to the pillows. I was nineteen years old, quite a woman now, but still young enough to giggle. She smiled at me, but our forced levity did not chase away the darkness.

I struggled through the Greek without the least idea of what I read, and we waited for news of Mary and to discover what Northumberland would do.

❈

MOST INTERESTINGLY, THE first person Queen Jane Grey summoned to court was me. Riders came in the night, a hundred or so with lances and horses, and made a great clatter around

Hatfield. I was terrified they meant to cart the entire household off to the Tower, but Northumberland's man seemed quite courteous when he asked to see the lady Elizabeth.

Of course we told him he could not—it was impossible, she was at death's door, we'd sent for a physician, Aunt Kat had bled her, we had no way of knowing if she might live. Elizabeth would certainly not survive a journey. Why did the King want her? we asked.

The gentleman smiled ingratiatingly and said they'd wait. But he had a message from the lady Elizabeth's friend and former playmate, the lady Jane Grey, asking to borrow the little seamstress of whom they'd both been so fond.

No mention of the King's death, no mention that the King had died proclaiming Jane Queen. Aunt Kat and I retreated to Elizabeth's chamber and held our council of three. Elizabeth was at first furious and refused to let me go to Jane, but her mercurial character changed again before long.

"Yes, you shall go, my dear Eloise. You shall sew and you shall listen and tell me every single thing she says and does. She and that blasted Northumberland and his cohort the Duke of Suffolk. Be my eyes and ears, Eloise."

Eyes and ears are dangerous things, I thought to myself. But I could keep my eyes on my needlework and my ears wide open. Servants gossiped and few paid attention to a needlewoman.

"And discover what you are able of Robert Dudley. Does he follow his father or counsel him to prudence? The Robert I know is not much for prudence, but even so, tell me of him."

"Shall I write?" I hesitated.

"No." Elizabeth paced the room. We advised her to stay abed, but she could not keep still, so we at least made sure no one could see into the room. "Keep your knowledge in your head, as I know you can, and tell it to me when you return. I will send a messenger. You will know this messenger—I will find a way. Do this for me, Eloise. Or do you love Jane better, who once treated you so kindly?"

Her eyes held fire. I quickly said, "You are foremost in my heart, Your Grace. You ever will be."

Elizabeth gave me a skeptical look, but only said, "See that you do. Godspeed, my lamb."

�֍

THE TOWER OF London was a paradox. The original square keep and its surrounding walls and towers and gardens housed royal families in great state. New kings and queens stayed here the night before they progressed through London to be crowned at Westminster. Knights were dubbed in the great hall; storage houses held plate and jewels worth the kingdom's fortune. And the Tower was a royal gaol from which there was generally no escape.

Some prisoners did leave the Tower with their heads intact—the Duke of Norfolk, uncle to Elizabeth's mother, had been reprieved by the good luck of King Henry dropping dead the day he was to have signed the writ of execution. Aunt Kat and Thomas Parry had been released after questioning about the Seymour affair, although Elizabeth had had to plead with Somerset to bring it about. But all lived in shadow of the scaffold, watching the blackbirds strut about the green, waiting for word that they would join the toll of those before them—queens, dukes, lords, cardinals, bishops, and great men of state.

Jane Grey had been brought here by her father, the Duke of Suffolk, and her father-in-law, the Duke of Northumberland, to be proclaimed Queen. I, arriving by a rather dirty cart in the night in the rain, was not supposed to know that. Ostensibly I'd heard only that Jane needed a needlewoman to help her with the new wardrobe she'd have now that she had married. Why Northumberland thought he could keep his plot all so secret I scarce knew, but those in great power sometimes thought all those around them blind fools.

The courtyard in which the cart stopped teemed with activity. Men in armor, guards in livery, hurrying pages, and servants—everywhere were men, swords, pikes, weapons of war. My mouth dried as I scurried past the soldiers and followed my guide inside.

This late, I assumed they'd shove me into a servants' room and Lady Jane would send for me in her own time in the morning. To my surprise, a woman met me at the door and chivied me toward a back staircase, hissing that "she" needed me.

I was tired, dirty, smelly, and irritated, but I had no choice but to obey. The woman took me by the elbow and propelled me up staircases and through passages until we emerged into the rooms in which King Henry's queens had lived before processing through London to take their crowns.

Jane Gray had changed little from the days when she and Elizabeth shared lessons under the tutelage of John Aylmer in Catherine Parr's household and at court. Jane had large eyes in a small face and was slender and small for her sixteen years. She looked even smaller standing under the hall's vast beamed ceiling in an enormous embroidered robe with sleeves belling over her small wrists. Her hair had been dragged back and pinned under a French hood, which made her pale, rather rabbity face jut forward. Her figure was as slim and slender as I remembered, so even if she had shared a bed with Guildford Dudley, she had not obviously conceived.

Jane was not alone—her mother, the Duchess of Suffolk, paced the long room, eyes shining. The duchess did not even glance at me as I hurried in following the servant, but lifted a long finger and pointed to a corner full of bolts of cloth. "Over there."

I'd grown up in corners sewing for royal women. I had learned early in life how to discover the most comfortable corners of a room and make them my own. Sometimes I, sewing with all my might in a nook by the fireplace, was far warmer and more content than the great people who shivered across the room in cushion-strewn chairs. The corner to which the duchess directed me was dark and shadowy and not to my taste, but the July night was hot, the shadowy corner the coolest in the room. I took up my place without a murmur.

The duchess paced and fanned herself vigorously. Jane stood out of her path with beads of sweat rolling down her face, eyes following her mother back and forth, back and forth.

"It must be done by morning," the duchess snapped. Her eye fell on me, and I dropped my gaze in deference. "You will finish, won't you, girl?"

My temper rose. I was the daughter of a gentlewoman, a Champernowne. Though my mother married unfortunately, I was not and never had been of the serving class. I did not mind waiting on great ladies I respected like Elizabeth, or even Jane, but I was here at the insistence of Northumberland, who had risen to a dukedom from nothing, *on* nothing but ambition. But Frances Grey, née Brandon, niece to Great Harry and now Duchess of Suffolk, had royal blood in her veins and never let anyone forget it. Thus she glared at me from before the cold fireplace and called me *girl*.

I did not speak directly to Jane, but I made it plain my words were for her. "The cloth is fine. 'Twill make up in no time, as long as I know what it is I am making."

The duchess glared. "Everything is there. You will sew."

"I will need light." I could hardly cut a pattern and seam

a gown without being able to see. "And perhaps assistance. There is enough for two or three garments—how many did you wish?"

As I hoped, I goaded Jane into speech. "Bring her light." She waved to the servants who occupied the other corners. "Bring it now, and I will assist her."

"You will *not*," the duchess roared. "Remember who you are."

I thought Jane would crumple to the floor. She had never been one to defy her elders, and the duchess her mother had a personality that flattened all before her.

But then Jane, like most quiet people, had a stubborn streak that, when invoked, hung on like death. Jane didn't quite look the duchess in the eye, but the corners of her mouth firmed slightly, a look I'd seen before. "I will sew with Eloise," she announced. "It is something I *can* do."

The duchess went green with anger. I could point out that sewing was a most royal pastime—Henry's wives sewed his shirts and helped in the making of linens. Mary sewed quite well and so did Elizabeth, although Elizabeth preferred pursuits more active to the mind than the hands.

My corner had a bench so I would not have to sit on the hard floor, and I busied myself sorting the cloth while Jane had her quiet confrontation with her mother in the middle of the room. They had certainly supplied her with sumptuous fabric. Cloth of gold, gold and green brocade, thin silk taffetas, sumptuous velvets, damask lined with silk and fur—*fur*, I thought, *for hideous July weather.*

Jane must have won her small rebellion, for she plunked herself onto a stool next to me and snatched up a skein of silk. "It is because I am married. A matron must have a larger wardrobe than a maid."

A ridiculous explanation for cloth fit for a queen. I smoothed the velvet in her agitated fingers, catching her hands before she could tear the fabric, and found her skin ice-cold.

Jane did not have to say a word. I saw the gown in its completion and felt Jane's fate in the beautiful green on gold. She'd wear the green overskirt open over an underskirt of gold brocade, and the same brocade would trim her sleeves. The costume would be beautiful on her, a walking sculpture, and I would create it for her.

A halo of light touched the window above her head, the rising sun, but the light changed as a cloud passed over it. Inky darkness seemed to surround Jane, eating the golden light like hungry snakes. In my mind the dress changed to dull black and rose to cover her face like a shroud.

I tried to banish this dreadful vision, and gasped with the effort. The duchess, who hovered to watch Jane in case she might whisper something to me she should not, strode over to us and dragged my face up with a hard hand under my chin.

"What is the matter with her?" the duchess demanded of Jane, releasing me. "Is she ill? If she is ill, she must go from this place at once. You cannot take sick."

I was exhausted and longed for bed, but I held my tongue. If the duchess sent me scuttling back to Hatfield, I would have little to report to Elizabeth but that Jane was having new clothes and the duchess loved to harangue her.

I forced a laugh and waved my hand in front of my face. "Indeed, no. I had a long journey and not much to eat, and the room is close."

"She ought to sleep," Jane tried. She put a cold hand on my forehead, and it was all I could do not to shrink back. A corpse might have touched me.

"No," I said quickly. "I will sew."

The duchess regarded me with a stony face and hard glare but ceased her questions.

I sewed. Jane helped, or pretended to, but she was fairly useless, the cloth slipping from her nerveless fingers, and I could not trust her at all with the scissors. The duchess did nothing but storm up and down the room and demand servants to bring her wine and sweetmeats, which she devoured without offering any to Jane or me. Jane recoiled at the sight of the food, but I, healthy and in no danger of being Queen of England, was hungry.

Though the duchess and Jane were cryptic, I knew quite well that I sewed Jane's coronation wardrobe. I saw no evidence of stately robes and ermine, but the gowns that would come from this cloth would be for the banquets and balls and ambassadorial visits she'd attend after the crowning itself.

The weight of these clothes would crush Jane. She'd crumble and fall no matter how much the Duke of Northumberland and her mother stood behind her to hold her up.

I could better see Elizabeth in them, her slim, upright form regal, watching with steely eyes as ambassadors from foreign lands bent knees to her. But with Edward's dying deed, Elizabeth might never wear the robes of a Queen, and it might have been Elizabeth's shroud I'd seen in the green velvet that Jane had touched.

The dawn light that had brushed the window grew brighter as the duchess swallowed sweetmeats and Jane and I quietly worked. When the window lighted fully, we heard horses in the courtyard below and then the tramping of many feet.

I had not thought it possible for Jane to go whiter, but her face became as pale as linen, her pupils widened, and she began to sway on her stool. Her mother thrust a hand under Jane's arm and jerked her to her feet.

"Get *up*. Stand. Meet them. And you." She kicked my bench over as I scrambled up. "Do not sit in her presence. Ever. Do you understand?"

I held my breath, understanding very well. They were going to do it. The ambitious, turbulent, heroic, handsome Dudleys, aided and abetted by the Duke and Duchess of Suffolk, were going to turn England upside down. I thought of Robert Dudley and the wicked kiss he'd shared with Elizabeth just before his wedding, and wondered if he was party to this conspiracy to keep Mary and Elizabeth from the throne. Robert stayed mostly in Norfolk these days or attended Parliament, intent on his own career, but his father could have compelled him to obey.

The duchess nearly dragged Jane from the room. With no one watching me, I followed, keeping well behind the crowd of servants who lighted the way. The large hall was filled with people—the Duke of Northumberland himself, looking excited and pink; the Duke of Suffolk, standing as far from his wife as he could; and Northumberland's sons, Guildford Dudley and the handsome Robert, in Norfolk no longer. Other men had come as well, men of the King's Council I did not know, William Cecil with nervous, darting eyes, and old William Paulet.

A canopy had been set up at one end of the room, which I recognized as King Edward's own cloth of gold. My heart thumped as I squeezed into the room, unnoticed. Northumberland had a paper in his hands that dripped with seals, including the large red round one of the dead King.

Northumberland bounced on his toes, waiting for silence, though I had the feeling every single person in that room already knew what he would say.

"This *Devise*," he began in a loud, clear voice, "was drawn up by Edward the King of England and signed by the Council not many days before he died. For yes, as I stand before you, I bring you grievous news. King Edward is dead. Long live Queen Jane!"

"Queen Jane!" Suffolk bellowed, his face already red with hock. He dragged his daughter forward and placed her under the canopy, forcing her to turn and face the room.

The crowd took up the cheer: the Dudleys in enthusiasm; the men of the Council less so. Jane, the regal Queen, looked upon the faces of her subjects and dropped to the floor in a dead faint.

II

I WAS AT last able to sleep because with everyone hovering around wretched Jane I could slip away and find a bed. I slept in one that a maid had just abandoned to serve the invading Northumberlands. It was warm from her round body. I slept hard for a short time and then awoke, restless and worried.

What the bold servant had reported to Aunt Kat and me was true. The darling Dudleys had somehow persuaded the Council to let them steal the throne from under Mary's nose. I did not doubt that however much they put the crown on Jane's head, it was Northumberland who'd truly have the power. He would rule England, and Jane would let him. Guildford Dudley, another dashing, handsome fellow, might try to put his hand in, and Suffolk obviously thought he'd have much say himself, but I knew Northumberland would be the true monarch.

I stared at the ceiling awhile, watching a spider crawl back and forth across a crack that must seem a chasm to him. So must the abrupt accession to the crown seem to Jane, with

Northumberland and her own mother and father standing behind her to push her into it.

She would not have chosen this for herself, I knew. Jane loved books and learning, not the trappings of power. Her tutors had praised Elizabeth's quickness, but loved Jane for her devotion to books and languages. Elizabeth used learning for her own gain; Jane loved it for its own sake.

I wondered what Mary would do—where she was, what she planned. Someone would have gotten her the news by now, and I doubted Princess Mary would bow her head and step aside. She had accepted King Henry pushing her aside because she'd had no choice; he'd been much stronger than she. But I knew that Mary with her fixed stare and deep convictions would never accept an upstart like Northumberland and a mouse like Jane keeping her from her rightful place.

I threw back the covers and climbed from the bed, wondering what the day would bring. I had to shout for a maid to stop and help me dress, and then I followed her down to the kitchens to demand breakfast. The cooks wanted nothing to do with me, but I told them I'd come at Lady Jane's special request and that they wouldn't want to anger the new Queen on her first day. The kitchen staff gave me evil looks, but they also gave me a good helping of stew.

After I filled my stomach, I returned to the room we'd abandoned and found it still abandoned. The cloths spilled from the bench, my needlebox in a jumble where it had fallen. I quietly tidied up and folded the cloths, brushing dust from them. I resumed my sewing, my head bent, so that if anyone peeked in I would look as though I'd virtuously stayed at my post all morning.

The first person to peek in was sweet Robin himself. Robert Dudley sailed in dressed in finery fit for a Queen's brother-in-law.

"Is it Eloise Rousell?" he asked, peering into the cool shadows. "But it is. Dear Eloise. Dear, dear, dear Eloise."

"Leave off your dears, my lord," I said. "Or have they made you a duke, too?"

He gave me a smile, his handsome face lightening. "Always impertinent, is our little Eloise."

We were near the same age, so why *little*, I did not know. "You have not answered my question."

"My father has all the duking," Robert said. "Tell me why you are here."

"My lady Jane asked me to help her with her wardrobe," I said calmly, but my heart raced. Robert Dudley was no fool, and he knew Elizabeth. He'd know she would not lend her favorite servants willingly, which meant either I had abandoned her or she'd sent me for her own purpose. I did not know where his loyalties lay—with his father and Northumberland, or with Elizabeth for whom he felt friendship and more?

Robert could easily tell his father that Elizabeth had sent me to them—a spy in their midst. He could easily use me for his own purposes, perhaps to feed me information to tell Elizabeth, true or false. I saw in his eyes, which danced with possibilities, that he hadn't decided what to do with me yet.

Our conversation might have turned in a dangerous direction if we'd not been interrupted. I recognized the man who entered as Robert's friend with whom I'd danced at Robert's wedding—James Colby his name was, I remembered. Colby had fiery red hair and a look of the Welsh about him, though I knew he was English, from Shropshire. He was tall and rawboned, his face not particularly handsome, having seen a fight or two, but he possessed eyes of keen blue.

The blue eyes swept over me without much interest and fixed on Robert. "Dudley, they're looking for you."

No *my lord*, no bowing and scraping, just a blunt "Dudley."

Robert bowed to me as fairly as he would a court lady. "Au revoir, my little seamstress. Colby," he nodded to the man at his side.

Colby swept another gaze over me, an assessing one this time, trying to decide why Robert favored me with his courtly bow. Was I a mistress, friend, Northumberland's coconspirator? His reddish brows lowered over his blue eyes as he tried to reason it out. Robert, tired of me, swept from the room, boot heels clicking, and Colby, with a final baleful look at me, followed in his wake.

❋

LATER THAT DAY Jane, for the first time I had ever seen, stood up to her mother and father.

William Paulet, now the Marquis of Winchester, who had come to arrest Aunt Kat and Thomas Parry that fateful night, who'd had a hand in the trials of Anne Boleyn and the Duke of Somerset, arrived in the hall with a casket in his hands. He moved to Jane and bowed to her.

"What is it?" Jane asked, her tone barely curious.

For answer, Paulet opened the box. Jane stared inside it and blanched. Not until Paulet lifted the heavy pointed crown studded with jewels did I understand—he held the imperial crown of England.

"I did not ask to see that," Jane gasped. "Why have you brought it?"

"To see how it fit," Paulet answered.

Jane drew herself up. "I will not put it on. It is not time. I did not ask for it, please do not make me." She had tears in her voice, but her back remained straight; no more fainting fits.

"You must take it boldly," Paulet answered. "Soon I will have another made to crown your husband."

Jane stopped. Her tears ceased to flow, drying on her face in the July heat. "My husband?"

"Aye, Your Grace. Your husband, who will be King beside you."

Jane looked past old Paulet to her father and Northumberland. "There is no need to make a crown for my husband. Guildford Dudley will never be King."

Father and father-in-law stared back at Jane, lips parted, as though they'd heard a dog suddenly speak English. Northumberland was the first to recover. He walked quickly to Jane, his dark eyes bent on her.

"Guildford is your husband. Of course he will be King, he is married to the Queen."

Jane faltered beneath his glare, but her neck remained unbent. "I am Queen because my mother is the daughter of King Henry's sister. I am Henry's grandniece—his sister's blood is in my veins. Guildford is a Dudley. He is not royal born; God has not decreed him King."

Northumberland's glare became a snarl of fury. "Suffolk, tame your daughter."

It was not the Duke of Suffolk but his duchess who sailed to Jane and slapped her across the face. "You will obey your father. He has made you Queen, Jane, so that the Reformed religion may go on. You do not want Mary and her popery to rule us all, do you?"

Jane cried again, but she stood on her feet. "I have as much right as Mary—more, because I will never deliver England back to the Pope." She swallowed, dashing the tears from her eyes, the pearls in her hair shining in the summer sunlight. "I will be Queen, but only if Guildford Dudley is never King."

Northumberland stared incredulously. He had underestimated Jane, and that made him a fool. However quiet she was, however beaten into obedience she was, Jane was a Tudor and shared with Mary and Elizabeth, and Henry and Edward, the conviction that God's will brought them to the throne.

Northumberland lifted his gaze to Jane's father again. "Suffolk."

The duke lifted his shoulders in a shrug. "If she will not, then she will not. We will make Guildford a duke in his own right."

"Duke of Clarence," Jane said. "A lofty title."

My estimation of Jane rose again. Clearly she had thought long and hard about this, as though she'd known it was no use fighting her father and Northumberland, but she could impose her conditions. I was willing to believe she'd exerted the same stubbornness to stay as long as possible out of Guildford's bed.

William Paulet watched all this with a canny eye. I wondered if he'd brought the crown jewels to Jane just to provoke her declaration, to make certain Northumberland knew where things stood. His countenance was blank, but Paulet, in his late sixties and having survived the long reign of Henry and the short one of Edward, was a wise old bird. I had no way of knowing whether he supported Northumberland, but I had the feeling he'd be among those standing at the end of the day.

Northumberland gave up. He stormed from the room in fury, the Duchess of Suffolk vented her feelings on Jane, and the Duke of Suffolk sighed heavily. Paulet returned the crown to the casket and walked unnoticed from the room. Jane would be Queen, but Guildford Dudley would never be called King.

✤

THE NEXT AFTERNOON, Northumberland made another announcement, this one more somber. Mary had staked out a territory in East Anglia and declared herself Queen of England.

She had plenty of men-at-arms swear loyalty to her, and she was raising an army.

Jane paced and wrung her hands, face white, eyes wide like a frightened child's. The Duchess of Suffolk swept an icy gaze over her husband. "You did not secure Mary?"

I sewed in the corner, forgotten in the dark, plucking at the velvets meant for Jane. Robert Dudley lounged by the fireplace, one booted foot propped behind him on the grate. His friend James Colby stood in the shadows on the other side of him.

"She eluded us," Suffolk said in a hard voice.

"You let her," his wife boomed. "Go retrieve her then. You have London, you have an army, your daughter is Queen."

Northumberland looked as though she were a roach he barely stopped himself from stepping on. "She is a cunning woman who uses the most of the devil's wits. An army shall be dispatched, and a ship is standing by to take her. 'Twill all be over by the week's end."

"And what of the lady Elizabeth?"

I kept sewing demurely, trying to shut out the picture of death dancing in the velvet cloak I sewed. I did not wish to see death with red-gold hair and steady gray eyes, so I kept my focus on each stitch of my seam.

"My men report that Lady Elizabeth is very ill and cannot travel," Northumberland said. "That is no matter. She can be held at Hatfield as well as anywhere, and moved when she is better. The Tower is reinforced. It was meant to be a stronghold, and a stronghold it will be. Suffolk will lead the army against Mary and bring her to heel."

At this Jane shrieked again. "No, Father, do not leave me!"

Northumberland's face clouded. Perhaps Jane had the correct blood to be Queen, but she had not a Queen's mind. Were it

Elizabeth they'd elevated to the throne, she would be pacing, her eyes glittering as she thought who had the best chance to capture Mary. Her own feelings in the matter would be kept tight, tight under her white face, but she'd not beg any man or woman to stay with her, nor would tears roll down her face. She might rage but only against fools.

Jane's mother frowned at her. "Your father will not be gone long. He'll command the army and bring Mary easily back to London. You will be so busy preparing for your coronation that you will scarce know it."

But Jane was as stubborn in her own way as any of them in this room, as she'd shown yesterday, standing firm that Guildford should not be King. Like many gentle souls, she could dig her heels into a point so much that an army could not move her.

"You cannot leave me, Father," she bleated. "No one will listen to me. They will listen to you. You must stay."

Suffolk's face softened. He went to her and took her hands in his. Jane sank to her knees before him, lifting her hands in piteous pleading, while her mother rolled her eyes in disgust.

"Please, Father," she said.

On the other side of the fireplace, James Colby murmured to Robert Dudley and then the pair of them looked at me. I met their eyes briefly before returning to my work, not liking how they stared. Robert Dudley winked, but Colby's eyes burned with a strange light.

Meanwhile, Jane was busily getting her way. "Do not worry, I will stay." Suffolk held her hands, letting her weep against him. Her mother and Northumberland looked annoyed. But Jane's weeping was effective. Northumberland himself, along with his sons, was dispatched to snatch Mary from the east of England and deliver her to the Tower.

�֍

THAT NIGHT I was awakened by a hard hand across my mouth. I gasped for air, hitting out at my assailant, and tried to scream. I heard a satisfactory grunt as my fist connected with flesh, and then a strong grip forced me down to the pillows.

"Do not rouse the house, you idiot woman," a male voice grated. "I am here to help you."

Immediately my thoughts flashed to the hands of Thomas Seymour, his fingers tight on my breast as he admonished me not to call out, lest his wife hear. Fear washed through me, but I banished my panic. Thomas Seymour was dead, and this voice was nothing like his. The man was urgent, his words tinged with alarm.

I strained to see who he was, but the darkness was complete, and I could not place the voice. Not Suffolk or any of the Dudleys, not a servant. He kept his hand over my mouth, a broad, calloused hand without gloves.

"You must return home at once," the man said. "Without anyone seeing you. Get up and dress yourself. Dudley said you were sensible—do not give his words the lie."

I finally realized who he was, James Colby, Dudley's friend who had shown him no deference and little enjoyment when he danced with me. As my eyes grew used to the dark, I made out his tall body, rather long face, and glint of red hair.

I lay still to convey that I would not scream if he released me, but I do not think he quite believed me. He lifted his hand very slowly, ready to seize me again if I cried out.

"Why must I return home at once?" I asked in a whisper. "What has happened?"

He made a noise of annoyance at my question. Had he expected I would humbly obey a man who entered my room in the middle of the night, pinned me to the bed, and hissed orders at me? From the look on his face, he had. He'd underestimated me as much as Northumberland had underestimated Jane.

"There is danger here," he said. "Mary will win. Her sister must be protected."

"By me?" I sat up, hugging the bedcovers to my body. "You are optimistic. Shall I fight with my scissors and my needle?"

"You must go to Elizabeth and do as she tells you. There will be much confusion here, and you may not have another chance."

He knew me for the spy I was, knew that Elizabeth had sent me to report to her all that happened. Robert Dudley knew. Why the pair of them had not simply dragged me to Northumberland I could not tell.

Colby backed away from the cot and stood waiting. The July night was hot, but a cool breeze blew in from the window, bringing with it the sounds in the courtyard: horses stamping, chains rattling, men's shouts. They were going to fight Mary. Whoever won, Mary or Jane, Elizabeth might be the loser for it. Northumberland wanted Elizabeth secure, and I shuddered to think what that might mean.

I did not really trust Robert Dudley or Colby, but I knew I no longer wanted to stay with Jane. I slid from the bed and padded to the hooks on the wall that held my clothes. It became apparent that Colby had no intention of leaving the room or even turning his back while I dressed, so little did he trust *me*.

Nothing for it. I threw off my night rail and let the cool air touch my naked skin, raising goose bumps on my flesh. It was so dark he could not possibly have seen anything, or so I assured myself as I pulled on my chemise. I slid on stockings and laced my skirt around me, then held my bodice against my chest and looked over my shoulder at Colby. "Lace me, please."

He hesitated a moment, a typical man who did not realize how much assistance a woman needed getting dressed.

"If you want us to be so secret that I cannot call a maid," I said, "you will have to do it."

Colby's breathing grew louder as he approached me, and his fingers fumbled until he found the laces in the back. I held the bodice in place as he did the tricky bit of threading laces through clasps. He seemed somewhat competent at it once he started, and tied off the laces with the ease of practice.

"Do you have sisters?" I queried as I tied the skirt to the bodice and looked about for where I'd tossed my sturdy shoes.

"I had a wife."

He spoke in a neutral voice and I could not see his face. "Has she died?"

"Two years ago, in childbed."

Colby was young, perhaps only a few years older than I, but that was plenty old enough to have married and sired children. A woman dying bearing one was not unusual but still sad. "I am sorry." I touched his arm. "That is a tragedy."

He did not answer, and I had to leave it at that.

He twitched in impatience to get away, scarcely giving me time to gather up my needle case and tuck it into a bag. I suppose he'd have liked me to simply throw on a cloak over my night rail and flee with him, but sewing accessories were expensive and mine precious to me. He would simply have to wait.

Once I was ready he took me down through back ways that were deserted, the old Tower cold and musty, even in the heat of July. We wound through a narrow bricked yard in the pitch dark, the torches of the main courtyard and the sounds of men and horses not a breath away. He led me on down to a water gate, our feet slipping and sliding on the damp stone stairs. The tide was out, but a tiny boat rocked not far from the sludge of shore.

Colby propelled me to this with his fingers biting my arm. The two of us alone entered the boat, and Colby took up the oars. I sat in the bow, watching him row us down with the current, my bag of accoutrements at my feet.

I was certainly trusting him. He could be taking me straight into the arms of Mary, who might not be happy that I'd been helping Jane the so-called Queen. Also I was deserting Jane, poor Jane, who had no one on her side at the moment. But for some reason I believed that he wished to aid me to return to Elizabeth. Dudley cared for Elizabeth, though Colby seemed a man who might be more loyal and less flirtatious.

Also I could not object to leaving the Tower. A palace it might be, a fortress to protect kings and queens, but I could never forget its bleaker function.

I sat still, huddled in my cloak against the wind off the river. Colby strained at the oars, moonlight brushing his tunic and dark trousers tucked into riding boots. No flashy court colors, no hat with plumes, just plain garments for escaping. We moved as silent as smoke, my cloak and Colby's subdued clothes blending in with the shadows.

Colby rowed for an hour or more at an even tempo, resting only briefly from time to time. After a while he angled the boat for a dark bank and rowed to the shore. The boat bumped a deserted dock jutting into an inlet, but I had no idea where we were. The village on the banks was small and quiet, and no lights shone as we disembarked.

A horse waited for us at the other end of the village, held by a lanky young man who sent both me and Colby a relieved look when we appeared. The man, Colby's servant or squire, I could not tell which, helped boost me into the saddle and then Colby swung up behind me. The servant mounted a more placid-looking horse, and we rode off into the night.

The sun began to tinge the horizon with gray by the time we were well away from the village, heading north and west. Colby's charger moved swiftly, though I sensed Colby holding the horse back to keep from winding him.

I felt it safe to talk, so I pried the fold of cloak from my mouth and twisted my head to look up at him. "Why did you and Lord Robert decide I should return to my lady?"

Colby took his time answering, as though debating what to tell me. At last he spoke through tight lips, his white face stained pink from the wind. "Mary is Catholic, and she will return the old religion to England."

I waited, but Colby pressed his mouth closed, no more forthcoming.

"Every simpleton will conclude that," I said. "Let me see if I understand you aright. You supported Jane at first because she and Northumberland would retain the Reformed faith. You now believe Northumberland cannot stand against Mary, and so you want Elizabeth safe. Her claim on the throne, her Reformed claim, is likely to be restored when Northumberland is overthrown."

Colby said nothing for three or four of his horse's strides. "Women gossip overmuch."

"It is not gossip," I said indignantly. " 'Tis simple reasoning. You want to save the Reformed faith, not the throne. At least *you* do. What Lord Robert wants is anyone's guess."

"He wishes you to keep watch. And to report any difficulties to him."

"I will not spy on my lady," I began indignantly.

"You will do as you are told."

"I will do what is good for my lady Elizabeth," I retorted. "I will watch over her as I always have and keep her from the grip of conspirators like you. If you drag her into your secret dealings, you will lose the very cause for which you strive. She must be free of your schemes and plans, and be able to prove it."

"That is why we will speak to *you* and never to *her*."

"I see. Because if I am caught and executed for treason, 'twill be no great loss for you. You can easily find another informant but not another princess."

Colby actually smiled, a brief showing of teeth that disappeared as soon as it came. "You learn quickly."

"I am not a fool. Nor a silly prattler whom you can pay to repeat everything that occurs in my lady's household. I serve her, not Lord Robert Dudley. If our interests coincide, then of course, I will help you. But at her command, not yours."

We rode in silence for a time until we came to a turn in a road that I recognized ran to Hatfield. Colby muttered something under his breath that sounded like "bloody women," but the wind was in my ears, and I could not be certain.

12

WE WAITED TENSELY for news of Mary's defeat for the next several days, but no news came at all. I thought over James Colby's bidding that I look after Elizabeth and be his go-between. I didn't trust Colby, but well I knew that times were dangerous, and Elizabeth needed all the friends she could find. I determined to be a good one.

Aunt Kat had set free the poor servant who had come to us in the night to tell us of the King's death. Now that everyone knew that Elizabeth knew, we had no reason to keep him confined. He cursed us under his breath, but did not turn up his nose at the meal with which we rewarded him.

And then we heard. Once Northumberland had gone to fight Mary, the Council had weaseled their way out of the Tower, including old Paulet, who had escaped to his country home. Most of the Council declared for Mary, seeing quite well which way the wind blew.

In her castle at Suffolk, Mary won the day, Northumberland's men turning against him to join Mary. Northumberland finally conceded that he'd lost, turned his back on Jane Grey, and said loudly, "All hail Mary, the Queen."

At the Tower, the Duke of Suffolk tore down the gold canopy in Jane's chamber. "These things are not for the likes of you," he said. Jane, despite her fright, could only bleat relief that she did not have to be Queen, and sat down to write to Mary to beg forgiveness for what her father and mother had made her do.

The people of England cheered Mary—Catholic or no, she was the rightful heir, and Northumberland had no business meddling with the succession. They had tolerated Jane as Queen for nine days, and now they danced in the streets to rejoice that Mary had prevailed.

"What of Jane?" I asked John Ashley worriedly. I thought of the white-faced girl I'd deserted, kneeling at her father's feet, and the flash of stubbornness she'd shown when she refused to let Guildford be King. "Surely Mary will never believe that the plots were Jane's. She knows Jane better than that."

"Jane remains in the Tower," John Ashley told me. "But Mary has said she will be merciful to Jane and Guildford Dudley, and she has no reason not to be. She has already released Suffolk and his wife—as ambitious as they are, they would have been harmless without Northumberland. Northumberland will pay, of course, and he knows it."

"It wasn't Jane's fault," I repeated.

Aunt Kat sniffed at me. "Well, why do you not run to White-hall and tell Mary? I am certain she will listen to you and release her right away."

Her ironic tone made me flush. "I feel sorry for her, is all."

"As do I." Aunt Kat softened. "Pray for her, Eloise. Her innocence is sure to touch Mary and all will be well."

"It will be," John Ashley reassured me. "Mary will release her, in time, you will see."

I thought of Jane crying pathetically at her father's feet, and I realized that her very innocence would be her downfall. Both Northumberland and Suffolk had believed she'd be the perfect pawn-queen. If Northumberland had chosen Elizabeth as his pawn, things would have been much different.

Elizabeth, in the first place, would never have been coerced into marrying Guildford. She'd learned a hard lesson with Seymour about men using a woman to put forward their own ambitions, and she would never have meekly gone to the altar. She might have been tempted had the suitor in question been *Robert* Dudley, but with Robert safely married to Amy that was not to be. Now sweet Robin was in the Tower with his father, having obediently raised men against Mary in Norfolk. He waited, with Jane and Northumberland and Guildford, to see what Mary would do.

In the meantime, I hastily designed and sewed clothes for Elizabeth, who would ride in Mary's coronation procession. I had progressed in the world enough to have two seamstresses working under me, so that I drew designs for gowns and chose the fabric for each from the vast store Elizabeth either purchased or received as gifts.

I still sewed when we were in a great hurry. I could put together a bodice quickly to near perfection, and other ladies of the court envied Elizabeth having me all to herself. Elizabeth once speculated, with a frown, that Mary might steal me away to make clothes fit for a queen.

"Not for her," I said. "Everyone knows I am of the Reformed religion, and she would have much difficulty converting me."

"Guard your tongue." Elizabeth's frown deepened. "She will bring back the Mass, and you will be required to say it."

"You as well?" I challenged.

"That remains to be seen."

I had learned that with Elizabeth, it was always a battle of wills, even if she fought silently. She was a good fighter, and I wondered who would win in wars between her and her much older sister.

The wardrobe I had assembled for her was tasteful and subdued in keeping with her role as the virtuous Protestant princess, but I used lush satins and velvets and tissues, including the velvet with the burst of flowers I had been working on when we heard the news of Jane. I made her bodices simple and narrow, her overskirts draping modestly over a rather plain kirtle or underskirt, and kept the sleeves close fitting and uncomplicated. I made most things in pale colors, using much white and silver, thinking it could not hurt to draw attention to her virginal state.

At the end of July, Elizabeth rode to London accompanied by her household of two thousand riders and her ladies and gentlemen. I rode with her ladies, dressed like a lady myself. Aunt Kat stayed behind, admonishing me to look after Elizabeth in her place.

Our journey was not only to greet Mary as Queen, but to remind all we passed that Elizabeth was her sister and heir to the throne. Our company was splendid, dressed in green and white to proclaim Elizabeth's Tudor heritage. We had outriders with swords, men of Elizabeth's household in armor, we ladies in our best. Elizabeth rode bareheaded, surrounded by men with banners to both protect and proclaim her.

People turned out to watch as we passed from Hatfield down to London. They cheered and waved, and children gave Elizabeth gifts of garlands and fruit. She took it all as her due and smiled at them.

"They like a princess to look like a princess," she told me when we stopped to rest at a house along the way. "They shall always have that, I assure you."

As we rode on, I a little behind the other ladies, an outrider came close to me, his cloak streaming in the wind. A fold of it bared his sword and fluttered about his long legs, and I looked at the rawboned body of James Colby.

"Greetings, Mistress Rousell," he said formally.

I did my best to nod at him without encouragement. "I do not remember you joining Her Grace's household."

"But I have joined it, at the request of John Ashley. He is a friend of my father's and obtained me the position."

We rode a little apart from the others, so I could speak with no one hearing us over the thundering of hooves and snapping of banners.

"Why are you not in the Tower with the Dudleys?" I asked. "Keeping Jane and Guildford company?"

He gave me a wry look. "I managed to be on the right side, Mary's side, when it mattered. I am pleased Northumberland did not prevail, no matter what I think of Mary's religion. Most of the Council and Parliament agree."

"Did you betray them? Did you ride to Mary?"

"There was no betrayal. What I did was meant to happen, though I can say no more of it here."

"You are determined to draw me in to dangerous intrigue. Why do you trust me?"

Another glance, this time his blue eyes assessing. "You have proved yourself trustworthy. Elizabeth told me the ladies she would most trust in her household, and you were the first she mentioned."

"She spoke to you?"

He inclined his head. "She granted me a short audience with herself and her estate manager, Cecil. She knows where my loyalty stands."

"But do I?"

"I serve the princess, and I have been told you do as well. Mary is very Catholic, and Elizabeth sees that danger. Mary can be fair-minded, but when her religion is challenged she is blind. I have seen this."

I had seen it, too, in a distant sort of way. I had not paid much attention to Mary ere this, because I had expected Edward and his sons to rule, and Mary not to matter. Now everything about her was of severe and sharp importance.

Colby left me then, and we soon arrived in London. We paraded through cheering streets to Fleet Street and through the gate to the Strand and Somerset House, which had been granted to Elizabeth after Somerset's downfall. The house was enormous, its gates leading to large grounds and a pile of buildings backing onto the Thames. My lodgings were high in the back, over the river, the damp and stink of the water wafting into my chamber. It could not be healthy, I thought, but we did not linger in London. We rode out again the next day to meet Mary north and east of the city at Wanstead.

I again rode off and on near Elizabeth, keeping my eye out for James Colby. Elizabeth did not take her full retinue today, but there he was, dressed in her colors, one of her gentlemen. I still did not know what to make of him, and whether he truly had Elizabeth's best interests at heart or whether he and Robert Dudley worked schemes of their own. Robert Dudley, in his own way, could be as canny and manipulative as his father, Northumberland.

Once we were outside London I felt better—while town could be much more entertaining after long stretches of time in the country, I preferred the air of the country to that of London: all those bodies pressing together, the stink of privies emptied into passages between houses, of animals living without air or sun or grass beneath their feet. I thought country air more healthy, justified by the fact that plague gathered mostly in cities.

Elizabeth rode to a great house where Mary waited for her. Mary had finished her little war for the throne in Sussex and had traveled then to London to be proclaimed Queen. I did not know what to expect of Mary. I remembered her only as a princess who had been much criticized at court, who had turned a frosty demeanor to the world that disapproved of her. Edward's courtiers had found fault with her expensive costumes and jewels, with her stubborn clinging to the Latin Mass, with her short stature, with her deep voice, with her dark brows drawn too often over her gray, piercing eyes. Mary had felt their disapprobation keenly and had responded by being more pious, staring, and disagreeable than ever.

All that seemed far away, now. Mary greeted us wearing cloth of gold and velvet, with large pearls drooping on her breast and seed pearls lining the French hood that almost delicately held back her hair. Rubies and sapphires glinted on her hands, and a diamond cross hung from her neck. She waited for Elizabeth to walk to her, and then she caught Elizabeth's hands, smiling a wide smile.

Elizabeth, at least a foot taller than her older sister, stooped so that Mary could kiss her on both cheeks. When they straightened up and stood toe to toe, hands clasping, the contrast between the two women was remarkable.

Elizabeth was nearly twenty, Mary thirty-seven. Mary had a rectangular body: shoulders, waist, and hips almost the same girth. I noted that her seamstress had padded out her breasts and that she wore a Spanish farthingale in order to make her waist seem smaller in proportion. Mary's face was rectangular also, barely curving at her chin, her eyes wide spaced, her mouth small.

Elizabeth stood tall, her posture naturally upright with shoulders thrown back to show off her slender waist and small curve of breasts. Her hair was red-gold, as King Henry's had been; her brows and lashes fair; her eyes dark and glittering. She too wore diamonds and sapphires, but they were small and tasteful. The white gown I and my assistants had made spoke of simple elegance: a bodice closed at the throat, a dark velvet surcote drawn back to reveal a skirt of white and silver brocade. The dress was a work of art, more subdued than Mary's showy finery.

Mary, I could see, also compared Elizabeth to herself but in a different way. Her eyes lit with pride when she perceived that her own jewels were more numerous, more costly, and larger than Elizabeth's, that her gown rippled with velvet, her sleeves trimmed with fur. Most important, Elizabeth was still princess and possible bastard while she, daughter of Catherine of Aragon, granddaughter of Isabella of Spain, was Queen at last. After years of being shunted aside, ignored, and brutally treated, Mary had got her own back.

The Catholic Queen and the Protestant princess. Foreboding filled me, even as Mary turned to Elizabeth's ladies, her smile welcoming. Each was presented to Mary in turn, by rank, including me, as a gentlewoman.

A heavy wave of perfume engulfed me as Mary raised me from my curtsey and kissed my cheek, but the perfume could not quite hide the musty smell of warm body under many layers of clothing. She pressed a gift into my hand, as she had the other ladies: a small brooch of gold, unadorned, with the cross of Christ emblazoned on it.

"Your Grace does me honor," I said, hoping my voice was not too hoarse. "I am not worthy of the gift."

Mary's indulgent smile faded a bit, and she looked me up and down. "You are the seamstress?"

"I have that honor, Your Grace."

Mary glanced over my gown, which was a damped-down version of Elizabeth's—I could copy the style but never presume to wear the fabrics of a royal princess. Her gaze then flicked to Elizabeth, and her mouth turned down in one corner in contempt.

She disapproved of the plainness of the gown, a sign of Elizabeth's religion that did not favor ornamentation—not on the body and certainly not in the Church. Simplicity was the Reformed way. Mary's garments spoke of her convictions that God was to be worshipped with the most glorious jewels and precious metals money could buy, his followers draped in scarlet velvets and silks.

Mary said nothing of this—and she likely never thought it in these words—but she saw the contrast, and it annoyed her. Even so, she turned to the next lady with her smile in place and gave her the kiss, the compliment, and the gift.

Elizabeth dined with Mary, we ladies having the privilege of waiting on them. The topics Mary chose were safe ones—the weather, the ease of the journey, Elizabeth's health, her own health, the coming coronation. Not one word of Northumberland or Jane trembling in the Tower or Edward's duplicity in changing the succession at the last moment. Nothing that would bring anger or bitterness to this festive occasion.

Next to Mary stood a woman I knew—Jane Dormer. Jane was only a few years older than Elizabeth, and unmarried. Jane's delicate hands carved a slice of meat out of the haunch presented for Mary and laid it on a plate, using her knife again to cut it for her. She lifted her sleeve out of the way as she poured the wine, and sent a glance at me and a nod.

I nodded back. Jane and I were friends, of a sort, but Jane's family was very Catholic, and what's more, her family in

Buckinghamshire was close friends with the man my mother had married. Mary's gaining the throne, I had well to worry, might not simply restore the nation to the old religion, but it might make my stepfather and mother insist that I be restored to it as well.

"For the coronation," Mary was saying to Elizabeth. "What say you, sister, that you'll wear as fine a cloth of gold as any ever saw? I will send you the material myself."

"You are kind," Elizabeth said, taking a delicate sip of wine. "My seamstress is an artist. Perhaps the sleeves puffed over the shoulders in the new way?"

"Have you kept up with fashion then, in the country?" Mary asked, with a hint of derision.

Elizabeth's eyes glinted like a snake's. "As well as can be expected, Your Grace. I have been fortunate to be instructed on the subject by ladies of the court. They have given me much advice."

Which she obviously had not followed. Some whispered that Mary depended far too much on the counsel of her ladies; Elizabeth was declaring that she, for her part, did not.

"You are a Tudor, and a princess," Mary said, missing the reference. "You must now wear clothes as befits your station. Perhaps another seamstress can be found?"

Cold washed through me. If Elizabeth dismissed me, I would have to return home to that awful man for whom my mother had gladly left me.

"Mistress Rousell sews to *my* dictation," Elizabeth said. "If I am to be more at court, then of course, my wardrobe will reflect this, and she shall prepare gowns worthy of my position. I wish to do honor to the Queen."

Mary only smiled and inclined her head.

I did not seek my bed until late, waiting on Elizabeth and

helping her ladies undress her for the night. She bade me to stay even after that and listen to another lady read from the Bible—in English—as she lay abed. By the time I sought my own pallet, I was exhausted, and dropped off to sleep quickly.

I dreamed of Mary, her musty odor hidden by perfume when she embraced me, and behind that, a cloying odor of smoke. Incense, I thought, but the scent grew and the emotions that came with it tumbled over me—despair, anger, fear, and determination. All very odd.

The dream changed and I saw Mary and Elizabeth standing together, facing each other. Elizabeth seemed to grow in stature while Mary shrank, until finally Mary put her hand over her face and screamed in despair.

I woke abruptly into the quiet of the night. Royal houses were never completely quiet; somewhere servants dashed about waiting on the ladies and gentlemen who waited on the royals. Men outside patrolled the grounds and looked after horses, but this night not much sound reached my bed in the attics. I could smell the smoke of the kitchen fires, the cooks already roasting the meat for the next day. I reasoned that the smoke must have tickled my nose and entered my dreams, nothing more, but still the vision troubled me.

We stayed only a short time with Mary at Wanstead, and then the two sisters rode back to London together. We bedecked Elizabeth in a gown with enough gold brocade and velvet to please Mary, but we were careful to not let her outshine the Queen.

The people of London cheered as she and Mary rode into the city side by side. It was early August, the weather warm and clear, which seemed a good omen. Men tossed up their caps; children threw flowers and women gifts to both Queen and princess. Bells rang from every church tower, and the City guard had turned out, in livery, to salute them and escort them through.

Mary radiated pure happiness, and Elizabeth seemed content to ride a few paces behind her and nod regally at the crowds. *The people of England have much power,* Elizabeth always told me. *Their happiness or unhappiness can make all the difference to a prince's reign. Contented and serene or angry and rebellious.*

Under the summer sun with the crowds Elizabeth called the "people of England" rejoicing, it was difficult to believe that Mary's reign would be anything but joyful.

❈

"NO," ELIZABETH SAID in a hard voice. "I cannot possibly do as she wishes. Let me speak to her and explain why I cannot."

She sat on a cushioned chair, weeks later at Richmond, facing Mary's Council, who had been sent by Mary to Elizabeth's chambers. Their task: to make Elizabeth explain why she and none of her ladies had heard Mass since their arrival at court.

We had come to Richmond at Mary's invitation, where she prepared for her coronation with the enthusiasm of a bride for a wedding to a beloved. She lavished much attention on the pageantry and who would have a prized position in the procession, and would for hours pore over details of what she was to wear and who would sit with whom.

Thus far Mary had given every sign of being a tolerant ruler. She made no secret that she wanted the old religion restored, but had proclaimed not many days ago that she'd be merciful to those who had grown used to the Reformed religion, and would not force them into conversion. They would understand their error soon, she was certain, and turn back to the Church quietly and of their own accord.

Generous Mary released the Marchioness of Exeter and her son, Edward Courtenay, from the Tower, where they'd spent many years in a kind of limbo since the reign of Henry. She made the marchioness a lady of the Privy Chamber and had given Edward Courtenay a ring, which he romantically said made him her prisoner. Mary had also, as John Ashley had told me, released the Duke of Suffolk and pardoned him for his part in Northumberland's attempt to take the throne, along with others who had conspired with Northumberland against her.

But her tolerance began to wane as Elizabeth evaded attending Mass with her or having it said in private. Elizabeth had not out-and-out refused, but her excuses for not attending chapel since she'd come to court were many and varied. We ladies of her household had done nothing overt against the Catholic faith, but we continued to read our daily devotions in English and, like Elizabeth, contrived to be elsewhere when it came time to hear Mass. Now Elizabeth faced the Council, who stood before her and interrogated her about this lack.

"The opportunity to hear Mass is given to you six times a day," Bishop Gardiner said dryly. "Perhaps your duties have been too strenuous to allow you to attend the chapel, Your Grace?"

"Indeed," Elizabeth responded coldly. "I have much to do."

"Your tasks will be lightened," the bishop said without pause. "So that you may attend Mass with your sister. The attempt at Reformed religion is over, Your Grace. It failed. Her Majesty the Queen has come to restore the nation to the true faith."

And restore you to power, you old goat, I thought from my place among Elizabeth's ladies.

Mary had also released Bishop Stephen Gardiner, an old and wily man, from the Tower, where he'd lain for five years, having displeased the Council of Edward's reign with his opposition to Cranmer and the Book of Common Prayer. Gardiner had knelt at Mary's feet and smiled when she set him free and told him she'd make him her Lord Chancellor.

Mary had let it be known that those of the Catholic faith

would gain under her rule and would not be shunted aside as many had been by Edward. Gardiner rubbed his hands with glee and plunged into restoring the Church to its old glory, which as far as I could see meant rich robes on his back, money in his coffers, and permission to cuff those against whom he held a personal grudge.

Today he decided to cuff Elizabeth. Elizabeth represented what Gardiner hated, and he decided to relieve his pique by making her life miserable.

"It distresses the Queen," Gardiner went on. "To have a sister who leans dangerously toward heresy. She is in fear for your soul."

"I have no doubt," Elizabeth returned. Her gaze swept him and the rest of the Council. "I have been ill. My headaches are frequent, and my ladies stay to attend me."

"I am sorry to hear of your poor health," Gardiner said, looking not the least bit sorry. "The Queen will be happy to send a priest or myself to your chamber to read Mass in the event you are too ill to attend it."

Elizabeth sat up straighter, her white face even more icy. She was not going to win; the flash in her eyes told me she knew that.

She would also not give the Council the satisfaction of hanging her head, mumbling an apology, or weeping and begging Gardiner to intercede with the Queen for her forgiveness. She rose to her feet, indicating the audience over as far as she was concerned.

"I will give some thought to what you say." She nodded to the Council, who had the manners to bow to her, and swept from the chamber, leaving them staring after her. Gardiner's eyes sparkled in fury, which worried me not a little.

⁂

MARY HERSELF HAD not spoken much to Elizabeth since we'd come to Richmond, which I took to be a bad omen. We did attend the Queen's entertainments, dancing and cards and little plays put together for her. Elizabeth liked to dance. She would rise from her sickbed for that, and also to see Edward Courtenay, who had swiftly become a popular courtier.

Edward had spent most of his life in the Tower, and now, at twenty-seven, he found himself a member of Parliament, the restored Earl of Devon, and a favored gentleman in the Queen's court. I found him rather pale and foppish, but rumor had it that the Queen's Council hoped Mary would marry him. Courtenay was of the correct blood, being descended from Edward IV, of the right age to sire a son, and very English.

I could not tell what Mary thought of him; she treated him with courtesy that came more from pity than interest. After the gift of the ring he made it a point to smile at her and flatter her and flirt with her, but I heard scurrilous gossip that he enjoyed walking about London of nights and romping with low women. I supposed being locked away for so long had deprived him of the ordinary pleasures of men, but from what others whispered he was now rather overdoing it.

He and Elizabeth made a good pair, despite his character, I thought as I watched them dance. Both of them were young and energetic, sunny haired, and graceful. He knew he had the attention of both Mary the Queen and Elizabeth, her sister, and preened under their interest.

"The Queen considers him a match for her sister," a voice said in my ear. I did not jump, because James Colby had the habit of popping out of nowhere and beginning a conversation in the middle of it.

"I would hope for someone rather better for her," I answered, keeping my eyes on the dancing ladies and gentlemen.

"Are you a snob, Eloise?"

"Not really. It is just that I do not think much of Courtenay.

I've also heard rumors of a foreign marriage for Elizabeth, that sending her from the country entirely would be best for Mary."

Colby's nod told me I'd heard aright. "They debate it in Parliament. But after Elizabeth, the heir is Mary Stuart of Scotland with her very French ties. The Queen prefers Protestant Elizabeth to a French-Scottish Queen, no matter that Mary of Scotland is so very Catholic."

"Then Elizabeth had better stay. But not Courtenay." I studied Edward Courtenay and his oily smile. " 'Tis a pity Robert Dudley is already married and so obediently raised an army in the Jane Grey affair."

"Dudley is too ambitious and flies too high," Colby replied. "He will bring himself to grief."

I glanced at him. "I thought Lord Robert Dudley your great friend."

"He is." He gave me the ghost of a smile. "Which is why I know he overreaches himself. He and the princess are matched in spirit, but that may not be a good thing."

I sighed. "It is a bit worrying."

"More than a bit."

The music had ended, the musicians resting, but Mary clapped her hands. "Another. A pavane. It is most diverting."

Ladies and gentlemen returned to the floor, and James held out his hand for mine and led me out.

James danced well, as trained as any courtier, and I realized I still knew very little about him. He came from Shropshire, he had been married young and was now a widower, and Robert Dudley counted him a friend. Nothing more.

"At Lord Robert's wedding, you danced with me," I reminded him.

"Yes, I remember."

"You seemed quite bored. With the dancing, that is."

He did not apologize or even look apologetic. "My mind was on other things."

"Some scheme you were concocting with Lord Robert, no doubt."

"No doubt," he said.

"I saw little of you at court before this," I remarked.

"I spend much time in the country."

"In Shropshire?"

"And other places."

"You have many lands then?"

He bent a cold blue glare on me. "Not really. Why do you want to know?"

I wanted to know because I was curious about this man no one ever talked of, and of whom I knew nothing. Growing up in Elizabeth's house, I could recite the family trees of almost everyone she came in contact with and where they lived and what estates they owned. I could pin them down almost as well as Elizabeth herself. Against this knowledge, James Colby was an enigma. It was clear he resented my prying, so I gave him a banal smile and a little shrug and dropped the subject.

He danced the rest of the pavane with a frown on his face, and after the dance finished he led me back to Elizabeth's ladies and spoke with me no more. I watched him stride away, more curious about him than ever. I wondered what he had not wanted me to know.

No one seemed to have noticed me dancing with James Colby or speaking to him in the corner, but when we returned to the princess's chamber that night, Elizabeth said to me sarcastically that she hoped she'd not have to search for another seamstress once I married myself off to a nobody. Marriage being the furthest thought from my mind, I only gaped at her until she told me to close my mouth.

"I've had few good examples of marriage that would make me want to pursue the state," I told her. "Aunt Kat perhaps, but none other."

"Good," Elizabeth said, her eyes hard and glittering. "I dislike it when my ladies leave me. I have too much affection for you to lose you."

I assured her again she would not lose me to marriage, and the subject was dropped.

13

SEVERAL DAYS LATER, the agate-hard look reentered Elizabeth's eyes as she marched through Richmond Palace to have an audience with Mary. I wondered if she would express her rage to Mary or be coldly offensive as she had been with the Council.

Mary herself was in a temper by the time we reached her chamber. She thrust out her hand for Elizabeth to kiss, then snatched it away, leaving Elizabeth on her knees.

"My Council is displeased," she snapped. "And this displeases *me*."

Whatever sisterly affection Mary had expressed in the euphoria of her rise to the throne had vanished. She glared at Elizabeth with her small eyes in a look of outrage that reflected Henry Tudor.

Elizabeth suddenly burst into sobs and pressed her hands tightly to her face. Her body shook, but she never took her hands from her eyes, perhaps waiting to manufacture the tears before she looked up at Mary again.

"You must forgive my backwardness," Elizabeth moaned. "I was raised in a household that taught nothing but the Reformed faith. I am ignorant of all but that. How can I transform myself to something I have never known in the space of weeks? My upbringing is to blame—tell me, dear sister, what I can do to overcome it?"

Mary's expression did not soften, but I could see her unbend slightly at Elizabeth's contrite plea. She'd steeled herself for a long argument with heated, perhaps hateful words, and here was Elizabeth at her feet, weeping and begging for forgiveness.

"I am pleased to hear you acknowledge your error," Mary said, somewhat stiffly. "So many refuse to even admit they have been led astray. You will come to Mass with me, sister, and show the world what it is to repent your sins and beg God and the Virgin for forgiveness."

I held my breath, wondering what Elizabeth would do. I knew, through James Colby, that many in England were pleased that Elizabeth remained of the Reformed religion, hoping it meant that the Reformed Church could remain intact. If Mary did not force her own sister's conversion, they could believe the Queen sincere in her wish for tolerance.

Mary looked anything but tolerant as she stood over Elizabeth, her small hands clenched in fists, her bosom pressing at her tight stomacher. "Will you be willing to do so?" she growled.

Elizabeth looked up, the tears on her face real. "I beg you to give me books to read and a priest to instruct me. Help me to learn."

Mary leaned to her, the sapphire crucifix at her neck swinging. "You will attend the Chapel Royal with me next week at the Feast of the Nativity of the Virgin. May I send a litter to you for your convenience?"

"I will come," Elizabeth said with a quaver in her voice. "You are a kind, dear sister."

Mary's face softened with hope. She lifted Elizabeth to her feet and embraced and kissed her. Elizabeth, daintily wiping her eyes, returned the kisses, and then Mary dismissed her, watching her go with some suspicion despite the hope.

Her suspicions would have been justified if she'd seen Elizabeth storming through her own chamber when we returned, overturning tables and throwing anything she could get her hands on.

"Fool," she cried. "She's buried herself in her piety all her life and now she wants to drag me down with her. Can she not see that people do not want her Church, can she not hear their muttering?"

One of her ladies, Elizabeth Sandes, a staunch believer in the Reformed religion, snorted. "Not over the droning of Latin and the ringing of chancel bells," she said.

Elizabeth whirled about, her hair wild with her rage. She glared at Mistress Sandes for a few seconds, then burst into uproarious laughter.

※

ELIZABETH BEGAN THE morning of the Feast of the Nativity of the Blessed Virgin by being sick in a bowl, tainting the air of her bedchamber. She had not been fabricating when she'd told the Council she was the victim of severe headaches. Some headaches could keep her in bed for days, with her ladies in constant attendance, laying cool cloths on her brow and dosing her with herbs.

"I am wretched," she whispered. She clenched her teeth, her skin white as the linens on her bed. "The pain tears at me like claws."

I hoped we could send word to Mary to beg her to let Elizabeth rest, but Elizabeth put out her hand and stood up, determination in every limb. "Lace me into my gown, Eloise. She shall see what I am made of."

We got her to her feet and dressed, though it took most of the morning, and the escorts come to take us to the Chapel Royal grew impatient and annoyed. It took much time for us to traverse the grounds of the palace in the litter Mary had sent, since we had to move very slowly to not upset her head. Elizabeth lay against the cushions, pressing a cloth to her forehead, while I and her ladies hovered beside her with herbal balls and worried looks.

Inside the chapel, Elizabeth descended the litter and, with a gray-white face, entered the box she would occupy with her sister to listen to the Mass. She pressed her hand to her stomach as she sat and dragged in deep breaths. Jane Dormer, sitting behind Mary, shot her a glance, frown deepening.

Mary glanced sideways at Elizabeth, then stole a hand out to pat her. "I am pleased you have come. I shall not forget this."

"My head pains me something terrible," Elizabeth groaned. "Let me sit quietly, or I am undone."

Mary nodded, looking understanding. Jane Dormer continued to frown. Below us the bishop began his chanting, the Latin syllables filling the chapel, echoing to the beams. The Prayer Book was nowhere to be seen, the huge Bible on a lectern open and accessible only to the priests. As the bishop read the Magnificat, the Song of Mary, his assistant priests waved smoking censers about him, coating the air with the thick scent of sandalwood and patchouli.

I coughed. Elizabeth groaned audibly, her voice mixing with the priest's intonations. "My head. Mistress Sandes."

Elizabeth Sandes, who had pinched her face up as soon as the priest had started singing the Latin Mass, leaned over her lady and presented a silk ball filled with chamomile and lavender.

Elizabeth pressed it gratefully to her nose, closing her eyes and shutting out the heavy smell of incense.

Below us, the ambassador from the Holy Roman Empire scowled, his face set in irritation. Mary only looked concerned. She held Elizabeth's hand and chafed her wrists.

"*Gloria Patri, et Filio, et Spiritui Sancto,*" the bishop sang in a high-pitched voice.

The words were echoed by soft retching sounds from Elizabeth. Mary stroked her hand. Jane Dormer frowned, as did Elizabeth Sandes, and Simon Renard, the Imperial ambassador, openly glared.

The wretched service finally ended, and Elizabeth retreated to her rooms, complaining not only of her head but her stomach all the way.

But her theatrics worked. Not a few days later, several of Mary's ladies came to Elizabeth's rooms and presented her with jewels from the Queen, a ruby-studded crucifix among them. Elizabeth sent thanks to Mary and took them as though they were her due. The crucifix she pushed to the back of a jewel case and never withdrew again.

⁂

AUNT KAT AND John Ashley and I were privileged spectators of Mary's coronation, allowed to watch the new Queen enter the Tower one day and then leave it the next morning for Westminster. Elizabeth, dressed in white and silver, rode in a carriage behind her with Anne of Cleves, her father's fourth wife. I witnessed firsthand the cheers that rose when Elizabeth appeared, the Tudor princess, beautiful and shining in the sunlight.

Luckily, Mary thought the adulation was all for her. Wine ran freely in the streets, pipes flowing from wine shop to wine shop to dispense the drink to all. At Westminster Mary stood proudly, the crown on her head and tears in her eyes as every man bent knee to her.

"They say Elizabeth looks more the Queen than her sister," Aunt Kat remarked to me as we celebrated that night in Elizabeth's chamber at Whitehall. During the coronation banquet, Elizabeth had again sat with Anne of Cleves and was paid every honor. Aunt Kat sniffed. "In many's opinion, the crown was on the wrong head."

"Kat," John admonished, his eyes flickering in alarm.

"I've learned my lesson," Kat said, somewhat coolly. "No more dabbling in politics. But I cannot help what others say."

"Mary is Queen now, whatever that may bring," John Ashley said. "Though it did not look well, Mary having a lord dub knights at her coronation instead of doing it herself. She only emphasized that she cannot do what a man can do. She cannot don armor and lead an army, and she cannot dub the naked knights of the bath."

"Will she marry Courtenay, then?" I asked, my mouth full of sweetmeats, in which I had overindulged today. "I cannot imagine Courtenay as King. He would cause more trouble than Mary could soothe, I should think, from all I have heard about him."

"Mary is old," Kat said, forgetting that she herself was at least ten years older than Mary. "Courtenay is the sort who will always want a young and pretty woman. Like our princess."

John Ashley rumbled in his throat, and Aunt Kat blushed. "Never mind, John. I shall not give it another thought. She looked well today, our Elizabeth. She would make a fine Queen."

I squeezed my eyes shut a moment. "Please tell me you have not turned conspirator, aunt."

"Of course not. Mary is not married; she might be too old to bear children now—she is thirty-seven, after all. Elizabeth is the heir. We may all see Elizabeth Queen before our time on earth is out. No need for conspiracies at all."

James Colby, I mused, thought differently. He did not seem a man willing to sit back and wait and see whether Mary married and bore children. I had decided he wanted me to keep an eye on Elizabeth for two reasons—first to keep her safe, and second to ferret out when she might be likely to support any schemes dreamed up by him or Robert Dudley.

It made sense that Colby would plot to put Elizabeth on the throne—he did not want Mary there, Elizabeth was of the Reformed Church, and she was much more popular than her sister. Elizabeth was English, born of King Henry and an English gentlewoman. Mary was Spanish and sympathetic to Spain and the Holy Roman Empire. Mary wanted to drag England back under the harness of the Pope and Rome. Elizabeth wanted England to remain English.

Colby and Dudley were English and clever and popular and rash. Colby had dragged me right into the heart of things by confiding too much in me and admonishing me to watch over Elizabeth. If I were sensible, I would flee at the very sight of him and refuse to speak to him again.

But secretly I agreed with him, and when the plot came to oust Mary, I would be in the thick of it, risking my neck to help my princess. I knew this as well as I knew my own name.

�֎

"SHE IS SLY," Simon Renard said. "Not to be trusted."

Mary nodded reluctantly. I could see the reluctance in the strain in her neck, the way she dipped her head and quickly stilled it.

I had no business eavesdropping on the Queen and the Imperial ambassador, but I took the opportunity that had dropped into my lap. I'd come to the Queen's rooms to visit Jane Dormer, who had told me she had messages and gifts for me from my mother. She saw my mother far more frequently than did I; I'd had little to do with her since leaving her home for Aunt Kat's guardianship.

When Jane left to fetch things, I remained behind a screen in the little room, and Mary and Renard strolled inside for a private chat. They did not see me, and Renard began talking before he ascertained whether the room was clear.

"I do not trust her," Mary responded.

Not trusting Elizabeth made her unhappy, I could see in her eyes and the pucker on her forehead. The lonely Mary who wanted a happy family was having to acknowledge that rising to be Queen had not ended all hardship in her life.

"She has wriggled out of Mass for nearly a month," Renard went on with relish. "And she has not made use of the books you send to her. I hear she laughs with her ladies about them and openly defies you."

My skin prickled with anger. Not true that Elizabeth openly defied Mary, but her actions could be taken as such. Damn Renard for interpreting them so.

"I open Parliament tomorrow," Mary said. She put her stubby fingers to her lips, rings flashing. "Where the old religion will be restored and my mother's marriage to my father reinstated."

"A perfect time to remind others that your father's marriage to the Boleyn woman was never valid."

"No, it was not, was it?" Mary's eyes took on a kind of glow. "My mother was England's true Queen, as am I. My father's second wife was—inappropriate." Pious Mary could not bring herself to say the word *whore*. "I have always wondered, you know, whether my sister was born my father's daughter at all. She bears resemblance to that musician from her mother's court, Mark Smeaton, who was condemned to death for having improper relations with the Boleyn woman." Her lips trembled as she warmed to the subject. "I imagine that it is true, that Mark Smeaton is Elizabeth's father. Why should such a one be heir apparent to my throne?"

The words shocked me, and I knew them for a lie. I had never known Mark Smeaton, being a tiny girl when he died days before Anne Boleyn was executed, but I remembered Henry, and I had seen Henry and Elizabeth together. Elizabeth had Henry's red hair, his flashing eyes, his mercurial moods, his temper. When she worked herself into a rage, her look, her stance was all Henry's.

But I knew enough of court politics to realize that truth did not always matter. If Mary persuaded enough people to speculate on Elizabeth's legitimacy, to cast doubt on her possessing any Tudor blood, she could effectively bar Elizabeth from the throne forever.

"I will speak to my Council about it," Mary continued. "You are right that she is dangerous, and she has deceived me with her promises to attend Mass. Her blatant disregard of my wishes over her conversion sets a dangerous precedent. I am willing to forgive those who have strayed from the Church, but not her if she is so obstinate." Mary paced a little, the light from the windows catching on the pearls on her French hood. "She will not have the throne. She will rusticate in the country or be married off abroad, but she will not rule. Never. That is my wish."

Renard smiled an oily smile. "As for marriage, dear lady," he began. "The earl—Courtenay—he is too frivolous for you. A wiser, steadier, better man is what you deserve, one who will love you and help you rule in your best interest."

Mary sat down in a rush, color flooding her face. "Courtenay is too fond of worldly pleasures, I agree. I have seen that."

From the rise and fall of her bosom and her easy dismissal of Courtenay, I guessed she'd already entertained the notion of someone else. Courtenay had meant nothing.

"I believe we are of one mind, Your Grace," Renard said.

"Indeed."

They fell silent, and for a moment I thought they would go without revealing the name of this sainted man Mary would woo, but Renard chuckled. "Philip, the son of Charles our Emperor. A perfect match. I believe your affection lies in that direction?"

Mary smiled, her blush almost girlish. "I am a woman, Your Excellency."

A foolish one, I thought. I knew nothing about this Philip, but I sensed a foreign marriage would be a mistake. Courtenay, for his faults, was at least English.

Mary sprang up on light feet. "I believe we will deal well together," she said. "I will have another proposition to put before Parliament."

She shared a smile with him. Then he bowed as she turned and walked from the room, leaving the ambassador alone.

I tried very hard not to move or make a sound, but perhaps a breath escaped my lips, for Renard turned sharply and surveyed the room. At that moment, the open window moved a bit in the sharp breeze, rattling a tapestry that hung nearby. Renard glanced at it, relaxed, and followed his Queen out the door.

❈

I REPORTED THE conversation to James Colby, who started out looking grave, and by the time I had finished he regarded me in pure alarm.

We stood in a little-used corridor, I with my arms full of fabric, he having come in from outside. We'd arranged the meeting, but to anyone passing it would look as though we'd come upon each other by chance in the middle of errands, perhaps even stopping to flirt.

"She cannot possibly cut Elizabeth from the succession," he said in a low, savage voice. "Nor can we tolerate her marriage to Philip. We shall be in the hands of the Empire, and England will be swallowed whole. If she pushes this marriage through, we will have to act."

"Act?" I repeated.

"Yes, act, Mistress Rousell. Did you believe us full of pretty words and ideas?"

I had not been certain what to think. Conspiracies were fashionable during any reign, when young, wealthy, and well-born men grew bored and decided they'd change the world to suit them. Their need for change often dwindled into nothing more than bold words sworn over ale in taverns. But Colby's eyes told me he had moved from words to careful planning. Planning meant raising money and gathering men-at-arms, leaving hearth and home to march against the monarch. He had told me too much; he could not risk that I would not run straight to Mary or her Council.

He read the worry in my eyes and put his hands on my shoulders. "I trust you, Mistress Rousell. It is not blind trust; I know you love Elizabeth and would do anything to keep her from harm. I would do the same. You may put your trust in me."

"I am not reassured," I said.

His fingers tightened. "There is danger coming. Much danger, to you, to me, to her. If you cannot bear that, then leave her household now and return to your mother. Stay quiet in her Catholic household and forget about Elizabeth."

"You know much about my family."

"I know everything about you, Eloise Rousell. I would not

have approached you did I not know all about you and believe I had measure of you."

I blenched. "How comforting."

"Dudley trusts you, although he can be more of a fool about people than I, but in this instance, he is correct."

"More comfort. You know much about me, but I know nothing about you. How can I be certain I can trust you?"

His cheekbones stained red. "You know all you need to know."

"I know next to nothing, not even the name of the wife you married."

"She came from no important family. You would not have known her."

He looked white about the mouth. I wondered what he was hiding and resolved to find out. If my fate was in his hands, I wanted to know everything.

"There is someone approaching, Master Colby," I said as footsteps sounded in the passage. "Perhaps you ought to let go of me."

Instead of complying, he leaned forward and pressed a brief kiss to my lips. He stepped back quickly, as though not wanting to be discovered, just as one of Mary's ladies came around the corner. Her brows went up and her mouth down, but she passed with only a nod. I permitted Colby's liberty without fuss, because better Mary's ladies spread the news that I kissed James Colby in back corridors than have it reach Mary that we were speaking of preventing her marriage scheme, by force if necessary.

I took my leave of Colby and returned to my duties with Elizabeth, determined to discover everything I could about James Colby. But strangely, though I asked questions and poked and pried over the next several days, I could find no one who truly knew the man or what his life had been before he joined Elizabeth's household. The one man who might know—Robert Dudley—remained locked in the Tower.

❖

I HAD INFORMED Elizabeth of Mary's conversation with Renard about cutting her out of the succession. Elizabeth fumed and raged that Mary had implied she was the bastard daughter of a whore, and not even Henry's child. The knowledge that Mary would try to cut Elizabeth from the succession made her nearly mad with fury.

She stewed in a foul temper all the day that Mary opened her first Parliament, but Elizabeth's anger turned out to be premature. Mary did restore the legitimacy of Catherine of Aragon's marriage to Henry (implying that his marriage to Anne Boleyn was therefore not), but Mary's wish to disinherit Elizabeth was never mentioned. I learned later from John Ashley that Mary's Council had persuaded her that cutting Elizabeth out of the succession was more dangerous than keeping her as the legitimate heir.

All Mary had to do, the Council said, was marry and provide an heir, and Elizabeth would be moved down the line of succession naturally. Mary seemed to have capitulated, though her words on the matter were harsh, or so I heard.

If Mary could not do anything to Elizabeth in law, she could do things to her in private. In the cold days of early winter, Mary invited Margaret Douglas, King Henry's niece and a firebrand in her own right, to sit beside her in her chamber, ride beside her when they went out, and follow just behind the Queen when she moved through the palace—forcing Elizabeth to trail behind.

Elizabeth would have none of that. Her temper soured, and her headaches grew worse. When Mary grew angry with

Elizabeth for having long private chats with the French ambassador, Elizabeth came to the end of her patience. She sought out Mary and asked stiffly to be allowed to retreat to her estate at Ashridge in west Hertfordshire for Christmas. Mary's crowded, hectic court hurt her health, she claimed, and she needed to heal in the country air.

Mary smiled and acquiesced. She bade Elizabeth a pretty farewell and bestowed on her lovely furs to keep her warm during the journey.

14

THE PROBLEM WITH returning to Ashridge was that we were isolated from court and its gossip. The Privy Council might persuade itself that all decided within its body was secret and private, but rumor of every discussion and decision ran through the halls almost the moment they happened. In the country, however, the news we received was days stale, but Elizabeth made it clear she was determined to rusticate in the country.

And we would rusticate with her. She wanted her ladies close by at all times. I asked Colby what on earth I could do to help Elizabeth, stuck in her drafty chambers, but he told me that watching over Elizabeth and reporting news to her through him was enough.

Elizabeth allowed Colby to come and go as he pleased, and because he was not an important noble, he was often able to discover information others could not. Most of what we learned of court came from him and John Ashley.

Thus we heard when Mary succeeded in ramming her proposed marriage to her Philip down the collective throats of

Parliament. The men of Parliament had gotten her to agree that Philip, a foreigner, would not rule as King over English subjects. Mary conceded, though reluctantly, vowing that Philip would have more sway when he fathered the heir to the English throne. She was a would-be wife who longed to have a husband to tell her what to do.

I did not need to be at court to learn that the proposed marriage was opposed by all. Even those in the village at Ashridge shared their sentiment.

"They'll sing Spanish songs in the streets and outlaw the good English tongue," one woman said to me. "No good will come of it."

I heard the phrase over and over: *No good will come of it.* No more, *Blessed Mary, Queen of England.* It was grumbling that a woman could not rule; she needed a husband, but an English one. Philip was heir to the kingdom of Spain and son of the Holy Roman Emperor—of course lofty Charles V wanted to pull England under his cloak as a prize against the uncertainty of France. England would become an adjunct of Spain and the Empire, and even the lowest, most illiterate farmer knew it. Edward Courtenay, too, who had fancied himself husband to Mary and someday King of England, was disgruntled, and styled himself ill treated.

Worries echoed all over England. "If the marriage to a Spaniard takes place, we should lie in swines' sties, in caves, and the Spaniards should have our houses, and we should live like slaves."

"No good will come of it," Aunt Kat said one afternoon as I supped with her and John Ashley. "Mary says her private wishes are more important than the Council's or Parliament's advice. Says *she* knows the hearts of the people." Aunt Kat sniffed. "She cannot be listening with her ears if she believes that. If she marries this *Felipe*, she will be hated as the Queen who let another realm rule England. Church bells will ring dirges instead of joyous peals."

For some reason I remembered my dream when we met Mary at Wanstead in the summer: the pall of smoke and the feeling of despair. "He is Catholic," I pointed out. "She loves the Church more than anything."

"Edward Courtenay is Catholic, but English," Aunt Kat said vehemently. "Even if he is ridiculous."

"Too fond of bodily pleasures," John Ashley agreed, he who rarely spoke poorly of others. "Gluttony, avarice, and lechery will be his downfall."

"And pride," I put in.

"How foolish you both are," Kat snapped. "He could be brought to heel by the Council. He could prance around with his crown and enjoy himself and not threaten the rule. This foreign prince will be the death of us."

Neither Uncle John nor I had any argument to that.

�֍

EMPLOYED BY ELIZABETH to gather information, James Colby left the household for long stretches of time. Elizabeth never discussed these absences, and when I once said, casually, that I hadn't seen much of Master Colby lately, she quieted me with an angry word.

I longed to speak to him because he was the only one who confided in me—John Ashley did, but Colby knew details that John did not. John Ashley repeated the common knowledge of London; Colby had ways to dig deeper and discover truths. Ashridge was cold and dismal, the buildings old and odd with huge empty halls and cramped tiny rooms above and behind them.

I began to lie in wait for Colby in the chamber he'd been given—his own alone, which was most unusual—for his return.

The first night I waited, he did not appear, nor on the second. The third night, my effort was rewarded when at the hour after midnight, his door scraped quietly open.

He beheld me lying on his bed by the light of the fire, and quickly closed the door. Lighting candles with spills from the fireplace, he said softly and angrily, "Mistress Rousell, what do you here?"

I slid off the bed. Cold radiated from the cloak he threw over a bench, and his clothes smelled of smoke and the outdoors. "Please tell me what is happening," I asked in a low voice. "I can hardly be your go-between if I know nothing."

His expression was hard and stern, more serious than I'd ever seen it. "It is dangerous, Eloise."

"That is most obvious. But I am already in danger—you put me squarely in it. I'll not be like Jane Grey, shutting my eyes to plots around me even when I am in the thick of them."

"Very well." He swept his cloak from the bench and indicated I should sit there with him while we warmed our feet at the fire.

"We have been meeting," he began. "I and others, and Courtenay."

"Courtenay?" I asked, surprised. "What on earth for?"

"Courtenay has money. And he is not happy with Mary for choosing not to marry him, and considers himself the next thing to royalty. He opposes the Spanish marriage as much as the rest of us, perhaps not for the same reasons, but it hardly matters."

"He was released from the Tower not even six months ago," I said. "Is he so anxious to return?"

"He will not have to worry. There is enough resentment against the Queen that many men will be with us, and we have a good chance to prevail against her. We will put Elizabeth on the throne, and Courtenay will not return to prison. I, like you, do not much fancy him as King, but one thing at a time."

A cold shiver ran through me. "So you mean to actually dethrone her. Not simply petition her to change her mind?"

Colby snorted. "She does not listen to her Parliament; she does not even listen to her beloved Bishop Gardiner. *He* wants her to marry Courtenay, but she's done the equivalent of stamping her feet and declaring she will do as she pleases. She would never listen to a petition by her nobles."

"You will tell me now that the men of Parliament will not meekly bow their heads and go on about their business."

He looked at me for a long time, the blue of his eyes almost azure in the firelight. "You have guessed correctly. I'll tell you no details, but things are in motion. There will be a French fleet. Elizabeth was able to speak to the French ambassador much before she left court. We will succeed."

I digested all this in silence. I remembered Mary's anger when she'd discovered Elizabeth's meetings with the ambassador— had she an inkling of what was going on, or was she simply angry at Elizabeth for complaining behind her back?

"You are putting her in grave danger," I pointed out. "Any move against the Queen will draw the Queen's attention to Elizabeth like a hound on the scent of the biggest hart."

"There will be no communication with Elizabeth directly. That is why we need you. You tell her all so she knows, but she must do nothing. Like you, she does not need details. If it comes to pass that the plot becomes known, she will know no more about it than do her questioners."

I thought of Aunt Kat's lurid descriptions of the dark Tower room in which she'd been confined with no fire to warm her and no certainty she'd live to return home. She was ashamed that the threat of torture had loosened her tongue, but I could wholly understand why it had. The same might happen to me or Aunt Kat again or even Elizabeth.

"I am not afraid," I said, my voice steady. "I can hold my tongue."

"You are good and loyal."

"It is more than that. Elizabeth has a nasty temper and is haughty and selfish and sometimes cruel, but that does not seem to matter. She is who she is, and I will protect her from Mary as long and hard as I can."

Colby gave me a look of growing respect. "You are an unusual woman, Eloise Rousell."

I shrugged. "Perhaps because I was cast off from my own family. Elizabeth rewarded me well, befriended me, and now trusts me. Perhaps I took to her like an orphaned lamb might take to a shepherd boy. Her family cast her off too when she was a child. We have that in common."

One corner of his mouth turned up. "Either that or you lie very, very well, and tomorrow my head will be on the block."

This was the first hint of humor I'd witnessed from James Colby, and I studied him in some surprise. "Let your head rest easy on your pillow tonight." I reached up and lightly patted his russet hair. "Although I must say, having slept here two nights, that Elizabeth might have awarded you privacy but punished you by giving you the most uncomfortable bed in the place."

"You slept here?"

"I had no way of knowing when you would return, so yes. No matter, I aired the bedding each morning, so you have no cause to worry."

"I'd not worry." His blue eyes fixed on me. "We must invent a better way of keeping you informed that keeps your reputation from danger."

I stood up. "There is no danger in that regard. No one notices what seamstress Eloise Rousell does. That is why you chose me to help you, is it not?"

"One of the reasons," he said.

We shared a long look that I could not interpret. I gave him a sunny smile as his lips parted, and then I left the room for the overly cold passages of Ashridge in December.

❈

COLBY DISAPPEARED AGAIN soon after that, and I saw nothing more from him. I reported our conversation to Elizabeth, to which she listened without a flicker of emotion. She ordered me never to say anything aloud about it again and to keep everything I knew from Aunt Kat. I agreed. After the debacle with Seymour I could not trust Aunt Kat not to gossip to someone if only to prove she knew something they did not.

We spent a quiet Christmas at Ashridge, which merged into a dark and cold January. Mary sent Elizabeth religious books, chasubles for her priests, and ornaments for her altar. Elizabeth packed them away and never looked at them. At court Mary held lavish entertainments and Masses to celebrate Christmas and Epiphany while Elizabeth seethed, knowing that Margaret Douglas celebrated at Mary's side.

"All at court will be pitying me, or gloating," she said darkly one evening as she played at chess with me. "The shunned bastard sister, festering in the country, while Margaret Douglas plays the virginals and smiles at the Queen. Margaret, Countess of Lennox, put in the Tower for behaving like a wanton before her marriage. A plotter and a schemer is Margaret. Now favorite of the Queen." She picked up a marble queen from the board and threw it into the fire. "Fine company my sister keeps."

I forbore to point out that Elizabeth had hated being at court and had begged to leave, not wanting one of the heavy chessmen fired at me. "Things may be different, come spring," I said.

Her temper did not quiet, but she lowered her voice so only

I could hear. "God save me from plotting men. Plans can go wrong, and here I sit, unable to direct them, a helpless pawn." The chess piece in question flew across the room to splinter on the hearth.

Earlier that day, a message had come to Elizabeth from Thomas Wyatt, a rather impetuous young man, son of the sonnet-writing Wyatt, who'd accepted Edward Courtenay's invitation to help him in his conspiracies. Thomas had sent a message encouraging Elizabeth to move to Donnington, one of her estates, carefully not saying why. "Ridiculous," she'd said to me. "How would it look if I fled beforehand? Guilty. I must sit here as though I know nothing, as though I am utterly astonished that anyone in the realm could move against the Queen. I will wait and do as I should see cause."

She began to write as much in a letter to Wyatt, but before she'd penned more than two words, I stopped her with the extreme caution I'd developed since the Seymour affair.

"Easy to deny a spoken word, Your Grace," I whispered. "But if anything goes wrong, and a letter by you to Wyatt is found . . ."

"You have become devious, Eloise." Elizabeth frowned at me, but removed herself from her writing desk and burned the sheet. "And more clever than you ought to be. But I believe you advise well. Say no more of this."

I swore my secrecy, and she sent one of her gentlemen ushers off to Wyatt with a message so neutral no one not in the know would be able to make anything of it.

Now Elizabeth leaned over the board to me, a bitterness in her voice. "The trouble with being the second person in the realm, Eloise, is that there are those constantly plotting to raise you to be the first—so that you will reward them well, of course."

"Not Colby," I said quickly. "He understands the damage

Mary's marriage will do. He knows that the best person for England is you."

"Guard your tongue," Elizabeth said, but she did not look angry. She serenely set up the chess pieces, though how we were to play without her pawn or my queen I did not know. "These are things *women* would not think to discuss."

"Of course, you are right, Your Grace," I responded with a nod. "Forgive me."

"I would devise a way in which I might speak to these men. Writing, as you say, is too dangerous."

"James Colby is trustworthy."

"Indeed, but he can be in only so many places at once. No, I have another idea, one with which only you can help."

"I would be honored, Your Grace."

"Good." Her eyes glittered as they did when she was excited and intrigued. In a low voice she described her idea. I grew as excited as she and agreed it would work, with a few modifications.

We drew back from the discussion and composed ourselves, resuming the interrupted game of chess.

"You speak of James Colby much," Elizabeth said after a time. "Are you in love with him?"

I blinked. "In love? Goodness no, Your Grace. I do like him, though. He is sensible."

"Because I could not do without you, Eloise."

"I have no intention of leaving, Your Grace."

"My affection for you is too strong," she said in a hard monotone. "And I would be brokenhearted to lose you to marriage."

"No fear of that," I said with conviction. The wrong husband, I had seen, watching Jane Grey and now Mary, could land a woman in a world of trouble.

15

TOWARD THE END of January, the worst happened. Mary's spies discovered that a French fleet was waiting and ready to come to England at a moment's notice. Mary recalled to court a man called Sir Peter Carew, but he, being too busy raising and training troops for the rebellion Wyatt planned, ignored the summons. Mary dispatched trusted gentlemen to ride to him and discover what he was up to.

Then Edward Courtenay, the weak link in the chain, lost his nerve. Taxed to tell what he knew, he broke down and confessed the entire plot to his mentor, Bishop Gardiner. Gardiner, horrified because Courtenay was one of his favorites, reported to the Queen. The conspirators panicked and began their armed rebellion two months too soon.

The gentlemen leading it—the Duke of Suffolk, Carew, Sir James Croft, and Wyatt—had rather counted on their countrymen rising with them, but only Wyatt was able to effectively raise a force. While the other conspirators gave up quickly,

Thomas Wyatt marched to London. On the way, London troops sent out to stop him turned around and joined him, and a large force made its way toward Mary.

The details of the entire affair I heard from Colby later. At the time, Elizabeth and I waited in cold, dark Ashridge for the outcome, while Mary brooded in Whitehall.

We heard that Mary had gone to the City of London, which at first was fervently on the side of the rebels, to speak to them personally. The City of London always fascinated me, a small area surrounded by walls, within which the men had their own laws, their own guards, their own lives, so different and removed from any other in London or, indeed, England. Even the monarch lived outside it, apart.

If the men of the City opened the gates and let Wyatt's men in, Mary was finished. Wyatt would arrest her and—then what? Would they dare execute their true monarch? Or would they imprison her in the country, as her mother had been imprisoned, stripped of her rank and wealth, a condition in which Mary had spent much of her young life?

She must have known this, because her speech, as I heard of it later, was impassioned. "I am your Queen," she began. "At my coronation, I was wedded to the realm and the laws of the same. The spousal ring, I have on my finger, which never hitherto was, nor hereafter shall be, left off."

I imagined her standing before the men of the Guildhall, perhaps on a bench or platform so that she might be seen over them, turning her hand so that her coronation ring flashed in the light.

"You promised your allegiance and obedience to me. And I say to you, on the word of a prince, I cannot tell how naturally the mother loveth the child, for I was never the mother of any.

But certainly, if a prince and governor may as naturally and earnestly love her subjects, as the mother doth love the child, then assure yourselves, that I being your lady and mistress, do as earnestly and tenderly love and favor you.

"Then I doubt not but we shall give these rebels a short and speedy overthrow," she continued, and added for the few unmoved, "I never intended to marry outside the realm but by my Council's consent and advice. I assure you now, I shall never marry anyone but he with whom all my subjects shall be content."

The speech was cheered as Mary swept from the hall, surrounded by her men and ladies. Now all she could do was wait for the outcome.

※

On Ash Wednesday, Sir Thomas Wyatt led his forces across the Thames and headed to Whitehall. Mary's speech must have been effective, because soldiers of the City of London barred them at London Bridge, forcing Wyatt to march his army to the west to cross the river.

Mary was sitting in the gallery above the Holbein gate when Wyatt's men stormed the gate. I heard that the palace was in hubbub, that her yeomen guards had fled the enemy and retreated into the palace. Only Mary herself stood fast, sharply telling those in the room to stay and defend her person.

As it happened they did not have to defend her to the man. The gates below stood closed, and they held against the onslaught. Wyatt headed onward for London, with Mary's soldiers, more heartened, after them. Wyatt found himself squeezed between the closed gates of London and the soldiers behind him, and was forced to surrender. The prisoners were led to the Tower to await Mary's judgment.

❄

THEY WERE ON their way. Elizabeth paced as usual, sunlight flashing on the gold threads embroidered on her gown.

"She tells me it is for my safety," Elizabeth said to Kat Ashley, who had just read the letter Mary had sent Elizabeth. The rebellion was over, Wyatt in the Tower along with the Duke of Suffolk and Sir James Croft—all the men who had wanted Elizabeth on the throne and Mary off it.

Mary had sent a pleasantly worded letter just before the rebellion began, inviting Elizabeth to join her at court, where she would be safe. She'd sent a second letter now that the rebellion had been quelled; Elizabeth might still be in danger, she said, if any who had escaped arrest decided to retaliate.

"It is nonsense," Elizabeth snorted. "She knows it. *Run to me, sweet sister, and I will keep you safe.* In a nice locked room in the Tower, no doubt. I hear that Jane Grey's father has returned there to his beloved daughter and son-in-law Guildford. Mary was a bloody fool to let Suffolk out, and he was a greater fool to get himself tossed back in. She cannot let them live now, you know."

I thought of Jane sitting innocently in her prison, by all reports happy that people left her alone with her books. She was guilty of nothing but obeying difficult parents.

"You should not answer this summons," I said. I didn't like the letter—it oozed false sympathy.

"I have no intention of answering." Elizabeth ceased pacing and glared at us both. "I am ill, and it is far too cold to travel. Mary must make do with keeping me penned here. What can I, stifled in the country, do? I had no knowledge of these deeds, and I will hide here from the bad men. Bring me paper, Kat Ashley, I will write it to her."

The letter was written, and dispatched, and not long later came Mary's curt reply that Elizabeth must attend her—now. She would send an armed escort, she said, to see that Elizabeth arrived safely.

Elizabeth truly was ill; she had been all winter. Her head ached worse than ever, and her body had swollen and bloated until she could put on none but the loosest clothes. Hard on the heels of the summons came a physician, who closeted himself with Elizabeth and then emerged declaring she was fit to travel at least to London.

"The man is a damned fool," Elizabeth said when I went in to see to her clothes. "If I drop over dead en route it will be laid at his door, but small comfort that will be to me."

Her fury made her sicker still, but there was nothing for it. If she did not go, Mary might simply arrest her and drag her to the Tower with the rest of the rebels.

We started out on a chill day in February, Elizabeth in a litter accompanied by two hundred horses, me with the rest of her women. A fine day for a journey, crisp and cold, but fair. Banners snapped in the wind; the men wore red livery; and as we passed, people ran to the road to cheer.

Elizabeth's illness slowed our progress, and we'd traveled only six miles before the cold and her pain made us put up for the night. Her outriders took us to a large house well off the road, the gentleman who owned it scrambling to accommodate us.

"Lord, help me." Elizabeth spoke the words not in pathetic weariness, but in anger. She hated to face Mary and whatever waited in London in weakness, although I suspected she'd find a way to use the weakness to her advantage.

The house that emptied for us was cold. Aunt Kat ordered fires built in every room, chivying the house's servants, much to the country gentleman's dismay. She bustled about shouting orders to Elizabeth's ladies, many of whom were weary and almost ill themselves.

Being of robust nature, I found myself recruited to make Elizabeth comfortable in her small chamber, to lay rugs and hang curtains, to bring warm drinks and wine. I supported Elizabeth's head while she drank wine from a cup, and I chafed her wrists. Her hands and face had again puffed and swollen, and she groaned in earnest when she fell back to the bed.

"Now will they believe me ill?" she demanded. "I hardly could have invented this. Oh, take the wine away, Eloise, and cease your fussing."

I backed away, secretly pleased at her barking, because it meant she was not in grave danger. Mistress Sandes, Elizabeth's favorite, took my place, and Elizabeth turned her groans and snarls to her.

I did more running about for Aunt Kat and for other ladies who were cold and unwell, working far into the night. When the chaos inside wound to a dull clamor, when Elizabeth at last slept and the ladies and gentleman of her household began to settle themselves, I wrapped up in a cloak and slipped out into the darkness.

My goal was the stable yard and the houses that ringed it, where Elizabeth's and Mary's soldiers and many of the gentlemen had put up for the night. I had seen one among them I was anxious to interview.

The stable yard had calmed by this time, the horses fed and bedded down, saddles and harnesses being cleaned by the stable lads. The men were eating or drinking and talking, and I stood in the shadows, not wishing to be noticed.

As though he'd been waiting for me, James Colby walked out

of a warm, lit brick building and casually strolled in my direction. A cluster of trees stood not far from the outbuildings, and we met beneath the deep gloom.

"The princess truly is ill," I said as soon as he stepped next to me. "We cannot race to London, and you may tell that to Her Majesty's men."

"I hope she will tarry as long as she can," he answered.

He was so tall his voice came from a long way up. I shivered for no reason I knew—the night had not grown colder; in fact, the absence of wind made the chill tolerable.

"Why?" I asked sharply. "What has happened?"

"Guildford Dudley and Lady Jane Grey were executed today on Tower Green."

"Oh, no." I pressed my hands briefly to my mouth, nausea stirring in my stomach. "I'd not thought she'd truly send Jane to her death. She claimed to be so forgiving. What has happened to the world?" Tears slid silently down my cheeks. "Jane was innocent. She had nothing to do with plots—how could she? Without a word to say for herself, with her nose buried in books, how could *Jane* threaten anyone?"

My voice rose in my distress, and I found myself pressed against Colby, his arms around me. I leaned against him in gratitude and cried my fill.

My imagination filled in the details, which were confirmed when I heard the entire story later. Jane dressed all in black, being led across the Tower Green by her ladies, her lips moving as she read from a book of prayers she carried. Her white, strained face as she faced the people come to see her die and her stammered words that she was guilty of loving the world and worldly things too much. *Jane*, saying these things.

Then her ladies helping undress her to her chemise and Jane stepping to the straw. I shoved myself away from Colby, trying to blot out the vision, but it insisted on playing itself out to the end. Jane stepping to the block, tears running down her face, and the final, sharp blow. The vision did not spare me the blood, the wails of Jane's ladies, the *thump* of the executioner's ax.

I learned later that, more horrible still, she'd not been able to find the block once she'd been blindfolded, and a man had come out of the crowd to help her to it. Then Jane's blood, innocent blood, on the straw.

I gave a strangled cry and fell to my knees in the mud, trying to beat the vision out of my head. It vanished suddenly, and I saw only the frozen mud under the trees, a thick root that had risen above ground, the folds of James Colby's leather boots, and the glint of spurs as he crouched beside me.

I gasped for breath, drawing in the sweet scent of the night, welcoming the cold.

"Mistress Rousell?"

I could not say if Colby was upset at my distress or annoyed that I'd broken down.

"I am unhurt," I said, the only words that came to my lips. "I simply . . ."

Colby's hands were large and warm, lifting me to my feet. "I told you too abruptly," he said.

I wiped my eyes with cold fingers. "I knew Lady Jane, you see. I grew up side by side with her, I designed gowns for her. I started to sew her Queen's wardrobe. I knew . . . I knew at the time I was sewing a shroud but I dared hope that Mary would spare her. She was innocent."

"She was a banner to flock to, just as Elizabeth is," he said grimly. "Whether Jane had any desire to become Queen was not the point. While any man could use her, she was a danger to Mary. Elizabeth is an even greater danger, which is why we must take our time traveling to London. If Elizabeth arrives too soon on the heels of Jane's execution, Mary may simply follow with another. A lightning trial, a night in the Tower—"

"Enough," I hissed. "I do see the danger, though I am but a foolish woman, weeping on your cloak."

"Not so foolish. Robert Dudley is sometimes led astray by a pretty face, but not in matters of importance."

I looked up at him, barely able to make out his features in the shadow. "Were I to think that through long enough, it might twist into a compliment. Thank heavens you were sensible and stayed away from Thomas Wyatt in the end."

"But I was in the thick of it." Colby put rough-gloved fingers on my chin. "I fought with the soldiers in London against Mary. Wyatt sent me to protect Elizabeth when he saw that it was futile. They battled at the very gates of Whitehall, and the Queen's personal guard were nearly too cowardly to protect her. Had not the City stood by her, we would have gained a foothold in London and it might have ended in victory. But it did not, and I slipped away and rode here."

I absorbed the story, cold fear in my stomach. Elizabeth could well share Jane's fate if Mary saw fit. Perhaps the fact that Elizabeth was her sister, perhaps the fact that she was a Tudor would save her. But if Mary was angry enough, if she could be convinced that Elizabeth had set Thomas Wyatt and his soldiers on her, she would be merciless.

"Damn them," I said between clenched teeth.

"We will protect her," Colby promised. "You and I."

I thought him too certain. "We are doing naught but gossiping in the mud in the dark. How can this protect her?"

He seized my shoulders and squeezed hard. Even through the thick fabric of my cloak and the sleeves beneath, his fingers were warm. "You will. You must. There may come a time soon when all she has is you, when Mary will take away everything but you. Then you must stand by her. You must insist on it."

He gave me the feeling he knew much more than he was telling me. "I will always stand by her," I said.

"It will be difficult. And dangerous. But I believe if anyone can keep her from falling, it will be you."

"You have much faith in my ability, James Colby."

"I have come to know you. You are clever, though you try to hide it behind that guileless face and your childlike blue eyes. I knew at once that the method Elizabeth used to communicate with the rebels was invented by you."

"Not so. It was her idea. I simply made it practical."

"No one else could have." He released me. "Go to her now and persuade her to tarry as much as she can. And prepare for the worst. Do not let my faith in you be misplaced."

"It shall not be," I said stiffly. "You give and take back compliments quite easily, Master Colby."

"If we survive this, I will toast your many accomplishments."

"Elizabeth would not approve," I said, drawing my cloak about me. "Good night."

He stood apart from me and let me go, his eyes glittering in the darkness. I walked away from him, uncertain as I always was after I spoke to him. But he was not wrong about Elizabeth's danger. Jane was murdered, Elizabeth could be next, and we were heading directly into Mary's waiting arms.

16

 ELIZABETH'S ILLNESS SLOWED our journey to a crawl. We managed at best five or six miles a day, and even that taxed most of her strength. Her body ached and her limbs and belly swelled as before. Her physician bled her, Aunt Kat and Elizabeth Sandes gave her herbs, and I tried to take down the swelling with warm cloths.

Elizabeth and I had had a long talk after I'd spoken to James Colby. She lay in bed, pale and sweating, as I told her of Jane's execution and Colby's suggestion that she take as much time as possible arriving at London. We should give Mary's temper time to cool, I said, and keep out of sight while Mary was signing execution orders.

"I did not need you to meet your dashing adventurer in the dark to tell me that," she snapped at me. "I could not manage a faster pace were I in a tearing hurry to get to London. Can you credit what Anthony Denny has told me? That there is a rumor that I hide myself and will not come to court because I am great with child, probably by one of the rebels."

My gaze dropped to her swollen belly and she glared at me in fury.

"A servant mistook your illness," I suggested. "And spoke to others of it."

"And if I discover who, they will be sorry they have a tongue."

"The day we ride into London," I said. "We ought to go in full daylight. You should wear your white and silver gown and travel with the curtains of your litter open."

"And show them how slim and *not* pregnant I am?" She smiled at me from her pillows. "Clever girl. It will not stop Mary doing as she pleases, but I'll not let her tarnish my reputation. The people of England want the pure princess, and that is what I shall be."

❁

THE SLOW JOURNEY did give Elizabeth time to heal and compose herself. By the time she reached London, she was much better and the swelling had dispersed. I carefully resewed the plain white bodice to one of her white and silver brocade gowns and laced her into it.

As planned, she rode through Smithfield toward the city, surrounded by her red-garbed guardsmen. She wore shining white, her body slender and erect, every inch the Tudor princess.

The city turned out to cheer her home. The road was lined with well-wishers who not only removed caps and waved and shouted, but handed her gifts as we rode along. She acknowledged them with the stateliness of a monarch, smiling her thanks. They loved her, and she absorbed that fact as though she'd known it and expected it.

We rode across Fleet Bridge and through Fleet Street to the Strand and so on to Whitehall, where Elizabeth's men dispersed.

I accompanied Elizabeth and her ladies to Elizabeth's chambers, where she waited for Mary's summons.

The summons never came. Elizabeth paced, her health regained, her anger evident. She demanded of everyone to know what went on outside the walls. What of Wyatt, what had he said to his questioners, had he named her? What had her gentleman servant, accused of delivering messages to Wyatt, said? What was the rumor about the French ambassador having a copy of one of her letters to Mary?

James Colby kept an eye on comings and goings and reported to me, and I in turn reported to Elizabeth.

"Wyatt has said nothing against her," he told me when we met one morning in a chill passage. "The men of the rebellion name each other, but not her. One of her gentlemen has been accused of taking a message to Wyatt thanking him for his suggestion she remove to Donnington, but nothing can be proved."

"I remember that."

"Please God you forget it, Eloise. You do not want to be questioned in the Tower."

"Why haven't you been?" I asked curiously. Colby, who knew what was going on better than most, who had been among the fighters in London.

A look of some self-loathing crossed his face. "I am too careful. I abandon honor to keep myself alive."

I wondered what he meant. "I for one am happy you do. She needs friends; she needs information. She needs you."

"The greater good," he finished bitterly.

"Indeed. Do not flog yourself for not being tortured in the Tower with the others. We need you. They are the fools for getting caught."

His eyes flashed the self-loathing again. "They have not

named me—they truly believe they die for the betterment of England, but they will leave enough of us alive to try again."

"Try again?" I echoed hopefully.

"God in heaven, Eloise, you sound eager. This is dangerous business. Women should cringe in their chambers, not run to be in the thick of things."

"You do not know women well then. We are more ruthless than the men, I believe, when we see a need. I am willing to fight for Elizabeth, and not Mary. Why should this puzzle you?"

A smile crossed his lips. "Thinking on my mother, I well believe in the ruthlessness of women."

Learning that James Colby had something so human as a mother interested me. "Your mother? Have I seen her at court?"

"No. She died years ago. My father as well, the better for this business. If something happens to me, I cannot harm others connected to me. I have no more connections."

He had lost his wife as well, and he'd never spoken of brothers and sisters. A man alone in the world.

"Is that why you are willing to risk your life for all?"

"Not the only reason, but knowing no one else will be punished for my crimes allows me to act more resolutely."

"Well, I shall be sorry if you are put to the block," I said, keeping my voice light. "Even though you dragged me into your plots—quite literally. But I should not like to see you suffer, so I am glad they have not named you."

He looked at me for a long time, his red hair framing a strong face, his chin dusted with red stubble.

"I am sorry now I did drag you into it." He brushed my cheek with the backs of his fingers. "You should be creating famous costumes for queens, not mucking about in conspiracies."

"Elizabeth's downfall would likely be mine. I may as well help keep her safe."

He sighed, and his hand dropped to his side. "Take care, Eloise."

"I always take great care, Master Colby."

❖

WE STAYED AT Whitehall for three weeks, without word from Mary. Thomas Wyatt went to his trial and was pronounced guilty and condemned to die. Wyatt admitted to sending messages to Elizabeth, but always declared she'd provided him with no answer and made no sign of condoning the rebellion. Elizabeth's gentleman who had carried a verbal response to Wyatt admitted to Elizabeth's vague reply, but the Council had nothing in writing and nothing could be proved. It began to look as though Elizabeth might be spared.

I dared hope Mary would simply send Elizabeth home and ignore her again. As the days dragged by and nothing happened, my hopes increased. But I had not calculated the influence that Simon Renard and Bishop Gardiner had on Mary.

"She brings evil to this realm," they whispered into Mary's ears. "Courtenay and Elizabeth should lose their heads," Renard the Imperial ambassador said. "It is the only way to keep peace."

Bishop Gardiner had grown fond of Edward Courtenay in the Tower, and it was likely that only his affection saved the young man. Gardiner had no affection for Elizabeth, however, and sat beside Mary, feeding her malevolent thoughts.

A few days after Wyatt's trial, I heard running feet in the passage outside the room where I sewed with Aunt Kat. A maid I had posted to report to me what went on in the castle outside our chambers suddenly burst in upon us. Out of breath, her hair hanging, she panted, "They are coming. They are coming for Her Grace. We are undone."

She wailed and wrung her hands. Aunt Kat slapped her and I hurried to the inner chamber to Elizabeth. I found her rising from her chair, her books falling to the floor, her face white.

"Quickly, Eloise, fix my gown."

I knew what she wanted. I hurried to the wardrobe and gathered up a bodice of velvet and gold I had made since our arrival, and hastily laced it on her. I stood her near the window, angling her body to catch the light on the fabric, and arranged her velvet overskirts to coyly reveal the glittering brocade of the underskirt. Her ladies grouped themselves around her, not protectively but in a little tableau that put Elizabeth in the middle as the sun and they the stars around her.

When the first man, the Earl of Sussex, came through the door, ramrod straight, no bowing, he found Elizabeth regal and haughty, awaiting an inferior. The entire of Mary's Council piled in behind him, from Bishop Gardiner, eyes shining in righteous triumph, to William Paulet, looking carefully neutral.

"We have come to arrest you." Sussex had a slightly apologetic note in his voice. Henry Radcliffe, Earl of Sussex, was one of Mary's staunchest supporters, but he was very aware that Elizabeth, too, had Tudor blood, despite Mary's peevish insistence that Mark Smeaton had fathered Elizabeth. Sussex had a wife who drove him a bit mad, she not only being very Protestant but having also once been arrested and confined in the Tower for sorcery. This accounted, I thought, for the worried lines about his eyes.

The rest of the Council, save Paulet, turned hard faces to her. Paulet managed to reflect some reluctance—after all, Elizabeth might be Queen someday herself. Paulet had survived three Tudor reigns thus far, why not four?

Sussex cleared his throat. "Sir Thomas Wyatt has been convicted of treason," he said to Elizabeth. "You have been accused of knowing of the plot and aiding and abetting it, with evidence brought forth. You are to be taken to the Tower of London, there lodged at Her Majesty's pleasure until such time as you will be tried for your crime."

The Council remained a stern wall of men turned against a woman. They waited for her to fall to her knees and weep and plea, or faint as Jane Grey might have done. Instead Elizabeth raised her head, and her nostrils flared.

"What evidence?" she snapped. "There is no evidence that has not been manufactured, for I am innocent of this charge."

"Nonetheless." Sussex's voice hardened slightly. "Tomorrow you will be escorted to the Tower. Tonight you will remain here to prepare yourself."

"Let me speak to my sister," Elizabeth demanded as though she hadn't heard him. "Let me speak to Her Grace. She promised before I left court that she would hear me were I accused of any conspiracy as I have been accused today."

"Her Grace, the Queen, does as she pleases."

"Tell her, my lord, that I beg humbly to see her."

Sussex looked her up and down, clearly seeing no humility about Elizabeth. "I will deliver your message," he said. "Though I cannot speak for the Queen."

"But you do speak for her, my lord Sussex. You tell me from her that I am accused."

Sussex flushed, but he made no other sign of emotion. "Even so. We will return in the morning."

The Council turned their backs on her. They walked out, neither shuffling nor ashamed, their hats firmly on their heads, their backs straight. The insult was complete.

"It is Gardiner, I will wager," Elizabeth seethed when the doors had shut again. "Gardiner keeps her from seeing me. He fears that she will soften with sisterly affection. I doubt she will, but I wish to plead my case. If Mary hears me, she will change her mind. She is not stupid."

No, but she was careful, I reflected. This was made evident when, not much later, the Earl of Sussex returned without the Council but with a contingent of armed guards.

"You are to remain in this room," he told Elizabeth. "And your ladies must go, save two needed to wait upon you. You will not leave nor will they, nor will they pass on any communication from you to any other person."

Elizabeth's face was linen-white, her red-gold hair standing out like fire from her brow. "Mistress Ashley and Mistress Rousell shall stay."

"Not Katherine Ashley," Sussex said dryly. "Mistress Rousell comes from a pious family; she may stay."

I did my best to look pious, or at least to keep the flush from my face. I knew how to get word to and from Elizabeth under Mary's guards' noses, but I could not if I were sent away.

"Mistress Norwich, then," Elizabeth said without argument.

Sussex nodded as if he did not much care as long as dangerous Katherine Ashley were far from Elizabeth's side.

I tried not to smile at the irony that I, with sympathies heavy with the Reformed religion, should be allowed to stay with Elizabeth because my mother had married a good Catholic. Elizabeth regarded Sussex coldly, pretending she was not gleeful that she'd gotten her own way. I knew she'd named Kat first because she would obviously be rejected—then by contrast she could choose who she truly wanted.

His task done, Sussex went, again without bowing. But his look before he left the room conveyed that he was sorry he'd been chosen for the task.

"It will help," Elizabeth muttered to me after the earl departed. "These gentlemen are reluctant to choose which royal they will offend. They wish me to remember, if I become Queen, who disliked to see me so harshly treated."

I agreed, but I wondered whether Mary's Council's divisiveness would make her bring about Elizabeth's end that much faster.

Elizabeth did not sleep much that night, and neither did I. Mistress Norwich and I saw to her needs at table, undressed her, put her to bed, and read to her. Her English Bible and Prayer Book had been confiscated, but she had books of devotion and poetry, and Elizabeth Norwich could read Greek and discuss Herodotus with her.

At last we snuffed out the candles, and the night dragged on. When I looked out the window, I saw men in armor below, pacing back and forth in the courtyards. Mary was risking that no rescue attempt would whisk Elizabeth away.

In the morning, Elizabeth Norwich and I dressed the princess again, and we were ready and waiting when Sussex and Paulet came.

❧

"IF ANY EVER did try this old saying," Elizabeth wrote, anger evident in every curl of ink, "that a king's word was more than another man's oath—I most humbly beseech Your Majesty to verify it in me, and to remember your last promise and my last demand: that I be not condemned without answer and due proof."

Elizabeth had gotten her way around Sussex, who had allowed her at last to write a letter to Mary. Elizabeth had taken her time, writing carefully in her own hand, with me nearby, so that I could see every word.

"And to this present hour I protest afore God (who shall judge my truth, whatsoever malice shall devise) that I never practiced, counseled, nor consented to anything that might be prejudicial to your person . . . therefore I humbly beseech Your Majesty to let me answer afore yourself and not suffer me to trust your councilors—yea, and that afore I go to the Tower."

In the next paragraphs Elizabeth reminded Mary of the words of the Duke of Somerset, who'd said that if he had spoken to Thomas Seymour before condemning him, letting his brother explain himself, Seymour might not have been put to death. "I pray God as evil persuasions persuade not one sister against the other . . ."

She ended with a bolder tone. "And as for the traitor, Wyatt, he might peradventure write me a letter, but on my faith I never received any from him. And as for the copy of my letter sent to the French king, I pray God confound me eternally if ever I sent him word, message, token, or letter by any means, and to this my truth I will stand in to my death."

Elizabeth's letter ended near the top of a second page. She drew heavy diagonal lines across the remaining empty space so that Mary's councilors might not fill in something unwanted, then added a last plea and signed it.

She handed the finished letter to Sussex with a glint in her eye, not bothering to hide the words from him. "I thank you, my lord, for delivering that to my sister, before setting me in the boat for the Tower."

He took the paper, his nostrils pinched. "We cannot leave for the Tower now. The tide has turned and we must wait for tomorrow."

Elizabeth shrugged her slim shoulders, the set of her mouth telling me she'd known full well that she'd taken too long over the letter. If I calculated aright, the tide would turn again near midnight, but Sussex would never chance taking her on the river so late—one of her gentlemen might arrange for her to be plucked from Sussex's care and rescued.

Sussex left the chamber to deliver the message, his pearl and ruby cap jammed firmly on his head. He did return later to say that he'd taken the letter to Mary and she'd read it, but that there was no reply.

I saw the hope leave Elizabeth's eyes, but she did not droop. She thanked Sussex loftily and called for her supper. He did not admonish her, only gave her a slight bow and ordered the servants to see to it. I saw the look on Sussex's face before he turned away. Though Mary was firmly Queen now, the possibility that Elizabeth might someday be Queen lingered, and he hoped she would remember the deed he had done for her this day.

17

THE JOURNEY DOWN the Thames was one I would remember forever. The weather had turned with the tide, and a cold rain beat on us as I and one of Mary's armed gentlemen assisted Elizabeth into the barge that would carry us downstream.

Water ran from her cloak and pooled in the bottom of the barge, the canopy flimsy against the cold and wind. The two of us huddled together and Elizabeth Norwich huddled on her other side, both of us trying to protect Elizabeth from the worst of it.

I had been able to get word to Colby about what was happening, using our method, though there was nothing much he could have done. The guards had looked at me most suspiciously when I'd thrust my head out along with a pile of handkerchiefs and snapped at him that someone needed to bring clean linens. He had inspected the cloths to see whether I'd buried a letter between the folds, but of course I had not. I spoke the truth when I told Elizabeth that day at Ashridge that a thing written was tediously difficult to deny. The guard had let a serving maid take the handkerchiefs away and bring me clean ones.

The barge made its way downriver, past the pile of Somerset House, past the Temple to the north and the fields of Southwark to the south. The streets were empty, but bells pealed from the churches and cathedrals—it was Palm Sunday, and ordinary citizens rejoiced at the coming end of Lent.

The City wall flowed past, then the shadow of London Bridge, the houses on it looking in danger of tumbling into the water at any moment. Under the bridge, the boat rocked and tossed, the rapids threatening to carry it into the pilings on either side of us.

The boatmen strained, their sweat mingling with the rain while I held onto the gunwale with both hands, my heart beating in terror. I imagined Aunt Kat explaining to my mother how I'd gone to a watery grave with the princess they despised, but I could not picture their reaction. Somehow I did not imagine my mother or stepfather would be very sorry.

The boat at last shot from under the bridge, the speed sending us toward calmer river. We passed Billingsgate and all too soon saw the Tower draw close.

The boatmen guided the craft out of the current and to the landings, they being the only ones happy to see journey's end. The boat bumped stone, the relieved boatmen throwing ropes to those waiting above to tie us fast. Sussex immediately sprang ashore, as did Paulet, the elderly man hunched against the rain.

Elizabeth's face was set in icy anger. When her gentleman usher climbed out and reached a hand down to help her to shore, Elizabeth glared at him from under the canopy, then folded her arms and sat still.

He looked at her, perplexed, the rain streaking his beard and matting his hair to his head. "Your Grace, we must go in," he tried.

Elizabeth set her teeth and remained under the canvas. Paulet put a fold of his cloak over his nose, looking irritated that his task of bringing the princess to the Tower might result in a bad cold. He was nearly seventy years old, far too elderly for capers in the rain.

Sussex set his mouth. "Your Grace, if you do not leave the boat, I can give the guards instruction to lift you free. I do not wish to do so; I do not wish anyone to lay hands on your person."

Elizabeth said nothing. She looked at Sussex with all the fury she could muster, letting it spill beyond him onto Paulet. Then without a word to either of us ladies, she scrambled to her feet and launched herself up onto the stone wharf.

"Here landeth as true a subject, being prisoner, as ever landed here," she said through her teeth. She sat herself down on the stone steps, full in the rain, and folded her arms again.

I climbed out of the boat, my limbs cold and stiff. It was a black day, quite literally. The rain pelted from dark clouds, and afternoon didn't seem likely to be brighter than the morning.

I expected Sussex to growl at her to move, but he stood very quietly, waiting for her. *Hedging his bets,* I thought again. The other councilors waiting with him copied his stance. Only the gentleman usher, one of Elizabeth's own men, seemed distressed.

"Your Grace, you must not sit here in the rain," he said again. He was nearly as elderly as Paulet, with a wife and children and six granddaughters. I knew him as a gentle person, and now his kind eyes leaked tears. "Please, Your Grace, this is a bad place."

"Better here than a worse place," Elizabeth countered.

Her gentleman continued to cry. Elizabeth looked at him in exasperation, and then she sighed and nodded. Perhaps she took pity on her gentleman; I could not tell. Elizabeth could be impatient with even the kindest people; then again, she could soften her heart and do everything in the world for them.

She held out her hand for me, and I and the gentleman usher helped her to her feet. She flung her cloak about her in a dramatic gesture and ordered Sussex to proceed. Behind us, Paulet sneezed.

We walked along cold, wet paths that skirted the ancient stone walls, the way lined with yeomen of the guard. A few pulled off their hats as she passed. "God save Your Grace," one said. Elizabeth acknowledged him with a gracious nod.

The accommodations to which we were escorted were bleak, though not the rat-infested dungeons I feared. It was terrible enough, plain rooms that were warmed for us but nonetheless dreary. The ladies Elizabeth had been allowed to bring would be prisoners with her, not permitted to leave for fear we'd conspire with outsiders to rescue her. Mary had sent a few of her own ladies to wait on her as well, and to keep an eye on us.

Mary's women waited in the long chamber that was to be Elizabeth's, near a bed hung with heavy curtains. Elizabeth looked around, not with despair, but with anger.

"Did Jane Grey stay here?" she demanded of Sussex.

"No, Your Grace."

Jane had been housed in the palace when I'd been sent to watch her, but she'd been moved to the half-timbered L-shaped Lieutenant's Lodging after that. From the windows of this room we could glimpse a corner of Tower Green, where Jane had met her death.

Elizabeth refused to look out the windows. "You may leave us," she said to Sussex, a royal personage dismissing him.

She turned away from the retreating gentlemen so she would not have to see them refuse to bow to her again. She winced slightly when the heavy door of the outer chamber closed and the keys turned in the locks, but I was the only one who noticed.

❧

WE STAYED IN the Tower nearly two months to the day. During that time I saw few save the ladies waiting on Elizabeth and the elderly gentleman usher with whom I was allowed to run the occasional errand, inside the Tower, of course. Anything that was needed from outside the Tower—food, linens, and the like—was brought carefully by men loyal to Mary and passed to the ladies Mary had sent.

I did my best to be guileless and try to find out what was happening in the outside world. Pretending to be no more than distressed that I was locked away with Elizabeth, I managed to pry some information from the ladies and gentlemen who were allowed to go back and forth from the Tower.

First was that Wyatt refused to say anything against Elizabeth, even when he was promised pardon for admitting that everything had been instigated by her, or even known by her. Wyatt stubbornly would not speak. Neither would any of the others so questioned.

Second, the most damning evidence the Council had against Elizabeth was the belief that she had been preparing to remove herself to her house at Donnington, and that she had been fortifying it. This Elizabeth denied at her preliminary questioning, pretending to forget she even had a residence at Donnington. *Of course she had not forgotten,* I mused. William Cecil oversaw all her properties, and she consulted with him often, asking question after question about all her estates. She was careful of her money and properties, and we all knew it.

She denied then that she'd decided to go to Donnington, and no one could come up with a scrap of evidence to prove she had.

So what if Sir James Croft and Thomas Wyatt had advised her to go? she asked over and over. She had no idea why they'd wanted her to, and she'd thanked them for her concern and stayed put at Ashridge. She stuck with that story, and the Council could get no more out of her.

I began to hope. If the Council could not come up with evidence against Elizabeth, they would never bring her to trial. Why try her before a jury who might acquit her? The juries seemed lenient with the conspirators as it was. Thomas Wyatt and Suffolk had been the obvious ringleaders, and they were condemned—Suffolk already dead. Courtenay, who did not hide the fact that he'd hoped to be King one way or another, was in the Tower, but Bishop Gardiner's friendship kept him from trial. After all, Gardiner argued, Courtenay had not actually *done* anything.

Other conspirators, such as Nicholas Throckmorton—who I knew had been in it up to his neck—were pardoned. James Colby as well eluded capture and no one named him, for which I fervently thanked God.

I held on to hope through the long weeks, and on the dreadful April day on which Wyatt was executed, he declared on the scaffold that neither Elizabeth nor Courtenay had anything to do with his plots. I knew it to be a lie, of course, but Mary could do nothing about it. The condemned man's last words had done much to keep the Council's actions toward Elizabeth cautious.

I knew Elizabeth's fortune had changed when Mary sent word that Elizabeth was to be moved to better accommodation, though still within the Tower. The change scarce put Elizabeth in a better mood. Elizabeth expected every day to be dragged to trial, for Mary to have manufactured evidence, for a scaffold to be built for her. She wavered between fear and anger, choosing the latter to relieve her feelings.

As we waited, spring days lengthened and warmed, the chill dank of winter waning. Elizabeth was allowed to walk in the privy garden, supervised by Mary's ladies, of course. We strolled slowly, soaking up as much of the outdoor air as possible before we had to return to the rooms inside. As the conspirators, one by one, were let go or ignored, Elizabeth walked among the pruned hedges with a lighter step. Daffodils and crocuses burst up through the soil, perhaps a promise of coming freedom?

One morning a little girl came to Elizabeth and handed her flowers. Elizabeth bent down to her and smiled sweetly, calling her a dear child. Mary's ladies hovered behind them in disapproval, and a guard came over to see what they did.

While they were thus distracted, I walked to the far end of the garden and out through a gate to a little walk between two towers. On another side of this narrow passage lay another gate, behind which a dark-haired handsome man waited impatiently.

"God grant you good health, Mistress Rousell," Robert Dudley said to me. "And how is our princess this fine morning?"

"She is very well. How is your good wife?"

Dudley laughed, sounding as merry as though he'd not been held prisoner here for many months. "I have not seen her, and she is usually sickly, poor thing. Whereas our princess is robust."

"She is."

Robert smiled again. I remembered the passionate kiss he and Elizabeth had exchanged the night before his wedding and wondered if he was thinking of it, too.

"The weather warms," he said.

"Indeed." I chafed with impatience, wanting to speak of something more interesting than the weather.

"A mutual friend speaks highly of you," Dudley went on.

Assuming he meant Colby, I kept silent. Dudley was far more informed than I at this time. I had directed a few messages out, but none had come *in*. Would there be a rescue, another rebellion, or had Elizabeth's followers abandoned her?

Dudley read my expression. "Knowledge is dangerous."

"I dislike speaking in riddles, my lord."

He laughed again. His dark hair was trimmed and neat, his small beard framing a sensual mouth, his body lithe and well built. I could not blame females for being captivated by his handsomeness, although his nose, in my opinion, was rather on the bulbous side. But I found his charm overblown. I preferred plain speaking and sense to extravagant compliments and clever witticisms.

Elizabeth was no fool. She would not have liked Robert if he hadn't been learned and hadn't had intelligence to match her own. Still I could not help being glad that Robert had already married and could have no husbandly domination over Elizabeth. A man in a flirtation was the slave; in marriage, he was master.

The ironic gleam in his eyes made me wonder if he knew what I was thinking. I realized I'd been staring at him, assessing him most carefully, and I blinked to erase my expression.

"I have nothing to speak of apart from the weather," he said and gave me a smirk.

"No message for the princess?" I asked, voice low.

"None at all. Save to greet her, fellow prisoner, and to think of what joyous days we will have when we are past this place." He winked. "That is, if we walk out *our* way, not Mary's."

"That is nothing more than you have told me before."

"What do you expect of me, Mistress Rousell? That I send you ten written messages that rescue is at hand, naming all those who will be involved? Perhaps a map she may follow as she runs before Mary's army? Nay, my dear lady, look not to me for those."

A lady of my station—a mere gentlewoman—could hardly admonish a duke's son, but I wanted to scold him for his flippancy, maybe tweak his nose to relieve my disappointment.

"I am a plain woman," I said. "With plain understanding."

"You are hardly that," he drawled, and dragged an impertinent gaze down my body. "But if you insist, I will speak plainly." *At last.* "She is to do nothing. Sentiment changes; she is liked. Our mutual friend has other ideas. You are to stay close to her." Dudley smiled again, his haughty face lightening into the charm other ladies loved so well. "Is that plain enough? Or shall I write it in my blood?"

"Plain enough, my lord. I thank you."

His smile died, and he straightened. "Excellent. Now go back, Mistress Rousell, before you are missed."

He turned and walked away, not bothering to say farewell. Another reason I did not like him—he expressed courtesy as it pleased him, only toward those he wished to please. It was not me he wanted, but her.

�֎

IT WAS NOT until May that Fortune stepped in to help us, and then in an odd way. One morning a man called Henry Bedingfield came to the Tower to take charge of Elizabeth, and soldiers came with him.

Sir Henry Bedingfield had a large face; a long, wide nose that he tended to peer down; and close-set eyes. His long mustache drooped into his beard, giving him a perpetually woeful look. Not that Bedingfield smiled much. He regarded Elizabeth in sorrow, clearly wondering how a young woman could turn against her sister and her Queen, and told her he had come to take charge of her as his prisoner.

Elizabeth had measure of him before their first interview was over. "The Tower is being fortified," Elizabeth declared, staring Bedingfield down. "Am I so dangerous a prisoner? All this for one weak woman?"

Bedingfield, on his knees before her, took her statement at face value. I had watched Elizabeth fence and win with Tyrwhitt over the Seymour affair, and Tyrwhitt had been a much worthier opponent than Bedingfield. This match would be ugly.

"You are too humble, Your Grace," he answered. "But no, the guards have nothing to do with you."

His eyes shifted, and I knew he lied. Elizabeth knew, too. From what I could gather from the cryptic hints Robert Dudley gave me whenever I could see him at the garden gate, Elizabeth's prisoner status had changed. I could not discern—and Robert seemed not to know—whether that change was for good or ill.

"I have asked Her Majesty, my sister, whether I might walk in the great chamber," Elizabeth continued. "Have you brought her answer?"

"I have not had word on this." Bedingfield's eyes turned upward as though he were mentally reading from a long list. "But she does forbid you to speak with anyone in the gardens who are not your attendants."

"But I do not."

Again the eye shift, again reading from the list inside his head. "You speak on occasion to a little girl named Alison who is the porter's daughter."

Elizabeth's brows climbed. "The child? Who kindly brings me wildflowers because she thinks me beautiful?"

"Such an easy messenger to bring you news from the outside world."

Elizabeth gave him a look of lively contempt. "A little girl—a messenger—from whom? Thomas Wyatt? He is dead and can dream up no more plots. Edward Courtenay? He is watched most closely, I believe, by his beloved Bishop Gardiner and the Queen herself. There is no one to send me messages, Sir Henry. I am alone."

At the dramatic statement, Bedingfield cleared his throat. "Nevertheless, you must not speak to anyone again. The child's mother has been warned to keep her close."

"Dear God in heaven." Elizabeth sent the pretty vase of crocuses on a table next to her crashing to the floor. Bedingfield, stuck on his knees, could not scramble out of the way of the water and flying porcelain that rained across his person.

Elizabeth raged. "An innocent child of seven years as a conspirator. It is scarce to be believed. Let me write a letter to my sister, I beg of you."

Bedingfield wiped his beard, and shards of porcelain tinkled to the floor. "Out of the question, Your Grace."

"Out of whose question? Mine? Or yours? Or hers?"

"It cannot be done, Your Grace. I have not leave to give you permission."

She glared at him. "You must ask her leave, then, and her permission to give you leave to give me permission."

I watched Bedingfield's eyes move as he tried to unravel this. Elizabeth sent him a smirk that held no humor.

"I will inform Her Grace," he said at last.

"See that you do."

When Bedingfield finally left her alone, Elizabeth fumed and threw things that we ladies dutifully retrieved. Her anger pleased me, however, because I knew she hadn't given in to despair. Mary's preoccupation with and suspicion of the poor innocent child pleased me as well, not because I had any desire for the child to be hurt, but because it meant none had noticed Eloise Rousell dashing away to whisper to Robert Dudley in a grille between the gardens.

Elizabeth's walks continued, her guard watched her very closely, the little girl was kept away, and everyone ignored me. I continued to pass Dudley's messages—helpful and otherwise— to Elizabeth with none the wiser.

18

ON THE NINETEENTH of May, a great lot of armed guards filled the halls and courtyards of the Tower, alarming us not a little. Bedingfield appeared and gave the peremptory command that Elizabeth was to come with him, her ladies to pack her things and follow.

Elizabeth paled until her brows stood out in fiery red lines. "Am I to have no trial, then? Is Jane's scaffold still there, waiting for me?"

"You are to be moved from the Tower," Bedingfield said, tight lipped. "I am to accompany you far from London, there to live in a house at Her Majesty's pleasure."

"It is a trick," Elizabeth insisted. "You will get me out into the country, and your men will assassinate me there."

"I assure Your Grace," Bedingfield began. His tone and manner were anything but reassuring, and Elizabeth turned her back on him and would not let him finish.

I wondered if Mary *would* have the audacity to kill Elizabeth outright. She would not dare, I thought. If assassins knifed

Elizabeth in the night, all the world would guess that Mary had ordered her death. Elizabeth's popularity had not waned with her sojourn in the Tower, and had even, if Robert Dudley's information was to be believed, increased. He told me stories of men sentenced to the pillory for declaring loudly that Elizabeth was innocent, of people everywhere voicing concerns about Elizabeth's health.

Assassins in the night would only fuel more conspiracies to topple Mary, though I scarce could guess whom they would try to put on the throne in her place—the weak-kneed Courtenay? I had also heard via Dudley that Mary had tried again to disinherit Elizabeth but her Council had strongly advised her against it. This time, unlike her stubbornness over her upcoming marriage, she had listened.

And the Council's hesitancy, I thought, was why we were hustled into a barge that moved upriver to Richmond this fine May day.

For my part, I was happy to have the sunshine on my face and the wind in my hair, no matter where we were going. Even the presence of Bedingfield's men when we disembarked, a hundred of them, all armed, could not erase the feeling of freedom. I never wanted to see the Tower of London again.

That I was allowed to accompany Elizabeth at all had been difficult to finagle. Mary had wanted every one of Elizabeth's ladies dismissed and replaced with Mary's own, but she had relented at the last minute and allowed her to keep three, as well as three gentlemen. Elizabeth had begged for me to accompany her on the journey itself, saying she had need of a seamstress who knew her well. Again, because of my mother's marriage to a staunch Catholic, Mary agreed.

So the rest of Elizabeth's household was turned away with

many tears, and she and I, Bedingfield and his outriders, began the journey from Richmond north and west.

✣

THE ROYAL ESTATE we reached after five days of traveling reeked of isolation and mildew. Woodstock was a huge place, rebuilt by Elizabeth's grandfather, but run down now, as neither Mary nor Edward had been inclined to stay there.

Elizabeth surveyed the mess in some dismay, then briskly asked if it was to be their last stopping place.

"Indeed, Your Grace," Bedingfield told her. He surveyed the courtyard and the enormous house with some of the same trepidation. In the outside world of Oxfordshire, through which we had just traveled, spring had arrived, with lambing and flowers and greening of fields. Here at Woodstock the dark and forbidding air of winter still clung to the wood and stone buildings.

Elizabeth gave it a grim look, then demanded to be taken to her quarters.

✣

"I LOVE TO dance." Elizabeth threw her arms out and twirled around the room.

I chuckled because I knew she did not mean it in the literal sense. We had settled into life at Woodstock, May blending into a warm June and then moving into hot July. Elizabeth walked the unkempt gardens, read and studied, played tunes on the virginals, and had her daily verbal fencing match with her gaoler Bedingfield. I enjoyed watching her feint with him this way and that, and I knew she quite despised him.

Bedingfield knew it, too. His hesitancy annoyed her, as did his mulelike stubbornness in writing almost daily to Mary for instruction and to note to her anything Elizabeth said. Elizabeth knew he'd never be swayed to her side, but at the same time his obvious reluctance to upset her because she might become Queen someday irritated her.

"He tries to play both sides," she complained. "I would respect him much more if he were stern with me and meant it."

"Would you listen to him?" I asked.

"Of course not," she answered, and we broke into peals of laughter.

Our laughter was always strained, however. Elizabeth still worried that she had been brought out here to be killed, far away from court and prying eyes. From what we knew from covert messages, Mary's advisors had strongly warned her against such an act, but advisors could die or be dismissed and replaced with those who told Mary what she wanted to hear.

All of Elizabeth's ladies had been dismissed, save me and two others, but we'd had to be deemed "safe" first by Mary. Aunt Kat herself was under house arrest far from us; Elizabeth Sandes had been summarily packed off and fled to the Continent, along with others who were considered to have too much influence on Elizabeth. Anyone, like Elizabeth Sandes, who loved the Reformed religion and enjoyed waxing sarcastic about the Catholic faith was immediately dispatched.

But while Elizabeth's former ladies and gentlemen could decry the return to Catholicism, they could do nothing to prevent it. Mary had already made Parliament obedient on the subject, although the wealthy men in that body and on her Council who had eagerly hugged to themselves the monastic lands doled out by King Henry balked at returning them. Accept the Catholic faith? Yes, if we must. Return our lands and wealth to monasteries? A fervent *no*.

Queen Mary did not always get her way.

In mid-July, I received a message, delivered via one of Elizabeth's gentlemen, who took me aside in the garden and told me that James Colby would wait for me at a woodcutter's hut not far from the grounds.

"How am I to get away?" I whispered, mindful of one of Mary's appointed ladies approaching.

"You will know when to go," the gentleman answered. "Linger in the garden tomorrow when Her Grace takes her afternoon walk."

Mary's lady, a tall woman with a beaked nose, swooped down on us and told me there was mending to do. She gave Elizabeth's gentleman a severe look, which he returned blandly.

All the next day Elizabeth was in foul temper. She'd at last gained permission to write directly to Mary, and had received a reply that said, more or less, that Elizabeth was ungrateful for the bounty Mary had given her and that she should be more humble. Furthermore, Elizabeth was not to write again. Elizabeth fumed, and our garden walk was swift as she strode out her anger.

I still wondered how I'd escape the grounds. Elizabeth's gentlemen were allowed to come and go, but we ladies were prisoners with her. But I lingered as instructed in the garden after Elizabeth and her ladies had stormed back into the house, pretending I needed a bit more air. As I ostensibly studied flowers that covered a hedge in a riot of color, I heard a commotion at the gate of the outer courtyard.

I skirted the house to see what happened, taking care not to be noticed by Bedingfield's guards. A young man who looked vaguely familiar stood in the courtyard surrounded by armed men. A red-faced Bedingfield interrogated him at the top of his voice.

"Books?" he shouted. "What business have you got to bring Her Grace books? There will be messages in them, I'll wager."

"Indeed, no," the young man replied haughtily. I recognized him now as the son of Thomas Parry's wife by her first husband. Young Fortescue was presently reading at one of the colleges at Oxford not far from here. "They are tomes my stepfather thought Her Grace would want. She is a learned woman."

Bedingfield gave him a look, then turned to his guards. "Search them, and search him, for any messages."

The guards looked unhappy, dipping thick fingers into the books, grumbling as they did as they were bid. John Fortescue complained about having to turn his clothes inside out like a common thief. Under cover of the noise, I slipped back to the garden and out a small gate that had been unbolted for me.

I found the abandoned cottage not far up a woodcutter's track but deep under a canopy of forest. The tiny house boasted one window, whose shutter, worn and paint stripped, looked as though it should have hung askew, but someone had fastened it quite firmly over the window. Likewise the door had obviously been broken once, but its hinges were newly mended.

The rest of the house was ramshackle: thatch sliding off to leave patches like a balding man, whitewash now gray, bricks crumbling. Seedlings surrounded the house as did undergrowth, nature reclaiming what man had abandoned.

I stepped into the dim interior and waited for my eyes to adjust to the gloom, but I appeared to be the only one there.

"Close the door."

I stifled a shriek as Colby's voice came out of the darkness, but I obeyed and pushed the door shut.

"If I am caught, Bedingfield will write of it in great detail to Mary," I said.

He gave me the hint of a smile. "Surely a young woman slipping into the woods might only be keeping a tryst."

"You do not know Bedingfield. Should Elizabeth sneeze he

writes the Council to inquire whether they think it a code. All her friends are suspect and even some of her enemies."

"I tease you, Mistress Rousell. It is put about that Elizabeth's enemies might think to infiltrate her ladies by flirting, but none will dare try it with you."

I thought a moment as I laid my summer cloak over the back of a chair. "That is vaguely insulting."

"It should not be. The words mean you are shrewder than most and see through guile disguised as flattery. Your head is not easily turned."

"I had no idea I was such a paragon."

"The primary source of the idea is Robert Dudley," James said. "He finds it difficult to take your measure."

"Perhaps because I've taken *his* measure. He knows his own charm and uses it to his advantage."

"When his advantage runs parallel to my needs, I concede him his charm and let him use it."

"I grant that," I answered dryly. "Is it law that conspirators have to love one another?"

"Decidedly not." He grinned at me, looking like an ordinary person when he did that.

"What are we conspiring today?" I asked.

"Nothing. We only wish to know how Elizabeth fares. Bedingfield, we hear, is a strict master."

"He attempts to be. Elizabeth is far more intelligent than he and plays upon it. I've seen him clutch his head trying to decipher what she has said to him. She speaks in roundabout ways, trying to wheedle him into permitting her to do more than Mary would like. It is a good source of amusement, where we have few."

"I heard that she was cheered on her journey here, given many gifts as she passed through villages," James said. "That everywhere there is rejoicing that the princess is free."

"Yes, and I wish they would cease. It must fuel Mary's fear of her."

"It does."

" 'Tis a strange imprisonment," I went on, idly pacing the little room. "Elizabeth's every move and every word is reported, but her gentlemen freely visit Thomas Parry in the village, where he is come to oversee Elizabeth's coffers."

"Bedingfield's own fault," Colby shrugged. "Mary gnashes her teeth every time she receives a letter from Bedingfield, and she receives one nearly every day."

"Good." Mary on her righteous high horse deserved to be annoyed.

"Every plotter in the land goes to The Bull to see Parry," Colby said. "So much so that they will ruin all if they are not careful. Every day a new idea is dreamed up for rescuing Elizabeth, but none so far have proved plausible. The gathered gentlemen enjoy a good talk of treason."

"Do they endanger her?" I asked in alarm.

"They are hotheads. I hope I bring a measure of reason to their discussions. We want to win in the end, not simply stir up trouble. Parry brings a measure of reason, too—he knows that anything planned must be paid for in real money. He has at least kept Elizabeth's estates running smoothly and her tenants paying—though I imagine she'd turn pale at the state of the books."

I didn't smile. "She is frustrated not being able to attend to her own business. Bedingfield spends most of his time with his brow permanently puckered. Poor man. Mary could have chosen a shrewder gaoler."

"Not really. Bedingfield will do exactly as he is told, no more, no less. He will not be won over by Elizabeth and betray Mary, and Mary knows it."

I made a derisive laugh. "That is obvious. Turning against a monarch takes imagination."

Colby went silent a moment, then said, "Philip arrives in a few days' time."

"So the marriage will take place." I had not doubted it would; the servants Mary had appointed to Woodstock talked of it and wished they could attend the wedding. I had nursed some hope that Mary would see that the only person in her country who desired the marriage was herself, but I'd finally relinquished that hope.

"She purports to love him," Colby said.

"Love him? She's never met him."

"But he has written, he has sent a portrait, and she is convinced he has esteem for her that will develop into love. But the rest of us know that the Emperor only wishes to secure England in his ongoing fight with France. That and to use it as a wall against the German heretics. Charles the Fifth thinks an alliance with England worth sacrificing his best-loved son."

I sat down on a rickety chair, sighing. The thought of England, having struggled to stand on its own and putting its tongue out at the world when it did, reduced to a satellite kingdom of the Empire made me weary. I knew that world politics did not always benefit the ordinary people, but I had thought England different. Here, if the people did not like the monarch, they could and did say so forcefully, as they had rejected Jane Grey and rallied around Mary—never mind that Edward had assigned Jane to the throne himself.

They had once declared themselves tired of the Yorkist and Lancastrian battles by letting the grandson of an upstart Welshman take over the throne and end the bloody struggle. Now the Empire would create an heir through Mary and Philip, and England would belong to it.

I clenched my fists. "I will not have it."

Colby's sober countenance dissolved as he chuckled. "You are a spirited fighter, Mistress Rousell. A seamstress against the mightiness of the Holy Roman Empire."

"Do not tease me. You would not have asked me to come here if you did not need my help to stop the marriage."

"We cannot stop the marriage short of assassinating Philip, and such a thing would bring the wrath of the Emperor upon us. I am not certain we could survive a direct fight at the moment, even if France came to our aid. It is precarious. The only thing we can do is keep Mary and Philip apart as much as possible and hope Mary does not conceive an heir."

"That is all?" I leapt to my feet. "Sit by the fire and hope she does not become with child?"

"The Spanish already know they are not welcome here. They will want to stay as far away as possible. Mary will die childless and Elizabeth will inherit. Elizabeth likes loyalty, Eloise. She will reward well those who stand by her."

I studied him. "Is that why you do this? For the hope of reward?"

"Not the only reason. I do it for the good of England."

My eyes narrowed. "Many who say that they work for the common good or the good of the people often mean they work for the good of themselves. Why do you so much want Elizabeth to succeed?"

His expression revealed nothing. "I have told you. To keep England free from Spain and from domination by Rome."

"But why? Why should you wish this? Why do you hate Mary so much and her Catholicism? Or do you simply fear Spanish food?"

He did not smile at my witticism. His hands curled up at his sides, his blue eyes tight. "If the heresy laws are reinstated and

Rome and the Inquisition take root here, things will be very bad, Eloise."

"That fact is remotely obvious. I do not wish to be dragged off to be tortured because I recited the Paternoster in English. Which Bedingfield would immediately report to Mary, of course."

"Mary chose Elizabeth's gaoler well—stubborn and blind at the same time."

"You are wandering from the subject," I said.

We were both silent a moment. A crack of light from the shuttered window touched his red hair. By his stance and his hair he looked very Tudor-like—Elizabeth's hair was red and gold, Mary's dark but tinged with red as well.

"Why do you wish to know all my reasons?" he asked softly. "Suffice that they are good ones. I want Catholicism to stay away from England."

"I haven't quite decided I trust you. I know nothing about you, not who your people were or why you did not remain in Shropshire puttering about your estate. I do not see in you the feverish obsession of a fanatic, and so I must wonder what you gain by helping Elizabeth."

We squared off, his face red with the effort of holding in his temper.

"What must I do to gain your trust?" he asked, voice strained.

"Tell me the truth. You are not an idealist, like Sir Thomas Wyatt. You are not a cocksure courtier looking for adventure, like Robert Dudley. You do not have ruthless aspirations to rule through a puppet queen, like Northumberland."

He avoided my gaze. "You ask too many questions."

"Because you refuse to answer I will have to give you my guesses, and you will not like them."

"I have no interest in your guesses."

I came to him and curled my fingers around a lock of his red hair. "Tudor red," I said.

He moved impatiently. "Many a man in England can have red hair. It is not unusual."

I touched his chin. "You stay clean shaven, and you do not put yourself forward. You are taller than he was and quite slim, but when you are out of temper . . ." I drew back. "I should take care with that, were I you."

His breathing was hoarse. "You know nothing, Eloise."

"You cannot trust me with this secret? You trust me with so much, and not, I believe, because Robert Dudley assured you about me."

"My secrets are dangerous. Everyone who knows this secret is dead but me."

I remained standing close to him. His body was warm, his voice deep, and I placed my hand on his chest to feel his heart beat beneath it. "I must know one thing—do you plan to over-throw her or rule through her? Or blackmail her to keep silent that Henry has a living son?"

The room grew very quiet. When he spoke, Colby's voice was deadly soft. "If any of that were my intention, I would kill you before I left this house."

My throat tightened. "Then the fact that I remain alive means you have no designs on the throne?"

"None whatsoever. Why should I?"

"For one thing, Mary would not be Queen and preparing to marry Philip."

He shook his head, and the tension in him eased slightly. "I would have to fight hard for it, and even if I won I could not prove my claim. I was never acknowledged. My true mother was a milkmaid of Gloucestershire. I was taken off her hands and given to the Colbys of Shropshire to raise, and I never saw my mother again. She is dead. The Colbys are dead. And Henry is dead."

"Such difficulties never stopped men with lesser claim."

"Aye, 'tis so," Colby said. "But I have seen those who surround these pretenders to the throne—I have no wish to be jerked and manipulated by ruthless men for their own gain, and then executed when their plans go awry."

"You have some inkling how Elizabeth feels, then."

He grasped my shoulders. "Why do you think I've appointed you her guardian? To keep her safe and distant from the plotters, to keep her head on her shoulders. You are a good watchdog, Eloise."

"A fine compliment; I thank you. Does she know?"

"I have told you—everyone who knew is dead. Save for you."

I knew James perfectly capable of strangling me and leaving me on the floor, foolish Eloise who ran off into the woods alone to meet a stranger. It would be my own fault. I'd allowed myself to get caught up in the excitement of the rivalry between Elizabeth and Mary, the pride that I had been chosen to watch over her, my exultation that I'd come up with the scheme of using different kinds of stitching to convey messages out of Elizabeth's house.

Not only that, I'd much enjoyed meeting a handsome gentleman like James Colby in out-of-the-way corners. I knew he had no lover, because I'd have heard the gossip of it, nor any woman with whom he liked to flirt. The only woman to whom he spoke intimately was me, and I'd pretended to myself that his interest in me went beyond taking care of Elizabeth.

I was a fool. I let my ridiculous fantasies go and met his gaze squarely.

"No one would listen to the prattling of Eloise. Even if I blabbed far and wide that you were Henry's bastard, no one would believe me."

"Maybe not at first, but they'd start to look twice at me and to wonder. I am in your power now. What must I do to ensure you will keep my secret?"

"Nothing," I said. I put sincerity in every word. "I would never, ever betray you to a soul."

He looked perplexed. "Why not? Knowledge like this could do much for you."

I smoothed his cloak and picked up my own. "I will not tell you why not. That will be *my* secret."

I think he guessed, because he stopped me to press a brief, warm kiss to my lips. It was a sincere kiss, a kiss of gratitude, not an offering for my silence.

"Be well, Eloise," he whispered.

I told him I would take care to be, and departed.

19

"I AM VERY ill, Master Bedingfield," Elizabeth said in a hard voice. "This is why I am silent at Mass."

"But you are not silent," Bedingfield said, his drooping mustache bouncing with his words. "Only when prayers are said for the Queen."

"Perhaps that is when my headaches flare," she returned. "I do have them, sir. In fact, I have one now and must lie down. Mass must be sung without me, today."

Bedingfield looked more mournful than ever and scuttled away to write of the conversation to Mary.

Love was a strange thing, I mused as I went about my duties. When one is very selfish, love is about how the object of desire makes one feel. A cruel woman could make a courtier her slave and be kind to him only when he pleased her.

A less selfish love wants the happiness that person can give but wants to make the desired one happy as well. A mutual pleasing, as between a fond husband and wife. More selfless still is love that expects no return, a giving to keep the beloved safe or to ensure their happiness. This love could be good, as a mother to her children or a daughter to an elderly father, or it could turn dangerous and slide into obsession.

I did wonder as much as Colby why I wanted to keep his secret, why I, too, did not want to see him used by ambitious men or beheaded for the blood in his veins. I knew only that I wanted him to keep safe, and I admired him for his sensible acceptance of his position. If he'd been greedy and ambitious, he'd have tried to sail in and claim he was Henry's son upon Edward's death despite the difficulties he outlined.

He had not, I could see, because he did not want the throne. He wanted nothing to do with it, but he wanted Elizabeth to have it. Why he favored her over Mary I still was not certain, and one day I would make him tell me. He could just as easily have decided to throw his loyalty to Mary, because she was his sister as much as Elizabeth.

I thought of love for another reason that day that Bedingfield admonished Elizabeth. In Winchester, Mary had married herself to Philip of Spain.

I learned the details of the wedding and its splendor a few days later from a reliable source—John Ashley. He wrote to Parry, who in turn gave the letter to Colby, who in turn let me read it at the little cottage in the woods. Because I was searched whenever I returned from my walks outside the gates, I read the letter and returned it to Colby, remembering it to tell Elizabeth.

Philip had arrived in Southampton with great pomp and pageantry and progressed to meet Mary in Winchester. The Spaniards, I heard, were haughty and sneering, though John Ashley, a more charitable man, declared they were no more so than any other aristocrats. Philip, their prince, was handsome and fair-haired and supple of limb. Rumor had it that he put his beautiful body to much use in the bed of any lady who would have him, but his looks also made him regal and every inch a king consort.

He made it clear quickly that although he was glad to pull heretic England back into the fold of the mother Church, he would not oppose the fact that Mary was England's ruler. This much pleased the bishops and lords in Parliament and the Council, who had only at last given in to the marriage with that stipulation. Philip also was in the process of setting up tournaments, with all their pageantry, so that the lords of the land could compete as they had done in Henry's time.

Clever, I thought as I read Ashley's letter. *He knows he's not wanted here and softens the blow.*

Mary had emerged from their chamber the next morning a very blushing bride. Uncharitable onlookers claimed Philip pale and red eyed from having to fortify himself with much wine against the onerous task.

I read of the consummation with a qualm. A pregnancy would weaken Elizabeth's position and strengthen Philip's. The only hope was that Mary, in her late thirties, was far too old to carry a child. Even much younger women could have difficulties, so there was a chance she would not carry the child to term.

The royal couple was, at the time of John Ashley's letter, now traveling to London where they would continue their quest to pull England firmly under the dominance of Rome.

"And so it begins," I sighed as I handed Colby the letter. "Are you still willing to wait and see whether Mary conceives?"

"It is the best thing we can do," he answered. "For now."

I chafed at having to sit still, but I could think of no other course. He kissed me again before I left, but that day I was too distracted to take much pleasure in kisses.

When I returned to the palace, my basket and cloak and pockets were searched, as usual, and as usual, they found nothing. I went to report to Elizabeth what John had written, and found her in another towering rage. Bedingfield, rigid on his knees, regarded her from across the room.

"He refuses to return my Bible to me," Elizabeth flashed as I entered. "Can you credit such a thing? Shall I not read and study God's Word?"

"I assure you, Your Grace, you may have a Bible. Your Grace reads the Latin so well, I am certain it will be a joy for you to read the Word in that tongue."

Elizabeth screamed, fists at her sides. Bedingfield fled.

※

THE CHILL OF autumn gave way to winter. In November we heard, openly through Bedingfield—covertly though Parry— that Mary was with child. Elizabeth grew quiet as Bedingfield read the official dispatch, her face pale.

Cardinal Pole, in the meantime, returned from exile, read out the Pope's forgiveness to the nation of England for its heresy. England, apparently, was not to blame for its error in leaving the Church of Rome, never mind that two kings had led it astray.

So at one stroke, we were Catholic again. Mary had her handsome husband, her Church restored, and an heir inside her body. Her joy was complete.

"Meanwhile," James Colby said when we next met, "the rest of us wait and watch."

"She will have her child," I said unhappily, "and what will become of Elizabeth? And me?"

"There is rumor of a plot to make sure Mary miscarries the child. A poison that will cause her to lose it."

I blanched. "How awful. Is it true?"

"I do not know." Colby hitched his leg over the corner of the table. "It is not my plot, and it is rumor only. 'Twould be most difficult to get near enough to her in any case."

"I must draw the line at child murder," I said. "Even if such a child might be the death of us all."

"It might not be."

At his tone, I looked up, interested. "Why do you say so?"

"Philip is trying to persuade Mary to be more lenient on Elizabeth. That if Mary has a child there is no need to disinherit Elizabeth. That even if Mary does not have an heir, it is best to keep Elizabeth as a possible holder of the crown—Reformed Church or no."

"Philip, pawn of the Holy Roman Emperor, prudent?" I asked with a smile. "Who would have thought?"

"Better Elizabeth than Mary of Scotland, who is next after Elizabeth. Scotland is in the firm grip of France, and young Mary seems to be an easily manipulated person. She would make England become French, too."

"Besieged on all sides," I said.

"For now. Philip's presence keeps conspiracies at bay, because he has the might of the Emperor Charles behind him. But we shall see what the future brings."

I sighed, rose, and shook out my skirts. "I see nothing but bleakness for now. Please send my love to Kat Ashley."

"I will." He pressed my hand and kissed my cheek. "Godspeed, Eloise."

By tacit agreement we had not spoken again of his parentage, but it was there between us, an unseen specter. He still did not trust me completely, but as with Mary's pregnancy, he would wait and see what happened. My knowing was dangerous to him, but then he had passed himself off as the Colbys' son all these years—why would anyone disbelieve this now?

I had no idea what he meant to do. The games of intrigue were growing too deep for me.

❈

ALL THAT DARK winter at Woodstock we waited, uncertain of the future. The house was cold and the roof leaked. Fuel for some reason was difficult to obtain, and I had no fire in the room in which I slept. I admit I purposely ingratiated myself with Elizabeth in order that she might invite me to spend nights in her bedchamber, where a fire at least burned.

In London, in comfort, Mary made happy plans for her child to come. That she was quick with child, she had no doubt, and the news was broadcast to all corners of England.

Advent came and then Christmas. About that time I heard, through Parry who had heard it from John Ashley, that my sharp-tongued grandmother had died. I had never been close to her, but she'd taken my side against my silly mother and her pompous second husband, and I mourned her. Because of my grandmother, I'd been sent to Aunt Kat to be brought up, and Elizabeth had become fond of me, which had led to my present predicament, of course. But I had been ever grateful to the old lady for handing me over to Aunt Kat, with whom I'd been happy. Now my grandmother was gone, another sadness in this sad time.

The priests at chapel in Woodstock said many long Masses, which were supposed to be festive celebrations, but which we found tedious in the extreme. Elizabeth sat in sullen silence as incense wafted through the cold chapel to choke our throats and burn our eyes.

Spring came not too soon for me, with Candlemas and then the quietness of Lent. We waited for news of Mary's lying in, and while those around us prayed for her safe delivery, Elizabeth again sat in silence.

James Colby and I met regularly at the little house, and we were not the only spies. Elizabeth's gentlemen spent much time at The Bull in the village, where Parry lodged, and Elizabeth was never short of information. Bedingfield *had* to know what was happening, but he either was stupidly blind or simply did not want to deal with the complexities of the situation.

Colby and I drew closer to one another. Whether he was simply relieved to have someone with whom he'd shared his secret or simply wanted to keep an eye on me, I could not tell. I knew he could use my growing feelings for him to manipulate me, but I was so confused about what I felt that I did not care. All I knew was that I looked forward to my encounters with him and missed him when he roved about England keeping an eye on things for Elizabeth. When we met in private we kissed, though with none of the passion I'd witnessed in Elizabeth and Robert Dudley when I'd caught them on the eve of his wedding.

I said nothing out loud about what was between us, deciding to enjoy the friendship as I had it. Woodstock was a lonely place, and I knew I was luckier than Elizabeth to be able to stroll to the village and back and speak to Colby in the woods and communicate—even underhandedly—with Kat Ashley far away. It was the strangest winter of my life.

The loneliness at Woodstock ended in April. Mary had gone into seclusion at Hampton Court at Easter for her lying in, and now sent for Elizabeth to attend her. The summons stunned (and relieved) Bedingfield, but not me or Elizabeth, because, as Colby had revealed, Philip had been gradually persuading Mary to release Elizabeth and embrace her as sister once more.

As we prepared to leave Woodstock, Elizabeth walked the rooms that had confined her, looking about in distaste. "A horrible place," she declared. "Whenever I am Queen, I shall burn it to the ground."

One of Mary's ladies gave her a disapproving look, more because Elizabeth assumed she'd become Queen rather than for her vow of destruction.

As I departed, my gaze fell on the window frame, glass, and shutters where Elizabeth had inscribed verses, much to Bedingfield's irritation, but he hadn't stopped her. One in particular now caught my eye.

Much suspected by me, nothing proved can be. Elizabeth, a prisoner.

It was the last thing I saw of Woodstock.

❖

WE LODGED AT Hampton Court for several weeks in quarters built for King Edward when he'd been prince, without word from Mary. One morning we were awakened by bells pealing all over the palace and town.

"The Queen has had her child," one of Mary's women exclaimed. "God be praised."

Elizabeth quietly put aside her breakfast and returned to her bed. The bells continued to peal, and then quite suddenly faded away.

"It was a mistake." I passed the news to Elizabeth later that day, barely containing my glee. "Some poor fool thought the Queen had borne her child, a boy. They were so ready to believe it that the churches were ordered to ring their bells."

"Poor sister," Elizabeth said with a hint of genuine pity. "A cruel humiliation."

The pity was only a hint, however. Bishop Gardiner had visited Elizabeth during these weeks, after she'd demanded to see Mary, and attempted to badger her into admitting her guilt in Wyatt's conspiracy. Elizabeth stubbornly insisted on speaking only to her sister and would admit nothing. Watching Gardiner, aged, stubborn, and fire eyed, and Elizabeth, young and just as stubborn, face each other, I worried we'd spend another year at cold, dreary Woodstock.

One night shortly after we'd heard the bells, I was aroused from bed by a frightened maidservant. Wide eyes regarded me in terror over a single candle flame.

"She sends for you, miss. She is to go to the Queen now, in secret. I fear this is the last we'll ever see of her, miss."

I struggled to climb out of bed and dress myself quickly. Would Mary have Elizabeth murdered, here in her own house? She might, I thought darkly. Elizabeth had arrived with no pomp or pageantry, let in through the back gates like a servant. I doubted the populace at large even knew she was here.

I reached Elizabeth's room and found her dressed and waiting, with a heavy velvet cloak thrown over her gown. A gentleman with a lantern stood with her.

"This is your waiting woman?" he asked.

Elizabeth gave him an impatient look. "She is; my sister knows of her. Shall we go, and not tease the Queen's patience?"

Elizabeth as always stood tall and poised, but she gripped my arm with terrified fingers. "Do not leave my side," she whispered as we followed our guide out of the chamber. "I fear what this night may bring."

The man with the lantern seemed not to hear her. He hustled us down stairs, through a dark garden, and back into the palace through a door on the other side.

I disliked Hampton Court. It had been thoroughly refurbished by Elizabeth's father after he'd seized it from the unfortunate Cardinal Wolsey. Henry had remodeled it to woo Anne Boleyn, Elizabeth's mother, having the intertwined initials H and A carved on the moldings wherever he could. After Anne's quick downfall, workmen had hastily chiseled away the initials so that Henry could bring in Jane Seymour, but they'd had so little time that several had been missed. Here and there a lone *HA* remained high in the wall, a reminder of royal fickleness.

People heard ghosts at Hampton Court: the echoed screams of Catherine Howard in one gallery, a strange cold figure glimpsed stalking in another. I had no idea if the atmosphere rankled Elizabeth as we climbed the staircase to the Queen's privy chamber. She did look around us nervously, as though expecting assassins to spring from every corner, and kept tight hold of me. Whether my presence reassured her or whether she planned to thrust my body between herself and an assassin's knife, I could not tell.

We reached the chambers without mishap, and at the gentleman's knock, we were admitted.

Mary's chamber was deserted except for one lady attending her, not Jane Dormer but Susan Clarencieux. Mary sat in a chair by the window, her stomach distended, but not as much as I would have thought for being eight or nine months thick with child.

The Queen looked starkly older than when I'd last seen her. Her cheeks were heavier and the lines about her mouth had deepened. Her eyes held both satisfaction that her life was hers at last and frustration that it still was not all it could be.

With a pudgy, beringed hand, she beckoned Elizabeth to her. Susan detached herself from Mary and came to me to indicate we both must wait by the door. The gentleman who'd led us here disappeared, dismissed.

Elizabeth knelt before Mary and bowed her head, kissing the coronation ring held out to her. Mary remained silent, watching her. Candlelight touched Elizabeth's unbound hair, glistening like red-gold.

Mary's eyes flickered with anger, her mouth turned down in a sour frown. When she spoke, her deep voice rolled through the room. "You believe then, do you, that I wrongfully punished you? Your letter to me implied as much."

The red-gold head moved slightly, but Elizabeth kept it piously bowed. "I may not say so, not to Your Grace."

"You say it, I believe, to others."

Elizabeth remained in her posture of supplication. "I have never been, with one word or deed, unfaithful to Your Grace. I have always been—will always be—your truest subject."

Mary's face remained like stone. "I have heard of your behavior from Master Bedingfield, in tedious detail. Your conduct is not that of a prisoner; you did not accept your punishment as you ought."

"If my conduct was not all that it should have been, 'twas only because I was maddened at being driven from your side." Elizabeth dared raise her head, sending Mary a look of appeal. "I waited for one word, for one sign from you of sisterly forgiveness."

I curled my fingers into my palms, hoping Elizabeth would not take the contrite pathos too far. I'd seen sweet, penitent Princess Elizabeth unmercifully abuse Bedingfield, even tricking him into writing to Mary's Council what she dictated, claiming her own handwriting too royal to be read by them.

"Well, you are here now," Mary said. "Here you will remain until the birth of my heir."

She spoke stiffly as though she wished to say other words, but forced herself to speak these. As though someone stood behind the screen at her back and whispered lines to her.

"There *is* someone there," I hissed through my teeth at Susan Clarencieux. "Behind the screen. I saw her move through the crack."

"Hush," she told me in a severe voice. "This is none of your affair."

Mary glanced over Elizabeth at me, and I dropped my gaze as I should before the royal stare.

"You are good to me," Elizabeth was saying, "where I do not deserve it."

Did I detect a softening in Mary's expression? I could not tell from across the room. Mary's pregnancy, I think, had bolstered her confidence. She could afford to be generous to Elizabeth when the next heir to the land lay in her belly.

I jumped when I again saw a movement behind the screen. "Someone is spying on them," I whispered to Susan. "Friend or foe? And whose foe?"

Elizabeth had excellent hearing and looked up at my whispers. She turned and studied the screen behind Mary, while Mary turned a bright, angry red.

The tapestry-hung screen was suddenly shoved aside and around it stepped the last person I expected to see—Philip, King of Naples and Sicily, Regent of Spain, consort to the Queen of England.

20

"WELL MET, YOUR Grace," Philip said to the still-kneeling Elizabeth. Elizabeth remained fixed in place, saying nothing.

I admit I expected the Spaniard Philip, son of the Holy Roman Emperor, to be rather like comic Spaniards in theatre. Something inside me expected him to have a thick accent and greasy hair and to bumble about and fall down.

Instead, I saw a tallish man with hair so light brown it was nearly blond, a neatly trimmed blond beard, and a well-shaped, strong face. He had an athletic body hardened by tournaments and sport on horseback, wide shoulders, and an upright grace. On looks alone, I could understand why Mary had fallen in love with him—a dashing, handsome hero who'd ridden to rescue her and her country.

Not being Mary, I had no such compunction to love him and studied him with rather more objectivity. He did not carry an aura of evil or foolishness, but he exuded strength of character and the determination to have what he wanted. He might wait and watch and practice diplomacy to obtain what he wanted, but he'd achieve it in the end by pure force of will.

He did not love Mary. I saw that at once when he looked at her. Mary was another piece of diplomacy he'd use as means to the greater glory of the Hapsburgs. He'd put up with her deteriorating looks, her rages, and her stubborn piety so that he could have England in his hand.

"Dear sister," he said to Elizabeth. "We are pleased at this reconciliation."

By Mary's pinched mouth, she had not seen the interview as a reconciliation. A chance to vent her pique, perhaps, but never a reconciliation.

Philip took Elizabeth's hands and raised her to her feet, giving her a chaste kiss on the cheek. Elizabeth returned the kiss but warily.

"We should have wine," he went on. "To celebrate. And join in with the ladies."

Mary remained seated, her sour look more evident, but she nodded at her husband. "Have it brought," she said to Susan and me, and Susan slipped out the door, dragging me with her.

I wanted more than anything to remain in that room so I could report to Colby what Philip was up to. But Susan, a severe woman with gray hair under her French hood, curtly gave me orders, which I in turn gave the servants. We collected wine and sweetmeats from the kitchens despite the late hour, and carried them back into Mary's bedchamber.

The royals awaited us, Mary sitting stiffly in her chair, Elizabeth on a stool at her feet, Philip standing behind his wife. He gallantly crossed the room to us, and I juggled the tray while I curtseyed deeply to him.

With chivalric grace, Philip relieved me of the tray and then Susan of hers, placing both on a table while he poured wine for us all. I momentarily feared he meant to poison Elizabeth, and perhaps she did, too, because she glanced into the cup Philip handed her without enthusiasm.

He brought wine to Susan and me, Susan curtseying low again to receive it. When I curtseyed, he touched two fingers under my palm and raised me to my feet, the smoothness of his sleeve brushing my chin.

I studied his clothing. He wore a crimson silk doublet embroidered in gold and embellished with gold beads and small rubies. Over this he had put a short black velvet cloak also embroidered in gold. It was a beautiful costume, and the ease with which he wore it told me that he was used to such sumptuousness and thought nothing of it. I could easily picture him in the magnificent pomp of a coronation—a crown lowering to Philip's head. He gave me a bemused look before he turned away, and I contrived to appear innocent.

Susan and I remained in the corner while the three talked, or rather, Philip talked and Mary murmured responses and Elizabeth listened. They drank wine—Elizabeth, I noted, barely wet her lips with it. It became clear that whatever Mary wanted, Philip desired a pardon for Elizabeth. I thought about what Colby and I had discussed at our meetings in the cottage near Woodstock, how Philip feared Mary of Scotland inheriting England more than he did Elizabeth inheriting it.

His planned reconciliation had nothing to do with compassion or friendship or sisterhood, whatever Philip's silver tongue said. He played politics in this room, and Mary knew it. Elizabeth knew it, too, as did I, and Philip knew the two Tudor women knew it. It was a play in which only Philip knew all the lines. He fed them to the other two, who obediently said them back.

By the time Mary allowed Elizabeth to leave, she had tentatively agreed to bridge the chasm between them, repeating that she wanted Elizabeth near her during her lying-in. We returned to Elizabeth's chambers, she gleeful but cautious.

"Perhaps, just perhaps, we might return to better times," she said. " 'Twas a curious night."

I could not disagree.

※

MARY'S STAY AT Hampton Court lingered through May and June and into July, with no sign of a birth. Everyone counted on their fingers and Mary's midwives stammered that they must have been mistaken about how far along she'd been before she'd confined herself.

Elizabeth resided with Mary in the royal apartments, no longer a prisoner, but still not encouraged to leave again for her own estates. Mary wanted Elizabeth firmly by her side.

I found Philip's Spanish courtiers aloof and strange. The ladies wore their gowns spangled with gold lace and pearls and other jewels, wearing colors from black to silver to gold to deep blue and crimson. They had dispensed with low-cut bodices and sleeves that bared the shoulder for sleeves puffed high, linen wadding making the sleeve caps stand well above the shoulder. The long sleeves were then close-fitting against the forearm and wrists. Their overdresses sometimes closed all the way down the front rather than split open over the underskirt, though many of them did like to hook back the overskirts to show a sumptuous damask kirtle.

The gentlemen at all times wore velvets and silks and satins even when they rode out in the mud and rain. They tore their clothing and tossed it away, then complained when more was too slow to arrive from Spain. They behaved like a court in exile, but following Philip's commands, they stoically looked the other way when Englishmen jeered at them and threw mud and worse when they rode by.

One day I entered Mary's bedchamber to deliver fabric she'd ordered and found Mary on the floor, her knees drawn to her chest, her maids and midwives hovering anxiously over her. Mary's face twisted in agony, hanks of hair hanging down, and she let out a low, guttural cry.

"Is it the baby?" I whispered to another of her attendants.

The midwife shook her head. "She has had this illness since spring," the woman told me. "Naught to do with the child."

Mary moaned again, a piteous sound. She leaned her head back, the cords on her neck standing out. I handed the clothes to another attendant and slipped out of the room.

"Poor Mary," Elizabeth said in genuine pity. Elizabeth's headaches of late had gone, and the swelling that had plagued her in last year's spring and again at Woodstock had not returned. "I know well how frustrating pain can be. All I can say is she had better have this child soon, because what they are saying—it is horrible."

"What things?" I asked.

"That she miscarried, that the baby the bells rang for was a monkey someone tried to pass off as a newborn babe. That God is punishing her for marrying Philip. People wanted an heir, and now they are angry."

Mary in her chamber moaned again, the sound echoing with hollow sorrow.

Now that Elizabeth was not officially a prisoner, her ladies and gentlemen could come and go as they pleased—although her favorites like Aunt Kat had still not been restored. Elizabeth gave me leave to make visits outside Hampton Court altogether when she did not need me, and I happily went, rejoicing in freedom and the warmth of summer.

No longer did I have to meet James Colby in secret. He had friends near Hampton Court, a man and wife who had served

Queen Catherine and had been pensioned off by her will, and he stayed in their house. The Williamses were a kind family, friends with not only Colby but William Cecil, Roger Ascham, John Ashley, and others who had made up Elizabeth's household once upon a time.

In addition, the plotters who had surrounded Thomas Parry in Woodstock often paid visits. We would sit at Sir Shelby Williams's long board, our elbows on the table, partaking of fine joints of meat and warm wine, talking freely. The company was prudent enough not to openly speak of Mary or Elizabeth, except in a general, gossipy way, but we talked of many things long into the night. The time was made merry by song and good company.

Colby and I liked to have long talks alone in the hall after others had departed and retired, Williams and his wife making a tacit agreement not to disturb us.

"Rumor has it that Mary miscarried," he said to me one night in July. We sat side by side on a bench facing the fire, the summer night having turned cool. "Rumor in London has it that Mary is dead."

"Rumor is wrong," I answered. "Nothing has happened."

"She ought to show herself, then."

I snorted. "What nonsense. If Mary were dead, Philip would depart and his Spanish court with him. They hate the Spaniards in the village." I paused. "I cannot help feeling sorry for Philip's gentlemen and their ladies, but at the same time, I do wish they would go away."

"That time may come soon," James said. "Philip has other kingdoms to worry about, and England is only a small corner of the Empire."

"England is an independent nation," I said indignantly. "And part of no foreign empire."

James smiled. "You echo the sentiment of the English people."

"And of Princess Elizabeth."

"True."

"Mary's pregnancy is false," I said, sighing. "Something else has made her belly swell; she is ill with it. Everyone has guessed this, even Philip, but she will not admit it. She is so certain God will not desert her—she is so certain she is right."

"God *has* deserted her." James's voice was so stern I looked at him in surprise. "He has, Eloise, and for good reason. She has revived the heretic laws. We have not spoken of it here because it is so terrible, but she has already had people tried and burnt in London. Ordinary people who refuse to give up their English Mass, people who cannot afford to flee to Geneva. The Archbishop of Canterbury and his cronies gaoled at Oxford for writing the Book of Common Prayer at King Edward's command. It is madness."

I had known about Cranmer's arrest because he'd been housed not far from us at Woodstock. I heard that he'd already recanted his Reformed faith, but it is easy to recant anything when your fingers are being crushed.

"You are in no danger of being arrested yourself, are you?" I would not put it past Mary to arrest Colby out of pique because he used to work for Elizabeth. I wondered if the Colbys had made record of his birth and baptism or whether anyone going to Shropshire could discover that he'd been born a bastard and adopted. More than once I had wondered what the milkmaid in Gloucestershire had told of Colby's father, and whether any of it had been written down. No one had any reason to check, but if Gardiner and his Council decided to try him for heresy, who knew what might come out?

"Do not worry," Colby said now. "I mouth pious Catholic prayers and attend Mass like a good lad. Martyring myself will help nothing—I do what I must to stay alive."

"Good," I said fervently.

"Good because I work for Elizabeth? Or good for my own sake?"

"On both counts." I looked at him without blushing. "On both counts, James."

I strangely did not mind whether he returned the affection I felt for him. He kissed me with rather more warmth when we parted and looked at me thoughtfully, but I refused to be embarrassed.

�֎

AT THE END of July, Mary left Hampton Court, taking Elizabeth with her. No trumpeters or heralds ran before us; no lavish pageantry accompanied her progress.

Mary's melancholy ran deep. She had at last given up and admitted she had not been with child. And then Philip had told Mary he was leaving England. He promised it would not be for long, but everyone but Mary understood he was deserting her. The marriage and the attempt at an heir had been a failure.

None but Mary were sorry to see the Spaniards go, leaving from Greenwich where Mary and Elizabeth traveled to see them off. Mary mourned for days, her dream of a marriage and child and perfect happiness crushed.

"It shall never happen to me," Elizabeth said as we watched Mary's gaze return again and again to the window. Below her, the Thames on which Philip had departed ran wide and full. "I shall never ruin myself with a bad marriage. A woman must be careful whom she marries, especially a Queen."

I silently agreed. I had received an alarming letter from my mother not long ago musing that it was high time I wed. I hoped it a passing whim on her part, or rather, her husband's part—I knew who had prompted the letter. I determined that I would refuse any suit and beg Elizabeth to stand by me to keep my stepfather from marrying me off.

Not many weeks after Philip's leave-taking, I was allowed to go to Aunt Kat and ride with her to Hatfield, where we would meet Elizabeth, restored to her home once again. Mary had finally let Elizabeth off the lead—as long as she stayed home and behaved herself, she admonished.

Kat and I had a tearful reunion with much embracing and many kisses. I knew though, as we rode together north to Hatfield, that Kat's house arrest had not made her any more docile and compliant than had Elizabeth's.

"It does a body good to go about where one wishes," Kat said to me as we rode at our slow pace, the outriders happily dawdling with us. "Our time is coming, Eloise, you mark my words."

"What do you mean?" I asked, not really paying attention.

"Mary is barren, her husband is gone, and her old Bishop Gardiner is at death's door. Our princess shall be Queen and sooner than you think."

"Mary's health is poor?" I asked, doing my best to sound innocent.

"Child, you have been with her more than I. The people of London thought her dead before she paraded through with Philip on his way out. That is why she made such a to-do of it, to show herself."

"How do you know all this, Aunt Kat? You have been confined longer than I have."

She gave me a sage nod. "I had my ways. Oh, yes, I know all about what's been going on. I know Mary wants to confiscate the lands of those good Reformed Protestants who have fled to Geneva and other places, but that she is opposed. Well, we'll see if she gets her way, but I think not. A mistake, the burnings at Smithfield. London chokes on the smoke of her victims, and Mary will not last."

I could see that my aunt had not lost her taste for meddling.

"James Colby came often to see me," Aunt Kat continued, "and he got messages to me. No, Elizabeth's cause has not died."

"Mary watches her," I pointed out. "Philip may have persuaded Mary to let Elizabeth out of prison, but Philip is gone, not to return, I think."

"Mary will obey Philip whether he be near or far," Aunt Kat predicted. "She lives to hear a word of praise from him. No, there are those who want Mary gone and they hardly keep a secret of it."

"You hardly keep a secret of it either."

She spoke of treason, openly, with riders around us, though most were out of earshot. Her boldness showed me more clearly than the crowds cheering Elizabeth as she rode through London how much love for Mary had waned. Mary had taken shopkeepers out of their homes and burned them for reading English Bibles and refusing to recant. These people willing to die for their beliefs were those not rich enough to leave England and live in comfort abroad—they had to stay and face Mary's wrath.

Mary had bullied Parliament into letting her marry a foreign prince who cared nothing for England but how it profited his father's empire. Now the prince had run off to the Netherlands to make them behave, and Mary had not produced an English heir, a new hope.

Therefore, Elizabeth had become the new hope. I felt a qualm of foreboding.

❧

CHRISTMAS THAT YEAR was particularly festive. Elizabeth was home with her favorite ladies and gentlemen, including the Parrys;

her former tutor, Roger Ascham; and the Countess of Sussex, who was estranged from the husband who had led Elizabeth to the Tower. Aunt Kat and Uncle John had reunited with her, and she even had visits from Doctor Dee, the astrologer.

As Advent wound on, people came and went—one Master Kingston, two young men called Verney, James Colby. At Hatfield, excitement mounted. Because of Colby, I knew everything from the start.

"The French ambassador is with us," Kingston said as we sat at table one night in December. Outside the world was cloaked in darkness; a cold rain had fallen but it was still not cold enough for snow. "Sir Henry assures us that the money will come from France's coffers. He will lead a force from there."

The reason for this new eagerness to form an uprising was Mary. She'd abused her Parliament this autumn when they'd not wanted her to take away lands belonging to the Protestant exiles, and again when she'd wanted to return her own lands that had been stolen from monasteries under her father.

The crown had very little money, the men of Parliament argued. Returning the monastic lands would be a disaster. But Mary adamantly wished it—God had told her this was necessary, she said, to heal the rift her father had made. She'd gone so far as to locking the men of Parliament into the chamber until she got her way. They'd resisted and now they wanted no more of her.

"Mistress Rousell is our go-between with the princess." Kingston looked straight at me. "You know how to keep her informed with no one the wiser?"

"Better than you can know, Master Kingston," I assured him.

"Eloise is trustworthy," James said.

They had great courage, I thought, to sit and plot to overthrow the Queen over ale in Elizabeth's own house. Sir Christopher Ashton, a man fanatically devoted to Elizabeth had promised his support most fervently. He would depart to France and meet with Sir Henry Dudley, a cousin of Robert, and together they would raise an invasion force.

Kingston with Colby's help would put together an army in the west, and other loyal gentlemen would gather in the south and east. The French king would pay for much of this rebellion in return for driving Hapsburg Philip and Mary out of England. The armies would take London and Mary's person this time, placing Elizabeth on the throne before Philip could act.

Kingston fished a coin from his pocket. It had been severed in two, the cut half ragged. "When I am sent the other half of this, they will be ready in France. And we will see an end to this hideous farce."

I thought them rash, but I knew better than to state that opinion among these half-drunk, conspiracy-mad gentlemen. They wanted Mary gone, dead if she had to be.

I thought of Mary as we'd left her in Greenwich, ill and grieving. Her only desire now was God's work, to return the lands and money the crown received from the raided monasteries, to convert those stubbornly clinging to the Reformed Church.

"They should be punished with fire," I remembered her saying the day after Philip had gone. "It is God's will. The flames will free their souls."

The men in this room wanted it stopped, and they were willing to pay any price to stop it.

21

I DID MY duty throughout Christmas and Epiphany to keep Elizabeth informed of what went on around her. We never wrote or spoke a word that could be misconstrued or used in evidence, but I was able to convey to her, in my own way, what she needed to know.

When Wyatt's rebellion had come precariously close to losing Elizabeth her life, I was angry with the gentlemen who had put her into such a position. This time, my hopes lay with Colby and the conspirators, because this time things were different. Two years ago Mary had simply wanted to marry whom she pleased. Now she burned people alive because they clung to their beliefs.

I did not become very sympathetic to the conspirators, however, thinking them too bold and foolish, until early in the year of 1556 when I had cause to travel to London. My route took me near Smithfield on a day when several burnings took place.

I did not know the people led out to the pyres that day. Two women and a man, the women fairly young, the man elderly. The day was cold and misty, damp under leaden skies.

"Two shopkeeper's daughters," a woman said near me as I craned to see. "And their old uncle." She lowered her voice. "A shame to witness it."

She glanced at my fine clothes and fur-lined cloak and the servants waiting for me, gazing in fascinated horror. The woman I spoke to was middle class, and she knew as I did that most wealthy gentlewomen served Mary in some capacity or other.

"A shame, I agree," I said, then added. "I serve the princess."

The woman's grim countenance lightened. "Blessings be on her, I say. Blessings of God be on her." The woman closed her mouth and moved away as though she feared she'd said too much.

I wanted to leave, for the two women were being bound to their pyres, the man openly weeping, but the crowd was too dense and hemmed me in.

The crush kept me, mercifully, from seeing everything, but I could still hear and smell. Torches were lit and thrust into the wood, but the damp had got into the pyre and the sticks scorched and smoldered. Before long, the girls began screaming and pleading.

"For God's mercy, light it hotter. Fan the flames, good people, I beg of you."

"The wood's too wet," a man near me shouted. He swore. "It's too wet to burn 'em quick."

The cries of the girls turned to shrieks. I heard nothing from the old man, but I could see him standing in the midst of smoke and smoldering wood, tears running down his black face, his hair singed and gone.

"Please, fan the flames," one of the young women cried.

Several people pushed forward, trying to get to them, to let their lives end as they slowly roasted, but the guards pushed them back. I desperately scrambled the other way, squeezing between people who openly wept or shouted for others to help the victims. The smell of slowly burning flesh haunted me as I fled, as did the girls' pathetic screams.

"Stopped, it must be stopped." Tears ran down my face, and I growled the words between clenched teeth. I'd lost my servants and passersby stared at me as though I were a madwoman, but I did not care.

I walked all the way through London without knowing it, my skirts dragging in the mud and dung, my shoes ruined. Anger and horror dogged me every step of the way. The thought of Mary sitting in her palace, watching the river for any sign of Philip and feeling sorry for herself, infuriated me beyond reason.

"Stopped. It must be stopped."

I'd reached Somerset House, my feet somehow taking me where I knew I needed to go. Aunt Kat was there, and she came flying down as I entered the front door to enfold me in her arms. "It must be stopped," I sobbed.

"'Twill be, love," Aunt Kat said. She stroked my hair and let me cry. "That is why we work, my dear. To stop her and her damned Catholic bridegroom. We will win through."

I did not very well see how. Conspiracies were fine and good, but I began to chafe for something to do, but I was not certain what. Aunt Kat and the others were not idle. Kat had collected pamphlets against Mary and her Catholicism that she planned to distribute. Robert Dudley, though living mostly at Norfolk, still went to court from time to time and had many talks with his old friend James Colby, who in turned passed us information on Mary. Dudley even went so far as to sell a piece of land and give the money to Elizabeth, for which she thanked him sweetly.

In March, the Archbishop of Canterbury, Thomas Cranmer, was condemned to burn. During his imprisonment, he'd signed six statements recanting his conversion to the Reformed faith and affirming his loyalty to the Pope. But then Cranmer, who had made it possible for King Henry to divorce Mary's mother and marry Elizabeth's, who had created the Book of Common Prayer, did the remarkable. When he was condemned, he made a speech, much to the distress of his accusers.

"And now I come to the great thing that troubleth my conscience, more than any other thing that ever I said or did in my life, and that is the setting abroad of writings contrary to truth. Which here I renounce and refuse as things written with my hand contrary to the truth that I thought in my heart, and written for fear of death and to save my life, if it might be . . . and for as much as my hand offended in writing contrary to my heart, therefore my hand shall first be punished. For if I may come to the fire, it shall first be burned.

"And as for the Pope, I refuse him as Christ's enemy and antichrist with all his false doctrine."

I imagined the open mouths and angry growls of the host of Mary's bishops who'd put the old Archbishop on trial. They'd confidently thought they'd terrified Thomas Cranmer into admitting his heresy and confirming Mary's stance. But in the end, he died a martyr, another around which Mary's opponents would rally.

I heard that when Cranmer stood on the pile that was to burn him, he said in a loud, clear voice, "This is the hand that wrote and therefore shall it suffer the first punishment."

He thrust his hand into the flames and held it there until he died. Mary had been so angry, Robert Dudley reported, that she'd gone to bed ill.

Stopped. It must be stopped.

I would stop her. No matter if I died for it, as long as I stopped Mary first.

✠

WHILE IN LONDON with Aunt Kat that March, I received a message from my stepfather. He and my mother were lodging in their house in London, near Lincoln's Inn, and I must come to them. I ground my teeth and ignored their first message, but the second one came with a large manservant who would not leave until I went with him.

"Why should they be in London at all?" I growled as he led me toward Fleet Street and the Temple. "They have a snug house in Buckinghamshire in which to roost."

The manservant, whom I did not know, said nothing. I could not slip away from him, he guarded me so well, and presently we came to the modest house near Lincoln's Inn and I entered in trepidation.

My stepfather, Sir Philip Baldwin, was a wealthy man, and the house he'd hired reflected that he spared no expense. Tapestries hung on the walls and clean rushes with herbs were scattered across the board floors. A gallery circled the second floor of the house, the railings polished. A maidservant met me at the door and led me upstairs to this gallery, the steps creaking under her tread. The maid was as tall and strong as the manservant; their resemblance in build and taciturnity made me think them brother and sister.

If my mother had awaited me alone in the long room warmed with a large fire, I might have borne the visit well. As it was, my stepfather sat with her on a chair filled with cushions. It was the only chair in the room. My mother sat on a bench, albeit softened with hangings, her head bent over some stitchery. Neither my mother nor Sir Philip rose as I entered. They waited as though expecting me to pay them the deference I would a great lord and lady.

My mother was complacent and plump like a partridge in a nest, her fat face outlined by her French hood, large rings on every finger. My mother had been slim in my childhood—fine living and much food had put a good deal of flesh on her bones. My stepfather, as complacent as she, had dark hair going gray at the temples and a hint of ruthlessness in his eyes that my mother lacked. I knew that Sir Philip was loud in his support of Mary and Catholicism and had benefited from it. Mary had given him a sinecure with an income, and I heard he was as proud of his small position as though she'd granted him a dukedom.

I curtseyed with feigned respect, trying not to let my impatience show. My mother held out her hands.

"It is good to see you, daughter." Her gaze hungrily roved my bodice and velvet sleeves. "Are those facings silk? So pretty you look. A credit to us, I have always said."

Sir Philip looked less impressed. "You will sup with us, Eloise," he said—a command, not a request.

I took my mother's hands and kissed her cheek. "I cannot stay, sir. We return to Hatfield in the morning and there is much to be done."

Sir Philip gave me a chill smile. "You will not be returning to Hatfield, daughter. It is arranged. Tomorrow you will be betrothed to Sir Henry Felsham, a friend who is in need of a wife. Since you are in need of a husband, he has agreed to marry you."

The bottom could not have dropped out of my world more assuredly if I had fallen from the top of a tower. I stood gaping while the fire crackled pleasantly and a group of men passed in the street, talking loudly.

"I would have more words of gratitude." My stepfather's voice snapped me out of my daze.

I studied him with imperiousness worthy of Elizabeth as appalling anger washed over me. "I will *not*," I said in a clear, ringing voice.

The ruthlessness in his eyes turned swiftly to cruelty. I saw in them a man who would do anything to get what he wanted, and I sensed that my mother had long since learned to give in to him. "You defy me? I am your guardian, Eloise Rousell. I would think you delighted to rid yourself of a low name and take a higher one. Felsham is a wealthy man with three estates. You will be Lady Felsham and your son will inherit his baronetcy. What I have done for you is far, far more than one of your sort could hope."

"*One of my sort*," I repeated. "How dare you?"

"Eloise," my mother tried.

My stepfather rose and slapped me across the face. "Ingrate. Blood tells, as I knew it would. You will marry him, and he will have the keeping of you. That is all."

I put my hand to my cheek, barely feeling the sting. "I am two-and-twenty years old, and do not need your permission to marry as I please."

He put up his hand to slap me again, but my mother made a noise of distress. He glanced at her in derision but lowered his hand. "You are impudent and disrespectful. Felsham will cure you of that. He is not afraid to punish his wife."

My fury grew. "I cannot leave the service of my princess. She does not like her ladies to leave her. She will not let me go."

"Your monarch is not Her Grace Elizabeth, but Her Majesty Queen Mary. I am certain the Queen will give me every power to take you from Her Grace's household and marry you where I see fit."

Spittle flecked his lips. I had no doubt he could do just that. Mary was soppy about her true and loyal subjects—and she'd gleefully take away Elizabeth's favorite little seamstress if she had excuse to.

I forced my voice to cool. My gamble might not work, because Mary had the power to stop me, but I had to try.

"I cannot marry your friend," I said, drawing myself up straight. "I am married already. In a parish church in Buckinghamshire, to a Master James Colby."

My mother let out a little scream and pressed her hands to her face. My stepfather gaped at me exactly as I had gaped at him, and then he raised his hand and expertly and thoroughly beat me.

�֎

I MUST RETRACE my steps and explain how it happened that when my stepfather was ready to bind me into an unwelcome match, I was already legally sworn to a more welcome one.

After I'd received the letters from my mother, I had sought out James Colby at Hatfield, cornering him alone in the gardens one afternoon. He had been speaking of Ashton's plans and our part in them when I grasped his sleeve and said, "James, you would do me a very great favor if you would marry me."

James paused, his red brows climbing slightly higher on his forehead. "Marry . . ."

"Yes, right away. I would be in your debt."

He waited for another few moments while chill autumn wind whipped at my hood and threatened to dislodge it.

"May we wait?" he asked finally. "Elizabeth will be on the throne sooner than you think, and I need you where you are now. After that . . ."

"No, James, it must be now." I told him in quick words about my mother's letter and my fear she'd marry me off. "My stepfather will do it—I know he made her write the letters. If I marry, I will have to leave Elizabeth, and you will lose my help. I will have nothing to do but sit in a house saying rosaries all the long day. Please, James."

He watched me with his blue eyes, taking in every word. "Are you certain?" he asked at last. "Considering what you know about me? I can think of several gentlemen I could persuade to take you, who would be above suspicion. You could work that way, and Elizabeth would keep you at her side."

"No." I drew a breath. "Of all the gentlemen I know I could only think of myself married to you. That is why I have asked you."

He looked away from me, across the green to the woods beyond the village where Elizabeth hunted. "This is not what I wanted."

I had come to this interview prepared to make a business-like arrangement with James—if he married me, I would some-how make it worth his while, use my influence with Elizabeth to bring him money and perhaps a title, to assure him I'd do everything in my power to make certain his secret stayed bur-ied. I thought that if he was not amenable to this offer, I would ask him who might reasonably be.

Nothing, however, prepared me for the stab of hurt at his words. Prickles of heat spread across my face and my palms grew cold. I needed to respond, to say that it did not matter and ask for a recommendation. But I could not speak.

He gave me a half smile. "I wanted it to be much more than this. I wanted to wait until Elizabeth gained her throne—she has promised me a position in her government and a baronetcy. I wanted to offer you so much more than a hasty wedding to a nobody."

"Why?" I asked, my tongue heavy.

He looked away again, the smile remaining in place. "Someday

I will explain to you, Eloise, but the garden behind Hatfield is not the place. I will fix it, we will marry, I will hand you heaven and earth later."

I watched him in shock, almost afraid to understand him. "Are you in love with me?"

I truly wanted to know; I had no experience with men in love, at least not men in love with me. James turned his smile on me full force, and I moved back a few steps, so little could I take the promise of happiness in it.

"That is one of those things we will discuss later. What is your full Christian name?"

"Eloise Alice Rousell."

"Eloise Alice." He nodded. "I will find a priest we can trust."

My throat was suddenly dry. In the space of a few short sentences, I was betrothed. "You will make certain it is a legal marriage? Something not even Mary could put asunder?"

James gave me a decided nod, his grim businesslike manner returning. "If I take a wife, it will be legal and binding. You leave it to me. Will you tell the princess?"

I hesitated, glancing at the windows of Hatfield where no doubt someone watched us. "Not yet. I think—the fewer who know of this right away, the better."

"I agree. Very well, I will find a priest who will keep it from both royals. I will start at once." He paused and looked at me. "When we are wed, Eloise, even if none know it but us, I shall want to be your husband in all ways. Do you understand me?"

I flushed. "You mean, in the bedchamber."

"Will this change your mind?"

My flush deepened, but I was not embarrassed. "Decidedly not."

"Good." He touched my cheek, so briefly that anyone watching might miss it. "I am pleased to wed someone with whom I am in complete rapport. Thank you for asking me."

He was teasing me. I smiled back at him to show I did not mind.

❈

JAMES ARRANGED FOR the banns to be read three Sundays running in a little church in Buckinghamshire, just over the border from Hertfordshire. Four weeks after our agreement, I met him in that little church, where we married. He paid the priest handsomely to register the marriage but stay quiet about it.

We rode back to Hatfield separately. The household had assumed us on errands for Elizabeth as she went about fortifying her houses while pretending not to. Aunt Kat was too busy to pay attention to me, and no one was the wiser.

James and I had arranged to meet in secret to begin our married life. We chose an inn along a road leading west toward Ashridge where we knew none of Elizabeth's people stayed at the moment. The wind chilled me as I rode to meet him, my cloak hardly enough to keep out the February cold.

Hatfield was in an uproar because Henri of France had written his ambassador that Elizabeth should give up on her plan for now. The King advised Elizabeth to stay quiet and take the long view—in other words, France was pulling back from paying for the uprising. Messages flew to and from Hatfield, and in the midst of it I departed alone, wondering if James would be able to keep the appointment.

Elizabeth's ladies and servants had stayed often enough at this inn when we traveled from Hatfield to Ashridge that the landlord and his wife knew me. Assuming I was on business for Elizabeth, the landlord's wife gave me a private parlor without fuss.

I discarded my cloak and warmed myself by the fire, waiting, wondering if he'd come. When we'd married, he'd not said much to me, had barely even looked at me. Since then he'd been busy running messages or closeted with others who were secretly fortifying Elizabeth's houses.

Such things were more important than meeting with a new wife, I decided. Not an auspicious beginning to our marriage, but I supposed it was my own fault for rushing him into it. I paced the floor as the sun dipped behind the horizon. I'd have to stay the night here if it grew too dark, and I busily began inventing stories to explain my absence.

I never heard his step, but suddenly James was there. The chamber door closed and he stepped behind me, warm hands on my waist.

"Did any follow?" he asked me.

"No. I did as you instructed."

He loosened his grip and turned me around. I thought he would begin speaking but instead he kissed me. This kiss was different from the brief brushes of mouths we'd been enjoying whenever we met in private. He kissed me with a man's kiss, with the taste of passion I'd witnessed when Robert Dudley had kissed Elizabeth.

Strange to feel the rough of his unshaved whiskers against my lips, his strong mouth opening mine. The remote memory of Thomas Seymour squeezing my breast no longer haunted me. Seymour had been oppressive and demanding; James wanted the taste of me, Eloise. He saw me as a woman for whom he had affection, not as a female to conquer.

I liked the taste of him as well. For a long time we held each other, breathing in each other's scent and enjoying each other's warmth. I cupped my hands against his lower back, pressing him to me, and felt a blunt hardness against my abdomen, evidence of his desire.

"What do we do?" I asked him softly.

"Whatever we can."

The little chamber was cold but the bed had been piled high with comforters. James helped me undress, then lifted the covers so I could burrow into the freezing bed. His doublet and shirt came off quickly and soon the heat of his body warmed the little nest I had begun. He pulled the covers over our heads and for a moment, the newly wed couple simply lay together under the weight of the blankets and shivered.

The warmth of his arousal bumped my hand. I touched him, curious about this shape of male I'd never given much attention to before. He liked my fingers on him and gathered me close, moving against me and whispering my name.

His hands found my breasts, which he touched with utmost gentleness, raising his body a little to support the tent of blankets over us. I lay beneath him in the dark while he nibbled my neck and then to my wonder, moved to suckle my breast.

The feeling was strange but not unwelcome. My body lifted of its own accord, liking the warmth of his tongue.

He raised his head again and parted my legs with a steady hand. "Are you ready, Eloise? It might hurt a little."

"I know." I'd heard enough ladies laughing about the marriage bed to know what a virgin would feel when first lying with a man. James splayed his fingers over the petals of my opening, where I was wet and desiring him. I arched back, rubbing my body against his to show I was no terrified miss.

"Please, love," I whispered.

His kiss covered my mouth. The quilts began to slide away, baring us to the cold, but I did not care. My legs widened and he slid himself partway inside me.

I felt strange and stretched, but an excitement wound through me, tingling as though I were in a lightning storm. Like a wanton, I dug my fingers into his buttocks and urged him down to me.

He slid quietly in all the way, and I felt the pain then, like I'd been squeezed into one hard point. I gasped, and he stopped. His breathing came hard, his body slick with sweat, though it was freezing cold in the room.

"Are you well, love?" he asked.

For the first time in my life, I had no words. I nodded mutely, those wanton hands on his buttocks liking how smooth and strong and flat he was. This was a beautiful man, and he was my husband, and God had given him to me to enjoy him.

His eyes went heavy, and he made a sound in his throat as he slid a little out and back in again. His body was a welcome weight, his warmth covering me better than any quilt. As he rocked his hips, the wooden bedstead creaked, the headboard bumping the wall. I twined my legs around his, urging him faster, liking the feeling of my husband.

The bed bumped harder, patches of whitewash crumbling and falling to the bed to scatter like snow in James's hair. That made me laugh, and he opened his eyes.

"Does it amuse you?" he asked tightly.

"Yes." I began to laugh.

"Dare you mock your husband?"

"Yes," I repeated. "I dare." I grinned broadly, as though daring *him* to do something about it.

He punished me by loving me so well I stopped laughing. The little bed scraped across the floor and at one time I heard an ominous snap, but nothing collapsed.

22

MY STEPFATHER TRIED to petition Mary to have my marriage to James made illegal, but his plea never got further than Mary's secretaries. I doubt Mary ever learned of such a minor problem, and if Elizabeth did, she made no mention of it. I did not think she actually had heard of it, because Elizabeth made no bones about prying into the lives of her ladies and taking them to task over anything she did not like.

Elizabeth grew more assured and arrogant as the year wore on and as public opinion turned firmly against Mary. The many and terrible burnings, culminating in the deaths of Hugh Latimer, Bishop of Worcester, and Nicholas Ridley who'd been Bishop of London, in the autumn of 1555, and Archbishop Cranmer in the spring of 1556, resulted in Mary being openly hated. It did not help Mary that these men—supposedly evil heretics—died heroically. Bishop Latimer had said to his fellow condemned, "Be of good comfort, Master Ridley . . . We shall this day light such a candle by God's grace in England as I trust shall never be put out."

In March, even before Cranmer's death, Mary began making arrests of Ashton's conspirators. As with Thomas Wyatt's plot, betrayal had come from within the conspirators themselves— the greatest problem stemmed from trying to raise money. When Thomas Seymour had tried to rise against Somerset, he'd bribed a man at the Bristol mint; Ashton tried to corrupt those at the Exchequer. This part of the plan was found out, and arrests began.

I was blissfully ignorant of the crumbling of the plot at first. I had returned to Elizabeth at Hatfield that spring and had been walking about in somewhat of a daze. I had defied my parents, married the man I wished to marry, and fallen in love with him.

We had not been able to meet many times to share a bed, but the few encounters had been blissfully beautiful. I was new enough to bodily passion that it transported me to great joy, and I thought there was nothing more wonderful than a husband and wife in bed. James was always gentle, but he could be teasing and playful, and we laughed a great deal. Marriage so far had been a heavenly state, and I was hard pressed to keep a smile from my lips and tune from my throat as I sewed clothes and chivied my assistants.

The man who brought the news of the conspirators' arrests shattered my happiness.

"They've thrown them into the worst of cells," he reported grimly. "Mary cares nothing for their rank or family; all have been poured into a noisome pit that would turn your stomach and one of them has already been racked."

"Who?" Elizabeth asked, voice brittle. "Who has she arrested?"

"Lord Bray. Edmund and Francis Verney. Henry Peckham. James Colby. It's Colby who has been racked and then tossed into the foul hole without a blanket."

I dropped the bodice I'd been stitching, and the steel bands fell to the floor with a clatter. Elizabeth looked at me sharply. Aunt Kat quickly retrieved the bodice, but I sat frozen, the needle fallen from my fingers.

Colby, the wily, careful Colby, imprisoned and tortured. He'd be tried, certainly condemned, and executed. The husband that I'd loved for less than a year—short, sweet months—the friend I'd known for years, torn from me.

Sudden pain burst through me, bringing bile to my tongue. The stool I'd been allowed to sit on to sew slid out from beneath me, and I covered my mouth with my hand as I tumbled to the floor.

Aunt Kat cried out in distress. Skirts swished as Elizabeth rose to her feet. "Eloise," she said sharply. "What are you doing? Why do you dare?"

I heard Aunt Kat's small scream, then the voice of the Countess of Sussex. "She is ill. The poor child is bleeding."

I felt it then, the trickle of blood between my thighs, the hurt as though someone had gripped my insides and twisted them. I heard a wild cry, loud and wailing, and realized it had come from me. Hands reached out to me, some bare and worn and some ringed and soft.

"Miscarried?" Elizabeth's voice rang out among the chatter. "How on earth could she miscarry?"

Ladies parted and Elizabeth stood above me, glaring down at me like an eagle from an aerie. Tears poured down my face, my entire body aching.

"How could you miscarry, Eloise?" she demanded of me, her face sharp and white. "You were with child? By which of my gentlemen did you behave so unseemly? Master Colby?"

"I married him," I gasped. "I married him."

I saw the long fingers ball into hard fists, saw the rigid stance that meant her worst anger. "Deceitful, ungrateful girl. How dare you?"

I knew she wanted to say more, but I saw her realize that bullying me while I lay in pain at her feet would not look well.

She gave a scream of exasperation and turned away. "Get her off the floor and to bed. We cannot have her bleeding to death in my presence chamber. Clean her up and send for a surgeon."

Aunt Kat was there, lifting me to her bosom, and then a gentleman usher, a tall, strong man with a kind face, scooped me up and carried me away. Aunt Kat trotted anxiously alongside us and put me into her own bed.

I lost the child who'd been only a month old, then lay in bed, too melancholy to move. I had lost my babe, and my husband was in a foul prison, likely to leave it only to be executed. I cried for hours, tears quietly leaking from my eyes, and could eat nothing.

Aunt Kat hovered always at my side, trying in vain to make me take food. I wanted nothing but news of Colby, but I could discover no news stuck at Hatfield. Aunt Kat did not know what was happening, and John Ashley could find out only that James was being questioned, again and again, with the others.

Once when I awoke, it was Elizabeth's long-fingered hand holding the cloth to my forehead. She gave me a smile, her affection in place, which loosened a tightness in my heart. I had feared she'd not forgive me, that she would turn me away, and I would have nowhere to go.

"Poor Eloise," she said softly. "We must get you well."

"Are there gowns to be made?"

She laughed her charming laugh and shifted the cloth. "Always impertinent, is my Eloise. We must get you well for your sake and reunite you with your husband."

Hope flared in my breast. "He still lives then? Will she release him?"

Her smile died. "In truth, I do not know. I will do my best to discover what happened to him." She leaned to me. "This loyalty will be rewarded."

I could not stifle a groan, and I turned my head. The promises of royals were empty to me. The Tudor women were capricious and worked for their own gain, no promise could change that. Elizabeth had some true affection, I had seen it, and so did Mary, but they could put it aside at a whim when they wanted to.

I wondered very much if Elizabeth would be so generous if she realized that James Colby was her own half brother. Or perhaps she did know, perhaps Mary had found out the secret, and James would die for it.

I began to cry again, and Elizabeth called for Aunt Kat, some exasperation in her voice.

I woke each morning fearing to that day hear news of James's death, and every night dropped off to sleep being no wiser than before. John Ashley told us the entire conspiracy had been revealed, and while Ashton was safe in France, every other man had been rounded up and interrogated, including Kingston, who died before his questioners could get him to the Tower. But unlike two years ago when Thomas Wyatt and others had been swiftly arrested and executed, time ticked on, and we waited.

April dragged into May, which was tediously warm, and toward the end of May two men came to arrest Kat Ashley—and me.

"My niece is ill, she lost a child, she cannot travel," Kat babbled as the two men waited for us.

"I will go," I said quickly. I had recovered in body from my ordeal, although a sadness lingered inside me that I knew would never leave. "I want to go."

We were not allowed to see Elizabeth to say good-bye to her, and Kat was not even permitted to speak to her husband. The gentlemen made us ride side by side while they surrounded us and set a hard pace to London.

The metropolis was warming, mud from spring rains drying, and the streets teeming with ordinary people on ordinary business, ignorant of plots and plotters, queens and princesses, prisons and tortures. No smoke drifted from Smithfield today, and we passed southward through the City, not to the Tower, but to Fleet Prison.

The gaol was dank and cold, despite the warm sun outside, noisy and smelling of human waste and the Fleet River rushing below the grated windows. The gaoler, a large, taciturn man, gave me a look up and down with his hard eyes, and Aunt Kat stepped protectively in front of me. He shrugged and took our money—we had to pay for our keep—and gave us a cell to ourselves. The room had a table and stool and a narrow bed we'd have to share, and that was all.

"I have failed her," Kat said. She spoke in a low, clear voice, too weary for despair. "I have taught her since she was four years old. She liked to slap me when she was displeased, and I let her, but I knew she loved me as I loved her. I have tried to help her, to guide her, to raise her where she belongs, and I have done nothing but make a mess of it."

I laid a comforting hand on Kat's shoulder, though Lord knew I had little comfort to give. "You love her well, is all, Aunt Kat. Even if you are not politically astute."

Kat brayed a short laugh. "Ha. Politics are nonsense. I read too much in my youth and am happiest in my books—those classic tomes of ancient Rome. I never liked politics." She grimaced. "But you must understand, Eloise. When I first joined Elizabeth's household, she was nothing, a cast-off bastard none knew what to do with. Her father's household would not even send her clothing, and she went about in threadbare garments too small for her. She was restored as she should be at last, but she has been deprived of her rightful place for so long. I only want to see her achieve it, that is all I have ever wanted, but my husband is right—I am a fool."

"Love can make one foolish," I said, twining my arms around her and resting my cheek on her hair. It had made a fool of me, I thought with heavy heart as I envisioned James Colby in his cold Tower cell.

Now began the hardest days of my life. Kat and I stayed in the Fleet Prison all through the summer, enduring the heat behind walls that sweated with damp. At one point we were moved into better accommodation, two rooms with more comfortable furniture, but we were not told why, and we were not allowed to write to the princess or even John Ashley. I learned nothing of my husband, whether he was alive or dead, though no rumors ever came of executions.

Mary's men came repeatedly to interrogate us. Kat's chamber in Somerset House had revealed a box of pamphlets, diatribes against Mary and her Catholic regime. Kat feigned ignorance— "I know nothing about such papers"—but it was clear our questioners did not believe her. But still they did nothing but keep us confined here, wondering.

It was easier to learn of the princess's fate than James Colby's, because Fleet Prison was a font of gossip, and so many people liked to gossip about the princess. Those coming in eagerly told stories to those who had been imprisoned for a time, and the gaolers and guards readily talked.

Elizabeth had been confined to Hatfield shortly after we'd been arrested, rather than being taken to Mary or to the Tower. Though Mary was in fury again, she'd done nothing to punish her sister. Instead she'd told Elizabeth that her servants—including me and Kat—had confessed the conspiracy but claimed we acted in Elizabeth's name without her knowledge or consent. Mary then told Elizabeth she would not hold the actions of her servants against her.

Aunt Kat and I stared at one another in disbelief.

"Has Mary gone mad?" Aunt Kat wondered. "I cannot imagine her smiling sweetly and telling Elizabeth she believes in her innocence."

I could not imagine it either. But I remembered the handsome Philip concealing himself behind a screen in Mary's chamber to make certain Mary reconciled with Elizabeth after our confinement at Woodstock. I had no doubt the same voice guided Mary this time, although from farther away.

"If Philip told Mary to cover herself with feathers and cluck like a chicken, I believe she'd do it," I said darkly.

"Eloise," Aunt Kat admonished, but I saw by the twinkle in her eyes that she agreed.

✲

IN AUGUST MARY'S guards released us from the Fleet but told us we still were not allowed to return to the princess. Aunt Kat cried bitterly. We stayed with John Ashley in London, and I hoped in vain for news of my husband.

James was still alive—or at least he had not been executed. If he'd died of illness or his injuries from torture, I had no idea. Elizabeth, Uncle John said, continued living at Hatfield under house arrest but was allowed to retain most of her household. We had to be contented with that.

I tried to contrive ways to find James. I thought to go to Robert Dudley, now one of Mary's courtiers, to intercede for me and discover his friend Colby's whereabouts. But Robert—

despite the fact that his cousin had been up to his neck in the conspiracy—was sitting quietly at home in Norfolk with Amy. William Cecil, Elizabeth's friend, was carefully watched and I had no chance to get close to him.

I had no way of knowing whether James had been informed of my arrest or of my release, or if he even knew I had carried his child before I lost it. I'd not had a chance to tell him he was to be a father before his arrest.

"No more intrigue," I cried to Uncle John. "I want my husband and my life. I want to never hear a prison door shut on me again."

Kat and her husband exchanged glances. "She has been like this since she lost the baby," she excused me.

I fell silent, frustrated. Aunt Kat lived for Elizabeth, so she had revealed while we stewed in the Fleet, loved her even before her own husband. I was beginning to realize that despite my loyalty to her, I did not love Elizabeth as much as I might. She would be better for England than Mary, I knew that, but I did not love her.

Aunt Kat and I removed to the country in September, but not to Hatfield, because Mary still considered Aunt Kat a dangerous person. Elizabeth lived on, doing as she pleased, ostensibly watched by guards, but having most of her entourage about her, save Kat Ashley. The wishes of Philip of Spain protected her, and Mary dared make no move.

Toward the end of the year, Mary must have relented still more, because I was allowed to return to Hatfield even if Kat could not. Kat sent me off with many well wishes for the princess, and I arrived in time for Elizabeth to be summoned to court to spend Christmas there. Her greeting to me after months of separation was to demand I help get her wardrobe ready.

"Your Grace," I ventured. "Have you word of James Colby?"

"Colby? My gentleman you married without bothering to ask my permission?"

"I have heard nothing of him, Your Grace, no word whether he be dead or alive."

My downcast countenance softened her a little. She took my face between her hands and gave me a fond look. "Foolish Eloise. Serve me well, and I will forgive you. Your husband, I believe, has gone to France."

"You believe?" My eyes widened. "Do you know for certain?"

She released me. "He was turned out of the Tower once he had recovered and put on a ship for France. He had no time to search for you; he had to leave at once."

My knees grew weak with relief and I had to sit down quickly. Sweet happiness flowed through me. My husband was not dead, not prisoner—in France, safe. Where and how safe and for how long, I did not know, but for now it was enough to know that he lived, in a place out of Mary's reach.

❊

I RODE WITH Elizabeth to London at the end of November. She surrounded herself with liveried outriders, traveling once more as a princess in fine style.

When we'd arrived at St. James's, Mary invited Elizabeth almost immediately to her privy chamber. No more ignoring the princess and leaving her to pace and stew; Mary sent an entourage to escort Elizabeth the day after her arrival to convey her to the Queen.

In her chamber, Mary grasped Elizabeth's hands and kissed her cheek. "You look well, sister," she said in her low-timbred voice. "The time spent in contemplation and study has been good to you."

Mary's countenance was smiles, her square face lit as though she had genuinely missed Elizabeth. But her eyes were as hard as ever, a darkness flickering behind her sunny gaze. Her sweetness rang false, and I could only wonder what she was up to.

"Indeed," Elizabeth answered. She imitated Mary's cheerfulness, not objecting when Mary threaded her hand through the crook of Elizabeth's arm.

"What a lovely gown," Mary said. She looked it over as she helped Elizabeth sit at a stool at her feet. The jewels bedecking Mary's gown and fingers flashed in the candlelight, a heavy sapphire crucifix hanging from her neck. Elizabeth had relegated herself to subdued pearls on her pale gown and a few plain rings.

"My seamstress is quite clever." Elizabeth nodded at me.

"I remember her. The niece of your gentlewoman, Katherine Ashley, is she not?"

"Indeed."

Mary glanced at me without much interest, although she must be remembering how Aunt Kat had been found with malicious pamphlets against her. Because both Kat and I had been at Somerset House just before the pamphlets were discovered, I was guilty by association. She'd arrested and tortured my husband and consigned me to several months in Fleet Prison. But other than giving me a slight frown of disapproval, Mary ignored me.

She and Elizabeth took their meal together later that evening, and both Elizabeth's gentlewomen and Mary's waited on them. Jane Dormer greeted me pleasantly enough; she had heard of my scandalous secret marriage, to a heretic no less. Jane did not have much sourness in her, however, and she chose to forgive me.

Elizabeth and Mary supped as we carried dishes to and fro, poured wine, handed them cloths, and performed various other chores to make them comfortable. Elizabeth sat as graceful and upright as a swan, her white gown showing her red-gold hair and brows and dark eyes to advantage.

Mary had once more covered her dumpy body with purple velvets, sleeves turned back to show bright gold silk, and a stomacher too tight for her broad waist. Vast quantities of sapphires hung from her French hood, the cross suspended from her neck tonight was crusted with emeralds and diamonds.

"His Majesty the King sends you his fondest thoughts," Mary said as she munched a sweetmeat. Elizabeth had finished her meal and sat quietly.

I half expected Elizabeth to ask, "He does, does he?" but she only inclined her head and murmured thanks.

Mary nodded in serene acknowledgment. "You well have cause to thank my husband, for he has kept your welfare and your future in mind above all things."

"Indeed?" Elizabeth asked, a touch of acid in her voice.

Mary missed her sarcasm. "He has. His last letter to me outlines a fine idea, and he has asked me to present it to you. His Grace has entered discussion with the Duke of Savoy to offer him as a husband to you."

Her words dropped into silence. Elizabeth's colorless lids slid over her eyes once, twice. "Savoy?" she asked in a voice like frost. "The dispossessed Prince of Piedmont, ruler of nothing?"

The temperature of Mary's reply dropped as well. "Emmanuel Philibert is courteous and a man of chivalry. He is neither a boy nor an old man, but ripe for marriage. I would think any young woman would be grateful for his offer."

"*Not too old, not too young*—this is a recommendation?" Elizabeth scoffed. "He is foreign and the King your husband has him on a tight lead. Savoy is dependent on Philip for everything."

"Philip thinks much of you," Mary said. She lifted her goblet, found it empty of wine, and snapped her fingers irritably at Jane, who hurried forward to refill it with fervent apologies.

"Marrying Savoy will strengthen your chances of staying in the succession," Mary continued. "After the fruit of my body with my husband, of course."

"It seems I would owe much to Spain and the Empire then," Elizabeth responded tartly.

Mary slammed down her cup, wine slopping over. "A woman needs a husband. You are young enough to find the married state pleasing, young enough to bear children." Her voice broke over the last word.

"I shall never marry," Elizabeth said. "The unmarried state is the one that pleases me."

Mary recovered herself. "You are young and have no idea what you mean. God has seen fit to bless you with this gift as he blessed me with the King."

"And I see what such a blessing has done," Elizabeth retorted. "You brought in a foreign prince to ruin the nation of England, and you wish me to follow in your footsteps? A fine example you have set—the people mock you and throw things at you in the streets because your husband is a Spaniard."

Mary shrieked. She swung her arm and backhanded Elizabeth across the face, knocking over her goblet at the same time. Elizabeth's head snapped back, and wine arced over her white dress to stain it like blood.

"How dare you," Mary shouted. "You impudent, ungrateful daughter of a—Jezebel. Blood will out. Get out of my sight and out of London. Get back to your house and do not put one foot out of it until I give you leave. Go!"

Eyes blazing, jewels flashing, she pointed to the door. She was panting, her face streaked with perspiration. Her ladies rushed to her at the same time Elizabeth's ladies rushed to open the doors, all of us watching each other with scared eyes.

Elizabeth rose and swept from the room with dignity despite her ruined gown, but I saw her mouth shaking. I reflected as we hurried to her rooms to pack what we'd unpacked only a few days ago that Mary's words were nearly the same as the ones my stepfather had used on me.

23

ELIZABETH RETREATED TO Hatfield and stayed put, grinding her teeth. She fumed over and over at Mary's high-handedness and vowed to anyone who would listen that she'd never marry a foreign husband.

Curiously Mary said nothing more about the matter, but March brought Philip of Spain back to England. Mary was in transports of joy to see her husband again, but he'd not come for love of Mary. He'd come to try to force the Savoy marriage upon Elizabeth as well as to persuade Mary to let him have an army to help him in his new war against France.

The Savoy issue, though Philip was furious that Elizabeth refused it, was finally dropped. Philip wanted the match, but Mary switched her stance to take Elizabeth's side. I thought I knew why. Philip wanted to marry Elizabeth to his cousin Savoy in order to keep England under his thumb when Elizabeth inherited the throne. Philip assumed Elizabeth part of the succession and England's potential Queen, no matter what sins she committed.

Mary did not want Elizabeth in the succession at all, and so for the first time, Mary disobeyed her husband. The two sisters stood against Philip, to his exasperation, and eventually the matter was dropped.

But to Philip's other request, the war in France, Mary was obedience itself. Despite her Council's advice to the contrary, Mary gave Philip his army. Philip departed to fight, taking Lord Robert Dudley and many other prominent gentlemen, including the spurned Duke of Savoy, with him.

Philip and the English won a glorious victory at Saint Quentin, but soon after that disaster struck. Calais, the symbol of English glory for two hundred years since its capture by Edward III, fell in the cold of January 1558.

"It is inconceivable that she has done such a thing," Elizabeth snarled when she heard of it. "A foreign war following her damned foreign husband—a man with the gall to look at me with wanting in his eyes. Philip knows his wife is a loss; I have refused his cousin, so why should he not have me?"

"He would have to get special dispensation since you are his sister," I murmured.

Elizabeth ignored my impertinence. "With this loss Mary has driven the last nail into her coffin. She hopes herself with child again, but it is a farce. She is ill, she'll not last now. Serves her right for handing Calais back to the French on a platter."

With that sympathetic remark, Elizabeth returned to raging, vowing to bring Calais back under English control during her own reign.

The fall of Calais brought me mixed feelings, because when the army returned, beaten and bedraggled, Robert Dudley brought James Colby with him.

He rode through the Hatfield gates following Dudley, and for a moment I scarcely recognized him. I saw a tall man with hair dark red under a cap, a thin beard on his chin. His left arm hung slightly askew as though it had been broken and not healed correctly, and a long scar marred one side of his face.

He dismounted and walked toward me as I stood in the court-yard trying to decide who he was. I saw Robert Dudley grin suddenly at me, and then I realized.

I abandoned all decorum. Letting out a shrill scream I ran straight to James and flung my arms about his waist. I'd not seen him in nearly two years, and anything could have happened in that time, my death or his, or him finding a lady in France he liked better than me, but at the moment I did not care.

He swept me up and held me hard, his arms shaking. He kissed me right there in front of everybody, and I heard Robert Dudley laughing.

"Such a display," Elizabeth said later when the gentlemen were welcomed home with wine and dancing. "I take it you were pleased to see your wife, Master Colby."

Colby did not look embarrassed. He'd worn a warm smile since his arrival and it never left his face. I could not stand next to him and hold on to him for hours as I longed to because I had to serve the princess, but I pushed aside all others to fill his wine cup, and he'd turn that warm smile to me each time.

"Devotion is touching," Elizabeth said, and laughed. "Dear Robin, you must show such devotion to me or I will think you forgot all about me."

Robert gave her a devastating smile and a mock bow. For the rest of the evening he served her with exaggerated courtesy, and Elizabeth laughed at him like a girl.

I had feared Elizabeth would not let me be with my husband tonight, just because she was not always sympathetic to married love, but she dismissed me without much interest early in the night, and I retired to my chamber to wait for James.

He was not long behind me, and we had a reunion in truth. He lay with me far into the night, loving me again and again with increasing frenzy. In the small hours of the morning I curled up next to him, not sleeping, and enjoyed the feel of my husband's warm body at my side.

He did not sleep either, touching or kissing me softly at intervals. I ran my hand along his twisted left arm, the skin mottled and smooth.

"It broke," he said. "In the Tower."

When he'd been racked, I knew. His arm had been pulled apart and then clumsily healed. "I was horribly afraid for you. I hate her for doing this to you."

I was not quite certain when I said it whom I meant—Mary, whose guards had tortured him, or Elizabeth, who had tacitly condoned the plots that got my husband arrested.

He touched the scar on his face, which twisted from his cheekbone to be hidden in the short beard he'd grown. "This I got in the fighting."

I traced the scar, too, which had ruined his handsome face but disguised any resemblance to his true Tudor father. "Why did you fight for Philip? Our enemy?"

"For a full pardon and a chance to come home. Philip cares nothing for these petty uprisings to put Elizabeth on the throne. He wants Elizabeth to be Queen and is taking a stern hand with his own wife."

"She should not have lost Calais."

He rumbled a low laugh. "Mary did not lose it. The French took it with their canny attack when those inside the fortresses least expected it. We marched to try to save it, but to no avail. Calais is French once more."

"Elizabeth is furious."

"Many people are." He traced my cheek. "As for myself, I am only happy I came home."

"I thought you would forget about me after all this time."

He chuckled again. "Eloise, how could I ever forget *you*?"

He kissed me for a while then, both of us drowsy and contented.

"Did you know Aunt Kat and I had gone to Fleet Prison?" I asked after a long time.

"Yes, I found out after I'd been hustled off to France." He pressed a kiss to my hair. "I wanted to rush back home and tear the walls down to get you out. Dudley restrained me. He had a better way, he said. He has some influence with Philip."

"Was that why Aunt Kat and I were released without a trial?"

"Very likely."

"And he pardoned you for joining his army. It seems we owe much to Philip of Spain."

"Yes." James pulled me close. "Ironic, that."

I had to agree.

※

THE LOSS OF Calais devastated Mary, and she never recovered. Later that spring she claimed she was again pregnant, although this time her midwives reserved judgment. When I made a journey to London with James to purchase cloths for Elizabeth—she now had me choose her fabrics and no other—Robert Dudley had us as guests and I saw Mary in passing at St. James's.

She did not look with child; she looked pale and bloated and ill, with a gray cast to her face. Her clothes hung on a body that was swollen in the midriff and bone thin in the shoulders and neck.

"She is dying," I whispered to James. He agreed with me, but we dared speculate this to no other, including Robert Dudley.

That visit was in August. By November everyone admitted what I had seen, that Queen Mary, abandoned and forgotten by her husband, faced her last days.

⁂

THAT NOVEMBER IN 1558 is a time I will never forget. On the sixth of the month, Jane Dormer approached Hatfield surrounded by outriders who bore the Queen's standard. She curtseyed low before Elizabeth and offered her the jewels Mary had sent.

Elizabeth took the casket without expression. "She still lives?"

"Yes, Your Grace. She is sore ill, but still alive."

"And she has named me as her successor, at last?"

Jane nodded. "On two conditions, Your Grace."

"Conditions?" Only Jane Dormer, the dearest and closest lady of the Queen, would be tolerated giving Elizabeth conditions. "How interesting. Name them, and I will give my answer."

Jane was not in the least intimidated. "First that you pay her debts. She fears others will be ruined if you do not."

Elizabeth gave a nod. "That will be done. And the other?"

Jane raised her head and gave Elizabeth a piercing look. "That you uphold the Catholic religion, the true Church. That you continue the work Mary has done."

Elizabeth's red-gold brows arched. "This is her stipulation?"

"Indeed, Your Grace."

Elizabeth laughed once, a derisive sound. "She need not have bothered with conditions. I will pay her debts, she can be assured about that. And I pray to God that the earth might open up and swallow me alive if I am not a true Roman Catholic."

Jane peered at her in amazement. So did I, although I strove to hide my expression from Jane and her servants.

"I may tell this to the Queen?" Jane asked. I could forgive her for sounding skeptical.

"You may. Also that my prayers are with her, and my hope that she goes easily and quickly to God."

Jane curtseyed. "As you will, Your Grace."

Elizabeth smiled, and Jane went, Godspeed, back to London.

A few days later, Jane's betrothed, Count Feria, now ambassador to England from Spain, rode to Hatfield to dine with Elizabeth.

Very few sat down with Elizabeth at table. She supped like the royal princess she was, eating alone with ladies waiting on her. She liked ceremony and etiquette and was very aware of where everyone fit into it on the vast chart in her head.

Once she had learned of Mary's impending death, Elizabeth carried herself even more like a queen. Her household expanded—prominent ladies and gentlemen deserting Mary in her last hours to find a place with the new monarch. I found it sad that more abandoned Mary each day, but I had to admit excitement about the coming change. No more leaky roofs and cold prisons like Woodstock.

Elizabeth had already appointed certain men to prominent positions in government, ready to slide into place as soon as they heard word of Mary's death. She had brought some of the highest-born ladies in the land into her service, and word arrived of the imminent return of some of her favorites who had fled into exile.

Gomez Suarez de Feria had become Philip's eyes and ears in England, and Elizabeth received him as an ambassador from a foreign land. She treated him with the courtesy due his rank, at the same time knowing that he would report everything she did or said to Philip. Even so, I do not believe he was prepared for her.

"I congratulate you," Feria said in his pleasant Spanish lilt. He approved of her, I could see that in the way he looked her over as though sizing up an unfamiliar horse to determine its soundness.

"You have survived dark times, Your Grace," he continued. "And ever in these troubles was His Grace Philip reaching his hand out to steady you. Because of my master Philip, you will be Queen of England. A generous gift from Spain and the Empire."

His words fell into cold silence. Elizabeth looked up from her venison, game caught in her own parks, her knife balanced expertly in her hand. "A gift from Spain?" she repeated.

"It was His Grace Philip who released you from your prison, he who prevented your sister from doing harm to you," Feria said reasonably. "And so you come to your inheritance."

Elizabeth laid down her knife. Candlelight touched her red-gold hair and her pale gown studded with pearls as she studied Feria, her gaze as piercing as Mary's ever had been.

"It is not Spain that gives me my crown," she said in a voice like winter ice. "It is the grace of God and the people of England who give it to me. I am an English Queen. The rule is mine by right of my succession as laid down by my father, King Henry. Not by a gift from Spain."

Feria stared back, openmouthed and red in the face. I felt a bit sorry for him, but the man was a fool if he'd expected Elizabeth to clap her hands in girlish glee and bestow hearty thanks on him and Philip.

Elizabeth had much more to say. "Your master Philip tried

to induce me to marry outside the realm. It is the Duke of Savoy I mean, as you doubtless will recall. My refusal stemmed from one thing only—seeing how my sister the Queen had lost much affection from the people by marrying a foreigner. And that I will never do."

Feria swallowed. "I see, Your Grace."

"It is clear you do not see. You have affection for my sister— you are to marry one of her most trusted ladies after all, and affection for your master. Commendable, Lord Feria. But do not expect me to share it."

She lifted her goblet, her eyes sparkling, the subject closed.

The abashed Count Feria returned to London to confide in Jane Dormer his forebodings on Elizabeth's accession. The Catholic faith, he predicted, was doomed in England. He and Jane later went together to Spain with other English Catholics— Jane from all I heard was very happy married to her Spanish count, who later became a duke.

Not long after his visit, I was awakened very early in the morning by a commotion in Hatfield's yard. Hatfield had so filled with people that they overflowed it, and the house was already stirring, servants running to build fires and ready meals for those staying in the house.

But this was more than the usual bustle of servants. I rose from my bed and looked out the window. James rose behind me, pulling on his nightshirt as he joined me.

A rider had come in through the gates and was pelting hard for the main doors. I felt a ripple move through the house, beginning with the rider and flowing all the way to the door of Elizabeth's chamber. I snatched up a wrap and ran downstairs, sliding into her chamber before the excited servants could reach her door.

"Who is it?" Elizabeth asked me from her bed.

"A rider." My mouth was dry, my words rasping. "I could not see who."

Elizabeth tore back her covers and scrambled out of bed. "Help me," she hissed.

I got her into a dressing gown to cover her night rail and pulled her hair into some semblance of order. Only when she satisfied herself that she looked calm and tidy did she let me open the door.

She glided regally into the outer chamber and observed the crowd of her householders who had hastened there. The man they let through was not who I expected. Elizabeth had told Sir Nicholas Throckmorton to send her word when Mary had at last died. The young man who entered was not Throckmorton, but he fell to his knees and thrust something up at Elizabeth.

Her face changed as she took it. What lay on her palm was a ring, plain and black, the betrothal ring Mary had worn on her finger since the day Philip placed it there.

Mary would only have parted with it on her death.

Elizabeth fell to her knees. I ran to assist her, but she motioned me away, tears running down her cheeks though she smiled as hard as she could.

"This is the doing of the Lord," she said, her voice clear. "And it is marvelous in our eyes."

24

THE DIFFERENCE BETWEEN being seamstress to a princess and seamstress to a Queen was that, from the instant Elizabeth received the ring in her chamber, I had not a moment to call my own. By the end of November we'd already made a progress to London, Elizabeth in robes of purple velvet that we'd hastily made for her. We stayed for a week at the Tower, then moved to Somerset House; all the while I was expected to pore over the fabrics and trims and jewels to bedeck the Queen at her coronation and beyond and make a start on the coronation gowns.

Mary was dead, and Elizabeth was Queen, and England heaved a collective sigh of relief. Mary and her Spanish husband were gone, and a pretty, young, Protestant, English Queen had taken her place. The English people were tired of winter and longed for spring.

Elizabeth had her councilors and courtiers in place within days of receiving official news that Mary had died. William Cecil was already busily making notes and charts and plans as

Secretary to the Queen. Katherine Ashley came joyfully to us in London and received Elizabeth's fond embraces. Elizabeth instantly made Kat first lady of the bedchamber—a gift that surprised everyone but me.

Robert Dudley she made her Master of Horse. John Ashley was now Master of the Jewel House at the Tower. To James Colby she gave a captaincy in her personal guard and a promised knighthood and baronetcy at her coronation, and I became first seamstress to the Queen.

Being official seamstress meant that though I longed to be near my husband at all times, we perforce saw very little of each other. A few stolen moments when we met in a passage, a few words before we fell, exhausted, into our bed at night—and that only when Elizabeth allowed me to sleep elsewhere than her chamber.

The coronation was foremost in our minds, and I spent every minute of the day consulting about Elizabeth's clothes, picking out the sumptuous fabrics brought in especially for her, drawing designs, bullying my assistants to sew faster, and taking up a needle when it became clear that we'd never finish in time.

The gown for the coronation itself we remade from the one Mary had worn. I held up the wide band that had been Mary's bodice and shook my head. Elizabeth was much taller and slimmer and the bodice would have to be remade.

Elizabeth was not the most easy of persons to fit these days. She was surrounded by people from morning to night, most of them men, most of them high placed, most of them trying to talk to her about everything at once. A lesser woman would have fainted away under all their fussing. Elizabeth simply told them what she wanted done and expected them to do it and moved on to the next crisis.

The coronation would be held very soon, on January 15, the

date chosen by Doctor Dee the astrologer as the one most favorable. Dee, I thought darkly, might believe it an auspicious day, but he was not the one who had to finish the wardrobe in time.

The state robes of red and purple velvets had to be got ready first, then the gown she would wear under them, a gold silk with a pattern worked on it in silver thread and pearls. The long, pointed bodice was trimmed with precious jewels, with ermine on it and the close-fitting sleeves. I attached a small ruff for her neck, which would make her rather long face seem rounder. The gold skirt had a train trimmed with ermine, which took a rather long time to make, and we hadn't much time.

Over this dress we put a mantle of cloth of gold, embroidered with red roses and lined with ermine, with gold tassels hanging at intervals. Her maids brushed out her hair until it shone like red-gold, letting it flow loose and long over her shoulders and back.

The entire costume was tricky and fussy, and I was never completely happy with it, knowing especially that all of London watched. The world would, too, because countless reports and drawings would be circulated throughout the kingdom and abroad.

I am not certain how we did manage to finish. A few of the gowns we did not—we'd have to pin them on her and hope—but on the appointed day Elizabeth was ready to travel through the streets on her progress to Westminster. She rode in a large litter carried by mules, Robert Dudley handsome on horseback just behind her. She would process slowly, stopping to take in pageants put on for her by the Guilds of London, each of which would be symbolic of their love of her and hopes for her reign.

I did not join the procession, but James, newly knighted in the Tower, marched with her guards. He dressed in white trimmed with her colors, his back straight, his crooked arm hidden by the fine silks of her livery. Aunt Kat rode with Elizabeth's train of ladies as well, she with her exalted new position, and John Ashley rode with her gentlemen.

I slipped from the Tower and joined passersby on the streets, where I cheered and waved with the rest of the Londoners. Conduits had been set up to allow free wine to flow in the streets, and I allowed myself to get lost in the frenzy.

The next day I attended the coronation banquet and waited on Elizabeth. Again I was actually far from her side, passing wine and cloths to ladies who handed them to ladies who handed them to Elizabeth. But I minded not at all. My heart was light—after so much darkness and so much fear, Elizabeth was Queen at last.

❈

A QUEEN, HER councilors told her, needed a husband. As with Mary they felt that a woman could not rule without guidance from a man—had not Mary made disastrous decisions such as returning the Church to Rome and reinstating the heresy laws, not to mention losing Calais? I longed to point out that Mary's *husband* had gone and lost us Calais, but the Council fondly believed that the right husband would make all the difference in Elizabeth's case.

What followed was a string of suitors—Philip of Spain himself; Archduke Charles of Austria; Sir William Pickering, one of Thomas Wyatt's conspirators; Eric of Sweden. Every eligible bachelor in Europe wanted to pair himself with Elizabeth, England being the jewel every man wanted to add to his crown. I knew, however, and so did James, that while Elizabeth let these crowned heads of the Continent woo her, only one man in the world existed that she could envision as her husband, and that man was Lord Robert Dudley.

Dudley had been made the Queen's Master of Horse, which meant he saw to it that she had the best horseflesh in Europe made available to her. Philip had brought Spanish horses to England, and now Robert ordered horses from Flanders and Ireland to add to English stock. Robert also became her most trusted confidant and her closest friend. This friendship grew and twined into something strange and complex, and by the time Elizabeth's reign was less than a year old, every person in the kingdom hated him.

"Is he so very terrible?" I asked my husband one evening in the first August of Elizabeth's reign. I sat by the fire as the day had grown cool, and stretched out my feet as I stifled a yawn. I was easily tired these days, as only a week before I had given birth to our daughter, who lay sleeping in a cradle at my feet.

Before I had pushed her out into the world—I wailing loudly no matter how the midwife tried to hush me—I'd had no idea how profoundly I could love one small person. I also never understood how profound was my fear for the mite who struggled to live. She'd been born a little too early, and James and I and Aunt Kat hovered over her, taking turns sleeping, terrified that we'd watch our Catherine drift into her final sleep.

"Dudley?" James mused, his eyes closed, his long legs also stretched toward the fire. "He is arrogant, he makes no bones about using people to get what he wants, he flirts with every wife but his own and has the Queen dancing in his hand. Do you consider that terrible?"

"A bit," I admitted.

"While his wife lives, Elizabeth can have only a flirtation with him, at worst an affair. He is not likely to be King."

"Yes, but I hear that Amy Dudley is often quite ill. And tongues wag that the Queen would not be sorry to see Amy die and Robert free."

"It is rumor only, Eloise. Have you heard her say this yourself?"

"No," I said grudgingly. "But when she becomes impetuous and imprudent she only endangers herself. We must stop her."

James opened his eyes and arched his red brows. "We must, must we? Elizabeth is Queen now, nearly six-and-twenty years old, and has ceased listening to the likes of us. She is no longer the little princess so careful with how she comports herself. And she can now send you to the Tower for twitting her about her behavior."

I pursed my lips, refusing to see this in an amusing light. "Perhaps she would not listen to you or me," I said. "But I know someone she might."

He caught my thoughts as he so often did, and nodded. "I believe you are right. Shall you ask her?"

"Indeed." I yawned again. "In the morning."

The next day, after a much needed sleep, leaving my daughter safely in the arms of James, I went in search of Aunt Kat.

※

ELIZABETH AND WILLIAM Cecil sat with heads together, speaking rapidly, but these days this was a common sight. Cecil had begun working not an hour after Elizabeth received word of Mary's death, and since then he'd worked almost ceaselessly.

Together they faced Parliament to revoke Mary's return of the Church to Rome and to end the persecution of heretics. They'd had to finagle and fight the House of Lords, many of whom had prospered under Mary and were reluctant to return supremacy to the monarch. The lords danced, but Elizabeth was firm—she was of the Reformed religion and that was that. No more Catholicism and popery, no more persecution of heretics.

I could not say that the instant Elizabeth put the crown on her head England became a smoothly running kingdom of peace and prosperity. At the time of Mary's death influenza ran rampant, and I came down with it after Elizabeth's coronation, one reason my babe came early, or so the midwife claimed. I suppose my illness had made the child ill, too, though at the time I'd had no idea I carried her.

So with half her kingdom ill, Philip's war in France continuing until April, and her parade of eager suitors, Elizabeth spent most of her time working.

Not all of it, however. Aunt Kat and I had come today to confront her about her private life.

Cecil gave us a courtly, if preoccupied, bow when we entered. He only nodded when Elizabeth said she would withdraw to speak to us, clearly wishing to return to the task at hand. William Cecil ever liked his work.

"You look well, Eloise," Elizabeth said after we'd made obeisance to her and she'd kissed us. "Motherhood agrees with you."

"I have become fond of its state," I answered neutrally. In truth I adored my little daughter, but I knew Elizabeth did not like mothers gushing about babies.

"One day I, too, may sample it," she said briskly, as though she did not care one way or the other. "What is it, Kat?"

Kat creaked to her knees, and I knelt beside her. "Lord Robert Dudley," Aunt Kat said without preamble. "You must leave off."

Elizabeth stopped. Her mind had obviously been elsewhere, she indulging us with this private audience because she was fond of us. Now her eyes narrowed to dark, hard agates.

"Oh, must I? Who are you to tell me I must?"

"Your old governess," Aunt Kat returned. "I have looked

after you since you were four years old, twenty years and longer. And never more than now have you needed me to chide you about your behavior."

"Chide me?" Elizabeth laughed, cold and shrill. "There is no need for your chiding. I have been friends with his lordship nearly the twenty years you have been looking after me. We were children together, as close as—nay, closer than brother and sister."

"Your flirting and dancing and laughing and kissing have nothing to do with being brother and sister."

Elizabeth reddened, the daughter of Henry working herself into a fine rage. "And you, Eloise Colby," she spat. "Do you agree with my aging governess?"

I nodded, bravely meeting her gaze. "I am afraid I do. It was I who persuaded her to seek you today. I who insisted she speak."

Aunt Kat looked offended. "I certainly know my own mind, Eloise, and can speak as I please."

Elizabeth stared at us for a moment longer, then suddenly flew into a temper, her eyes sparkling in fury. "My friendship with Lord Robert is none of your concern," she shouted.

Aunt Kat barely winced at her words. "Rumor says otherwise. They say you enter his chamber as you please day and night, that you might well be carrying his child. Your behavior is discussed at the courts of Paris and Spain; I'd not be surprised if it has reached the Saracen lands. Take a husband quickly, Your Grace, I implore you, and stifle these stories."

Elizabeth slapped her. The red imprint of her hand was stark on Kat's white face, but Aunt Kat set her mouth in stubborn lines. She had said much more than I would ever have dared, but Kat knew she'd needed to say it. Or rather, she knew Elizabeth needed to hear it, bluntly and without diplomacy.

Elizabeth curled her fingers into her palms and stepped back, her breathing hard. A muscle in her jaw moved as she strove to master herself.

"I know, Kat, that you are devoted to me," she said, her voice icy. "Because of that devotion you see fit to speak to me of this. But I cannot simply take a husband because you wish it, you know, or because you think it will be good for me. Such things need to be weighed carefully, because I must marry for the good of the realm and nothing more."

"If ever you marry *him*," Aunt Kat said. "I believe your realm will oppose it."

Her smile was brittle and terrible. "How lucky for me then that Lord Robert is married. Your concern is noted, Katherine Ashley. Now, go from my side and never speak to me of this again."

"I will take any punishment you choose to give me," Aunt Kat began. Her lip stuck out slightly, and she made no move to rise.

"I do not wish to punish you." Elizabeth's eyes flashed. "That is, unless you do not *get out*."

Kat did not flinch. "Help me to my feet, Eloise. It is difficult for me to rise these days."

I sprang to my feet and assisted Kat to stand, then we got ourselves out of the room under Elizabeth's incandescent glare. Outside Cecil pretended to have heard nothing, but his quick glance at us showed he had. He, too, disapproved of Elizabeth's excessive flirtation with Dudley, and I could see a small smile hovering about his rather pompous mouth.

❋

I HAD HOPED Aunt Kat's words would sink into Elizabeth's very sensible head, and this would be the end of the matter. But alas, it was not to be.

August merged into a blustery September, then autumn gave way to winter and spring came again. My daughter grew and against the odds became robust and strong, for which James and I fervently thanked God. I still did not see as much of my husband and daughter as I wished, but I did enjoy my domestic bliss.

Elizabeth, vivacious and flirtatious and a natural coquette, teased the men who wanted domestic bliss with her and drove her Council mad with her procrastination. Ambassadors and go-betweens continued to parade their masters before her, and English hopefuls flirted with her at court. Each one she pretended to consider, some longer than others, before saying either *no* or a provocative *maybe*.

And all the time Robert Dudley was at her side, with her when she rode out on the hard-to-handle horses she favored, she as spirited and reckless as the horses themselves. Whenever she invited me to ride with her, a coveted and much-sought-after position, she would gallop into the woods and make me stand lookout while she and Robert kissed and fondled each other in the shadows.

When Cecil went north to Scotland with an army to help the Scots noblemen tame the French there, Robert stayed behind with the Queen. James stayed behind as well; as the captain of her personal guard, he was to be with her at all times. James did not want to leave me or our child, I knew, but I could tell he'd prefer a clean and simple confrontation with an angry French soldier to the complex intrigues of court.

Elizabeth's flirtation with Robert, if anything, increased. They were not often out of each other's company. He stayed with her when she received ambassadors and teased them with her. He lounged on barges next to her, he ran his fingers through her satin and velvet jeweled skirts that I'd sewn. He took ribbons from her gown and tied them around his wrists. One of his servants told me he twined the ribbons she gave him around more intimate parts and wore them under his clothes in her presence.

In short, they said she was a wanton, her behavior was that expected from a wanton's daughter, although no one dared mention the name *Anne Boleyn*.

"I hear that your wife has sickened," I said to Robert one day while we rode side by side. Elizabeth had galloped ahead a little, her guards fanning out to keep watch over her, and Robert dropped back to a walk to spell his horse.

"Indeed, the poor lady," Robert said. "A sickness in her breast she has had for some time now. It makes her weak and wretched. I send her gifts and hope they cheer her."

Charming, smiling, handsome Robert playing the devoted husband. I restrained myself from making any skeptical comment. "Please convey to her my wish for her swift recovery."

"I will. You are kind, Lady Colby. Your daughter does well?"

"We are most pleased with her, my lord. She grows by the day."

I was unable to keep the pride from my voice, and he laughed at me. "A fine hit by my friend, Sir James Colby," he said, and gave me a bawdy wink. "My felicitations."

I flushed, which only made him laugh the harder. "Thank you, my lord," I said stiffly and wished he'd go away.

Amy Dudley continued quite ill, and my kind hopes for her recovery did not help her. She grew sicker and a bit deranged in her mind, I heard. She knew of Elizabeth's attachment to her husband, and she lived on in Dudley's houses, unwanted and alone.

Court gossip speculated that Amy Dudley would not last much longer. When William Cecil returned from signing treaties with France and Scotland, he was greeted with the rumor that Elizabeth had secretly borne a child by Robert. This was nonsense, of course, but it was everyone's firm belief that Elizabeth would marry Robert, and she only waited for Amy to be out of the way.

25

 WILLIAM CECIL WAS a hardworking man. He had a wife, an intelligent woman who loved learning as much as he, and he enjoyed gardening when he had an hour to himself, which was rare these days. He dove into the business of running Elizabeth's kingdom with dedication, helping her restore the Church in her own way—not to the austere Protestantism of John Calvin but doing away with the elaborate ceremony of Catholicism. Elizabeth wished her priests to retain their costly vestments and some of their ritual, but she frowned coldly at excessive ornamentation, hordes of candles, and blanketing incense.

Cecil had had to persuade her to take the threat of the French getting a foothold in Scotland seriously and to commit troops, threatening in tears to resign if she continued to dismiss his advice. And he also had to contend with a Queen who was evasive on the question of marriage and who put off her Council when asked to name a successor.

"Marriage is a dangerous undertaking," she said. "And naming a successor is equally dangerous if not more so. See how many plots and intrigues revolved around me without my approval when Mary was Queen. I would never advocate a subject rising to overthrow a ruler."

She had never condemned the plots, though, I remembered. She had pretended not to know about them and had quietly fortified her own estates while the conspirators planned to raise armies against Mary.

All in all, Cecil had a difficult job, steering the Queen in the right direction without incurring her displeasure. Elizabeth was generally reasonable and intelligent, but she had her blind spots and Robert Dudley was one of them.

"He makes me laugh," Elizabeth said when she learned of more complaints about her flirtation. "He understands me better than anyone and raises my spirit high. Why should I not have that?"

"She makes good argument," I told James after this. "She spent so long alone, keeping quiet and never putting a foot out of line so people would think her the good, plain Protestant princess. Why should she not enjoy herself in the light after such a long darkness?"

"No one minds if she enjoys herself, Eloise," James said patiently. "Her entertainments are becoming legendary and invitations to them much sought after. She is making it extremely fashionable to be part of her court, and the ploy is working. She is generous to those who support her, and every man wants to be a star to her sun. But she stirs anger and disgust with her favor to Dudley. She will divide the kingdom over him as Mary did with Philip."

"I remember." I shivered. "I spent the winter in horrible rooms at Woodstock and had to meet you in a ruined house if I wished to speak to you."

"You enjoyed the duplicity."

"Of conspiring under Mary's nose?" I smiled, reflecting that it was easy to romanticize hardship in a comfortable chamber before a warm fire with one's beloved husband. "Of course I enjoyed it. If I had sat meekly sewing during that winter, I should have been wretched."

"You ever like to meddle, Lady Colby."

"John Ashley says that about Kat."

"It must be a trait of the Champernownes, then. But do you see, Eloise? If Elizabeth has an affair with Robert Dudley or marries him, she will divide her Council and Parliament as much as Mary did—more, because Dudley is fairly widely despised. He is too . . ." He stopped, groping for words.

"Handsome and charming?" I supplied. I understood. Dudley was the sort of man susceptible ladies swooned over but whom other gentlemen did not like. Add to that the fact that his father, Northumberland, had been executed as a traitor, and King Henry had executed *his* father, citing the same reason.

"No one wants him to charm the Queen into molding England into what he wants," James finished. He leaned to me, the firelight catching on his red hair and serious expression. "I speak not because I do not wish happiness for Elizabeth; I speak because I fear she will ruin all she has begun. There will be rebellion and evil once again. At this moment she is the sun to England, the golden princess who became their beloved Queen, but if that ever changes, England will be plunged into chaos."

"I do understand, James." I sighed. "What a shame she does not love a stodgy, ugly gentleman who would give her many children, make friends of her advisors, and fade into the woodwork."

James laughed out loud. "Is that your description of a perfect husband?"

"For a Queen," I said severely. "For a Queen as radiant as

Elizabeth. She is a Tudor, and she will rule, not her husband. Make no mistake about that. Even Robert Dudley, I am afraid, would not be able to tell her what to do against her own wishes."

"I agree with you. And if he should rise up against her? He obediently rose against Mary for Jane Grey and condoned conspiracies against Mary, even if he was trying to keep his own nose clean. What if Robert decided he should have more from his wife the Queen than her smiles? What if he wanted her kingdom?"

"She would have to fight him."

James nodded. "England will not be stable if Robert Dudley becomes its King. Too many do not trust him. We cannot let that happen, Eloise."

His voice rang with determination. I had seen that determination before—in Elizabeth, in Mary, in Henry. I had speculated ere this that Henry's descendants seemed to possess his temper and unwavering belief in himself in pure form, undiluted by their mothers' blood.

"What are you going to do, James?" I asked in some trepidation.

He subsided. "Nothing, for now. But if she makes a foolish mistake, I will have to act."

"And I will have to decide where my own loyalties lie."

"Yes," he said softly. He leaned closer to me, a watchful look in his blue eyes. "You will."

I sat silently for a long time. I wanted my life to stay as it was, I in a privileged position with the new Queen, working with fabrics I never dreamed I'd be able to touch—costly cloth of gold and gold tissue, velvets so fine they were like rippling silk. The clothes I designed for Elizabeth's portraits, her balls, her entertainments, her progresses had already begun to become famous.

Great ladies of the world wrote to me begging for my advice or trying to tempt me from Elizabeth's service, which of course I could not leave.

I wanted to stay here with my husband by my side; I wanted my daughter to grow up unharmed and happy. I wanted this, and I wanted James to be an ordinary gentleman, son of an ordinary gentleman of Shropshire.

But he was James Colby, ever driven to act for England. He had once told me he worked for the greater good, and I had not believed him. I believed him now.

He wanted England to prosper as much as Elizabeth. He had always thought Elizabeth would make a great Queen and had worked to install her, but I realized now that if he thought she would be bad for England, he would not hesitate to remove her. He had told me he did not want the crown for himself, but he might decide he had no other choice.

"Oh, James," I said, heartfelt.

He gave me a faint smile. "Perhaps you should have married the dull Catholic gentleman your father offered you."

"No." I got to my feet and went to him, looking down where he lounged on his chair. "I pledged myself to you. I love you."

He said nothing. He pulled me down into his lap, and I buried my face in his neck, my heart thumping hard. I had never thought I would have to make a choice between James and my Queen, and I had no idea whether I could make the right one.

❖

ELIZABETH CONTINUED TO play with Robert Dudley. I watched courtiers grit their teeth when she and Robert made them the butt of jokes. She and Dudley were shameless, heads together, whispering at each other, then smiling as one at the baffled and teasing them unmercifully. Elizabeth would play the lute and shoot fond glances at Robert as he watched her, in view of everyone at court. But she turned a dangerous glare on anyone who even looked as though they might rebuke her.

I never tried. Not because I was afraid of her retaliation, but because I knew she would not listen. If she would not listen to Aunt Kat and Cecil, she would certainly not listen to me.

William Cecil speculated one day in September of 1560 that if things continued as they were, he would have to resign. "Even if the Queen were to lock me in the Tower for the rest of my life," he sighed. "I cannot stay."

If Cecil went, I asked James in panic, how long would it be before the Council followed suit, and James's fears of civil war came to pass?

The decision was taken away from all of us. On September 8 Amy Dudley was found dead at the bottom of a staircase in Cumnor Manor in Oxfordshire, her neck broken.

The uproar drowned out every other interest. Had Amy killed herself in despair, because her husband was the Queen's lover? Her servants said she had been ill and melancholy and hoped her end would come soon. Or had Robert had her killed so that he could be free to marry the Queen? The staircase was not steep, everyone said. That the fall should kill her was unlikely. More likely someone had broken her neck elsewhere and arranged her at the bottom of the staircase, an attempt to make it look like an accident. More rumor put it that Robert and Elizabeth had talked about poisoning her—perhaps she'd been weak with poison when she fell.

Tongues wagged, gossip soared; the scandal spread across the channel to the courts of Paris and beyond, royals all over Europe shaking their heads at the English Queen's folly.

Elizabeth, to my amazement, remained oblivious, or at least she pretended to. Both she and Robert asked that Amy's death be investigated, and a jury was sent to look into the nature of her demise. The investigators decided it was indeed an accident, but this did nothing to still wagging tongues, and the uproar continued.

James said nothing, did nothing, until the day he learned Elizabeth had told Cecil that she would wait a short interval and then let Robert begin courting her.

James took me with him and requested an audience with the Queen. We were at Whitehall by this time, and we found Elizabeth in the very chamber in which Mary had watched the men of Thomas Wyatt's army swoop down the street and bang at her gates.

It spoke much of my trusted position with the Queen, and James's character, that Elizabeth agreed to speak with us alone. She dismissed Cecil and her other ladies, and led us to a smaller chamber where we were quite by ourselves. She glanced about the little room with a pointed look, as though to invite us to see that no screens were positioned for the convenience of eavesdroppers, no doors behind which conspirators could hide.

Elizabeth positioned herself in the exact center of the chamber and James and I arrayed ourselves in front of her, me slightly behind James. After we had exchanged the requisite greetings and inquiries into the health of our daughter, James began.

"You will not marry Robert Dudley and make him King."

Elizabeth's eyes, already hard, because she must have known what this requested interview was about, grew still more granite-like. "This is your command?"

"Mary made a husband of Philip against all opposition," James said. "She decided she knew, better than her Council, better than her government, better than the English people themselves, which man would be good for the nation. She divided England. She created rebellions against her. You know this, you were at the heart of those rebellions. You remarked upon her obtuseness; you remarked that her arrogance in the matter was her downfall. And now you run to repeat the terrible mistake she made."

He stopped. Elizabeth listened in pure silence, her face like marble. When he had finished, she turned and walked a few steps toward the window. The lovely gown I had made for her, silver fleur-de-lis embroidered on a black surcote over a gold skirt, shimmered in the sunlight. I made certain her clothes always caught the light, to ensure that she was brighter than anyone else in the room.

"And will you start this rebelling?" she asked in a quiet voice. "Will you find your adventurers and your rebels and rise against me?"

Colby said nothing, wise never to admit anything to a Tudor.

"You will not." Elizabeth turned back to him, her skirts swishing. "You are mine, James Colby, and you always have been."

He made a slight bow. "I never made any pretense otherwise. I work for *you*, Your Majesty, which is why I advise you thus. Though you do not like to hear it."

I relaxed a little, but I knew at once our mission had been for naught. She would not listen to Kat Ashley, she would not listen to William Cecil; she'd not listen to James.

"I am more careful than my sister," she said briskly. "There is no one to take my place. No second person in the realm to rally 'round. Who is left to take the crown? The Grey sisters? They are a pathetic pair and all of England preferred Mary to Jane Grey. No, the Greys will never do. There are a few more of the blood, but much removed. My father did his best to rid us of all our relatives and rivals. Courtenay, the last of the Yorkists, has died. Mary of Scotland? Would anyone dare bring about such an obvious tie with Catholic France? You have no one, and the people of England would quickly see through a pretender."

James went close to her. She had to look up at him—she was tall, but James was taller.

"There is someone," he said. "One other person who would—reluctantly—step into your shoes."

"Who?" she scoffed.

James said nothing. He simply looked at her.

"James," I said in alarm.

Elizabeth gazed steadily at Colby, and then her eyes, which were so like his, flickered. "I see," she said at last.

I held my breath, waiting for her to call for her guards, to command that James be arrested and taken to the Tower. Tried and condemned for treason because he bore her blood.

Her father would have done so without hesitation had James threatened him. Mary might have done so, perhaps hesitating a little. With Elizabeth I could only watch and wait.

"Would the English people rally around a bastard?" Elizabeth asked softly.

James did not back down. "I mean no offense, but there were many who said the same about you."

"My mother was a Queen and a noble lady."

"So many said otherwise. And yet they adore you."

Rage flashed into her eyes, Tudor rage so strong I knew we were both doomed. Both my head and James's would adorn pikes outside Whitehall and my poor child would be left alone.

"You are a bold and brave man, James Colby." She emphasized his name.

"I want what is best for England, as do you. I suppose it is in my blood to want England to be great. You will make it great, I know this." He paused a moment. "But if Dudley is King, all will come tumbling down."

She faced him in silence, her expression carefully masking the thoughts that raced behind her eyes. I knew Elizabeth. She might fly into rages, and her tart tongue could strip a man's flesh from his bones, but ever since the Seymour affair she did nothing without thinking through every possible outcome. Her flirtation with Robert had been the exception, and I saw her realize that.

I will never know what it cost her to bend her head and agree. I saw behind her eyes furious anger, deep sadness, the draining of hope for her personal happiness, and loneliness. She would always be lonely.

But I also saw vast determination, ambition, and need for her kingdom. I saw the strength of will that had served her through the Seymour scandal and her disgrace, through imprisonment in the Tower and the cold days at Woodstock when she had been certain that assassins would dispatch her in secret. The strength that had let her sail through the dangers of Mary's reign without falling. Jane Grey had fainted when she'd been handed England; Elizabeth took it and raised it high.

At last she gave James a nod, albeit a frosty one. "I will not marry him," she said in a quiet voice. "I will never marry, Robert Dudley least of all. You have my word on that."

James nodded, too, tension easing from his body. He bowed to her then, a deep courtier's bow, acknowledging her as his superior.

Elizabeth gave him an ironic glance, and then she transferred her gaze from James to me. "You keep secrets well, Eloise. All these years I have watched you, but you never revealed this knowledge, not in word or look or deed. I commend you."

I gaped. "You knew? You knew about James?"

She snorted, Elizabeth the confident. "Of course I knew, my dear. I knew when I saw him at Robert's wedding. I saw him from across the room and knew exactly where I'd seen that look, that stance, that bearing before. I admired Henry, my father, and studied him much." She smiled tightly. "A favor, Eloise. Bear him only daughters."

"If I can," I said doubtfully.

"You can, do you but put your mind to it. I will assist you with my prayers." She gave me a wintry smile. "Leave me now; I would be alone." She added softly as she turned away from us, her face to the window and the coming winter, "I will always be alone."

A beam of sun fell on her reddish-gold hair, gleaming from the gold threads of her gown, the jewels on her bodice. She was a piece of the sun, a new light for England.

Colby took my hand. He led me from the room and through the outer chamber, past the curious Cecil and creaky old William Paulet, now Elizabeth's treasurer. James led me through the winding pile of Whitehall Palace and up the stairs, and to our chamber under the eaves where our daughter waited. Aunt Kat held Catherine on her plump lap, and both looked up when we entered.

Catherine held out her arms for me, laughing. Kat rose as I scooped up my girl.

"Well," Kat asked abruptly. "Did she listen to reason?"

"I believe so," James answered. He slid his arm around me and the babe and laid a soft kiss on my cheek. My James, so gentle, when minutes ago he had been ready to face down his Queen, with force if necessary.

"Good." Aunt Kat sniffed. "Elizabeth has ever had a wise head on her shoulders, never mind how impetuous she can be, or how silly about men. She'll make England the best Queen it ever saw, before or after." She gave us a decided nod. "I have always said so."

26

To our collective and immense relief, Elizabeth did not pursue her interest in taking Robert Dudley as a husband. Cecil's mournful look gradually lessened, and he even twitted Throckmorton, who had been writing a stream of terse letters to Elizabeth about Dudley, to cease.

No one questioned why she let her friendship with Dudley cool slightly; most people at court were simply happy to let it cool. She never said a word about her private meeting with James and me, though her demeanor became quite chilly. She did not dismiss me, as I feared, and in fact I began working on designs for a gown of black satin that would open over an underskirt of cloth of gold. I thought it high time the high-capped mahoitered sleeves began to disappear—they being popular in Mary's reign—and made the sleeve caps on the surcote smaller, though instructed that they be much decorated with rubies and embroidery.

Gradually over the next two years, Elizabeth made it plain that the "love affair" with Robert was over, though handsome

Robert remained her favorite. There was no definite talk of him marrying anyone else, her gifts to him increased, and when war came again in France, she sent his brother to fight and kept Robert at home.

She took care, though, to show her courtiers and her council that Robert was distanced. Once she laughingly called him her *little dog*—"I wager that when people see him they are certain I am not far behind," she jested.

Robert swallowed his anger at this humiliation, at least in public. In private, Elizabeth reminded him coldly that she was mistress of the kingdom and would have no master.

I thought Robert would demand a post away from Elizabeth, perhaps in France, or at least wish to leave court. But he did not. Even though Elizabeth made clear to him she'd never marry him, she bestowed estates and gifts on him, and he remained at her side, reaping the benefits of close friendship with the queen.

But while Elizabeth relieved her councilors (and me and Aunt Kat and James) by not insisting she take Robert to husband, nor did she seem eager to take anyone else. She again refused to name her successor, reminding her Council what had happened when Mary had a clear successor—looking pointedly at those gentlemen who had conspired to set Elizabeth on the throne and depose Mary. Parliament petitioned her several times, in long, formal documents with well-argued points why a sovereign should marry. She countered every point in equally formal speeches, and refused. The virginal state, she hinted, was far superior, making spinsterhood into an honorable undertaking.

"Lastly, this may be sufficient," she concluded one speech by saying, "both for my memory and honor of my name, if when I have expired my last breath, this may be inscribed upon my tomb: *Here lies interred Elizabeth, a virgin pure until her death.*"

Her Council and Parliament were not satisfied, but Elizabeth was young, I reminded Aunt Kat, with plenty of time to marry and bear children. Aunt Kat had married late in life and found happiness, though she'd not been blessed with children, but if Elizabeth married within the next few years, children would be sure to follow.

I was fitting Elizabeth for another gown in October of 1562, this one a riding costume of black velvet with patterned cutouts in the overskirt that would reveal a silver tissue skirt beneath, when something dreadful happened. I had received the bodice from my best seamstress and wanted to fit it to Elizabeth myself in her chamber. I had spent the last two years watching her from the corner of my eye, wondering when she'd find an excuse to arrest my husband or send him to sure death on some enterprise for her.

I was in fact surprised when Elizabeth hadn't sent him to France with Robert Dudley's brother the month before, when the de Guises of France had begun hostilities against the Protestant Huguenots. But she kept him at home, and had told James to accompany her with her outriders on her now-canceled visit to meet Mary of Scotland in York.

Young Mary had returned to Scotland on the death of her husband, the King of France; won over her dour Scots councilors; and prepared to settle in, ever reminding the world that she was the obvious heir to the throne in England. Elizabeth had wanted very much to get a look at this queen her cousin, who was reputed to be tall and beautiful and very charming, but war with France and Mary's de Guise uncles and cousins had made Elizabeth call off the meeting, to her disappointment. She'd kept James nearby, however, one of her retinue whenever she traveled or made progresses.

"Keeping an eye on me," James told me. "If I run off to

France, I might muster some of her own troops to my corner, and then she'd have to worry about me and an uprising."

I held my little Catherine, who'd grown large and quite energetic. "She would have me as a hostage. And your child."

James smiled, but with a glint of shrewdness. "Elizabeth rarely lets sentiment get in the way of something she truly wants. She would reason that I would not either."

There were days when I wondered if Elizabeth was right. If James had the chance to overthrow Elizabeth and take over—for the good of England, of course—would he hesitate because of me? I had to admit that I did not know. I loved my husband, but I could not predict him.

There was nothing we could do but obey her for now, and so I continued to work on her clothes and James continued to drill and shine his breastplate with her other guards.

Today she was snappish while I pinned on the close-fitting surcote, though I most carefully kept pins away from her skin. "The bodice is a bit loose, ma'am," I announced, slightly surprised. We were always most precise in our measurements, which meant Elizabeth must have thinned of late, which worried me. "My lady will have to do it again."

Elizabeth turned quickly to examine her profile in the mirror. "Is Mary of Scotland too slender, do you think? She is tall; she must resemble a long-necked bird."

Her ladies tittered as expected. Elizabeth continued. "Her ambassador told me Mary is much taller than I. To which I replied that Mary was far too high, and that I was of the right height, being neither too high nor too low."

I joined in the laughter as I carefully removed the bodice and slid a silk robe over Elizabeth's shoulders. "You are very warm, ma'am," I said. "Shall I open a window?"

Elizabeth jerked the robe from my fingers and frowned. "I am very cold; I'll have no open windows on such a chill day."

I looked at her in alarm, for the room was stifling. The ladies exchanged glances but said nothing.

Elizabeth put her hand to her face. "I feel a trifle unwell. Eloise, call my maid to draw me a bath."

"Should you?" Aunt Kat asked from her other side. "Perhaps it would be wiser to send for your physician, to at least be bled if nothing else."

Elizabeth sent her a look of scorn and loosened her red-gold hair to flow over her shoulders. "When you become a physician, Katherine Ashley, you may advise me. I am cold; a hot bath will feel fine on my skin. Arrange it."

I quickly summoned servants and bade them bring a bath and fill it with kettles of boiling water. Elizabeth did look happier ensconced in its steam, but unfortunately, Aunt Kat was proved right. That night Elizabeth took to her bed, and her physician announced she'd contracted the dreaded disease smallpox.

⁂

AUNT KAT WAILED. "Oh, my beloved girl."

She sat in our chambers, wringing her hands. The physicians had sent Kat away, though she longed to nurse her as did I, but James refused to let me go to her.

"You've never had the disease, Eloise," he told me sharply. "There is no use in you contracting it yourself, or in giving it to Catherine." He did not add that our unborn child might also be at risk, for I had but learned that in a few months I would produce another baby.

I conceded his wisdom, for thinking of Catherine ill made me cold with fear. James himself had had the disease as a child and so had Aunt Kat, and for some reason, those who survived it never suffered it again.

So I agreed to stay put in our chambers while Aunt Kat hovered at Elizabeth's door, and James reported to me on her progress. Elizabeth showed no signs of the spots, he told me, but her fever was great and she lay in a stupor, unable to speak.

"You do see the problem," James said in a quiet voice. "She has named no successor. If she dies and Mary of Scotland makes good her claim as heir by blood, England is in danger of being Catholic again, and what's more, under the thrall of France."

I laid my hand over my abdomen and the squirming child beneath, remembering the days of Catholic England and the smell of burning flesh. I did not want my daughter to grow up in such a place, nor did I particularly want us to flee to Geneva to live out our lives in exile.

"You would never let that happen," I said, raising my head. "Would you? You'd take up the fight again."

James nodded grimly. "I would oppose Mary of Scotland. From all accounts, she is frivolous and featherheaded. A beautiful woman, they say, but not much for statecraft."

"Who then?"

James's eyes shuttered to me, and he kissed my forehead. "You would conspire in your chambers not far above Elizabeth's own? She is strong, she will survive this, and we will have no fears."

He left me filled with direst foreboding. James was in effect telling me to stay home and raise our children, leaving the conspiracies to him. This not only was contrary to my nature, but made me worry very much what he planned to do. If we were not to be caught in the machinations of a turnover of power and the revenge of the now-deposed Catholics, we would have to disappear the instant Elizabeth died. I would have to abandon her at the last, but if I did not, my child and my husband might be in gravest danger.

Poor Elizabeth. She lay by her fire, wrapped in blankets, unable to speak. She was ill and alone, and I hoped she did not understand that the thoughts of most people, aside from Aunt Kat's, were only fear of what would happen to the realm if she died.

Even if she survived, Elizabeth would lose her looks, which would upset her very much. She was vain of her pale skin, and to be forever scarred would enrage her. Already she did not like a very young and pretty lady to stand too near her lest a contrast be made, though Elizabeth had yet to pass her thirtieth year.

I prayed much and my small daughter learned to imitate me, on her chubby knees next to me, with her hands folded in supplication. I asked God that if it were his plan to take Elizabeth from us, to please change his mind, because England had much need of her.

Whether God granted my boon or Elizabeth had more strength than we knew, the Queen recovered. Within weeks of the day she'd fallen ill, I was allowed to return to her side.

"Did you finish that bodice, Eloise?" she asked me as soon as she saw me. Her voice was weak and gravelly, her face studded with raw, red scabs, but her eyes were as sharp and clear as ever.

❧

"DISASTER AVERTED," MY husband murmured to me as we walked in the gardens together a month later. Elizabeth had thrown a grand winter banquet, and we'd stolen away from the stifling heat of the hall to the clear chill of the evening. "You did hear that in her delirium, Elizabeth wanted Cecil to name Robert Dudley as Protector of England and bestow on him a ridiculous sum of money?"

"Yes, it has made him strut about," I answered. "Especially now that he is one of the Council. Cocksure that Cock Robin will be King one day. Will he never give up the notion?"

"He will." James sent me a secretive look, but amusement danced in his eyes. "Tell no one yet, but the Queen has decided that *he* will make the perfect husband for Mary of Scotland."

I stopped walking in astonishment. "She would never . . ."

"She would," James replied. "Robert is hers—he belongs to her, heart and soul. She would control Mary through him, and he has no royal blood to strengthen a claim on the throne. He is English to the core—he'll resist all attempts to become Scottish or French."

"But Elizabeth loves him. She'd never send him to another woman." Even as I spoke, I faltered, realizing that, indeed, such a thing was exactly what Elizabeth would do. James echoed my thoughts.

"She will enjoy playing the martyred woman who sent the man she loved to another to save her kingdom."

"Yes," I conceded. Such high drama would appeal to Elizabeth.

Aunt Kat had little to say about the scheme, though I knew she felt that the sooner he was off, the better. Aunt Kat tired easily these days, and I watched her with increasing worry. She'd nursed Elizabeth back to health and was never far from her side, but Elizabeth took to sending her early to bed so that Kat would not be forced to stand long hours in the Queen's presence.

Kat enjoyed taking care of my little Catherine, and when my second child was born in 1563, another girl called Elizabeth, Kat held the baby in her plump arms and gave her a proud smile. So far I was fulfilling Elizabeth's wish for me to bear James no male children, though I knew James longed for a son of his own.

Mary's Scots council was not so keen on the Dudley match,

but Elizabeth went at it with vigor. She made Dudley the Earl of Leicester in 1564 to make him more palatable, but even that failed to please Mary or her Scots. It pleased Robert, however, who'd been chafing for a title and lands for a long time. His father had been a duke, but of course lost everything during the short reign of Jane Grey. Elizabeth had teased him with the promise of a peerage since she'd become Queen, but had held it up and snatched it back exactly like offering a dog a treat and then whipping it away.

Elizabeth grew exasperated at the Scots' resistance. "Who will Mary have then?" she demanded. "If she turns up her nose at my sweet Robin?"

We would be surprised at the answer.

All the while Elizabeth played matchmaker for Mary and Scotland, I worried about Aunt Kat. Her duties were light and gave her much time to sit by the fire, but I knew I was watching her fade.

Kat Ashley, who had taken me under her wing when my mother had married her Catholic gentleman and no longer wanted me, who had raised me with more affection than my mother ever would have, who had taught me much about the ties of family and friendship, was slowly dying. I would lose her, my anchor to the past and to innocence.

When Elizabeth had become Queen, she'd surprised everyone and displeased many by appointing Kat first lady of the bedchamber. But despite the troubles Aunt Kat had dragged Elizabeth into in the past, Elizabeth loved her, and she, too, saw Kat as the last link to innocent days.

"She raised me," Elizabeth had written as a girl to Protector Somerset, pleading for Aunt Kat's release from the Tower. "And we feel as much or more love and loyalty for those who raised us than even those who gave birth to us."

Elizabeth had never known her mother, the disgraced and fallen Anne Boleyn, but Aunt Kat had always been there at her side. She'd been at my side as well.

Aunt Kat liked to gossip as much as ever, though. "Young Lord Darnley is on his way to Scotland," she said one day as we sewed in her rooms. I asked her to help me these days with easy work because she still enjoyed being useful, even though I had a host of seamstresses, drapers, mercers, milliners, and glovers at my beck and call. "Lord Cecil and Lord Leicester have convinced Elizabeth no harm will come of it. For all that Darnley's mother seems to enjoy the Tower."

Darnley's mother was Margaret Douglas, the lovely daughter of King Henry's sister. She'd been given in marriage to the Earl of Lennox, but had been imprisoned as a young woman for betrothing herself to Sir Thomas Howard against Henry's will, and narrowly escaping execution.

Nearly fifty now, Margaret Douglas was as ambitious as ever, and she and her husband Lennox were leaders of the nobility who remained steadfastly Catholic. Margaret doted on her young son Darnley and did not hide the fact that she considered her children ripe to inherit the throne, and in fact had recently been placed under house arrest in London for her open ambitions for her son.

"I must advise her against it," Kat said decidedly. "Margaret Douglas is not to be trusted. I must tell her." She gathered herself to her feet, but suddenly sat down again with a little sigh and remained still.

"Darnley is a young pup," I said, patting her weary hand. "He will trip over his own feet, like as not. Mary's court will be amused by him, and he'll slink home with his tail between his legs."

Events unhappily proved me wrong. Darnley *was* a puppy at nineteen, but he charmed Mary and she charmed him. He had the misfortune of falling somewhat ill during his visit, and Mary enjoyed herself nursing him back to health, and hence fell in love with him. No more thoughts of Robert Dudley, new Earl of Leicester, were entertained, and the following spring, in 1565, Lord Darnley and Mary, Queen of Scots, were betrothed and sent an envoy to seek Elizabeth's approval. Elizabeth remonstrated with her, trying to reintroduce the idea of Mary's marriage to Dudley, but as spring slid into summer, Mary grew more giddy about Darnley and proved immovable.

Elizabeth was livid. "Mary is a stupid woman," she declared, eyes blazing in a perfect likeness of her father's rage. "Darnley is a fool, a spoilt boy who does what his mama bids him. I'd not be surprised if Cousin Margaret caused him to sicken so Mary's pity would turn to love."

"She was nowhere near Scotland," Aunt Kat pointed out. "Though an agent could have done such a thing. I advised against his going, you know, my dearest. You must listen to your governess."

Elizabeth made a noise of fury and raised her hand to slap her. She stopped herself, her hand frozen, when she noticed that Aunt Kat's eyes were half-closed, her body swaying. Both Elizabeth and I caught Aunt Kat as she went down, and Elizabeth cradled her against her bosom.

"Send for a physician," Elizabeth said, her voice subdued. "Now, Eloise. Hurry."

❋

AUNT KAT DIED peacefully. On a warm June day I sat in her chamber, my fingers idle, having no interest in sewing or fabric that day. James came to sit by my side, and we watched all afternoon as Aunt Kat drifted in and out of sleep. John Ashley stood at the foot of her bed, his lined face worn with grief.

There was a noise of many people in the outer chamber, and Elizabeth herself entered the room. She angrily waved the others to stay outside and came to the bed where her governess lay.

She stood over Kat for a long time, taking no notice of me and James, though we'd risen at her entrance, or of John Ashley. Her back was straight, the pearls on her silk bodice catching the light. I ordered pearls sewn on all her clothes now, pearls being a symbol of virginity and purity.

Elizabeth bent over the bed, pressed a kiss to Kat Ashley's cheek, and turned away in a rustle of skirts. As she passed me, she closed her long fingers around my arm, lifting me from my curtsey and dragging me away with her.

She walked fast, Elizabeth ever robust. We quickly left her entourage behind, Elizabeth hurrying me down long passages and up stairs, ducking and dodging through rooms until we were quite alone. At last Elizabeth stopped in an empty chamber. I laid my arm across my tight stomacher, trying to catch my breath, while she marched to a window and gazed out at the warm summer afternoon.

"Stepmama loved days like these," Elizabeth announced after silence had stretched long between us. "She said they made her feel like a girl."

"Yes," I answered. I remembered Catherine Parr when she'd first married Thomas Seymour, happy and in love.

Elizabeth swung around. "You know what she was to me."

I understood that she now spoke about Kat Ashley. "Yes," I said again.

"*You* know, Eloise, better than any of them. Better than your husband, better even than John Ashley. You were friendless, as I was, you were unwanted, as I was. In the middle of it all, was *her*."

My eyes filled. Kat Ashley, the rock in our turbulent stream, who sniffed at my frivolous mother and told me I'd be better off without my real family. In the same way, she'd become indignant if anything was withheld from Elizabeth's household—Elizabeth was a princess, a Tudor, Henry's daughter. And amid her dudgeon and her scoldings were fierce hugs, her comforting touch in the night, her beaming smile when she said, "You are quite clever, my girl."

Tears trickled down my face. "She loved you."

Elizabeth's tears echoed my own. "I know she did. No matter that I was bastard or queen."

She enfolded me into her arms. She had not done so in a long time, not since she'd become brittle and so careful. "I will need you now, Eloise," she whispered. She kissed my damp cheek and eased away but kept hold of my wrists. "I will need you to slap my hands when I am foolish and give me disapproving frowns as she used to."

I tried to smile. "I do not know if I can be her equal."

"You were when you came to twit me about Robert Dudley. I was so angry, and yet the two of you stood your ground."

"I thought you would dismiss us then and there," I said, remembering her rage and my nervousness.

"I might have. But I knew, you see, that Katherine Ashley was right. She was my conscience. When all others were afraid, she told me of my foolishness for my own good. You must be my conscience now, Eloise. Promise me. For her."

She was asking me to become Kat Ashley. I felt foolish and inadequate, a woman of nearly two-and-thirty, even though Kat had been about the same age when she had become the governess of small Elizabeth. But I knew Aunt Kat would want to know that Elizabeth was looked after, that someone at court and in the kingdom put the interests of Elizabeth the woman before all else.

"I promise," I said.

She held me again, and we wept for the woman who had been better than a mother to us both.

We returned arm in arm to the passages below, where Elizabeth's worried ladies waited for her. Elizabeth wiped her eyes, held her head high, and walked with me to Aunt Kat's chamber. She pushed away the attendant who bathed Kat's face in fragrant water and took up the task herself.

I seated myself on the other side of Aunt Kat, Elizabeth paying no attention to etiquette for this hour. Together we held Aunt Kat's cool, wrinkled hands as she slid into her final sleep.

※

ELIZABETH TREATED KAT'S passing as she would that of any highborn noblewoman, with a period of prayers and mourning. Her grief was as genuine as mine, and she called me more than once into her private closet to speak of Kat and mourn her.

Gradually Elizabeth returned to her routine and the problems she faced—what to do about Mary and Darnley, the continuing question of her marriage and her successor, and the everyday management of her kingdom. I watched her as she stood in her great hall at one of her feasts that Christmas, upright and regal in her gold tissue gown and black velvet surcote, her head thrown back, the lights of a thousand candles glinting on her sleek hair. Her face had healed well from the smallpox, with only some scarring that she covered with cosmetics.

She was Queen of England, a woman in a world dominated by men, and she was winning those men to her side. Every gentleman and lord now wished to be in the court of Elizabeth instead of opposed to it, waiting for benefits to be heaped on them by their glorious Queen.

An idea for another gown sprang to mind as I watched her, one studded with pearls, glistening and glowing in patterns to show both her purity and her power. Her headdress too would be studded with pearls, and the entire ensemble would show her mastery of her court and of the world, Elizabeth our great monarch.

A gentleman at the table raised his goblet and made a toast to their fair Queen, echoed by a cheer. Elizabeth's eyes narrowed a bit at the obvious toadying, but she graciously inclined her head. Candlelight danced on the pearls in her red-gold hair and reflected on the golden canopy above her.

Across the great hall, her eyes met mine, and she gave the barest twitch of lips. We would do it, she and I, she the ruler, and I her conscience.